Bruce THE **GENTS**

"Bruce Thorstad offers us a great read, and a breath-taking authenticity, based not only on careful research, but an intuitive understanding of how things were. *THE GENTS* has a delightful comic quality and two unforgettable heroes. But there is an underlying seriousness to the work: Thorstad writes movingly about the dark and tragic sides of human life. This is a grand book by an author who is destined for the top. Readers are going to treasure every page of *THE GENTS,* and when they reach the last sentence, they'll rush out to buy Thorstad's other books. He's that good."

—Richard S. Wheeler

"In *THE GENTS,* Bruce Thorstad has woven a complicated plot through which a whole mess of characters, good, bad and ugly, ride. Read *THE GENTS.* You won't forget any of them."

—Robert J. Conley

"As memorable and colorful as Thorstad's best. This is the first 'Gents' book and I'm thinking of calling Thorstad up to tell him to hurry up with another one."

—Dale L. Walker,
Westerns columnist, *Rocky Mountain News*

Books by Bruce H. Thorstad

The Gents
The Times of Wichita
Deadwood Dick and the Code of the West

Published by POCKET BOOKS

THE GENTS

BRUCE H. THORSTAD

POCKET BOOKS

New York   London   Toronto   Sydney   Tokyo   Singapore

This book is a work of fiction. Names, characters, places and incidents are either products of the author's imagination or are used fictitiously. Any resemblance to actual events or locales or persons, living or dead, is entirely coincidental.

An *Original* Publication of POCKET BOOKS

POCKET BOOKS, a division of Simon & Schuster Inc.
1230 Avenue of the Americas, New York, NY 10020.

ISBN: 0-671-75904-3

First Pocket Books printing March 1993

10 9 8 7 6 5 4 3 2 1

POCKET and colophon are registered trademarks of Simon & Schuster Inc.

Cover art by Tim Tanner

Printed in the U.S.A.

For help in the shaping of characters in this work, I'm indebted to the Siu family—Ron, Pauline, and Kevin.

And to the Mings—Jessica (Sweetwater), Jeannie (Prairie Weet), and Dennis (the illustrious China Camp).

And finally, a tip of the Stetson to the founders and members of the Single Action Shooting Society, as savvy a bunch of supporters as a Western writer could have.

THE GENTS, 1872

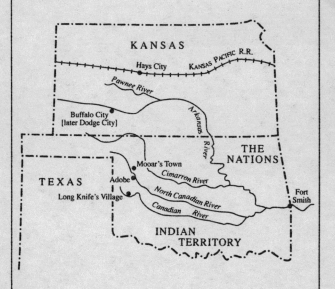

THE GENTS

1 · RILEY

RILEY STOKES, WOUNDED AT CARDS, TURNED HIS BACK ON SCRAP-
ing chairs and men's voices and stepped out of the Railway
Advance Barroom, his sore eyes squinting at the morning.
He'd been heading for the street, but he slowed at the
realization it would only lead places he'd been to already.
Bad luck, he supposed, signaled a need for avoiding old ruts.
Hard thinking seemed called for. He sagged a shoulder
against a balcony post—as good a spot as any from which to
review his prospects.

He was a dark-haired man in a rumpled black suit and a
blue cotton shirt lacking both tie and collar. On his back he
wore thirty years, making him young by most standards, but
old for a man on the Kansas frontier having no trade to fall
back on.

His squint deepened. Such a generosity of sunlight after a
poor night of poker was fazing, so that he was tempted just
to go down to the Hays House and on up to bed. In respect
of his losses, he would have welcomed a drizzly morning, a
day that sorrowed with him. Instead, he was dealt the usual,
giddy Kansas sunup—a yellow blaze climbing a roofless sky
and the rising, curing smells of prairie grasses.

Riley found such mornings fraudulent. They showed up
promising fresh beginnings, then turned hotter than hellfire
by half-past breakfast, and by noon had reneged on all such
promises. Give a person a day that starts out rainy, he
thought, and it can only improve as it goes along.

He supposed, though, he was remembering the nourishing
rains of Kentucky. Kansas rains were different—in a word,
fickle. For weeks you scorched to a cinder, but take those
broad skies for granted and they'd cloud up ugly and come
at you like an army with a grudge. Then you'd get rain in
riverfuls, hailstones like grapeshot, and maybe your
behinder chased by a cyclone in the bargain. It was a
wearing, all-or-nothing sort of weather, oddly similar, now

1

that he thought of it, to the boom-or-bust business of poker luck. Riley preferred rain that doled itself out predictably in gentle showers. More like, he realized with discomfort, the regular salary of a workaday job.

Well, he had come a stretch since Kentucky, mostly downhill. His pants were thinning in the hinder, his coat ripped along one sleeve. The money in his pockets tallied less than four dollars, fifty-one fewer than he'd sat down with at the poker table. The sum total of the Riley Stokes estate consisted of his father's old watch and a cap and ball revolver, neither of which he fancied selling just to pay his room rent. Wherever had he got the notion he was cut out to be a gambler?

Behind him, voices toned. Then boots scuffed wood and the batwings strained against coil springs. From the blue haze of the barroom, three of the four players who'd spent the night at Riley's table came into the morning, their faces fisting to shelter night-owl eyes, their expressions as aggrieved to meet the sun as Riley's own. A round of coughing erupted as they hit the fresh air. Two of the players set off down the boardwalk, trailing pipe smoke, leaving the other standing with his hands in his pockets.

"Ah, morning on the prairie," he said expansively. His eyes played toward the town's outskirts and he inhaled conspicuously, demonstrating the morning's bracing qualities. Riley turned and looked behind him, seeing only dazzle coming off dirt street. His squint became fierce. Someone—so it seemed—had thrown another log on the sun.

"Say, I didn't clean you out of breakfast money?" the man inquired.

"No, I . . ." Riley patted a pocket. "Of course not. I'm not much hungry in the mornings anyhow."

Riley's listener nodded absently. He was taller than Riley, with a keg of a head and barrel torso to match, but with long, oddly slender arms and legs. He wore a nut-brown, tailored coat, a double-breasted hound's-tooth waistcoat, and a citified hat with abbreviated brim. His face was reddish, meaty as a ham, framed by side-whiskers that were white and feathery. He stood with his weight on his heels, a big man, looking as though he had never missed a meal in his life.

"Well, sir, it is clean sheets for me," the man said. He stretched and yawned, his chin retreating to swell a full throat. With an exaggerated shrug he resettled his shoulders, then smoothed his lapels to his satisfaction and bade Riley a good-morning.

Watching him set off down the boardwalk, Riley had a momentary, useless urge to ask for his money back, for the man was the night's big winner, a Chicago salesman named Powers. "Purveyor of agricultural implements of the most modern patterns," he had told Riley the evening before, then flourished an illustrated catalogue. Riley, still watching the drummer, had not felt hungry until the man had mentioned breakfast.

The swinging doors parted again for the last of the night's players, an even taller man than the other, though uniformly lean, with a narrow face and sandy mustache. His coat was good charcoal broadcloth trimmed in black velour. Under it was a blaze of white shirt and a brocaded vest. All the man lacked was a riverboat, Riley thought sourly; he'd never had much use for dandies.

Riley found himself irritated. He said, "That damned drummer about cleaned me out," not so much to inform the dandy as to lodge a protest in front of a witness. He nodded down the boardwalk at the salesman's diminishing back. "When one player gets all the luck, it leaves a bad taste."

The tall dandy did an odd thing: he laughed—abrupt, sarcastic, a kind of snort. "That fellow's no more drummer than I am," the dandy said.

Riley's scrutiny rotated, then elevated. He had studied this dandy off and on all night. With his straw-pale hair and darker mustache, the fellow looked no older than twenty-eight, yet he had a self-assurance more common to older men. Now he stood amused at Riley's expense, eyes crinkling, the sole possessor of superior knowledge.

"The man's a drummer from Chicago," Riley said. "I saw his prospectus."

The dandy lit a cigar, the kind called a twist, crooked as a dog's leg. "I guess anyone can pick up a prospectus," he said through blossoming smoke. "Lest I'm bad mistaken, that sport walking off with our money is Terrible John Parrott."

"Him—Parrott?" Riley said, surprised. He took a hasty

look at the disappearing, now slightly malignant form of the implement salesman. Suspicion bunched his brow. "He gave his name as Powers."

"Naturally he'd hide his identity," the dandy said. "Folks knew he was Parrott, who'd be fool enough to share a poker table with him?"

"For damned sure not me!"

"I'm surprised to see him this far west," the dandy said. "During the war, he was supposed to have run the shady side of Memphis till Federal troops shut him down. Last I heard he was a big operator on riverboats. I expect he's just stopped off the Kansas Pacific to clean out us rubes. Heading to Denver, I'll bet, looking for new ore to mine."

Riley imagined himself a mine, his pockets excavated by this Terrible John Parrott. He felt invaded. "Whoever he is, he's one lucky bastard."

The dandy laughed again. "A gambler of his caliber, luck has naught to do with it."

Riley scowled. "Let me understand this. Are you saying he . . . *cheats?*"

"You'd best draw your own conclusions. As a sporting man myself, I say nobody's fortune's sweetheart. I figured going in this Parrott would cut himself some margin or other—he's got the reputation for it. I expected it to cost me, bucking a big-time sharp, but I hoped to learn something in the bargain." He chuckled ruefully and savored his cigar.

"So did you?"

"Not a blessed thing," the dandy admitted, "except he's slicker than I thought."

Riley was getting the hollow, untethered feeling that came before his humors turned around. If he weren't careful, he was liable to get mad. "Well, by God, no wonder we got skinnt! I got a mind to sic the marshal on him."

"I'd not advise it," the dandy said mildly. "Lest you can prove your charges, you'll just make a bad enemy."

Riley exhaled frustration. Here he—Riley Stokes, professional gambler—had been cheated without even suspecting it, and by a man he still thought of as an implement salesman. And here was this brocaded dandy, a fellow who seemed about as smooth as warm butter, and it turned out there were players even *he* was no match for. Riley had a feeling he'd spent too long in the wrong line of work.

"I looked for hole cards," the dandy said. "I checked for readers and strippers, but I couldn't get a thing on him. About the only trick left is using a shill." For a moment, the dandy seemed lost in wonder and contemplation up there at his six-foot-and-something; cigar smoke settled around his head like a cloud on a mountaintop. Riley himself was five feet, ten inches, a height he found satisfactory. More height than that was purely show-offish, he believed, often downright annoying.

"Well, *hell and hallelujah,*" Riley said, "you could've said something about the man being a card cheat! That game cost me fifty-some dollars and I didn't learn a thing either, other than now I'm flat busted!"

The dandy's dreamy expression resolved. His eyes settled on Riley and cooled by notches. Riley looked away, first to the man's too-extravagant cravat, then to the vest, which swirled in an elaborate print—intertwining maroon and gold somethings, maybe tadpoles mating—the whole business as gaudy as a hotel carpet. On the front page of Riley's thinker, the term "tinhorn" coalesced. He was suddenly all done with gaming and gamblers.

"Let's not go off half-cocked," the dandy warned him. "What I told you were only suspicions. Besides which, I assumed we were all grown men at that table. A wise man, as I'm sure you've heard said, never risks what he can't afford to lose." Then he shrugged, a subtle, superior gesture accomplished solely with the eyebrows.

Riley didn't know what most stuck in his craw, what the man had said or the way he'd said it. Hot words were rising in Riley's throat, but he didn't trust himself to unlimber them. He glared at the dandy, then muttered something he did not quite catch himself. The dandy's face went mystified, giving Riley one small satisfaction.

Riley turned and took a long, angry step off the boardwalk, which was higher than he'd expected. He momentarily stumbled, recovered, then steamed rigid and erect across Main Street, crossing obliquely behind a passing freight wagon, his gait complicated by sun-baked ruts. He felt unwashed, unshaved, and unhappy; the grit of sleeplessness was itchy behind his eyes. Floating like a lithographed ghost before him was the image of that brocaded vest, its tadpoles mating in frenzy.

A wise man never risks what he can't afford to lose, indeed! A person's whole life was a risk, and some lives riskier than others. Here was this brocaded son of a bitch thriving in a profession that was sending Riley to the poorhouse. Where was the fairness in it? The dandy was fussed up in fancy clothes, tall as a flagpole, and what was worse, probably just the sort that women found good-looking. He was some rich man's son, probably, with a head start on life that would carry him forever.

In front of the *Star-Sentinel* building, Riley reset his hat and stepped up on the boardwalk, careful to keep his back to the dandy across the street. Somewhere in the washboard ruts between the saloon and the news office he had crossed a threshold. He would put the sporting life behind him; he would get a fresh start. In short, he would buy a newspaper. It was high time, Riley considered, that he found himself a job.

2 · RILEY

FORBIDDINGLY, A GREEN SHADE WAS DRAWN THE LENGTH OF THE *Star-Sentinel*'s door. Riley tried the doorknob and was relieved to find it unlocked. It was the day the new edition came out. His plan was to read the Situations Offered advertisements before anyone else got to them. Riley Stokes, Kentucky poor boy, would get a head start of his own. He stepped into a high-ceilinged room that smelled of the woody stuffiness of newsprint. An ink smell overlaid it—oily and biting. A newsman, probably the editor, and his boy helper were running the press, laying a fresh double sheet of paper on the typeboard and then cranking it with an elliptical rumble under the rollers. Then they cranked it back again, carefully peeled off the printed page, and laid it on a table. Finally, the editor looked up at Riley, his expression owly over round-paned glasses.

Riley stood like a parson—hands clasped behind him,

weight on his heels—clear indications, he felt, that he was willing to be patient. "Morning," Riley said pleasantly.

The newsman scowled and turned on the boy, a bright-looking lad behind an ink-stained apron. "I thought I told you to lock the front door."

The boy blinked and said, "No, sir," at which the editor made a sour face and then started forward to confront the intrusion. He wore sleeve garters like a grocer.

"Yes?" the newsman said, still looking over the spectacles. He gave off exasperation.

Riley displayed a five-cent piece, survivor of the night's poker. "All I need is the new paper."

The newsman assumed theatrical weariness. "I'm afraid I have a policy. On press day no one gets a copy till the whole edition is printed. Otherwise, everybody wants to jump the gun on merchants' sales, et cetera, et cetera."

Riley felt his cheer souring. "A policy," he repeated. Having policies reminded him of certain army sergeants, who'd had various policies of their own, all contrived to make their own lives convenient and a poor private's miserable. Riley eyed what were surely finished *Star-Sentinel*s stacked on a table by the press. The coin in his fingers was faintly greasy. "You mean you won't sell me a paper?"

"What'd I just now say?" the newsman asked him. "I start doing that and I'll be besieged by every bummer off the street. We couldn't get our work done."

"Ah," Riley said, enlightened now, "you don't want to be bothered."

Wicks of gratification came alight in the editor's eyes. He said, "Discerning of you." The corners of his mouth made a brief, tight smile.

Riley knew sarcasm when he heard it. He looked at the fresh papers, then at the editor, then at the boy assistant. A night of losing poker was a tiring business. But if he toddled up to bed and slept away the morning, he would be beaten to his paper—and thus to any job that showed promise—by that race of ordinary men who slept nights, got up mornings, and were resigned to working for wages.

Again Riley proffered the five-cent piece. "How about you?" he asked the boy. "You have the same policy?"

The boy looked stunned to be asked. He glanced at the older man for a cue. "Of course," the boy said.

Riley whistled. "You two sure stick to your guns. I bet even was I the mayor or the marshal you would not sell me a paper."

The editor said, "Well, I hardly think—"

"I guess, was he in town, even the president of the Republic would not get the new paper to enjoy with breakfast," Riley said, letting his face hang comfortably in no particular expression. One reason he'd gone into poker was that folks had praised his deadpan.

The editor crumpled his forehead, showing a hardening of attitude. "We're very busy."

"I guess if you made exceptions, you wouldn't have much of a policy," Riley said. There was more he could have said, but he saw it would not prove useful. He turned to leave, the editor following. When he opened the door the editor held it for him.

"Good day," the editor said stiffly.

"I sure do hope so," Riley said. He stepped onto the boardwalk and had the door closed behind him. The bolt shot home a little abruptly, Riley thought, considering he was a paying customer.

The dandy no longer stood in front of the Railway Advance; he'd been replaced by a swamper with a broom. Riley put the five-cent piece in his pocket with the rest of his meager stake. Feeling so little money in there reminded him of having been cheated, which reminded him he was mad at himself for not detecting it. Then he was mad all over again at the riverboat dandy, who'd been wise to the cheating throughout the game.

Riley's room was on the second floor of the Hays House, down in the next block. Until the new paper came out, he had nothing to do but go on up to bed.

Traffic was picking up on Main Street. Riley crossed, watching two soldiers riding into town on the tailboard of a granger's wagon. They sat facing backward, their legs swinging, probably having bummered a lift from nearby Fort Hays. He looked at the blue uniforms and thought of the army and then of how he hated officiousness. Give a man a dash of power and he liked to thwart you with it; the army had taught Riley that much. On the other hand, the army had also taught him there was nearly always a way to get what you wanted. All a person needed was a lick of smart and sufficient brass to use it.

Riley stepped onto the far boardwalk to look back at the *Star-Sentinel* office. Sun glistened off curling shingles, still dark with the night's dew. The notion of comeuppance had always been dear to him. Abruptly, he was a man inspired.

Riley dashed back across the street, one hand keeping his hat in place. He leaped to the boardwalk and with the heel of his fist attacked the *Star-Sentinel's* door, his pounding rattling the panes. "Hey in there—*quick!*" he called, then pounded again.

The door opened warily on the editor's face, its expression teetering between alarm and anger.

"Is that *smoke* I see coming off your roof?" Riley jigged in agitation and jabbed a forefinger skyward. A passing farmer stopped to follow Riley's gesture, his eyes wide, brow furrowing. "Up along the shingles there!" Riley said.

The editor's face stretched. *"Where?"* he breathed, and he erupted through the doorway and dashed past Riley, eyes nailed to the eaves, his young assistant right behind him.

Riley slipped through the office doorway and in four strides reached the stack of fresh newspapers. He grabbed one, folded it, stuck it in his waistband under his coat. He got out through the door to see the editor stalking him, the man's face as purple as spoiled meat.

"Smoke, indeed!" the editor said. The boy again looked stunned. "Dew!" the editor fumed. "Nothing more than dew steaming off the roof!"

"It was?" Riley said. Innocence settled over him like a benediction.

Face congested, deeply suspicious, the editor peered beyond Riley into the news office. The farmer stood looking from the roof to the editor to Riley as though he were watching a minstrel skit and not expected to make comments.

"Then it's one time I am tickled to be mistaken," Riley said easily. "My eyesight never was the sharpest first thing in the morning." He held the door for the editor and his assistant. "No harm done," Riley assured them. He touched his hat brim, genial as a politician.

"Your experience with mornings, sir, appears very limited," the editor said. He glared at Riley and then at the farmer, as though he too were implicated. "You *will* excuse us." The editor closed the door with violence. Its bolt went home like a pistol shot.

"By gosh, there's gratitude for you," Riley told the farmer. "It just as easy could've been smoke I saw."

He recrossed the street, whistling no particular tune, and went up past Walker's Harness Shop and the partly finished new dry goods store. Someone had penciled NOTIONS on a wooden signboard and then had painted in only half of it.

He walked to the Hays House before withdrawing the newspaper. He had a renewed sense of himself. He still had his old pluck. It was possible, Riley Stokes conceded, that he was a gambler at heart. If so, what he needed was not a permanent job but merely a way to rebuild his stake. With money in his pockets, he'd be ready to face a poker table again. Certainly in the past half year he'd found it easy enough to fleece grangers and soldiers, buffalo men and railroaders. The conclusion was plain enough. It wasn't gambling he ought to steer clear of; it was big-time sports like Terrible John Parrott.

He sat on a bench under the Hays House balcony and spread out the pages, finding Situations Offered, the small advertisements placed by those seeking men. Hays City was supposed to be a booming town on a booming frontier; even so, there were not many listings.

The Kansas Pacific required a telegrapher, which was not in Riley's line. Roofers were needed in the construction of commercial buildings, probably a hot and dirty business that held no appeal for him. Riley bit a fingernail.

In the last column he found what he was after. The Herbert Express and Drayage Company wanted a pair of messengers for what it called "hazardous employment of limited duration." The ad further specified "unmarried gentlemen skilled with firearms." The phrase "generous remuneration as commensurate with risk" especially pleased him; risk, he remembered, was part of life. Job applicants were to report at 6 P.M. that same day at the Lincoln Street office of Julius Herbert, Company Director.

Riley stared vaguely out at Main Street. The lesson of the morning—to apply initiative in the face of adversity—was fresh in his mind. The thing was to strike while the iron was hot. He would leave waiting till evening to men less enterprising. He stood up from his bench. He would apply for the position immediately.

3 · TAI HEI

"SEE THE HAPPINESS OF THE GRASSES," HER HUSBAND, TWO Horses, admonished her. "They offer themselves to the buffalo, who in turn give themselves to us. Must you dwell so upon yourself? Find something of the day in which to take pleasure."

Her Kiowa name was Bird of Morning, but she felt little like Bird of Morning at that moment; rather she felt like Tai Hei, her old self. Tai Hei did not answer, did not nod, for she knew the proper way to act while being instructed. She held her dark eyes still and looked ahead in the attitude that said she was listening respectfully. Two Horses gave her a look, sympathetic and exasperated at the same time, and then heeled his pony and surged back to the head of the column, making a fine sight even in his paint of mourning.

Tai Hei did not resent her husband's scolding, for his words were meant to encourage rather than punish, and came anyway not merely from his own heart but from the shared wisdom of the people. Whenever new situations arose, Tai Hei supposed the entire band became aware she was still unused to their ways. Her husband's words amounted to this: be a Kiowa. Which was to say, accept a life of sacrifice and there will also surely be victory. Be of strong heart and endure awhile longer.

So Tai Hei shifted her weight on the horse's pumping withers, trying with little success to ease her back. Her pumpkin front was tighter than ever, her breasts heavy to bursting and her nipples sore under the buckskin dress. The kicking heels of the little one within her did not bother her, being reminders of new life. But when the kicks went down to where her urine was stored, it made her want to wet herself. A procession of honor such as this one could not stop at each point on the sun's path to let one woman urinate. She shifted again on her precarious seat and shut out thinking about it. Be a Kiowa, Tai Hei told herself.

The plodding hooves and dragging travois raised only a little dust here where the wide valley shallowed toward Buffalo Water Creek. Because of nourishing water, the grasses grew thicker than on the high prairie. She would be thankful for the lessening of dust and take comfort in that, for her place was at the procession's rear. At its head rode her husband, Two Horses, followed by the shrouded body of his great father, Eagle Man, in his day one of the Principal Dogs—the *Koitsenko*, or ten bravest. Then followed Sky Calf, Tai Hei's sister-wife, and Hears Snow Falling, mother of their husband, and then a few others, some of them old warriors who owed Eagle Man some debt that had not been repaid in life.

Iron Bow, today honored despite his youth by being made outrider, loped in from a far rise, his face shining with news. He drew up and spoke excitedly with Two Horses.

The procession stopped, so that Tai Hei had hope of getting off her pony to squat hastily behind a soapweed patch, and even, if there were time, to lie flat against the earth to ease her back, both of which would be very good. Ahead, the men conferred and pointed to the horizon while the line of women sat patiently, some dozing, their ponies beginning to graze.

Tai Hei was not born a Kiowa, and perhaps could never become Kiowa, for that part of her that was not Bird of Morning and properly patient craved to hear what words were being spoken, what matter was being decided. Did it not affect her as much as it did the men?

Then she heard the distant booming of guns, the shots coming evenly spaced, as measured as drumbeats and therefore ominously foreign. These gun-shooters were the white hunters, who plucked the buffalo day upon day as methodically as the ants working. Tai Hei had seen their blasphemous leavings—whole buffalo carcasses, sometimes vast fields of them, with only the skins taken, or the skins and tongues taken and the rest rotting under an angry sun. The stench of their hunting was an offense against heaven.

The Kiowa way was to swoop in on ponies and reap the animals wholesale, sending a vast herd to rumbling life with a *yi-yiing* of cries and crackle of guns. The warriors killed joyously what they needed and no more, and through many skillful and daring feats gave an honored prey its due.

Then came the women's job—the skinning and butchering, which went on for a day or longer, each woman working with tired arms and glad heart, the older girls and the smaller children helping. Finally, the procession would return to the village, to a clamorous welcome, followed by feasting and celebration.

In the Kiowa way of hunting there was great honor, for each had his or her own duty. Much meat was prepared and hides tanned for robes and lodge skins, all things to sustain them through the coming winter. The buffalo spirits were honored by such a hunt; they did not begrudge the people their harvest, for they knew that winter was long and the people needed nourishment in order to continue the circle of hunter and hunted.

But these whites . . . Tai Hei pitied them, these men who hunted badly. How, she wondered, could they return home and show themselves to their women after their grim way of hunting? Where was the honor in it? And when these white hunters died, as all men someday must, how could they go to their sky father after committing such offenses? Would not their sky lives be endless anguish and punishment?

She was angry with them, these beings who did not know how to act. To the extent that she was not a Kiowa, and thus had that small thing in common with whites, Tai Hei was even embarrassed for them. Though she knew it was foolish, she bore unbidden a small portion of their shame.

Again, Two Horses pointed to far-off horizons. Beside him, Wolf Running was still, meaning that he did not disagree. Another distant gun sounded. Two Horses turned forward, his back telling Tai Hei nothing, and the procession resumed its slow pace, but with its course now veering west, proceeding by indirection toward the particular stand of cottonwoods that Two Horses had decided would be his father's resting place.

Ahead, Sky Calf, Tai Hei's sister-wife, turned her pony from its place in line and circled back, her broad face bemused, for Sky Calf's friendship, though tender, was of the kind that was extended through teasing. Sky Calf was well aware of, and cheerfully tolerated, her young sister-wife's occasional failings. She knew Bird of Morning's love of gossip and news, her questioning of the why of things.

The company was welcome. Tai Hei managed a smile, and called her sister by her formal title, which was Wife-of-My-Husband. It was good to share a life and household with one such as Sky Calf. "You have words for me?" Tai Hei asked her hopefully.

"Yes, little mother. I feel your ears aching back here to hear the words of our husband."

Tai Hei was impatient with the formalities, for Kiowa speech could be as roundabout as wild turkeys mating. Though she was being mildly rebuked, Tai Hei asked, "Why is it that we are now veering westward?"

Sky Calf smiled all the more at that. "I hear your questions back here also. It is on account of the guns of the white hunters," she said. "It is said by the men that we should swoop down upon them and rub them out, for white men are wasteful and they make the hunt that is never finished."

"Yes, why do we not rub them out?" Tai Hei said. She thought meting out quick deaths might be kinder to these bloody-handed ones in the long run.

"Because we have few warriors today, and a somber task, and the shoots-far guns of the white men would take some of our ponies, if not also our men."

"This argument our husband agrees with?"

"He admits it is an indignity, but we must go around the white men to reach the burial place. He says our men will fight them some other time."

"His heart is too heavy for fighting," Tai Hei said.

"Yes, and he is too proud to say so," Sky Calf said. "And also he will not make war while women are with him. He does not say this, but I know it." As the first-wife, Sky Calf was proud of how well she knew his mind and heart.

"So it is," Tai Hei said, which was the saying of her people. Once it was out of her mouth she disliked the finality

of it and hoped it would not cut off the talking, for she badly
craved diversion. Sky Calf guided her pony closer. Some of
the men looked back to see what was delaying the rear of the
procession.

"How is it with you really?" Sky Calf asked, still looking
amused. She flicked her eyes to Tai Hei's bulging belly.

"My heart swells with pride over the new little one," Tai
Hei said.

"Why then is your brow so troubled?"

"I burst to urinate," Tai Hei admitted.

Sky Calf laughed. "Get down and relieve yourself, silly
pup. I will hold your pony." Her face was merry. Tai Hei
slid gratefully from her blanket saddle. When her legs
touched the ground, they could hardly hold her. A woman
so pregnant had little modesty left; she squatted behind sage
no higher than her knees. Even squatting was difficult.

"We are sure to be scolded," Tai Hei said as she eased her
insides. The easing was a great blessing.

"I will catch any sharp words aimed your way," Sky Calf
said. "After all, our husband does not rule in everything."

4 · RILEY

AT THE HERBERT EXPRESS AND DRAYAGE COMPANY RILEY
Stokes learned Director Julius Herbert took his breakfast at
the Big Creek Cafe. Riley backtracked to the business
district, imagining the man just finishing his meal, leaning
back with a last cup of coffee, probably in more expansive a
mood than he'd be in all day. Meet adversity with initiative,
Riley told himself, hurrying. A lick of smart and sufficient
brass to use it.

The Big Creek Cafe was awash in coffee aroma, cigar
smoke, and the thick, hot-grease smell of fry pork. In
response to Riley's question, a waiter pointed out Julius
Herbert at a nearby table. He was compact and dark
bearded, bearing some resemblance, Riley thought, to Ulys-
ses S. Grant, though on the whole considerably tidier-
looking than the president. Herbert breakfasted with three
other men, all dressed similarly in business clothes.

Riley approached the table just as one of the men wound up a story and let off abruptly, leaving his listeners in some astonishment. "Mister Herbert?" Riley said. His timing was unlucky; the three others erupted in laughter, but leaving Herbert sour-faced, as though the joke had been at his expense.

"What is it?" Herbert said when the laughter rattled away.

"About the position you are offering?" Riley's statement climbed unintended, coming out a question. "The limited and hazardous one," Riley said more firmly. "I believe I answer all your particulars."

Herbert flicked his eyes to Riley's newspaper. "That thing out already? If you could read English you would see I want applicants no earlier than six tonight." He was annoyed, making Riley regret he had not waited. Except for Terrible John Parrott, the whole town seemed to be having a disappointing day. It confirmed Riley's opinion of workaday men.

Riley said, "I thought I would demonstrate initiative."

Herbert frowned. A second man at the table laughed and said, "He gives a good answer, Herbie."

"As a banker, I insist that my own employees exhibit high moral character," the third man said. "This fellow looks a bit of a ragamuffin."

"I was up working all night," Riley put in. "You will seldom find a more industrious person. I was raised by Methodists." Again, the second man laughed good-naturedly.

"You can show up at six and be considered with all others," Julius Herbert said, then turned his attention to his coffee.

"For pity's sake, Herbie," the second man said. "A nice-looking fellow and eager to work. I'll wager you could do worse. I'd hire him myself had I a hole to fill."

"Obliged," Riley said.

"I don't muck about with army contracts," Herbert answered gruffly. "I mean to have the best pair of men I can find for the job." He turned back to Riley. "Until six," he said. "A good day to you."

Dismissed, Riley touched his hat brim and turned for the door. While he hadn't got the job, he hadn't yet lost it either—although his victory in getting a newspaper had gone for nothing. There seemed nothing more to do but go catch up on lost sleep.

As he approached the doorway, he was conscious of a figure striding up briskly behind him. Riley swung open the door and obligingly stepped aside. "Pardon me," he said, and then was appalled to see the tall dandy of the poker game sweep past him—fancy cravat, brocaded vest, frock coattails and all.

The dandy turned and seemed flustered to recognize him. "Uh . . . you there," the dandy said. Riley came through the doorway, straightening to his full height. He would not be taken for anybody's servant.

"I am glad to run into you again," the dandy said. "After giving the matter more thought, I'd like to offer my apology." He choked a little on "apology," as though the word cost him an effort. Riley looked for a joke or trick of some kind, but the dandy's manner seemed deferential, the blue eyes earnest.

"For a fact?" Riley said.

"I probably ought to have told you beforehand this Parrott was a slick," the dandy said. "More to the point, that he was likely playing it shady."

"Well, I wisht you would've," Riley said.

The dandy looked Riley over. "Especially if you could not stand the losses. If you don't mind my saying, you seem down on your luck." Riley noticed the dandy carried another twisty cigar. He had a way of drawing on it that made Riley wish he had one.

"Not at all," Riley said, frowning. He nestled his left hand in his pocket to hide the torn sleeve. "I'm in the express business myself. Honest outdoor work. There's no call for me to dress up like a . . ." A riverboat gambler, Riley thought. ". . . like a banker," Riley said. "I don't hang my head on account of working for a living."

"Of course not," the dandy said. "I surely never meant—"

"It's a regular job of work," Riley told him. "Employment a man can depend on." He noted that some of the difference in their heights was due to the dandy's high-heeled boots. It made him feel a little better.

"Well, like I say, Mister . . ."

"Stokes," Riley said.

"Stokes. And I'm McCasland. So like I say, I'm sorry I didn't—"

"It's all right." They stood awkwardly, their topic already threadbare. "I appreciate you mentioning it, even if it comes a smidge late," Riley said.

"I ought to have told you sooner," the dandy said firmly. Again they stood. Riley found it hard to keep from studying the vest's mating tadpoles.

"I expect that's the new paper," the dandy said.

Riley looked under his own arm, surprised to see the rolled newspaper, which suddenly took on an aspect of criminal evidence. But the new edition should be safely distributed before long, he thought, thus erasing his crime. "Yes sir, fresh off the press," Riley admitted.

"I was just going to pick one up," McCasland said.

The paper was suddenly hot in Riley's armpit. He had a vision of the dandy going to the news office and saying he'd already seen a copy of the new edition. "You just take this here one," Riley said swiftly. The dandy protested. "Being all through with it, I insist," Riley said. The notion of giving the dandy something he no longer had a use for appealed to him. "Anyhow, it only cost a five-cent piece."

"Then I'll repay you for it," the dandy said quickly, digging into a trouser pocket.

"Oh, horse turds—I couldn't take that," Riley said. But the dandy insisted all over again and Riley acquiesced, telling himself no man of means would make a to-do about five cents one way or another. He looked down, expecting to see the dandy's hand come up with an impressive roll of bills or a handful of gold eagles. Instead, the palm held only a scattering of small coins. Riley accepted a five-cent piece. "Obliged," he said and handed over the paper with a small flourish.

The dandy tapped his palm with the paper, oddly fidgeting. "Tell you what. I just ate, but I'll stand you to breakfast."

"I've eaten already," Riley lied. He was not taking charity from any brocaded gambler. They stood wordless. With some relief, Riley thought of the express job, the day's mission. He made a show of looking at his watch. The lid spring was broken and he had to pry the lid open with a thumbnail. Looking at the watch, he felt, gave the impression of a man with appointments. He was only sorry it was not a better watch. At most, he'd get only two or three dollars for it.

"Well, sir, pretty quick here I've got a man I need to see," Riley said.

"You said the express business," the dandy said. "The salary is sufficient, I take it?"

"Fair wages," Riley said, "regular as clockwork."

"No hard feelings?"

"Nothing of the sort."

"I'll maybe see you again," the dandy said. Riley nodded and backed a step and the two men moved off in opposite directions, though Riley soon realized he was going away from his hotel instead of toward it. He made sure the dandy didn't see him when he changed directions. As he walked, he transferred the dandy's coin to the pocket holding the rest of his money. At least his fortunes had risen five cents' worth. He took it as an important sign that his luck was changing.

5 · EUSTIS FALK

BUG-EYE HOLLENBECK GOT HEAVILY OFF THE WAGON SEAT TO look at the groaning wheel and the next thing he did was kick it. "What cheese-headed coon was supposed to've greased this son of a bitch?" he roared. "Grubb, you lard-arse, fetch out that tar bucket. Somebody give a hand with that frigging screw jack. By the bleeding Jaysus, do I have to do everything in this outfit?" Behind his back, the teamsters called him the German or the Dutchman, but Hollenbeck liked to say *Jay-sus*, like an Irishman, because it stretched the word out longer.

Grubb and a younger man, Sile Cooper, set to work jacking up the rear of the wagon. Turning the screw jack, even with a long iron handle, was heavy work with the load aboard.

"Useless!" Hollenbeck yelled, "you being a-horseback,

ride up the rise yonder and see can you spy the Pawnee River. I been thinking it's over the next rise all the damnable afternoon. Must be we are pret' near on top of it."

Without answering, Eustis yarded out a rolling block rifle from his saddle boot, wheeled his horse, and loped toward the rise. He was a tall, loosely connected man and he rode with flapping elbows, as though there were no more to him than bones and clothes.

It was the curse of any man named Eustis to be called Useless now and again, no matter how handy he might be in any number of situations. Eustis Falk normally counted himself a fair hand in any company. In the whiskey trains of Bug-eye Hollenbeck, a man with a brow as black as a storm coming on and a voice that cut like a bullwhip, Eustis had worked his way up to being more or less foreman, even though it was not Hollenbeck's manner to acknowledge it.

Eustis had no more than topped the rise and seen the scraggly line of distant cottonwoods that indicated the river when a movement caught his eye. A little buck of an Indian, more boy than man, had been lying on his pony's neck, holding the pony flat on its flanks on the prairie, both of them together lying quiet as snakes while the boy spied on the whiskey wagons. Eustis was amazed the little buck had let them get so close; probably Eustis suddenly loping over the rise had been the surprise of the boy's life. No grown warrior, especially not one out ranging on his lonesome, would have let a wagon party get within half a mile of him. There was a youth's bravado in it.

"By God," Eustis said aloud. He had never cared for being spied upon, and the fact of the spy being an Indian made his anger run all the stronger. Eustis pulled up sharp and craned his turkey neck, making sure, before he got too indignant, that no other Indians lurked on that rise. Then he raised his rifle.

Bent on escape, the little Indian had got up with his pony, hanging tight to its neck, and was now thumping heels into the pony's belly and switching its flanks with a bow for more speed. Eustis steadied down and touched off a shot that spilled the pony in a roll of dust. He loaded a fresh cartridge and kicked up his mount. The little buck was up in an instant and launched a wobbly arrow, which fell short.

Eustis loped in, holding the long rifle with its buttstock under his arm like a lance, and triggered off a second shot, smashing the boy's chest with a .50-70 ball.

When Eustis swung off his horse he saw the little buck was still struggling so he went over and busted his head in with the rifle butt, figuring his two shots had already raised enough racket, especially with more Indians likely about. Eustis didn't care to see any creature's suffering, even an Indian's. The pony was stone dead with a bullet through the neck and Eustis couldn't help but admire his own marksmanship.

Then he had two considerations. The first was whether the little buck had pals in the neighborhood, as in Eustis's experience, young bucks, when they wanted to raise hell, mostly went out in bunches. The second was how Bug-eye Hollenbeck, a man as touchy as gunpowder, would react to his having killed the Indian—or more exactly, to his calling attention to their presence by such casual gunfire.

His conclusion was that even Hollenbeck's cyclone temper was less of a threat than prowling Indians. The little buck was Kiowa, if Eustis knew his markings, and Kiowas were a serious business no matter what their ages or numbers. He put his foot on the boy's face and stooped over and scalped him, being careful not to foul the scalp in the pulped brains. The long hair was like a handle and made the job easy. The scalp came away with a sucking sound.

Eustis reloaded the rolling block and swung up into the saddle. He scanned the horizons, seeing no Indians, but it was when you didn't see them that you most had to worry. As he loped back over the rise and down to the wagon party, he saw the German standing out front in his tall boots, planted like a tree. The man's whole stance was a challenge.

"By creation, if you shoot off a gun, you had best kill something," Hollenbeck roared at him.

Eustis raised the scalp. "Kiowa, most like."

Hollenbeck grunted. He was the kind of man who, if he failed to attack you for something, it passed for approval. "Got him afore he could tell his pals about us," Eustis said carefully. "That little river's real pretty. Just a mile or so ahead."

Hollenbeck grunted again. "Only one of 'em?"

"Only one I saw." Eustis was not a man to volunteer information. He knew lone wolves who went ranging were rarely such youngsters. This one hadn't been much of an Indian at all, but by God it was the best-looking scalp Eustis thought he'd ever taken. Thick and glossy. "It don't mean there ain't more," Eustis added.

"Then they will already know we're here," Hollenbeck said sourly. "Thanks to your ruckus."

"Not likely. With all the buffalo men hereabouts, you hear a couple shots on the plains, it don't necessary tell you much." For Eustis Falk, it was a lot of talking. He generally husbanded his words to no more than a handful a day, but killing the little Indian had excited him.

Hollenbeck apparently considered it. One hand consulted his beard, a sure sign of deep thinking. "Maybe so," he said finally. He appeared to forget all about Eustis sitting his skinny horse; he turned instead to his crew, who had left off struggling with the axle jack and were regarding Eustis and the bloody scalp. Evidence of Indians had a sobering effect on men on the plains.

"What you coons standing around for?" Hollenbeck thundered at them. "Grease the frigging wheel and let's get a move on!"

Eustis made a move to swing down. He had a tow sack in a wagon where he would put the scalp. "You stay put," Hollenbeck told him, and then ordered Sile Cooper to saddle him a horse while he fetched a rifle, a pair of buffalo sticks, and his brass spyglass. "If there's more Injuns in these parts, I want a look-see," Hollenbeck told Eustis. He swung into the saddle and gave Eustis one of his crooked looks, with the bug-eye staring off to the horizon someplace. Eustis shrugged. It seemed they were going Indian hunting.

Bug-eye Hollenbeck had a black beard as stiff as broom straw, a face that apparently hadn't felt soap and water, and of course, that damned old bug-eye. He wore leather breeches, a red woolen shirt, well faded, and a battered hat the circumference of a ten-egg fry pan, the brim tacked up flat in front.

Eustis had worked for Hollenbeck for three years and knew him as well as anybody did, which was to say not much. Running whiskey to the Indian Territory was miles wide of the law, a situation guaranteeing high profits while behooving a person to be closemouthed about it. Hollenbeck's jaws, though, worked steady from sunup, mostly cursing out his men, calling them coons and cheeseheads like they were either niggers or farmers or some combination. And yet, while he liked to hear the blaring of his own voice, Hollenbeck rarely said anything of substance about their business.

Hollenbeck let others in the Territory, white traders, do the retailing, mostly down southeast to the so-called Five Civilized Tribes in the part called the Nations. Settlement Indians liked their whiskey as much as any wild Indian on the plains. Hollenbeck, though, stuck tight to just wagoning, for while an outfit was hauling, there was little danger.

The Lighthorse—Indian police—would not bother them, having no authority over white men. And if stopped by the army or Federal marshals out of Fort Smith, Hollenbeck could face down authority with the coolness of a gun slick, staring a man full in the face with that bug-eye roving and claiming he was bound for Adobe Walls or Fort Griffin or Jacksboro in Texas, or most any other damned place, and the officer would have to accept the explanation. Hollenbeck cozied up to some officers by handing out free liquor; others he scared the bejesus out of by popping out his bug-eye—about as startling a sight as most men ever witnessed and one Eustis never got used to. On the whole Eustis would rather see him give away good whiskey.

Hollenbeck punished his horse till he got up a good speed, heedless of prairie dog holes. Eustis loped in behind him. They topped the rise where he had surprised his Indian and there they lay, pony and boy sprawled no more than a hundred yards down the gentle incline.

"Killing that pony was good thinking," Hollenbeck said grudgingly. He got down and steadied the spyglass on the buffalo sticks and scanned a long time. Eustis shaded his eyes with his hat and examined the plains as well.

"I don't see nothing," Hollenbeck said finally. "A'course looking into that sun is a trial on anybody."

"Injuns would likely be near water this time of day,"

Eustis offered. "Iffen you wanted, we could flank the river a mile and let the wagons follow. If there's Injuns, we'd soon see 'em." It was another long speech, especially considering it was Hollenbeck he was talking to. Eustis licked his lips when he finished.

"Might could," Hollenbeck said, running fingers through his beard. "We might could at that." He stood up and said jokingly, "Useless, one of these days we might have to leave off calling you Useless."

The sun was three fingers lower when they spotted the Kiowa. The Indians were a ragged line a mile distant heading toward the fringe of trees along the river. Their ponies plodded, then stopped. Hollenbeck got down immediately and set up the telescope. "Confederate spyglass," he said, pointing proudly to the brass tube. "Man told me it says 'Made in Richmond' on it someplace."

"That right?" Eustis said, being polite. He himself never had much luck looking through spyglasses. Usually he saw no more than blackness, then a sudden and nervous circle of brightly colored world and then back to blackness again.

"It don't look to be no war party," Hollenbeck said. "Chrissakes, they got women with them. What in holy hell you make of such a party as that?"

"Hardly enough for a hunting bunch," Eustis said. Without aid of a telescope, he made out only dots of horses. "They would want women, though, for their skinning."

"No more'n ten, eleven all told," Hollenbeck said. He squinched his face to see through the telescope and it made his voice come squinched too. "They're dismounting by the river. Hell, they're cutting poles."

"For tepees," Eustis suggested.

"They ain't got no bundles with them as is big enough to be lodge skins."

"Burial party, I would wager," Eustis said with sudden conviction.

"Now you hit the mark."

"Damned burial scaffold is about the only thing a redskin ever builds permanent," Eustis said. "'Course, you can pull them down easy enough when looking for valuables."

Hollenbeck said, "I make out three, four women and

some old geezers. There's no more'n a couple braves who look up to fighting." He studied the far distance awhile longer, then closed up the telescope with the sound of metal parts sliding. "A burial party sure. Let's bring up the whole outfit before it gets too dark."

"What you fixing on, Bug-eye?" Eustis had let a little worry into his voice, which was rarely wise around a man like Hollenbeck.

Hollenbeck looked at him, one dark eye fixed squarely while the damned bug-eye strayed off to admire the sun-down. Eustis often got the feeling Hollenbeck could look clear around behind him. "Why, Useless—you are generally game for a frolic."

Eustis stood, unsure if he were supposed to answer.

"Ain't you?"

"Generally," Eustis conceded.

"Then let's by God get them other coons and hop to it," Hollenbeck said. "I don't mind taking time now and again for a little bit of fun."

6 · RILEY

IT WAS FIVE-THIRTY IN THE AFTERNOON WHEN RILEY AGAIN walked the boardwalks of Hays City. He'd washed and shaved and finally eaten a late-afternoon meal big enough to catch him up in the victuals department. His funds remaining totaled just over three dollars.

This Julius Herbert fellow, Riley decided, had probably had the morning grumps. It was a malady to which many were susceptible, Riley included. Herbert might turn out to be a decent egg otherwise. As he walked, Riley enjoyed a pleasant vignette in which Herbert had a change of heart toward him, welcoming Riley into Herbert's office at the drayage company with a handshake and an important job. Sustained by the daydream, he walked tall and his boot heels rang cheerily.

As he walked, however, Riley met a fair number of men straggling back the other way, burly workmen, most of them, all sour-faced and hangdog looking. He pitied these men, who apparently found life disappointing, their prospects limited. By contrast, the job Riley looked forward to had sounded both interesting and lucrative.

Riley reached the yards of the Herbert Express and Drayage Company just minutes before six, timing himself carefully with his father's old watch. He could have come earlier, but showing an extra measure of initiative in front of Julius Herbert only annoyed the man. Now he would demonstrate punctuality, and a rare ability to follow orders to the letter. This time, Riley would give his future employer nothing with which to find fault.

As he turned off Lincoln Street, a particularly dejected-looking man was coming out of the drayage yards, his shoes scuffing dust. "No use going further," the man said. "Them express positions is already filled."

Riley tried to grin. "Most likely you're joshing."

"No, sir, I wisht I was. A sign on the office advises they got the men they was looking for."

"Damn it all, that just can't be," Riley said, and he felt and heard the desperation coming into his voice. "The paper said six o'clock."

"Some must've jumped the gun on it," the man said. Riley swore. A mix of momentum and rising anger carried him another thirty paces. The sign, freshly lettered on a piece of shingle, was propped against the porch railing. POSITIONS FILLED, it declared bluntly. JOB SEEKERS KEEP OUT.

Riley saw red lightning, outriders of approaching rage. Here this bastard Herbert had had the gall to tell him he'd be considered with other applicants, and then he'd hired men ahead of the deadline. Riley kicked savagely at the foot of the porch railing. The sign toppled. He toed the sign faceup, seeing dirt stuck in the paint.

He stood in his ragged coat, his hands useless at his sides, an awareness of his fourteen-dollar room bill at the Hays House gnawing at him. He would have to sell his watch after all, and then his Remington revolver, just to scrape by a little longer. He'd heard of men so broken-down on the frontier that they'd returned east riding the undercarriages of the Union Pacific, skimming twenty inches off the roadbed with the ties whirring underneath like reaper blades. Riley supposed that to be his future, eventually shambling into his ma's Kentucky kitchen, barefooted, his pockets turned out—if, at that sorry stage, he still had any pockets.

When he cut it loose, Riley Stokes had a temper like a cannonade. He decided he was just awfully angry, and the anger was well justified, and he was for damned sure going to let somebody know about it. He stepped up on the porch and stalked to the closed door. Inside, a man's voice droned. Riley thundered a fist and the voice stopped. Then it said, "For the love of Mike, don't break it down!"

Bordering on fury, Riley swung the door open. Beyond a seated figure in a gray coat with his back to Riley sat Julius Herbert, director of the Herbert Express and Drayage Company, pipe poised in midstartle, looking more like President U. S. Grant than ever, except as spook-eyed as a barn owl.

"You again," Herbert said, and snorted. "First you're ten hours early and then you come in late and busting my door down. I was beginning to think you weren't coming."

Riley said, "I—"

"Have a seat," Herbert ordered. "It looks as though you two are all that's going to show. Times must be better than I thought. I figured that advertisement would have brought out a crowd."

"Few men have the stomach for danger," the man with his back to Riley said smoothly. "It was probably that 'hazardous' business you mentioned that kept folks away." The speaker had light-colored hair. His flat-brimmed J. B. Stetson's hat was perched on a near corner of Herbert's desk. The hat carried familiarity; the voice fairly rang with it.

Hazardous be damned, Riley thought. What had kept job seekers away was the "positions filled" sign. Still dumbfounded, his anger throttled back but unreleased, Riley sat down in a rung-backed chair and looked across at the other job applicant. It was McCasland the dandy, the frock-coated son of a bitch who had bought Riley's newspaper.

Riley felt his face must have vaulted to surprise. In

response, the dandy gave him a brief, almost sheepish smile of recognition.

"Since it seems you're both hired," Herbert said, "we may as well skip the preliminaries." Riley sat blinking and bewildered while Herbert asked their names, writing them down in a marble backed notebook.

Herbert, a believer in dramatic pauses, pushed his chair back. While tamping his pipe, he eyed them soberly. His company, he told them, had secured an army contract to deliver goods—exactly what kind of goods he did not specify. For a job taking six to seven days, he required a pair of armed and steady-nerved men. "Each man to furnish his own weapons, of course," Herbert said.

"Of course," the dandy said.

"I think it best to withhold details till tomorrow," Herbert said. "You will understand my reasons for secrecy when the time comes. Let me say only that the job entails a considerable trip across the prairies. You should procure bedding suitable for sleeping on the open ground. Transport will be provided, as will all provisions *en route*."

"That's generous," Riley put in. He did not mean to be taken for a wooden Indian.

"The job begins when the Kansas Pacific arrives from Topeka—that'd be roughly two-forty tomorrow afternoon. Be here then, the both of you." Herbert tapped the desktop with an index finger, then replaced the pipe in his teeth. Another pause for effect. "Questions, gentlemen?"

"The advertisement mentioned 'remuneration as commensurate with risk,'" the dandy said.

"So it did. In light of possible hazards, the company offers sixty-five dollars per man for the job."

Riley was rocked. The figure came to ten dollars a day. "That's even more generous," Riley said.

"I'm afraid I'll have to hold out for seventy-five," the dandy said easily. Julius Herbert nearly swallowed his pipe. Badly affronted, he peered at the dandy. Riley was affronted too.

"I have a budget allowing sixty-five per man," Herbert said, more surprised than anything, "and not a penny more." The statement ended on a stern note.

The dandy's face opened to a grin. "Well, sir, no harm done. My daddy taught me to test every price."

"You'll find this one as firm as bedrock," Herbert said flatly.

The dandy dipped his head: an acquiescence. "Sixty-five it is," he said smoothly, and he shifted a leg across the other knee. There was an itchy silence in which Riley noticed he could see right through the sole of the dandy's boot.

"The advertisement also mentioned hazards," Riley put in.

"That matter is part of what is confidential," Herbert said. "I will say I've not lost a man yet." He smiled, delivering a punchline. "But then, this is to be the first trip." The dandy laughed politely while Riley struggled to smile. Herbert stood up, signaling an end to the interview. "Let us merely say that if certain situations arise, you will earn your salary."

Herbert shook Riley's hand somberly, so that Riley had to wonder what he was getting himself into. Then the dandy surprised them all over again by asking for an advance against wages. "Just to tide me over," the dandy said. "A man has expenses."

A new seriousness settled over Julius Herbert. "You are a very forward young man, Mr. McCasland."

"Yes, sir—I've been told that."

"What kind of figure would you require?" Herbert asked him.

"Only twenty dollars or so. I've been down on my luck."

Herbert looked doubtful, then slid open a desk drawer and took out a metal cash box. "It's irregular, but I suppose ambition is no crime. In fact, I admire a man with brass and initiative. You remind me of myself in earlier times."

Herbert smiled. Riley was flabbergasted. A twenty-dollar greenback passed from Herbert to the dandy. The thought clumsily gathered in Riley's mind that he could use an advance too; there was his hotel bill to pay. Riley formed up half a sentence. Herbert closed the cash box with metallic finality, then set it reverently into the drawer. The drawer bumped shut. The time to speak aged, then passed. Riley bit his lip.

"I extend my wholehearted gratitude to you, sir," the dandy had the nerve to say. He got smartly to his feet, a schoolmarm's brightest student. "Likewise, I will extend my utmost in service."

"Which I deeply appreciate," Herbert said, looking as happy as if marrying off his homeliest daughter. He reached out and shook the dandy's hand, ignoring Riley like he were part of the furnishings.

"Till tomorrow," Herbert said warmly.

"Two-forty on the button," the dandy said.

Ten seconds later Riley and the dandy stood on the office porch looking at a gathering sundown. The flip-flop of the day's fortunes had left him bewildered.

"I reckon this sign could prove embarrassing," the dandy said, and he stooped to pick up the sign lying where Riley had kicked it. "Looks like somebody got a little sore about it," the dandy said, and chuckled. As the dandy picked it up, Riley couldn't help but read the "Job Seekers Keep Out" part of it. It had looked so official.

"Clever idea, don't you think?" the dandy said, heading out of the yards toward Lincoln Street. He did not seem quite so much like a dandy when he walked. His long legs took purposeful strides, making Riley have to trot occasionally to keep up.

"Why, that trick euchred a whole bunch of fellows," Riley said. "I met them coming back. I expect it was a kind of cheating."

"Not at all," the dandy said. "Just improving the odds. No one was obliged to believe my sign. I see it didn't keep *you* out." He paused to sail the sign edgewise out over a vacant lot.

"I was just coming in to kill the bastard," Riley admitted, making the dandy laugh. "Anyway, I thought you were a sporting man," Riley noted. "Isn't taking a job more or less of a comedown?"

The dandy shrugged. "Any sporting man needs a stake. My fortunes at the moment are in a bit of a dry spell." They turned off Sherman Avenue toward Main Street. "And you, I believe, claimed to be in the express business," the dandy said.

"It appears I am," Riley said.

"'A regular job of work,'" you said. 'Something a man can bank on.'"

Riley felt his ears warming. "I can bank on sixty-five dollars for a week's work," Riley said, and once more the dandy laughed at him.

7 · TAI HEI

TAI HEI STOOD WITH HER PEOPLE, EACH THROWING SIDELONG glances at the lowering sun. The scaffold was a good one, incorporated on one side into a cottonwood, the other side supported with sturdy uprights and cross members lashed with green rawhide, soon to dry as hard as wood. The body of Eagle Man, medicine bundle beside him, lay eight feet above ground, a tribute to the high station he'd held in life.

When the sun's rim touched the earth's far edges, Tai Hei's husband, Two Horses, began speaking in the high, reedy voice appropriate when commending a spirit to the sky father. He called upon Taimay, the Kiowa sacred effigy, to plead in the afterlife on his father's behalf. He enumerated Eagle Man's attributes, which Kiowa gods already knew well: that Eagle Man was a great *Koitsenko,* one of the Principal Dogs or Ten Bravest, the highest rank among Kiowa military societies. In battle, he had been second to none; in loyalty, an outspoken follower of Little Mountain, greatest Kiowa chief and recorder of the tribal history. Then after Little Mountain's death, Eagle Man had pledged fealty to Satank, later killed by carbines while a prisoner of the whites. Surely, Two Horses suggested, Eagle Man would enjoy a sky life in the company of illustrious warriors.

Tai Hei listened and yet did not. She heard her husband's exhortation and reflected on it, but she thought also of the sun's fire, quenching itself now in the earth. Did not the sun rise anew each morning? The same was true, she saw, of the flame in the breast of the one who was her father-in-law. For as his flame flickered and died, and the shadow of that flame rose to the sky father, yet another flame on earth caught and climbed, the beginning of new life. She cupped her hand to her belly and felt tiny heels kicking as though in response to these thoughts. Joy welled up in her so that she wanted to laugh aloud.

She stood feeling again the truth of it, that it was the same flame burning in all the people, just as all flames were separate feathers of the same fire. In that moment a certainty descended. She felt her child would be a male child and that he in his life would be joined in some way to the old warrior Eagle Man. Perhaps linked by their names. It was so wonderful an idea that she gave a start, so that Sky Calf turned and with a look admonished her. Be a Kiowa, the look said. But Tai Hei went on with her thoughts awhile longer. She decided she must speak to her husband about a name when next she had the chance.

Her husband's voice droned on. Tai Hei's mind returned. And then she felt foolish, standing at her father-in-law's burial and beginning to think of names for her child, for the child was after all a Kiowa, and as such must find his own name, just as he eventually must make his own way in the world. She was foolish at such a time to let herself be Tai Hei again, and not Bird of Morning, a Kiowa.

She heard hoofbeats and looked about her, expecting to see the return of young Iron Bow. Instead it was Wolf Running, his face hot with import, gesturing toward the river. Tai Hei had a need to learn the reason for this disturbance, but she caught Sky Calf's eye and felt her sister-wife scolding her for curiosity. But then another warrior and Wolf Running were leaving the group, though Two Horses was now transported, his voice falling into the chant. It was a beautiful chant, Tai Hei thought. Surely this brave spirit, this *Koitsenko,* would ascend quickly.

There came a rattle of shots. Old Tall Deer, his face amazed, turned and fell. A pony screamed and reared. Two Horses opened his eyes, appearing lost between trance and disbelief. Sky Calf's usually merry face went gaunt with alarm. Across the river the brush erupted in foxtails of smoke. More Kiowa fell. Tai Hei held her palms to her ears to shut out her own screams.

Hooves thundered, the heavy, iron-shod horses of the white men. A few Kiowa were firing now, retreating as they went, protecting the women. But retreating to where? Behind them was the vastness of the plains. Bullets hissed like hot iron touching water.

A horseman bore down on her. Tai Hei ran, stumbled, scrambled to her feet. The man had a laughing, hairy face. He leaned out for her, missed, rode by, then wheeled to come back at her.

She ran crying, all Tai Hei now. She gripped her skinning knife by its bone handle and dashed into the trees. Hackberries slashed her. In the brush along the river it was already nearly dark. She ran headlong into a maze of dogwillow, plunging and then crawling forward frantically. Shots slammed behind her. Rough white men's voices were displacing the yells and screams of her people.

A heavy voice said, "One little doe-eye made off in the bushes."

"Watch yourself with her," another voice said. "Female or not, they're dangerous as snakes."

She understood the words and was astonished. Another shot sounded so nearby that she jumped. Bullets whispered angrily through the brush. She broke out of the dogwillow and gave a cry as she sprawled into the river, her heartbeat dinning in her ears. Chill, knee-deep water tugged her away. She rode the current until she again heard rough voices calling.

On the far bank was another stand of dogwillow, at its base a passage, perhaps a coyote run. In the brush from which she had come, a horseman blundered, cursing. She pushed through thigh-deep water, nightmarishly heavy and impeding, the current dragging her sideways. The bottom was uneven and she staggered, making splashes. But then she crouched low and got one knee up on the far bank and crawled into the passage, feeling panicked and awkward, vulnerable and afraid—both for herself and for her child.

Within the brush was a hollow. She recognized a deer bed, and felt the aptness of it. She crouched and waited as darkness enveloped her, and she knew the terror of the hunted doe.

8 · RILEY

THE DANDY, MCCASLAND, HAILED FROM TEXAS, OF ALL PLACES. He had been a trooper in the Confederate cavalry, though more lately a trail drover, hazing another man's cattle to the Kansas railhead. One three-month trip up the Chisholm Trail to Abilene had cured him of that profession. Cowboys called it a hell of a way to make a hundred dollars; McCasland heartily agreed that it was.

Once in Abilene and paid off, his saddlemates had gone on sprees, while McCasland himself had gone to a bathhouse and then a haberdashery. Following the hind ends of two thousand cattle, he told Riley, had fed him all the dust he ever cared to eat. Cowpokes used themselves up, he said, just making money for somebody else. He vowed he would become a town gent, a sport—in short, a gambler—making his living skimming his small portion of the plentiful beef money that flowed through Kansas cow towns.

"Well, dog my cats," Riley said. "Sounds like we're two of a kind." He maybe laid it on too thick, for, having been in the war, he did not much hanker to associate with ex-rebel Texans, frock-coated or otherwise. He figured, though, he might as well get used to this McCasland since he'd just hired out on a six-day job with him.

Riley himself, Riley told him, was from hardscrabble Kentucky farming country. They were Union people, the Stokeses, but by slim margins; the fact was he'd had cousins on both sides of the conflict. Riley himself had joined the Federal army and served out the war, which had started as a welcome respite from farming and evolved from there into pure and holy hell.

Farming, Riley said, was not so much dusty as plain dirty. And you didn't have to breathe it; it came in through your skin. He had followed a team of big-boned, manure-spattered ox hinders for what seemed like halfway around the world. He had plowed around enough stumps and straddled enough furrow to last him ten lifetimes. His sisters kept getting married, most bringing home husbands. The

34

home place was filling up. So when the railroads pushed west after the end of the war, Riley had pushed west with them.

McCasland said he had to agree, yes sir, it was two of a kind, was what they were, and Riley said yep, indeed it was.

They were passing square-shouldered false fronts of the business district, the unpainted siding that was the basic material of Hays City looking less raw in the dusky light. An almost palpable peace descended at dusk. The sun banked its fires; hot prairie breezes slackened and things relented generally. It was as though the plains had called a truce overnight to let the town catch its breath.

The swinging half doors of the Railway Advance Saloon were propped open to the evening. A rumble of voices flowed onto the boardwalk along with the popping progress of a banjo.

"Shall we?" McCasland said. "I figure Herbert's twenty dollars can buy me one last game. If my luck turns around, I won't have to take that job tomorrow."

"You'd do that?" Riley said, sounding to himself as disapproving as a schoolteacher. "Take his money as a stake, I mean?" McCasland avowed he would. "In my notion of a sporting man, he ought keep his word," Riley said.

"Well, in *my* notion, he adjusts his plans according to circumstances," McCasland said, and shouldered through the doorway. With nowhere much else to go, Riley followed, then came aware of the waistcoated bulk of Terrible John Parrott raking in a pot at the room's only poker game.

"That bastard again," McCasland noted.

"When it comes to that jasper, I reckon we learnt our lesson," Riley said sourly. They moved to the bar, watching Parrott as they went. Riley squandered five cents on a beer, seeing he as good as had an income.

"I still wonder what kind of play he's using," McCasland said. "You watch him from here and maybe one of us can learn something. I believe I'll have another go."

"He'll just take your money," Riley said.

"I'll quit after ten dollars."

"I'd be real careful," Riley said.

McCasland, winking, drew a nickel-plated derringer pistol from a vest pocket. "I'm always careful," he said, then put the little gun back with deliberation, as though it rode in some special arrangement in there. He picked up his drink, a brandy, and squared his shoulders. "I will see you later," McCasland said.

Riley watched him thread a path to the table, then introduce himself. A chair was pulled back for him, chair legs protesting. McCasland sat down and waited for the current hand to play out. He said something that made the other players laugh. Parrott, though, only smiled briefly and kept his eyes on his cards.

Riley leaned his weight against the bar, finding himself pleasantly sleepy. He couldn't follow the course of a poker game without staring over the players' shoulders, and most were too testy to allow that. He watched the game in the back mirror until the bar filled up enough to obscure his view. He took a seat at a nearby table, but a poker game started there too and he had to move again.

Forty minutes later, Riley was sipping a second beer right back where he'd started—boot heel on the bar rail, his short ribs lodged against the bar's rolled cornice. For a time his attention wandered to the banjo player. Riley had always wanted to play an instrument, both because he liked music and because it seemed clever to coax tunes out of what was essentially a contraption. His mother had played the fiddle, a pastime considered unseemly for a woman. To blunt criticism, she played sacred songs, mostly.

When he looked back to the poker game, one player had been replaced. McCasland smiled and joked. Other players laughed and drank and slapped the table. Terrible John Parrott tended to business, sober as a hangman.

Riley checked his watch, finding it eight-thirty. His daytime nap had not made up for a whole night's lost sleep. Tomorrow was a new day, with a new job to go with it. He caught himself yawning in the back-bar mirror, a clean-shaven man in a ragged coat.

Though McCasland had suggested he keep an eye on the game, Riley felt he owed him no particular obligation. On the contrary, because of his confounded signboard, McCasland had nearly cost him a job. Riley resolved to watch the game till his beer was gone, then nod McCasland a good evening and head down to the Big Creek Cafe. With his meal ticket as good as punched for a few days, he intended to splurge on a late supper. What he would do about the hotel bill he had no idea.

When Riley looked back at the game, he was surprised how the pile of currency in front of John Parrott had grown. While Parrott did not win every pot, he apparently took the big ones. McCasland, by contrast, was down to small change.

His face rueful, McCasland said something to the other players, touched his hat brim, and stood up. Then his blue eyes shifted to Riley, their expression grim, and he came toward where Riley was propping up the bar.

"I couldn't get a thing on him," Riley said. "Appears he's just sitting playing poker."

"He's doing more than that but I still can't figure how," McCasland said. "He's wearing two rings, but a shiner is no advantage unless you're dealing. He wins whether dealing or not."

Riley had to ask what a shiner was. McCasland explained how some players polished a flat in the underside of a finger ring, making it reflect like a mirror. "With practice you can read cards as you're dealing them. Parrott, though, is too slick for that one."

McCasland ordered another brandy and sipped thoughtfully. Riley remembered he'd been about to head out the door. "I've got just enough money to buy me some supper," Riley said. He lifted his beer mug and drained it.

A commotion kicked up at Parrott's table. Another player, a man no older than twenty or twenty-two, stood up in apparent anger, rigid as a fence post. "I reckon you'll take that back," he said, his tone shrill with youth. His voice, though thin, carried in the room, arresting three dozen men like they were posed for a painting.

John Parrott said something, quietly, genially, and then the youth's hand clawed at his holstered revolver. But before the long barrel came clear, the young man was looking at Parrott's extended arm, and at a cocked pistol pointed at his face. It was a pug-ugly gun, Riley thought, the kind called an English bulldog. If a pistol could have snarled, this one would have.

The youth stared into death's portal, the black hole of the muzzle opening onto unknown darkness beyond it. Riley whispered, "Kid—ease off it," though he was fifteen feet from the table and nobody heard him but McCasland. Behind Riley, the bartender said, "Don't pull guns in here." For a long moment, silence stretched, then the young man's shoulders let down a notch, his body easing like a spring releasing. He backed a step, his eyes still locked on the stubby gun.

Parrott's face cracked a smile. He said something so softly that Riley heard none of it, and then the young man turned and stalked out of the saloon with a metallic chinging of spurs, his face flaming, his eyes shamed.

A drinker next to Riley exhaled relief. A chair scraped. Parrott said something to the men at his table and they laughed in brittle, nervous laughter. It took long, uncoiling moments for the room's noise to rebuild. In the meanwhile Parrott tucked away his gun, shuffled the bank notes in front of him into good order, and folded the money away in a wallet. When he stood up, a man at his elbow slapped him on the back.

"I reckon I've seen about enough," McCasland said. He set his brandy on the bar.

"I sure am ready," Riley said. "Seeing death hovering close always did make me hungry." He followed McCasland into the night air.

An early summer evening in Kansas is a rare bird, as Riley was the first to admit. Surprisingly cool compared to the hell of afternoon, smelling of curing grasses, it was his favorite time of day.

Riley set himself for walking with a deep breath. He turned to wish McCasland a good night and saw the lighted doorway eclipsed by John Parrott, who walked out with an air of satisfaction. Parrott stopped at McCasland's shoulder. "Youngster forgot he didn't have his mama with him," he confided.

"Poker's not for everybody," McCasland said, to which Parrott said, "Now *that* is the truth," before moving on down the boardwalk.

Riley watched Parrott stroll to the end of the block. The

notion that this keg-chested man had cheated him was still unsettling, but without proof it was as McCasland had said: There wasn't much he could do about it. Then Riley remembered he had recently built himself into a good mood, and tried to call up the reason. In an instant, he had it: the new job, sixty-five dollars' worth.

"So what's this express job about, do you think?" Riley had always been the kind who couldn't stand suspense.

"Seems plain enough," McCasland said. "The boss man, Herbert, mentioned an army contract. 'Goods,' he says. It's dangerous work and is supposed to take six days, which I figure to be three out and three back, about the distance to Fort Larned or Fort Dodge down on the Arkansas."

"Meaning what, exactly?" Riley said. McCasland, still watching Parrott's diminishing back, took a while to answer.

"I'd guess an army payroll coming in on the Kansas Pacific from Fort Leavenworth. All we have to do is deliver it."

"Well, I thought maybe something like that," Riley said, stretching the truth. McCasland made it all sound obvious. Maybe Riley was not as smart as he ought to be, he thought; maybe he ought to just stay in express work permanent, and steer wide of gambling.

"I will see you tomorrow," Riley said. He was humbled.

"Just a minute, Stokes." McCasland was studying a figure who'd just emerged from the saloon. The man wore a cloth cap and toted a salesman's sample case. He seemed to Riley like a drummer who'd just stepped off a Pullman coach and was taking a look-see at Kansas before getting on again.

From an inside pocket, McCasland drew one of his skinny cigars. "I wonder if I might trouble you for a light, sir," McCasland said to the man.

The drummer's expression never altered. "It ain't any trouble," he said in a scratchy voice. He set the sample case on the boardwalk, struck a match, and held it up obligingly.

From his greater height, McCasland leaned forward. His cheeks hollowed; the flame mounted to illuminate the other's face, which wore darting eyes and a two-day stubble. "Obliged," McCasland said. He puffed speculatively as the man went down the boardwalk.

"I had a match," Riley said.

"I only wanted a close look at him," McCasland said. "You seen him before?"

"Wouldn't remember if I had," Riley said.

"I expect that's his talent," McCasland said strangely. "That little dustup inside just now—when Parrott threw down on that cowboy? All eyes went to Parrott's gun, but I saw that feller in the cap yonder pull a big Colt's Army from under his coat. It was that gun Parrott was banking on, every bit as much as his own little peashooter."

"By gosh, you don't miss much," Riley said. "Myself, I was just curious to see if cowboys go to heaven."

"That feller is Parrott's shill," McCasland said, "or I'm in the wrong business."

"His how much?"

"Shill. A plant."

"Like eyes in back of his head?"

"Exactly," McCasland said. "If you've got a minute, I'm curious about something."

"I guess so." Riley remembered that the Big Creek Cafe would not close for another hour or so.

They followed the cloth-capped shill, a shadow whose movements seemed aimless. He walked two blocks up Main Street and turned toward the railroad yards. For a time he was a faint, crunching sound on graveled back streets. Then he was a dark shape against newly arrived lumber stacked in the K.P. yards. They saw him stop and loiter, until, from between stacks of lumber, a taller, bulkier shape appeared. The two shapes nearly merged, conferring.

"Parrott," McCasland whispered. "I thought as much. Come on. Let's get our money back."

"How?"

"Once the cotillion commences, you dance with the shorter one," McCasland said alarmingly, and then he was moving forward, taking long, determined strides. Riley had been trailing along without much thought to where they might be heading. Suddenly, he had a hundred questions, though before he could ask one, here was McCasland initiating some action—exactly what, Riley had no idea.

There was a stiffening in the men's stances as they saw McCasland bearing down on them.

McCasland called out, "A moment there—Mr. Powers?" Riley remembered that Parrott had styled himself as a Mr. Powers, a drummer from Chicago.

"Who's that?" Parrott demanded. Riley was alarmed to hear revolvers cocking. Both Parrott and the shill assumed duelists' poses, gun arms extended. *"Stand or be shot!"* Parrott ordered. His voice filled the railroad yards.

"Here now, I'm a friend," McCasland said easily. He closed the last few rods between them. "We're unarmed. You know us from the poker tables."

"You," Parrott said gruffly.

"That cowboy you buffaloed," McCasland said, "he came back with some cowpoke pals swearing to shoot you down." McCasland slowed but still advanced, till he walked spang up to the waiting men. On shorter legs, Riley had to scramble to catch up. McCasland said, "I only thought somebody ought to tell you."

"Obliged, but we can handle it," Parrott said. "You just tell him he's making a big mistake." Parrott must have let his guard down then, for there was the sound of a pistol being eased off cock. Instantly, McCasland lunged forward, seizing Parrott's gun arm and pulling the big man to him.

Riley was caught flat-footed. He turned to see the shorter man extend a glinting revolver. Riley's sudden need to tackle the man came cleanly from some long disused part of him, some instinct left from schoolyard scraps, from the rough-and-tumble of growing up with brothers. He rocketed forward, spilling the shill to the ground. The gun exploded over his head and then he and this cloth-capped fellow were wrestling like ten-year-olds in the dirt of the rail yard.

"Hold it!" McCasland's voice commanded. Sometimes Riley wore his gunbelt on the streets of Hays City and sometimes he did not; tonight, he remembered tardily, he did not, since he'd begun the evening by applying for a job. His adversary was not much of a fighter, but Riley nevertheless had to be mindful of knives and hideout guns. Then too, he didn't know what was happening between Parrott and McCasland. It took him a minute, what with distractions, to pin his man.

"Hold it!" McCasland said again. Riley held the shill and looked around warily. Somebody was making wet noises, whimpering and choking. Riley was alarmed to see McCasland holding Parrott, one arm twisted behind the struggling prisoner's back and the snout of the nickeled derringer pressed into his fleshy windpipe.

"Get the six-shooters, Stokes." McCasland's voice came as everyday as please-pass-the-salt.

Riley eyed his fuming prisoner. The man's revolver lay on the ground some few feet away. Riley considered, measuring distance, then released his man and sprang for the gun, pounced on it and came up with it cocked and ready. The man McCasland had called the shill got warily to his feet. He had not been strong, but he was as intent as a wolverine and looked far from beaten.

"Jesus," Riley breathed. He sounded like a circuit preacher, putting that much feeling into it.

Parrott choked, the gun in his throat. "That sample case," McCasland said. "Let's see what we've got." Riley squatted to the case, keeping his captured revolver pointed carefully. Inside were a rumpled handkerchief, three fresh decks of cards, and—oddly—a beer mug, still smelling sourly of the Railway Advance's brew.

"Cards and whatnot," Riley announced. "A beer mug."

"We'll take the mug," McCasland said. "A lens, is that it? A prism or what-do-you-call-it?" He jabbed the derringer into Parrott's throat, choking him again, then brought his face almost lovingly close to Parrott's ear. "That was a question, Mr. Terrible John Parrott."

Parrott gargled. His eyes squinched with helplessness and reopened. He swallowed, then nodded.

"I remember," McCasland said. "It's called an eye. Damn me for an innocent, I should have spotted it last night."

"You can bet John is gonna get you for this," the other man said. He had a distinctively hoarse voice. "He ain't letting pass something this big."

McCasland laughed at him. "Well now, don't take this badly. We are squaring accounts, is all." He shoved the gun deeper into Parrott's throat. Parrott's labored breathing got a whistle in it. "There's the matter of my eighteen dollars and thirty-five cents tonight, and then thirty-seven-fifty from last night," McCasland said. "Then I believe you took

Mr. Stokes here for fifty-some. Meet Mr. Stokes there with the gun."

"Evening," Riley said uncertainly.

"I will tell you what," McCasland said into Parrott's ear. "We will just take potluck. We'll take whatever's in your wallet and call it even." Parrott's eyes widened; he strangled a protest.

"You got one free hand," McCasland pointed out. "Ease out that wallet and drop it." Only Parrott's eyes reacted. "Do it!" McCasland said. There was a rummaging as Parrott repositioned his hand. "I'd be awful careful about hideout guns and such," McCasland said, "or you'll breathe from now on through your cravat."

Parrott's wallet dropped with a considerable plop, like somebody landing a fish on a creekbank. McCasland peered down by his boots to locate it. He made as if to stoop, but instead gathered himself and pushed off powerfully, launching Terrible John Parrott into a pile of lumber.

Parrott sprawled. McCasland danced in, watching his chance. The moment Parrott got one hand—it was his right—behind him to push himself up, McCasland stamped a boot on it. Riley heard a muffled snap of finger bones and then Parrott bellowed in agony.

"Run, Stokes!" McCasland shouted, and he scooped up the wallet and sprinted, leaving Riley flat-footed, astounded, still leveling the revolver. Riley backed two nervous steps, holding the shill in the revolver's trance, then he spun and dug his heels and ran, seeing out of the corner of his eye the shill scrambling for Parrott's fallen gun.

Damn! Riley thought, why hadn't somebody thought to take that other gun? McCasland had a good lead and despite tall boots was a fair runner. As he sprinted, McCasland piped his voice up. Riley realized the bastard was *laughing* —high-pitched, delighted as any prankster.

From behind came the crash of a shot. Riley reached into himself, finding he had not run full-out in some years and having to remember which muscles to enlist. He leaned into it, running in earnest. Since the hammer of his captured revolver was still cocked, he angled his body and threw a shot, more to discourage pursuit than anything. Another shot popped in response and a pistol ball whined past Riley's ear. He overtook McCasland, who was gasping for breath at the back of a feed store. They had a choice of directions. From behind, footsteps were charging down on them.

"Cripes!" Riley said.

"Throw another shot to scare them," McCasland yelled.

Riley gulped air. He still carried the beer mug. "The hell with you!" he said, and he dropped the mug and was off running again. There was a shot alarmingly close behind. He heard McCasland's yell of protest but he figured the man was a better runner and was getting Riley murdered and so to hell with him.

Riley ran till his sides ached, wondering why he felt at all relieved when McCasland caught up with him, grinning, carrying the beer mug. The chase pounded through the back alleys of Hays City, flanking Main Street for a time, then veering off into the residential districts.

They dashed between carriage houses; they vaulted a wooden fence. Terrified cats streaked from underfoot. A tethered mule shied away from their ringing heels, pulling down its hitch rail. Dogs barked in outrage. They startled a man, suspenders a-dangle, just emerging from a privy. Riley trampled a vegetable garden, tripping on staked strings. McCasland hit a low clothesline and thumped flat on his back. He lay shrieking with laughter in high wet grass until Riley frantically hoisted him.

Eventually they pulled up gasping in a small barn somewhere. They barred the door with feed sacks and sagged down gasping.

"Sweet Mama," Riley rasped. "Don't ever . . . do something . . . like that . . . again." The smell of fresh manure hung thickly.

McCasland breathed. "And to think I . . . just had . . . this coat cleaned."

Straw rustled alarmingly near them. A vast weight shifted, rattling the far wall. Riley thrust a cocked revolver at the blackness. McCasland scratched a match on the door's iron strapping and held it high, his ridiculous derringer poised in the other hand.

In the wavering light of the match, a lone milk cow looked at them out of one baleful eye.

"Ahhh," McCasland breathed again. "If that wasn't the most fun I've had in a long time."

Riley snorted. When he could finally talk in whole sentences he said, "Your idea of fun is like my idea of getting my bowels scairt loose."

"When you knocked over those bee houses I thought I'd die laughing."

"Right," Riley said. "Great fun."

"Feel the weight of this beer mug," McCasland said.

"You still got that thing?"

"Hell, I wasn't leaving it."

Riley hefted the mug, which was surprisingly solid, nearly as heavy, in fact, as if full of beer.

"It's called an eye," McCasland said. "When it gets light out you can look through it. I saw a whiskey glass like it one time. It's got lenses built into it to work like what the Federals used in trenches. A periscope."

"Some spyglass kind of thing?"

"Pretty much. The shill positions himself near his partner's table. He's got beer in the mug and he sips it, except he's really spying out folks's cards. Thing is, he has to move around sometimes to get a better view. That's how I spotted him tonight, by how fidgety the man was."

Riley whistled, but quietly. "Now that you mention it, I guess that fellow was skulking around last night's game too. I suppose he gives Parrott signals about what cards everybody's holding."

"It must require quite a system," McCasland said. "Strike me a match." Riley did. McCasland opened Parrott's wallet, finding so much money it took four matches to count it. "Two-hundred-seventy-some is fair winnings," McCasland said. "I'd say the situation calls for an even split."

"I only lost fifty-one dollars," Riley said. "I couldn't rightly take more."

"They cheated you," McCasland said. "In Texas we would string a man up for such behavior."

"That is a point," Riley said. Having money again was an idea he could quickly get used to.

"Besides which, I'm not hunting those two down to give the rest back," McCasland said. It struck Riley funny, but his laughter, he noticed, subsided quickly. There was a quiet stretch.

"I got me a room in the Hays House," Riley said.

"Mine's in the Depot Hotel."

"Looks like we are stuck here till morning," Riley said. "I never did get my supper."

"This town will not prove much safer by daylight," McCasland said. "Fact is, on the contrary."

"Good thing we've got that express job," Riley said, thinking how comfortably far away a fort on the Arkansas sounded. McCasland grunted and passed him a wad of greenbacks.

"You can move pretty fast when you have to, Stokes. I suppose you have more name than just Stokes."

"I never been partial to getting shot," Riley said. "As for names, I've got a bushelful. Riley Andrew Jackson Stokes. My mother had grand notions. Plain Riley will do."

"A Yankee named for a Southerner?"

"A Kentuckian named for a distinguished general and president." Riley extended a hand.

"Mine's Prosper, which sounds like some church deacon. Most call me Cass."

They shook. After they had breathed awhile longer, there was little to be done but go to sleep. Being mindful of the cow, they ascended to the haymow and kicked up rude beds, causing roosting pigeons to slap up and resettle.

Riley lay back and pulled his coat over him; he wasn't chilly but he did it for camouflage. He decided he had passed nights under worse conditions. "Haven't slept in a barn in some time," he said.

"I hope whoever milks that cow in the morning doesn't shoot us," Cass McCasland said.

Riley waited for sleep. He had a hundred and thirty-nine dollars in his pocket but not a bite of food in his belly, which was poker luck all over again. In the ten hours he'd known McCasland, the world had become richer but riskier. Years later, when he first had a chance to look back on it all, he would conclude that, except for the war years, it had been

Cass McCasland who had got him into every tight scrape of his life. And one way or another—at least according to his own view of things—it was Riley Stokes who'd got them out.

9 · TAI HEI

IT WAS HOURS AFTER CREAKING WAGONS HAD CROSSED THE river, after a snapping bonfire big enough to roast the moon was lit and lived brightly and then faded, after cooking smells gathered and later diffused, after white men's voices had reached crescendo in drunken singing and yelling and had fallen away to mutters, after the night's stillness had drawn in to soothe away at least some of the horror.

Tai Hei came abruptly to herself, realizing she had slept, feeling terror constricting her chest, her heartbeat thundering. She listened, but except for an occasional pop of subsiding campfire or the wakeful stamp and jingle of a horse or draft ox, all was stillness.

After a time she slipped out of the deer bed and through the passage in the dogwillow. The river was a road, a long aisle opening between rustling plum trees and cottonwoods. She waded in stealthily, careful of splashing. Something spoke to her, and whether it came from the Tai Hei side of her or from Bird of Morning, she knew not. It bade her go upstream rather than with the current. She turned into the river's flow and waded with difficulty. The water's coldness was like her fear, sharpening her thinking and quickening her heart.

She walked the river, hiding her footprints, having to cross the deepest parts of the current in order to keep to the insides of curves where sandbars formed and the water flowed only ankle deep. She walked the river between the lines of cottonwood, barring from her mind thoughts of her people. She walked the river, seeing the stars parading in their accustomed order, unchanged and aloof, not deigning to reflect a merely human tragedy.

Cold crept into her, beginning with her feet and creeping

toward her center. She shivered violently but walked on until over her shoulder came the first glimmering in the eastern sky.

When the light was better she stopped to examine a bullet furrow on her thigh. It was more burn than gash, and had bled only a little. She scooped cold water and bathed it. Then, as she straightened, she felt a stirring, then a flood as her water broke, heralding birth.

Hurriedly, Tai Hei found a place within a thick stand of dogwillow and wild plums. Soon waves of pain were taking her, doubling her over, forcing her to lie down. The place was not so confining as the deer bed, yet offered shelter from the many eyes of the coming daylight. She lay back, exhausted. She had come a long way from the burial site, yet she was still close by the same river. The men had only to travel upcurrent to find her. What she feared was crying out in her birthing throes, drawing enemies to her.

With the skinning knife she sliced a strip of buckskin from the hem of her dress. This she folded twice, to be placed between her teeth when the next time came. Finally she drew up her dress, feeling her bareness and openness there on the ground. Her body shivered; her teeth chattered beyond her control. Once the sun was up, she told herself, she would be warm enough. Her baby would be born on a bright, warm day.

Nothing further could be done but wait. She had the knife to cut the baby's cord and to dig a hole so that the afterbirth could be deeply buried, for if coyotes should find and eat it, the baby's spirit could never be whole.

She smiled at such thoughts, for they were the thoughts of Bird of Morning, a Kiowa. The baby, also a Kiowa, would need her to be strong and clever and to protect its new life.

Then, deep in her center, she felt the movement: a gripping and rolling of muscles. She set the leather pad between her teeth and lay back, thinking she was ready to face the next part of her ordeal. And as waves of pain convulsed her, she felt the rightness of this thought, for indeed, she was offered no other choice.

10 · THE GENTS

HORSE TACK JINGLED IN THE FREIGHT YARD. SEVEN CAVALRY troopers from nearby Fort Hays milled around army nags, readjusting cinches and bridles, filling canteens from a wheezing pump. The detail comprised a newly minted second lieutenant named Bicknell, an Irish sergeant named Rafferty, and five privates carrying fifty-caliber Sharps carbines slung on wide belts around their shoulders.

The dray company's wagon was a fine Studebaker; its team appeared serviceable. Company Director Julius Herbert had an employee bore holes in the wagon bed with a bit brace. The treasure box was bolted down and covered with loose hay, then bags of oats for the horses were loaded in, followed by provisions for the men.

Into this bustle slunk Riley Stokes and Cass McCasland, wearing gunbelts, carrying bedrolls, their faces shaded by the five-inch brims of new hats. They showed nervous eyes; they shook Herbert's hand distractedly. While being introduced to the army detachment they shot anxious glances down Lincoln Street.

Julius Herbert, out of caution and love of secrecy, ushered them into his office to explain all particulars. Riley and Cass fairly bolted through the sheltering door, grateful to be hidden from the street. Herbert examined and approved of Cass's Winchester carbine, though he seemed less than happy that Riley had only revolvers, his own and the one he'd captured from Parrott's shill.

As for the express job, Cass had been largely correct. They learned they were to haul army pay first to Downer's Station, a minor post on the Smoky Hill River a half day away, and then to Fort Dodge, on the banks of the Arkansas near Buffalo City. The escort would remain at Fort Dodge, since posts nearest Indian Territory were being reinforced to meet the threat of rampaging Kiowa. Cass and Riley would return the wagon to Hays City. Only then, Herbert emphasized, would they be paid.

Herbert spoke confidentially, standing close to his new

charges and smelling of a barbershop. Abruptly, he took a step back and gave them an odd look. His eyebrows puzzled, struggling to merge.

"Did you not just yesterday have a rather sizeable mustache?" Herbert asked, examining Cass intently.

Cass looked pained. "I took a notion it made me look older. It's a young man's country out here."

"And Stokes—I believe you . . . you're *starting* a mustache," Herbert said, peering at Riley's stubble.

"I can't deny it. The real truth is, I won it off him at poker."

Herbert's disbelief cocked back another notch. "Let me understand this. You exchanged a *mustache* over a game of chance?"

"That's pretty much the way of it," Cass said. "We don't neither of us hold with gaming for money."

"I'm certainly glad of that much," Herbert said. "Of all things."

"I'll give him a chance to win it back one of these days," Riley said. "A man of his coloration looks awful pale without it."

At three-thirty in the afternoon the procession pulled out of the drayage yards amid a superfluity of shouted commands, the soldiers a-horseback and Riley and Cass driving the wagon. While rolling through the outskirts they both clutched their guns tightly, playing worried eyes over benign-looking porches and woodsheds and second-story windows.

Hays City thinned and gave way to prairie. The sun bore hotly on their knees and their necks prickled with a need to look behind them.

"You gentlemen take your work almighty serious," Sergeant Rafferty told them, plainly amused. He'd apparently noticed their grim faces. "I would not be consarned till we're well out on the plains."

"We're just sharpening our eyes for the real thing," Riley told him, and he tugged down his hat brim and encouraged the horses.

By nightfall they reached Downer's Station and were welcomed into a perimeter of dreary sod buildings by cheering, no doubt penniless, troopers. After dining on buffalo hump roast with the officers, Riley and Cass volunteered to have themselves and the pay box locked in the guardhouse. Sergeant Rafferty, the official paymaster, got an amused expression and said in that case that he'd have to be locked in as well. A Major Lucas remarked they were all admirably conscientious about protecting army currency.

Rafferty stripped to a dust-colored union suit, lay down on a mattress tick, and promptly went to sleep. Cass, however, lay with his Winchester beside him, staring for a time at the raftered ceiling. Riley slept fitfully with a revolver in hand, conjuring visions of Terrible John Parrott.

11 · BAYARD

LOUIS BAYARD SPOKE ABSAROKA AND PAWNEE AND SEVERAL Sioux dialects. He was fluent in the sign language shared by all plains tribes. He knew the rudiments of English nearly as well as the next man on America's inner border. The closest thing to French he understood, however, was "Louis Bayard."

He was compact and dark-eyed and his face bore the buckshot scars of smallpox. He was a half-breed, the whelp of a Crow mother and a flamboyant French trapper who had once wintered among the settlement Indians at Fort Laramie on the North Platte, spending enough nights with the kind of squaws considered communal property to leave behind mirrors and bright ribbons and uncounted doses of his seed—and also, though he did not know it, the name Louis Bayard.

When spring thaws came, Bayard the father disappeared into the upper Missouri country, where he might have become whitened bones along some trapped-out beaver creek—or be living yet in a well-chinked cabin just over the next rise, for all Louis Bayard the son knew. The son wouldn't have recognized him in either case.

Bayard's memory of his father was bogus anyway, based on obligingly fanciful yarns told by his Crow mother and aunts. But since the younger Bayard's people were hang-around-the-fort Indians whose old tribal stories were mostly forgotten, the tales of his father marked his mind, and were vivid enough, and himself susceptible enough, to leave him with divided loyalties, white and Indian, one foot in each camp.

As he grew, he became a lone hunter, sleeping outdoors except in the worst weather. He got along by being generally as Indian as he had to be and on occasion as white as he could manage. What that meant most often was scouting for the army. In all things, he was a man between, for he'd carved out a tenuous middle ground for himself between the fading visions of the plains tribes and the wholesale dreams of acquisition being carpetbagged west by swarming whites.

On a particular June morning in 1872, Bayard rode out to the fringes of Hays City in the employ of a pair of gentlemen, one of whom was dogging him as though Bayard were a hunting guide. With his charge in tow, Bayard rode a wide loop around the town, crossing the Kansas Pacific rails at the eastern outskirts, passing privies and woodpiles and kneeing his horse wide of the survey stakes—symbols of frontier optimism—that marked off imaginary streets and boulevards. Within two hours, still circling, he recrossed the tracks at the town's west fringes.

Where his loop intersected a skimpy wagon trail leading to the army post called Downer's Station, Louis Bayard slid off his horse to read what news the ground held there.

The white man finished yawning and said, "It's just a whole mess of old tracks. I don't believe a body could make out nothing." He wore a cloth cap that made his head look flat.

Bayard hunkered to finger a hoofprint; his eyes traced snaking wheel rims. The white man said, "You see any horse turds down there you like, I expect you can have them," and then laughed. He had dry laughter, like a crow calling.

Bayard looked in the direction of Downer's Station and said nothing. He considered he was working for the larger man with the bandaged hand and white side-whiskers, the one who had stayed in town, and he would not report his gleanings to this second man until and unless directed to. As was his practice when working for the army, he did not expend words on fools.

Bayard remounted abruptly, slinging a leg. He turned toward town, backtracking the wagon tracks and army-shod hooves, the white man following. When they filtered into the town's outskirts, passing boys rolling hoops and a string of milk cows idly swinging across the road, Bayard, still reading the ground, turned them onto Lincoln Street. At the Herbert Express and Drayage yards he veered in and slid down to examine the trampled dirt.

Julius Herbert had been talking feed prices with a wholesaler on the office porch when the half-breed squatting in his freight yard kidnapped his attention. "You there," Herbert called, getting no reaction from the half-breed. The white man sitting a-horseback turned to show a sleepy face.

"You'll excuse me," Herbert told his conferee, then strode proprietorially into the yard, although hatless and squinting. The half-breed still did not look at him.

"What the devil is he up to?" Herbert asked the white man, having to look up into the sun. The man wore a flat wool cap like a Scotsman, and with a cigar stub in his mouth resembled some eastern drummer for shoes or hardware.

"I'd advise you just to humor him," the drummer answered, standing up as best he could on overlong stirrups and massaging his rump. "He believes this here's where he lost his watch."

"His *watch?*" Herbert said, and shaded his eyes to see the squatting man better.

Bayard grunted and stood up. He passed by Herbert as an object of no consequence and slung up on his mount. Herbert backed two steps, as though Bayard were a lot to take in. The drummer said, "Redskin, I hope to hell you're learning something." For his response Bayard wheeled and set his horse into a fast walk out of the drayage yards. The drummer shrugged and jerked his mount's head around, while Julius Herbert stood with an anxious expression and watched them ride out.

12 · BAYARD

THE MOMENT BAYARD TURNED ONTO MAIN STREET HE RECOG-
nized his employer, a big man, standing under the Hays
House balcony and shifting his considerable weight from leg
to leg. Bayard saw that the man still had the white side-
whiskers and the bandage on his hand, still wore the black,
round hat with its little edge of brim. But since Bayard had
seen him last, the man had changed from his town suit; he
was dressed now in canvas trousers, tall boots, and a yellow,
knee-length buckskin coat fringed on the sleeves and the
skirting. Such clothes, though an impressive display of
wealth, looked ridiculous on a city white man, but he,
Bayard, would not be the one to tell him so.

The fact was, there seemed vast numbers of foolish white
men, many of them wealthy. Bayard had recently concluded
that wealth made fools of men as readily as did whiskey. In
fact—and exactly as with strong spirits—the more wealth
they had, the more foolish they were likely to be. Bayard
considered that a small portion of wealth, perhaps a herd of
ponies, would someday be good to have. He was wary,
though, of accumulating too much.

Bayard reined up in front of the big white man and sat his
horse, letting the smaller white man catch up. The big man
nodded to acknowledge Bayard's return, then lit a cigar. He
wore a toilet water smell as strong as any white woman's.
Even through this kind of floral fog, augmented by the cigar,
Bayard could smell impatience on him.

"It appears he wore you out, Legg," the big man said.
"You turn up anything?" Bayard had been told the big white
man's name and he struggled now to retrieve it: Parrott.

"Damned if I know," Legg said. "He don't say two words.
Alls we did was ride a circle around the whole pissant town
and then stop in some freight yard." Legg got off his horse
and stretched as though he'd ridden all day. "I think my arse
is broke," he confided to Parrott. "That there's some coat."

"Do you like it? It's my hunting costume," Parrott said.
"While you took your outing I examined the railroad

manifest. The agent in charge was uncooperative until persuaded."

"John, you are a one," Legg said, marveling.

"At any rate, they did not leave by rail." Parrott's eyes shifted to Bayard, who sat his horse impassive. "So out with your news, man," Parrott said. "I'm not one to be kept waiting."

Bayard did not look directly at a man when he spoke to him; it was the same way a true man approached animals. "They go in a wagon, these two you hunt. With seven who ride army horses." He pointed southwest. "To the little fort on the Smoky Hill which men call Downer's Station."

"Must we always grope for the meaning of these half-breed colloquialisms?" Parrott said. He smiled a bad smile that had no laughing in it. "You mean seven soldiers, I take it. Are you saying these bastards I'm hunting joined up with that half-arsed detachment we saw in town yesterday?"

Bayard frowned; he was saying what he was saying; he did not like to speculate about what might or might not be. Nor did he respond to questions to which he had no answers.

"I can hardly believe the army would shield them," Parrott said. He looked to Legg to have his opinion seconded.

"Don't ask me," Legg protested. "I don't claim to be no bloodhound."

Parrott looked back at Bayard, who did not react. Bayard disliked and avoided argument, for any man was free to think as he wished. In that respect he was pure Indian.

"The boot tracks you show me near the iron rails," Bayard said, "the place where these men took your money. These boots now travel on a wagon which goes with soldiers. This I know."

Parrott slapped his thigh thoughtfully with a pair of buckskin gauntlets and looked off to the southwest. "Very well. You're willing to track them for us?"

"I will track them."

"For what price?"

Bayard considered. When he worked for the army, he got ten dollars per job. That was for guiding a whole army, while these were only two men. Still, it was the same work. "Ten dollars," Bayard said, displaying fingers.

Parrott snorted, then Legg laughed his dry laugh that was like a crow calling, and the two white men smiled at one another to show they had some joke between them. "My good man," Parrott said, his face shining and foolish, "you deliver me these sons of bitches and you shall have a good deal more than ten dollars." Bayard looked at the ground beside his horse. It was not good to be laughed at.

"The other matter is what happens when we catch them." Parrott looked at Legg, then back to Bayard. "What I'm after is satisfaction. Look here what they did to my hand."

Bayard looked at the hand, wrapped thickly in bandages.

"He don't appear no squealer," Legg observed. "Did you tell him you went and got deputized? I figure that makes this manhunt all legal and official."

"Indeed it does," Parrott said. "Do you fathom what we are saying, Mr. Bayard?"

Bayard saw he was being patronized, but also that some response was expected. In his experience, men hunted other men for the same reason they hunted animals: to kill them. "I track these traveling men for you," Bayard said. "What happens to them is nothing to me."

Something near joy dawned on Parrott's face, causing his side-whiskers to curve out like horseshoes. "Splendid," he said, and whacked the gauntlets against his trousers again. "It appears we understand one another."

"I just hope it don't take too frigging long," Legg said. "I don't care for a lot of horsebacking."

Parrott smelled of impatience more strongly now, but it was the happy kind. "I suppose the next thing is to get outfitted. We'll start here in the gun shop." Parrott indicated a sign cantilevered over the boardwalk that had a picture of a gun on it. Parrott started for the shop with Legg following, but Bayard still sat his horse.

"Come, come, fellow," Parrott said, "you're working for me, are you not? Surely you've been indoors before."

Bayard moved stiffly when he thought he was being made fun of. Foolish men had to have their jokes. He followed them into the gun shop and stopped and stood awed; he had never seen so many different kinds of guns, and besides guns, canteens and canvas coats, stuffed animal heads, and stacks of ammunition in pasteboard boxes. His nostrils flared at the various smells.

"We're sportsmen," Parrott told the proprietor, his eyes appraising the racks of walnut and steel. "First off, we'll need something for long range."

"I take it you gentlemen mean to hunt our western buffalo."

"Whatever comes our way," Parrott said.

"Then a Sharps breechloader is the best you can do." The gunsmith handed down a heavy rifle. "This one's bored forty-four-seventy-seven. Some prefer a fifty, but a forty-four-seventy-seven kills them right enough and without so much fuss. Carries out farther, too. This is Sharps' Number One Sporting Rifle. As fine-sighted a weapon as I've sold."

"What I've heard, a man wants a Winchester," Legg said.

"That's more a short-range proposition," the gunsmith said doubtfully. "Though it's fine on multiple targets, being a repeater."

"Once I get to shooting, I do a lot of it," Legg said.

"What do you think, Bayard?" Parrott said. "Considering the task at hand."

Bayard was examining antelope heads, which were startlingly lifelike; it was a wonder the animals did not take fright with the white men talking so loudly. He turned, catching up with the question. "Any gun kills," Bayard said.

"There's a savage for you," the gunsmith said airily. "Your modern hunter is more particular about his accoutrements. I most strongly recommend the Sharps."

"All right," Parrott said. "And then something that cuts a wide swath. A shotgun."

"We stock the latest patterns, singles as well as doubles." The gunsmith let his voice expand with pride. "I'd venture to say we have a model at any price you care to name."

"Go ahead and impress us," Parrott said.

The proprietor blinked twice behind his spectacles. For a moment his eyes played over all of them, lingering longest on Parrott. "All right, sir, perhaps I shall." He fetched down a double gun and set it tenderly in Parrott's hands. "No less than a handmade English ten gauge is what we have here. What they call in London a best gun. I've not yet showed it to anyone."

"Confound this hand," Parrott said. "I can't even work a mechanism." He gave the shotgun to Legg, who cammed a lever to drop open the barrels.

Legg whistled at the gaping chambers. "Them holes look big as railroad tunnels." He closed the gun with an expensive clack, eared the hammers back, and brought the gun smoothly to his cheek. The hammers fell as twins. "That there is a piece of work," Legg said admiringly.

"Genuine Westley Richards," the gunsmith said. "First one I've been able to get. Examine the engraving on the sideplates. Faultlessly executed."

Legg looked. Bayard stepped in closer, wanting to see. "Some fellow hunting birds with a dog," Legg said.

"Grouse hunting, I should imagine," the gunsmith said. "The British are known for it."

Parrott said, "We can look at pictures later." He took the shotgun and laid it on the counter. "Let's take the three of them and be done with it."

The gunsmith's mouth worked a moment. "You'll take . . ."

"The Winchester, the Sharps, and the shotgun," Parrott said. "Sufficient ammunition for each." He leaned closer over the counter and rested his good hand on the English shotgun. "One alteration on these barrels, however."

"Sir?"

"They're way too long. You can whack them off about the length of your forearm."

The gunsmith strayed one hand to his spectacles. "Cut . . . ? Why, that would be a *sacrilege!* This is a Westley Richards of London, a two-hundred-dollar gun. It would spoil the balance. It would—"

Parrott's movement was vastly deliberate. He grasped the gunsmith by his tie and raised him several inches. The man appeared startled to the bone marrow; his eyes, magnified anyway by spectacles, swelled like a bullfrog's. Parrott drew his prey to himself, regarding the man tenderly. Bayard was curious to see what Parrott would do with him.

"Have you ears?" Parrott's tone was civil; he awaited an answer.

"Y-yes, sir."

"Then chop off the frigging barrels," Parrott said. Without shifting his eyes from the gunsmith, he said, "Legg—a penknife." Legg bustled. Parrott let go of his man, who very nearly collapsed. The man's hand went to his throat as though he'd been burned there.

An ebony-handled penknife appeared in Parrott's hand. "Just about so." Parrott drew the blade across the perfect, swirl-patterned Damascus steel of the English shotgun, leaving a bright line. "You have a hacksaw in the place, I trust."

"A cut right there—yes, sir. I have a saw indeed." The gunsmith wiped perspiration off his eyebrows and hurried the gun toward the back of the shop. Bayard heard him sawing back there.

"And a whole lot of shells," Legg called after him. "We don't want to go running out halfways to nowhere."

13 · RILEY

BY THE THIRD DAY OUT OF HAYS CITY, THE ALL-OR-NOTHING Kansas sun was roaring. Despite the rising dust, their pacing shadows looked as sharp as knives. Riley sweated happily and told the soldiers it was hotter than the devil's smithy. Secretly, he felt reprieved and wonderful. He had quit looking over his shoulder and now sat whistling "Old Dan Tucker." They figured to hit the Pawnee River sometime after midday. Riley was looking forward to bathing his feet, maybe lying up in the shade of cottonwoods. When he closed his eyes, he saw no more visions of Terrible John Parrott.

"It was a fine gait you set us formerly," Sergeant Rafferty noted, speaking equally to Riley and Cass. His mount, in contrast to most of the washboard-ribbed army horses, was a huge black that could have paced a locomotive. "But this marning I believe you gents have slackened the pace a bit."

"Well, it's danged hot." Riley didn't care to go into the real reason. "Best we spare the animals."

"Riley here is breathing easier," Cass said. "He was afraid

he had an angry female on his trail. She's taken a notion her little shaver bears him a resemblance and has convinced herself it ought to have its poppa's name."

Rafferty chuckled. "'Tis that way, is it?"

"He's chock full of horse turds," Riley said.

"Many a lad has been persuaded to join the military under just such circumstances," Rafferty said, ignoring Riley's protest.

"Let's close up there," Lieutenant Bicknell called from several places up the line. "Mr. Rafferty, a word with you."

"Mother, Mary, and Magdalene, deliver us from second lieutenants," Rafferty told Cass and Riley. "Coming, sir," he said louder, and surged ahead to join his officer.

"That lieutenant is government issue, all right," Cass said. "Another day and even we'll be saluting."

"I suppose there's some itch in you makes you stretch yarns like that," Riley said. "Some indisposition, probably, to telling the truth."

Cass sat a moment. "I hold truth in too high a regard to see it squandered," he said finally. Riley snorted. "Besides which, stretching a yarn now and again makes life more interesting. It's no fault in a person to crave entertainment."

"Life around you is more entertaining than safe," Riley said. "You could've taken Parrott's money without stomping his fingers."

"He needed a lesson."

"Well, I'm a man as can stand a strong measure of boredom," Riley said. "I don't find being shot at entertaining."

"Then here's your life's work right here," Cass said, gesturing ahead. "Following horses' behinds."

"A man could do worse than haul army payrolls. The money's nothing to spit at."

"Before you get too thick on it, remember we don't get paid till we take the wagon back," Cass said. "Parrott may be planning us some kind of welcome."

"Damn it, Cass—don't remind me."

Rafferty and Lieutenant Bicknell, riding ahead, had topped a rise and were gesturing beyond. The detail's pace quickened.

"I hope it's the river," Cass said. "I could use a swim."

"That lieutenant won't like it."

"That lieutenant is as puffed up at having his first command as if this were a regiment," Cass said. "He needs reminding I'm no part of his army. An unreconstructed rebel like me shouldn't be riding with bluecoats in the first place."

They rolled into the shade of wavery cottonwoods, whose leaves rattled dryly in the prairie breeze, blending with the calls of red-winged blackbirds into a kind of music. Cottonwood down drifted, the fluffs catching the sun. Riley flopped down in lacy shade. Before he even got his eyes closed, he was proved right concerning the lieutenant.

"We'll water the animals and push on immediately," Bicknell ordered. Cass, however, as calmly as a man going to bed, began taking off his clothes and draping them over the wagon's sideboards. Bicknell flustered up immediately. "Mr. McCasland, I intend to bring this detail into Fort Dodge at the earliest possible hour."

"Whatever for?" Cass said, standing on one leg to pull off a sock. He was already down to underwear. "We'll get there tomorrow anyway. What's the difference whether it's early or late?"

"To minimize risk," Bicknell said. "As long as this pay box is my responsibility, I mean to . . ."

Cass was grinning, a tall, lean, naked man. His face and forearms were well browned but the rest of him was white as cotton. "Last one in's a rotten egg," he announced and scampered into the water, which proved only waist deep. He spread his arms in a benediction and went over backward with a splash.

"Damn that looks good. I believe I will take the waters myself." Riley sat down on the riverbank and tugged off a boot. Cass's head broke the surface; he must have been sitting on the bottom. He slung wet hair out of his eyes and called, *"Whoo-eee,"* appreciatively.

"Mr. McCasland, I order you to get dressed at once!" Bicknell said, his face reddening. Cass's head disappeared. Riley, bare-hindered, hit the water like a mortar shell. Cass bobbed up and spouted.

"I'll remind you that I command this detail," Lieutenant Bicknell called out. Sergeant Rafferty and some of the troopers were chuckling.

"Mr. Rafferty, we'll have order here," Bicknell said, but they were schoolmaster words, more plea than command.

"Lieutenant Bicknell, sir," Cass said from the river. He had assumed an air of setting things straight. "I mean to have a swim and then a nap in the shade. Your boys changing guard all night spoilt my sleep."

Bicknell looked to Rafferty, who said, "Surely a short dip would be wondrous refreshing."

Riley noticed troopers suddenly conferring and looking off into the plum trees. Sergeant Rafferty noticed too. He got an intent look and unflapped his holster. Then his hand went up, calling for silence. The gesture was commanding; even Cass let off his horseplay.

There arose an eerie wail, muffled yet undeniable, its source such a mystery that Riley could not tell whether it came from there at the river or a mile out on the plains. Among the troopers, revolvers appeared. Anxious eyes scanned the horizons.

The cry came again, close by and chilling.

"By the bleeding Jaysus," Rafferty said in half a voice, and led a general rush for carbines. Cass and Riley scrambled buck naked and wary up the bank.

Sergeant Rafferty, assuming command, sent three troopers to surround the pay box. Cartridges slid home into Sharps carbines. Again the cry arced up and faded, plaintive, netherworldly, sounding of need.

"Spread out, the lot of you!" Rafferty ordered. "Beat that brush and mind you go gingerly. Be there murdering savages afoot, I mean to take them."

Lieutenant Bicknell, bowing to Rafferty's experience, obeyed as promptly as any private. Riley and Cass wrapped shirts around their middles, soaking splotches through the fabric. The men spread out, crouching, probing revolver muzzles into hackberries, kicking cautiously into dogwillow.

Once more the cry came, freezing them in tableau. It died abruptly.

"Here!" Cass said, starting forward. Among the troopers there was a cocking of carbine hammers. Riley came up behind him and they stood, toeing barefooted, two wet-haired men in swaddling clothes. The cry came again, frankly human, oddly familiar—and certainly not more than ten steps away. Cass's brow furrowed for trouble. He parted the brush, following his gun. They all crowded after. They gaped.

It was a young woman, drawn up into herself like a frightened deer, sheltered in a hollow among dogwillow saplings, a natural cave of vegetation. She showed dark, terrified eyes framed by tangled black hair. Her buckskin dress was open at the breast and a naked, new-born baby was held there, fuming vigorously, tiny legs and arms flailing in protest. For some reason, it refused utterly the proffered nipple. In the woman's free hand was a cheap trade knife, and her grasp on it appeared desperate.

"Sweet mother of mercy," Rafferty breathed.

Bicknell said, *"By Gadfrey."*

At the voices the woman recoiled, though the dogwillow penned her like jail bars. The baby's cry arose again, pathetically needful. Abruptly, the infant burped, then began to suckle.

"Why, the poor thing," Rafferty said.

"That is about as touching a picture as I ever did see," Riley said.

Cass said, "Kiowa, most like."

"Not hardly," Riley said. "Comanche sure as shoe polish."

"Hell, I've seen enough Comanche to know a Comanche," Cass said. "She's Cherokee or Choctaw maybe."

"'Tis some grip she has on that knife, at any rate," Rafferty said. "She would not kill her little one, surely?"

"I expect that skinning knife is for you and me," Cass said. "She'd like to gut open every one of us from piddle to gizzard."

14 · TAI HEI

AT EACH UTTERANCE OF THE HARSH-SOUNDING WORDS, TAI HEI drew back, expecting to be killed. And yet, as on the day of the attack, she found she understood. The words were English, the speech of white Americans.

"Here now. We sure ain't going to hurt you, little mother," one of them said soothingly. He in particular did not look so warlike, standing naked as he was, and shockingly white, with his men's parts covered ridiculously by a shirt.

Tai Hei opened her mouth, facing a half-dozen white faces, many of them fiercely mustached or bearded. Her upper lip trembled. The moment stretched: cottonwoods rustling, birds piping up, river chuckling steadily . . . The wet-haired man went on talking in a soothing voice, though she scarcely heard the words.

She commanded herself then to be Bird of Morning, a Kiowa, for she had her tiny Kiowa daughter who must be protected. But escape was hopeless; her way was blocked. She would die here, she recognized, she and the new life now two days old.

Once she accepted this fact, she began her death song, although she hadn't lived long enough among the Kiowa to know much about it. She forgot whether a death song should be a mere chant or if it ought to have words. Her voice trailed off uncertainly.

"I am of Kiowa," she said in halting English. The men stiffened; the faces before her went blank or shocked. She had said the wrong thing, and would now be killed. A sob convulsed her. She wavered and was Bird of Morning no longer.

"My name is Tai Hei," she said, between further sobs.

"Did she say *'tie hay?'*" one of them whispered.

"I am Tai Hei," she said. "A Chinese."

A very tall, wet-haired man said, "Well, what in the Sam Hill do you know about that?" in the kind of slowly dawning astonishment that sounded the same in any language, and then a blue-coated soldier said, "Mother, Mary, and Magdalene," in exactly the same tone.

15 · RILEY

THE WOMAN TREMBLED FOR A QUARTER OF AN HOUR, AND WAS coaxed from her hollow in the dogwillow only with great difficulty. That she spoke English and claimed to be Chinese were further marvels to be added to the already singular marvel of her and her baby's survival on the river-bank.

They spread out a horse blanket for her, clean side up, in the shade of the cottonwoods, and then took turns creeping up and speaking gently to her and laying out food on the blanket corners, as though they were taming some wild thing. Tai Hei gripped the knife in one hand and with the other held the infant, which now slept. She looked gravely at the food but did not reach for it.

"She's got to put the knife down to pick up the food," Riley said. "It's a heck of a big decision for her." He talked to her, saying how poor the food was but that it was all they had. He said she would have to eat soon or she would have no more milk for her little one. The young woman seemed to listen, and in two minutes speared a piece of army hardtack with the knife blade. The hardtack, dry as shingles, promptly split.

"Now that's sensible. That way you don't have to let go the knife," Riley said. "Try a piece of bread instead." She did so, spearing the bread and bringing it to her mouth, then eating warily. A canteen of water was placed near her. Clothing items appeared on her blanket. She selected a red bandanna for wrapping her infant. She ate steadily, although her eyes never left the men.

"Your heart kind of goes out to her, don't it?" Riley said.

"We've got to be moving." Lieutenant Bicknell had a way of bustling in place. "We've lost better than an hour already."

"You go and look for it," Cass told him. This time,

however, Bicknell was not dissuaded. He gave his orders and the troopers checked their cinch straps. Bicknell swung into his saddle.

"My people," Tai Hei said, and began sobbing. Cass and Riley squatted in front of her. Rafferty came over.

"What about your people?" Cass said gently. She began telling them how white men had attacked her group. Her English was scanty and hard to follow.

"I must look my people," she said at the end of it. "Some may yet . . ."

"Might still be alive?" Riley offered.

She sighed gratefully. He saw she was far beyond merely tired. "I must," the woman said. Riley and Cass studied one another's faces. Rafferty looked down current in the direction she had indicated. They talked it over. Riley and Cass were for investigating downriver, saying she'd been a captive of the Kiowa and that they owed her the same courtesy they'd give a liberated white.

"But it happens she ain't white," one of the troopers pointed out. "I reckon redskin or Chinee, she's just a heathen either way."

"Grimes, you sorry lophead," Rafferty said with some heat, making the trooper look away. Lieutenant Bicknell sat his horse, looking miserable and undecided. His inclination, Riley saw, was to push on to Fort Dodge.

"Surely you would not side with the likes of him, sir?" Rafferty said, indicating Grimes.

"Is it far, where this attack occurred?" Bicknell addressed Cass, as though Cass had to translate for the woman.

"It is not far," she said.

"Hell, how far could she have walked?" Riley said. "I think we are obliged to have a look-see."

Bicknell was clearly against going, but Rafferty, Cass, and Riley were arrayed against him, with the troopers wise enough not to venture an opinion. Bicknell looked at the trail to Fort Dodge and puffed his cheeks in exasperation.

"Begging the lieutenant's pardon, sir, but 'tis no more than the daycent thing," Rafferty said.

"If she'll even sit in the wagon," Bicknell said.

They coaxed her, demonstrating the wagon's comfort by lounging against the oat sacks, theatrically miming ease. She stepped out, walking in evident pain. When she sagged, they caught her and helped her to the wagon. Riley marveled that she was as light as a child.

They started, turning away from the trail and following the river's current, the woman sitting silently in the wagon bed and holding her infant to her. Riley wanted to ask about her being Chinese but it didn't seem the time to prod.

"I can't believe I'm allowing this." Lieutenant Bicknell's voice was fairly horrified. "My God—an army payroll!"

Despite the absence of any trail, the going was easy except where washouts and dry creeks slashed into the river's banks. Then they had to make wide detours with the wagon to get around them. After an hour they gave up trying to flank the river so closely and stayed a half mile out on the plains, where the air was hotter and the only shade their own.

"I expect in about two minutes she'll be sleeping like a baby herself," Riley told Cass, but despite her obvious exhaustion, the young woman clung grimly to consciousness. It was midafternoon when she began looking anxiously about her. "It is there," she said finally, gesturing ahead.

Cass shaded his eyes and looked down to where the river made an oxbow—a broad, lazy loop. The grass lay green and rich and stands of cottonwood and elm luxuriated near the water.

"It's possible we're being led straight into ambush," Lieutenant Bicknell noted.

"Carbines at the ready," Rafferty ordered in professional fashion, and there was a rattle of tackle. Whether he was genuinely concerned or merely humoring his officer, Riley could not tell. The troopers formed a line and edged forward. Riley slapped reins over the backs of his team.

"We could keep the woman in front in case there's firing," Bicknell suggested. Without slowing, Rafferty gave him a withering look and then leaned out along his black's neck and spat tobacco.

"Dead pony," Cass said, and as he spoke a pair of turkey buzzards winged heavy-bodied into the air. In the trees along the river, crows flapped up noisily and resettled a hundred yards farther down the line.

"If Indians were hidden in those trees, there'd hardly be

buzzards and crows," Cass said. "I'll take the birds' testament there's no ambush." Riley slapped his horses again and the wagon surged out ahead of the troopers. They could see another dead pony now, and soon after, widely strewn patches of clothing that denoted human corpses in the grass. Riley stopped the wagon. The woman, Tai Hei, sobbed and slid off the wagon tail.

"Here now, girl," Riley said, but she managed to walk out ahead of them, clutching the baby and moving stiffly because of having recently given birth. She walked uncertainly till she reached the first of the bodies, which looked like no more than tangled clothes from where Riley and Cass sat. Her free hand went to her face and she backed from the corpse and stood sobbing as the escort drew up to her. Riley thought he had never seen an Indian cry before, but then he remembered this one was no Indian.

In all, there were five men, two women, and six ponies sprawled in the oxbow of fresh grass. The corpses had been disjointed by wolves and then pecked over by vultures and crows and the faces were grotesquely swollen and blackened by sun. Lieutenant Bicknell gagged at the sight and smell and had to stand awhile upwind, taking deep breaths.

Tai Hei explained about the burial party, though she seemed to command few words of English that pertained to such matters. She found the remains of what she said had been her father-in-law's burial scaffold, torn down now and rifled through by her people's attackers.

"She insists on burying the bodies, Lieutenant," Cass reported to Bicknell. "One of them's her husband."

"I reckon we'll do it with scaffolds and trees in the Indian fashion," Riley said. "It's their favored style, and it'll be no slower than digging."

"Technically, these casualties are enemy," Bicknell said. He was slowly getting some color back.

For once, Rafferty was gentle with him. "Sir, there is nothing technical about her, surely." They looked out at the woman, who sat devastated in rich grass, her back to the plains, her baby cradled closely. "She says white men did this to her people. Sartainly there are wagon tracks all over," Rafferty said. "I believe we owe it to her, sir." Bicknell's response was to make a face.

"Look at the thing this way," Rafferty said. "The detail has rescued the poor girl from savages, and yourself in command, sir. The newspapers thrive on such happenings. Begging your pardon, sir, but getting your name in the papers is not the worst way for a young lieutenant to begin a new posting."

"I hadn't thought of it in such selfish terms," Bicknell said.

"Surely it pays to look at a thing from all sides, sir," Rafferty said shrewdly.

"Perhaps you're right, Sergeant. It appears I have a lot to learn out here."

"Yes, sir."

"Better start cutting poles, boys," Cass called to the troopers.

16 · TAI HEI

IN SOMETHING LESS THAN TWO HOURS THE LAST SCAFFOLD WAS up. The men, most with their shirts off and suspenders hanging, regrouped at the wagon, where they stood swigging water from canteens. Tai Hei understood she was being given a moment to inspect the work. The bodies were not wrapped in buffalo robes, nor were the scaffolds intermingled with the cottonwoods and perfectly constructed as Tai Hei would have wished them. Some of the Kiowa who had been among the burial party were not accounted for, though at this moment Tai Hei was too weary to sort out the missing from the dead. Her mind, exhausted, clogged with words of English, refused to work.

She placed her nameless baby on a blanket she had been given and walked forward, deliberately steeling herself, making herself be Bird of Morning. She stood beneath the elevated bodies, trusting the proper behavior would come to her if only she were worthy. She raised her arms to the sky father, then dropped them, useless. She began a low keening for the dead, bringing it up high and then letting it waver in tremolo as she had heard it wailed by women of her village. Conviction eluded her. She stopped, too exhausted to sustain grief, even for him who had been her husband. They were dead. He was dead. Wailing would not change it.

She turned and picked up her little daughter, pathetic in her vulnerability, yet beautiful too. A happy baby in spite of all, Kiowa and Chinese and wholly herself, this new little one. Tai Hei remembered the certainty with which she had believed her baby would be a male child, destined to be a warrior, eventually a *Koitsenko*. Yet here was the baby, a daughter. Surely she, Tai Hei, was a very poor Kiowa.

And then she remembered the flames—old flames flickering out, new ones gathering—and she saw her duty clearly. She approached the line of white men, who had had many chances to kill her and yet had not done so. Many had taken off their hats. In fact, all stood respectfully. In any case, Tai Hei was too tired to be afraid any longer.

"I wish to go from this place," Tai Hei said, and she clambered stiff and exhausted into the back of the wagon.

17 · RILEY

THEY'D ALL NOTICED THE ASHES OF THE TEAMSTERS' BONFIRE in the grassy oxbow flat. It was Cass who remarked on the wagon tracks.

"They're heading straight as a shot for the same place we're heading," he told the lieutenant. "We maybe haven't gone out of our way much at all."

"Then that's the only good news of the day, Mr. McCasland," Lieutenant Bicknell said.

They climbed the long rise away from the river. The well-watered grass of the river valley browned and sparsened into thirsty plains. When they topped the first rise, Riley jumped down from the wagon and spent a minute studying the tracks they followed.

"I'm no tracker but I'd say these wagons are hauling quite a load. Empty wagons wouldn't groove the sod so deep."

"So they're freight wagons," the lieutenant said. "What of it?"

"Well, it's interesting," Riley said. "This one rim leaves pretty near its own brand." He pointed out a raised, jagged wedge in one of the wagon tracks. He found the wedge imprinted again a few strides farther on. "I expect there's a chip of iron broke where the rim ends of one wheel meet," Riley said. "If a body wanted to talk to these murdering traders, he could follow this little mark as far as was needed."

"I'll make a point to include the information in my report," Bicknell noted, and he nudged his horse forward.

18 · TAI HEI

THE COLUMN STRAGGLED INTO EVENING. TAI HEI SLEPT, THEN woke to heartsickness when she realized her circumstances. Even so, the rhythm of the wagon was soothing. It seemed to her she had lost as much as she was going to lose, and that the coming days would be better. Her little daughter's safe arrival seemed proof of that feeling.

After a while Tai Hei began to sing. It was not a song of mourning for her dead, but one of hope and beginnings for her little daughter, a song of happiness for her. She sang of swans coming down through lush foliage to a river, moving awkwardly on the land but graceful once they got into the water, where they swam happily amid floating lotus blossoms. The song was repetitious and she altered the words now and then in a way that would please the infant. It was some time before she realized the words were Mandarin Chinese.

The dark-haired one driving the wagon spoke to his companion. "Darned if it don't sound like somebody tinkling glassware."

Eventually Tai Hei left off her singing. She felt unconnected to anything in the world, save her daughter, in a way that was both frightening and exhilarating. The white men were taking her to a place of which she knew nothing. Her people had sometimes spoken of the soldier forts, but she herself had never seen one. Perhaps she would see one now.

Her resolve was one of her duty as a Kiowa, to her people who were Kiowa. This resolve she placed firmly in her heart. Her thinking, however, she let run where it would, like spilled water finding its own path. The bodies had included Eagle Man, her husband's father. Then her husband, Two Horses, crudely scalped. Then old Wolf Running, and Swift Axe, and the woman Leather Maker . . . Yet, others of her party might still live, and if she did not save them, then who would? Surely no one, for she alone among her people knew of the captives' plight.

In time she would become truly Kiowa, connected to the people, to the sky, and the earth. But for the moment, she was both Kiowa and Chinese, and it was useless to pretend otherwise. She would use both parts of her as circumstances demanded. She would use her ability with American speech as best she could. But to save her people who were now captives, she would need her freedom from these blue soldiers. And more than that, she would need help.

"My son," she said after a time, using English and startling the men who drove the wagon. Their heads swiveled, showing concerned faces.

"What say?" the darker one said.

"My son has been taken. He calls now to me," Tai Hei said. The men looked doubtful. "I hear him crying—here." Tai Hei tapped her heart.

"Those butchering wagoners took your son?" the darker-haired man said.

"So it is," Tai Hei said. "My son, little Eagle Feather. Also taken are two others. Sky Calf, my sister-wife. Also old Hears Snow Falling, who is mother-of-my-husband." At these words both white men groaned. The two sat silently for some moments, their backs grieving.

"I can't tell you how sorry we are to hear that, ma'am," the lighter-haired one said finally.

Then the other said, "But as for helping you get these people back for you, we got our own worries to think of."

"He is right on the button there," the other one said. "We've been glad to help you this far, but getting your son and them back—that's just going to have to be somebody else's problem."

19 · BAYARD

IT WAS NIGHTFALL WHEN THE THREE RIDERS REACHED THE BANKS of the river the whites called Pawnee. Bayard thought of it as the Indians called it: Buffalo Water.

"The only reason this arse of mine ain't sore is on account of the feeling went out of it," the one called Legg said. He tottered stiffly off his horse and got laughed at by Parrott when his legs buckled and he sat down hard on the ground. Bayard enjoyed the sight too. Legg was a comical man in the first place, and this was a comical happening.

"No half-breed bastard better laugh at me," Legg said, ignoring that Parrott had laughed first. Parrott got down nearly as stiffly and massaged his legs. His shirt was sweated through in a wide swath down his back.

Bayard still smiled to himself, but inwardly, at the antics of foolish white men. He slid off his horse and set about reading the ground. Soon he grunted in satisfaction, for there one of the booted men had stood after getting off the wagon. And there had stood the other. The soldiers' wide-toed bootprints were splayed all over. But here were the naked footprints of one of the men—no, of two—and here the water had been entered. Bayard grunted again. It must have been good to lie in the cool water during the heat of midday.

Then the ground displayed a puzzle. Bayard squatted to study it carefully. Out of nowhere—the sky, perhaps—a small, moccasined print had appeared, an older girl's or small woman's. Bayard was sure that whatever female had made this track had not ridden on the wagon. He back-tracked, finding where the woman had come down along the riverbank. He read the ground even though the grass was deep and well trampled by army boots. Then he found a virtual path beaten through the fresh grass and he followed it to a hollowing in the willows.

He bent and sniffed, finding where a female had squatted to make water. A woman had lived in this space, one, perhaps two days. Then he found evidence of a little one: the mustard feces of the newborn. Where ground had been disturbed, he dug and found the sacred mystery of the afterbirth. Carefully he reburied it, then turned and went back to his gentlemen. The one called Legg had gotten a white man's fire going.

"I hate a man who keeps disappearing," Parrott said. "How far ahead are they?"

"So much of the sun's journey." Bayard pointed straight overhead.

"Can't you just say half a frigging day?" Parrott said. "I'm too tired for Indian guessing games."

"Also there is a new thing. A woman now goes with them. Also her little one." Bayard demonstrated the baby's size like a fisherman: so long.

Legg's mouth popped open. "Where would anybody get a woman way the hell out here?"

"They picked up a woman? Is she white or Indian?" Parrott said.

"Her feet walk in Kiowa moccasins." Bayard was certain of that much; in Indian fashion, he did not speculate.

Legg shook his head in wonder. Parrott tugged at his side-whiskers and his eyes drifted, seeming to look through Bayard. Then his focus sharpened. Strangely, he smiled.

"Well, those poor misguided Samaritans," Parrott said. "That ought to keep them occupied. Nothing slows a man quite so well as a woman."

20 · RILEY

THEY FOUND DR. TWEED'S OFFICE ON THE SECOND FLOOR OF A frame building whose first floor housed a barbershop. They led a slim and much bedraggled woman wearing a torn buckskin garment up the rickety outside stairway. The woman's eyes showed fright at the stairs and she clutched her tiny baby so closely that it began crying.

A clock, its brass-bolstered mechanism set into a cherry-wood housing shaped like the hat of Napoleon, ticked out some eighteen-hundred seconds, during which time its spear-point minute hand inched one hundred and eighty degrees across elaborately seriffed Roman numerals.

Cass rustled his newspaper, the Buffalo City *Beacon*. Riley paced, crossing and recrossing an oval of braided rug, painted floorboards creaking under his weight. The fragrance of bay rum and sounds of men's voices came up from the first-floor barbershop. Riley paused at the same point on each circuit to look out a water-spotted window, the glass wavy with flaws. In the window's corner, gauzy spiderwebs held the weightless corpses of flies.

He watched horse and jingling wagon traffic moving along Front Street. Across from him was a hotel, where a Negro in a sackcloth coat swept the boardwalk. Just down the street was a saloon, already leaking din into the street at this hour of late afternoon. The promise of both bed and beer were soothing to a man with trail dust for a gullet, a man who had slept in his clothes the past three nights running.

Riley heard a murmur of voices coming from the examination room. The woman and her baby were vast complications. Already he and Cass would get back to Hays City a day later than they were expected. Riley hoped the doctor would somehow know what to do with her, this friendless girl, all the while knowing with utter conviction that the doctor would not. He turned and looked at the inner door expectantly, then, after concluding that the door was not about to open, he shifted his weight and resumed pacing.

Cass turned a page and smoothed his paper. "I wisht you'd light someplace. You're nervous as a jumping bean. There's no reason to think they aren't perfectly healthy."

Riley looked about him. The carved-back settee with its red plush cushions did not look an apt haven for a dusty man. "It's not that," Riley said. A thought flitted ahead of him of how they couldn't very well just dump her on the streets of Buffalo City; but before he could snare it down, the inner door opened and Tweed came out, a slim man, and far younger than Riley's notion of a proper doctor.

Tweed closed the door gently behind him before speaking. "It's a remarkable story, isn't it? A Chinese captured by the Kiowa. And her English is amazingly good under the circumstances."

"It's getting better," Cass said.

"How is she?" Riley asked.

"Simple exhaustion, for the most part." Tweed washed his hands in an enameled bowl and dried them on a towel. "Otherwise they're both as hale as colts. Give her a day or so of rest and a few good meals—" The doctor had been rolling down his shirtsleeves but he stopped abruptly. "Well. And I suppose she'll be ready for whatever comes next. She's very keen, you know, on finding her son."

"We know," Riley said miserably.

"She asked if she gave me money, would I take her out on the plains after her boy." Tweed laughed in wonder. "Do I look like a frontiersman?"

"We talked to the colonel at Fort Dodge, hoping she might be taken care of somehow," Cass said. "From what we gathered from her description, the attack on her party was unprovoked."

"The colonel can't send out a patrol?" Tweed asked. "If the army won't punish these men, they could at least help get her son back."

Cass said, "Being the government lands for the Kiowa are in the Indian Territory, the official attitude is any bands roaming in Kansas deserve what they get."

"But she's *Chinese,*" Tweed said.

"There was a lot of shrugging of epaulets over that part of it," Riley said. "You know darn well had she been a white woman the army would see it different." He turned back to his window. "Anyway, what now?"

"For the moment, she's fine where she is," Tweed said. "I can sleep on the settee—Lord knows I've done it before. I'll get a bath for her downstairs, and I suppose I can find her something to wear." He was thinking aloud.

"That bed will be needed in a day or two, though," Tweed said. "We average four gunshot wounds a week. Some towns have opera, we have gunfights. It's our civic entertainment." He chuckled.

Cass studied the wallpaper. Riley looked out his window. "She can hardly remain with you gents, I suppose," Tweed suggested. "Till she gets on her feet, I mean?"

"We've got a freight wagon to return to Hays City," Cass said. "We're heading out in the morning."

"Hays is a rail town," Tweed said brightly.

Riley could see where that was headed. "You're saying ship her somewhere there's a Chinese community. San Francisco, most likely."

"It's the obvious choice," Tweed said, eyebrows shrugging. "After all, they're her people."

"Tai Hei says her people are the Kiowa nation," Riley said. He looked sourly at Cass, and then they both looked helplessly at young Dr. Tweed.

21 · RILEY

BY SEVEN-THIRTY THAT EVENING THEY HAD BATHED AND SHAVED and changed their clothes. They dined on plains steak—thick slices of buffalo hump along with coins of fried potatoes, both served with catsup.

After their supper, Riley went out riding, taking one of Julius Herbert's dray horses without a saddle. He found Cass two hours later, sitting in the company of four men at a poker table in the Bulldog Bar. Riley came in excited, repressing information with an effort. Cass beckoned him over.

"Why so worked up?" Cass looked back to his cards. "Fox in the henhouse?"

"I found where their tracks left town. South toward the Territory." Riley hated to say more because the men at Cass's table appeared a rough lot.

"That's something, at any rate."

"Fact is, I found out quite a bunch." Riley rolled his eyes toward the bar. "Stand me to a drink over this way a minute."

"I'm not doing myself any good here anyhow," Cass said. He moved a cloth-wrapped package from his lap to a safe spot beneath his coattails and clamped a wrist against it to hold it in place. He nodded to the men at the poker table and stood up. "Getting myself a drink or two. I always heard you give poor luck a rest and it might change on you."

"Anything's possible," one of the players said glumly.

Riley stood at the bar; he was too agitated to lean his

weight into it. "You remember that funny three-cornered chunk out of one of their wagon rims?"

"I do."

"I found that mark here and yonder all over town," Riley said. "Mostly, though, I had to ask a lot of questions."

"And?"

"The wagons belong to whiskey peddlers. I expect they hauled a load down from the railhead at Hays City."

Cass shrugged. "Stands to reason."

"So these whiskey men went around town trying to unload their liquor," Riley said. "It's evidently raw stuff. I only found two saloonkeepers who admitted to buying any of it, and they took just two barrels each."

"Meaning these men still got a lot of it," Cass said.

"Meaning just that. All told, they've got four wagons of the stuff. Bartenders tell me they stop here on their way to the Territory. Anyhow, once I figured they'd cleared out, I checked the trails out of town. There was the funny track, heading spang for Indian Territory. You know yourself that's a bad business, selling liquor to Indians. It tells something about the kind we're dealing with."

"Maybe we could work it so's the army caught them at it," Cass suggested.

Riley shook his head. "They'd just deny that's what they're up to. The story I heard is that they sell only to white traders, who in turn sell to Indians. That way these teamster boys keep their hands clean. Besides, the army's got no authority in the Nations or the Territory either one. The civil law down there is the Lighthorse—Indian police—but all they can do with white criminals is kick them out. You can easy figure how well that works. They come right back over the line again."

"And these whiskey men are a rough bunch, I'll bet."

"That too," Riley said. "There's some half dozen, the boss being a Dutchman name of Hollenbeck. I guess he scares the britches off everybody. Some saloon owners do a little business with him just to humor him. He is supposed to be something when riled."

"Wonderful," Cass said. "And these are the folks who've got Tai Hei's little boy."

They were served beers. "I miss a mustache when drinking beer," Cass said. "So since you're still jittering like you're scorpion bit, I expect you've got some plan or other."

"Me? I ain't got a notion in my head."

"Empty-headed, mush-hearted—that's you," Cass said. "You think we ought to do something but you got no idea what."

"I ain't too proud to pity unfortunates," Riley said. He sipped a moment and thought about it. "It's like some scraggly cat starts hanging around your barn. Wouldn't any fellow give her a squirt of milk now and again, while milking the cow or whatnot?"

"I reckon," Cass said.

"Surely he would. So the next thing, this kitty-cat is underfoot all the time, looking for that milk. And the *next* thing is, she's got kits mewing all over her, and it's all of a sudden your job to figure what to do with them." Riley sipped his beer without tasting it. "You ever have to drown kittens?"

"The moral is don't get involved," Cass said.

"We already are involved."

"Well, you wouldn't call me mush-hearted, but I was raised to honor motherhood," Cass said. "Where I come from, it's required of all gentlemen."

"Aha! Out of the woods comes the gallant Confederate, championer of lost causes."

"Have your fun," Cass said. "If you'd only listen a spell instead of telling cat stories, you'd hear me agreeing with you. We've just got our different reasons, that's all. I allow we could raise a stake for her. We already talked about doing that much."

"It's your method that's not to my liking," Riley said. "Too damned dangerous. We already have to take the wagon back to Hays where some big poker cheats are going to shoot us. That's all the danger my insides can stand. What you're talking about is juggling powder kegs. I am partial to boredom, remember?"

"Oh hell," Cass said, disgusted. "That Parrott is long gone. A big-time sport won't hang around some Kansas whistle-stop any longer than necessary."

"You stomped his fingers," Riley said.

"You're switching subjects. I'm still talking about Tai

Hei." Cass set a cloth bundle on the bartop, making a muffled clunk. It was about the size of their beer mugs. "Fact is," Cass said, "you know damned well what I'm talking about."

Riley said, "Oh, dang." Cass unwrapped the mug; it was no bigger than others on the bar but it appeared more heavily made, almost a solid chunk of glass. Cass poured Riley's beer into it, being careful not to spill any on the lens. The bogus mug seemed to fill up quickly.

"If that doesn't look convincing," Cass said admiringly.

"I don't think I got the nerve for this." Riley caught his own reflection in the back-bar mirror, the sorry face of the degenerate criminal.

"We went through that already. It's for the best of causes. Think how good you'll feel when we give Tai Hei some folding money and put her and her baby on a train to San Francisco."

"She don't want to go," Riley said. "Alls she wants is her little boy back, and then back to being a Kiowa."

"Give her time. As for her son, there's not much we can do. We're just two men, not the whole army." Cass put his back to the bar, lounging on his elbows. "What'll those whiskey peddlers do with an Indian boy anyhow? Sell him to Indians. He'll be back among his people in no time."

"You think so?"

"What else?" Cass said. "From that far table you'll be able to see almost everybody's cards. Then you amble over and stand at the bar awhile and you can see the other fellows'."

"Oh, double dang it."

"You got the signals straight?" Cass said.

"They're wrote down." Riley nervously checked a coat pocket.

"I'm going back to that poker game," Cass said. "Don't you leave me in the lurch." He parked the cheater's beer mug in Riley's hands and walked to the poker table. He sat down in his former chair and said, "Boys, deal me in," in a voice that rang like an auctioneer's. "I've got a notion my luck just changed."

22 · TAI HEI

A PARALLELOGRAM OF SUNLIGHT PIVOTED SLOWLY ACROSS HER bed. Then it climbed the wall, the hard line of its upper frontier overtaking a succession of unlikely looking wallpaper roses. The baby stirred, cried, nursed, slept again. The sunlight aged and weakened. In time it was dark.

It had been a long while since she had heard men's voices in the barbershop downstairs, and longer yet since she'd heard the white medicine man's creaking tread in the front room of his office. But as the sounds in the building gradually died, the street outside came ever more alive. Iron-shod hooves clopped by to the unfamiliar jingle of harness and skirl of wagon rims. Strange music reached her from various directions. Rough laughter vaulted up in the falling night.

She moved her legs under the covers, feeling all things clean and liking the sensation. The bath had been a revelation—the warm water, the medicinal smell of soap.

Another pleasure was being in rooms again. The sensation brought her brief, half memories of other rooms in far places of her earlier life. Sad memories, some of them, many best forgotten. Four years had been a long time to live among the Kiowa, so long that she had lost the habit of looking back. She saw the room for what it was: a wooden box for people.

Her little daughter slept, eventually stirred. Tai Hei sang to it, picking up the song of the previous day, the words telling about swans on the river. The baby opened dark eyes. Knowing nothing of attacks and killing, of people carrying away other people, the baby smiled.

The Kiowa way was to let the child name herself through some remarkable trait or deed. But in the meanwhile Tai Hei would have her own name for her infant. She opened her mind to let names float in to her, and was surprised that only Chinese words and meanings suggested themselves. One rose above the others. Her daughter would be Kam Loi— 甘來 or Good Things Coming—for truly had the baby's arrival been the only good amid a terrible time. And also because Kam Loi was the name of a particularly beautiful Mandarin actress Tai Hei had admired during her year in San Francisco.

Tai Hei had never attended the Chinese theater, had never seen acting on a stage. But she had heard retellings of the stories the plays told. She had seen lithographed posters of costumed actors, their faces painted to portray large emotions.

And she had seen the famous Kam Loi herself; yes, she had seen her. One day as Tai Hei walked out on some errand, her eyes properly downcast as befit a sing-song girl in public, a carriage had pulled up alongside her. A coachman scuttled to hold the carriage door. Tai Hei lingered, delaying her errand. A tiny foot, bound since childhood, probed out and found the step. A beauty appeared, face brightly painted in contrast to her black garment. Then another step and suddenly an emerald necklace swung forward from the wearer's throat, green against black, the jewel set in silver mountings. Tai Hei had gasped at such wealth and elegance. The beauty had smiled at her, then descended.

It was the famous actress Kam Loi, the other girls exclaimed when she told the story. She sat in the doctor's bed treasuring the memory. Then she resolved it: Until her daughter earned her own name among the Kiowa, she would be named for this pampered one. Little Kam Loi.

Then, as Kam Loi nursed, Tai Hei thought about money. She had forgotten the uses, even the existence, of this substance that had once so troubled the Chinese men she had worked for. A Kiowa had only a vague appreciation of money, of course, knew only that white men prized it and that captured coins made fine ornaments.

The two kind-eyed white men had spoken of money, and worried aloud over the lack of it. They had also spoken to the doctor about it. To those who lived in buildings, whether they were Chinese or whites, the getting and using of money seemed of great importance.

It was a puzzle, and yet not, for Tai Hei had once earned money, though never for herself. Most importantly, she remembered how to earn it. With money, Tai Hei could acquire a horse to carry her and little Kam Loi. And with it also she could acquire men with guns. What she had learned of the white men was that some were dishonorable and hunted poorly. Others yet were murderers. Confusingly, others yet were kind-eyed and offered food and clothing. So there were three breeds among them.

Tai Hei decided she would watch for the kind-eyed ones, and deal with them only. She would do what they wanted in the ways that men are pleased by women, and then they would pay her. Out of that beginning, she would accomplish her duty.

She got out of bed, thankful to see her way clearly. She put on the long shirt, smelling of soap, that the doctor had given her. Over it she slipped her buckskin garment, which smelled of Tai Hei herself (or rather, Bird of Morning!) and of her Kiowa village. She picked up Kam Loi and crept silently to the door. She opened it, hearing a clock, whose mechanism divided time into small, regular noises. Within moments she had let herself down the wooden stairway and was standing both terrified and determined in an easeway between buildings, looking out at the yellow windows and passing white men on Buffalo City's Front Street.

23 · MAGGIE ROSE

MAGGIE ROSE LAND BELIEVED IN PROTECTING HER OWN. SHE HAD set up her brothel in a succession of frontier towns, and had been pushed out, Bible-thumped out, quarantined out, or starved out of each one of them. Buffalo City was her bonanza, still too raw for blue-nosed town ladies, too wide open for any king pimp to have taken control.

She had built her parlor house at the edge of town, far enough out to be beyond the city boundaries once Buffalo City incorporated as a legal municipality, which was only a matter of months given the weedlike growth of the place. She was beyond the town and yet connected to it, for Maggie Rose kept her friendlies in the saloons of Front Street—bartenders, mostly, who steered hunters, freighters, and soldiers her way in exchange for the kind of special consideration only a whorehouse madam could dispense.

As in any frontier town, free-lance whores plied their trade in cribs and upstairs rooms the length of Front Street. Maggie Rose kept tabs on those, but rarely felt much challenged. For along with girls, Maggie Rose offered the comforts of a parlor house: hot baths, music and dancing, liquor, food, and gaming. She looked forward to a handful of good years, maybe a decade, before civilization and Victorian prudery caught up with her. With buffalo hide money flowing freely, a decade might well be enough—but only so long as Maggie Rose looked out for what was hers.

"The buggy's out front, missus," one of the girls said, on the scout at the parlor window. Maggie Rose accomplished the top button on her high collar and rustled to the door, her skirts sweeping the furniture. A hunter leaning against the ringing piano took notice of her passing, for she was impressive in a towering hat and black and bustled silk dress, as striking when fully turned out as a clipper ship under sail.

The door was held for her. Twin coal oil lamps on the porch splashed light across the planking. She swirled a shawl over her shoulders and went out and down the steps, mindful of june bugs, the heels of her high-button shoes knocking precisely. Dash closed the gate behind her, then helped her get a foot up, for her figure had fleshed out in the prosperity of Buffalo City. She settled herself: a henna-haired woman contained by whalebones, prow-bosomed, expensively gloved, an embroidered handkerchief peeking from one cuff.

"Front Street tonight, Dash," Maggie Rose announced. "We're on the lookout for new competition."

"Yes, missus," Dash said. The buggy listed as he climbed into the front seat. The rig was a good double-seat surrey, black with Brewster green trim, with a quarter extension top, side curtains, and a rigid rear panel complete with isinglass window. The rig had cost her eighty-five dollars out of Kansas City, and whenever, as now, she meant to be seen on Front Street, she felt it had been worth every penny.

Dash placed a long shotgun across his bony lap and reached for the whip in its cast-iron socket. He held the whip upright but did not prepare to use it. He said only, "Git along now, you hosses," in a scolding tone, as though the animals should have divined when to move forward. Attuned to his voice, the horses leaned together into their collars and hames and lurched into motion, the movement causing flickers in the twin lanterns mounted on either side of the driver's seat.

They passed a cabin with two barns and corrals, then a sod dugout that had collapsed with spring rains. Then they were in the town proper, first rolling past a scattering of hide and freight yards, then residences on surveyed streets and finally the bluff-fronted business buildings rising foursquare out of the prairie.

"Big night in town tonight," Maggie Rose said, noting the saddle horses and wagons strung along Front Street. "I'm sure we can expect some of these boys in a couple, three hours."

"Yes, missus," Dash said. He did not ask their destination, nor would he, Maggie Rose knew, for it was a game between them, he not asking and she finally explaining their errand at the last possible moment. She settled herself against spring-cushioned upholstery, sitting sideways on account of the bustle.

"I don't quite know what we're looking for," Maggie Rose said to the backs of her driver's prominent ears. The shotgun barrels glinted in the light of the side lanterns. "I'm told we've got new competition working right out on Front Street."

"Yes, missus."

"An Indian maiden, no less—though I can hardly credit it. Hannah says she saw her big as life down by the Long Branch, street-walking bold as you please and carrying a baby. But then, I expect we all know Hannah." Maggie Rose laughed harshly.

Dash's reaction was without precedent. He swiveled his bony rear on the front seat, Japan-waxed leather upholstery squeaking, shotgun barrels pivoting alarmingly, and looked into the rear as though perhaps the devil had taken his employer and left himself in her place.

"Injun woman?" Dash was all eyes and teeth and whiskers in the light of the side lanterns. "And her with some *baby?"*

"Have a care, you idiot!" Maggie Rose said.

Dash swiveled forward. "Yes, missus."

It was Dash who saw her first, her form sidelighted by a saloon window, taking hesitant steps toward a passing buffalo hunter, then tugging at his sleeve as he turned away.

"I expect that be her there," Dash said. "Injun woman, *hunh*. If that don't beat everything." He veered his team toward the slender figure.

"If she tries to get away, you'd best run catch her," Maggie Rose said.

They were almost up to her. Maggie Rose could see the sort of buckskin sack that served these wretches as a dress. Some Indian garments Maggie Rose had seen were elaborately decorated with beads and quills, but this one was plain and well dirtied, ragged to boot. The woman herself was young and small, standing bare-legged and holding a baby, which picked that moment to begin crying. She did not have the look of a pimp backing her, for which Maggie Rose was thankful, nor did she look to be much competition for Maggie Rose's three-story parlor house, but then one never knew what might strike a man's fancy.

The Indian girl turned in evident alarm, suddenly realizing the surrey would stop rather than pass her by. Maggie Rose saw the lank, dark hair, the black eyes shining like pieces of coal she had seen somewhere, cleverly shellacked and made into jewelry.

"You, girl," Maggie Rose said. Accustomed to command, her voice had come too sharply; the girl started like a deer. "There now, I ain't going to hurt you." Maggie Rose could see the baby, a tiny face dazzled by the surrey's side lanterns. "Come on over here, honey. Do you speak any English at all?"

Dash said, "Not too likely."

The girl's eyes widened, maybe at hearing a woman's voice from the carriage's dark interior. "Yes, I speak," the girl said finally.

"Why, she talk just about like we do," Dash said. "Look how she ready to scamper off to the prairies if a body more'n say boo."

"Hush," Maggie Rose said. "Come on here, honey. Come here to Maggie."

"You are an . . . actress?" the Indian girl asked her.

"What? Well, my heavens, every good whore's an actress,"

Maggie Rose said jovially. "Now I got a question. Just what is it you're doing in my town?"

"I wish to be a wife for money," the girl said, sounding hopeful.

Maggie Rose laughed hugely, partly in anticipation of the pleasure of retelling the line. "Well, don't we all, honey," she said when she could talk again. She leaned forward into what little light was spilling out of saloon windows. The girl stood, smiling sweetly.

"Why, honey, that child is no more'n a few days old," Maggie Rose said. "You can't be doing nothing with men after just having a baby."

"I wish to be a wife," the girl said again. "I must my people to save."

"Well, for the love of Mike," Maggie Rose said, stopped flat. She looked in wonder at Dash, who mirrored the expression right back at her.

"That ain't no Injun, I see that much," Dash said. "She look more like some kind of China girl I seen someplace. What folks call a Celestial."

"Hush," Maggie Rose said again, but she looked more closely and wondered if it were true. The baby had stopped crying, for the girl had given it a breast to suckle, right out there on Front Street.

"Dash, help her on up here in the buggy. Honey, you best come out to my place till we figure what you're all about." Maggie Rose slid over with a whisper of silk and patted the upholstery.

Dash got down gingerly, a lean and large-boned man of indecipherable age, and set out a buggy weight. "Now if this don't beat all," he told the horses. "Taking some China girl on out to our place."

The girl took one hesitant step backward.

"Now, Honey, don't be ascairt of Maggie Rose. Hell, I don't bite . . . lest I'm paid to," Maggie Rose said, and laughed so that the girl smiled again. She decided Dash had been right on two counts: The girl was certainly ready to run off if anybody made a threatening move, and she somehow did not look right for an Indian, the buckskin sack of a dress notwithstanding.

Dash went around in front of the horses and made the girl

an odd bow, like he'd already decided she was Chinese. Then he smiled and extended his hand.

"That's just old Dash," Maggie Rose said. "Now you look sharp, honey. There's a step right here." The girl put her foot out and found the iron step and Dash pushed her up from behind.

"She don't weigh hardly nothing," Dash said. Then there the girl was, sitting on the leather seat.

"There now," Maggie Rose said soothingly.

"I smell a smell of much flowers," the girl said.

"That's perfume," Maggie Rose said. The infant's eyes danced and focused uncertainly, looking at the side lanterns. The girl spoke to the baby in a reassuring voice. The language could have been Comanche for all Maggie Rose knew.

"It sound when she talk like little old bells ringing," Dash observed.

"We'll bring her around the kitchen entrance," Maggie Rose said. "It's going to take me a bit to figure out exactly what we got here."

"Yes, missus, yes, ma'am," Dash said with enthusiasm. "Well ain't you two ashamed, standing there doing nothing. Get you off to home now!"

24 · PARROTT

THEY FILED INTO BUFFALO CITY, A TRIO OF RIDERS, HORSES' heads pumping tiredly. They passed weedy vacant lots, darkened mercantiles, the canvas-bonneted bulk of smelly hide wagons, uncountable saloons in full swing, a yellow-windowed hotel with moths crazying around its porch lanterns. The half-breed led them, sitting straight and undistracted by sights of the town, reading the grooved street as though darkness were no different than daylight.

Their side trip to Fort Dodge had been a wild-goose chase, confirming only that the men they sought had stopped, had divested themselves of their army escort, and had then repaired to the town nearby, probably for the comforts of baths and beds. The half-breed still claimed to follow their prey's wagon, divining its tracks straight down what Buffalo City denizens forthrightly called Front Street, though how Bayard could tell one set of tracks from the tangled skein of others was more than Parrott could see.

Legg dozed in the saddle, the man's soft snoring a relief after his incessant complaining—about tender posteriors, mostly. Now and again Parrott reminded himself that Legg was worth putting up with, for the man had often demonstrated his uses, especially when debts were to be collected. Not that Parrott had needed convincing; he had recognized Legg's talents with knife and gun the first time he saw them, and had quickly latched onto him.

Parrott considered it his genius to be able to read a man—whether at a poker table or elsewhere. "I never play cards," John Parrott liked to say. "I play men."

It was true he could size a man up, determine what, if anything, the fellow was particularly good at, then jump from that judgment to the more cogent one of what use, again if anything, the man might be to John Parrott. And from that determination, proceeding to hire or beguile away that one valuable part of a man was usually easily accomplished, and usually at bargain rates.

For most men, Parrott found, sold themselves cheaply. Like Enoch Legg, who worked less for salary than for a love of the violence that cropped up inevitably in Parrott's line of work. Or like this half-breed, Bayard, willing to trade away his almost supernatural skills at tracking for a paltry ten dollars. It often seemed to Parrott that, of all men, only he himself knew his own true worth.

In fact it was that very thing—the high value Parrott set on certain aspects of himself, on his sense of invincibility, for one thing—that would soon cause these one-horse-town, poker-playing sons of bitches to be dealt the surprise of their lives. Parrott felt vengeance was well justified. He had only dealt them a lesson in the possibilities of poker, a demonstration (for those with the wit to appreciate it, it could have been an enlightenment) that once poker becomes a profession it ceases to be a game. For which lesson the gents in question had ungratefully stuck a gun in his windpipe, robbed him, humiliated him before an employee, then smashed his priceless, well-practiced hand. For each of which trespasses these fools would pay dearly.

A streaking cat caused their horses to skitter. Legg came awake with a snort, rubbed his eyes and looked over the town. "About time you joined us," Parrott said.

Still reading the ground, the half-breed turned down a side street, with Parrott and Legg filing behind, three riders seemingly towed by their moon-cast shadows, the clop of their horses slowly displacing the now diminishing roar of saloons. They stopped in front of apparently twinned barns, one fronted by a sign: L. VON SCHMIDT, LIVERY.

Bayard grunted. "It is the wagon," he said, looking squarely ahead of him. Parrott realized his own tired eyes were fixed on a lurking shape—a sturdy spring wagon with a raised seat and open box. A Studebaker, probably, or one of its imitations.

Legg groaned, slid off his horse, and sat down in the dirt, not even attempting to stand. Then he lay back and pulled his knees up and groaned again. "We go any farther, I'm gonna have to walk," Legg said. "My arse is raw meat."

Parrott swung down and massaged the insides of his knees. Then he straightened, took the shotgun from his saddle boot and walked stiff-legged to the wagon. He ran a hand along the sideboards, assuring himself by touch of the wagon's presence. He felt the whiskered wood grain, the scurf of paint beginning to peel. He levered back on the brake handle. He draped an arm on the backrest, thinking of the men who had lately sat there. He poked a finger into the whip socket, taking satisfaction. "They're ours," Parrott said.

"Probably sleeping comfy in a room someplace," Legg said. Because of lying on his back, his voice came raspier than usual.

"It's early yet." Parrott looked up toward Front Street. "If they're any kind of sporting men they'll be at a saloon." He dug into a coat pocket and took out a silvered object that became moonlight's plaything. He put the shotgun on the wagon seat and pinned a nickeled badge to his coat. He broke open the shotgun barrels and checked their loads. He slid a hand into his coat pocket to feel there the weight and cylindrical bulk of spare ten-gauge shells.

"And if they're at a saloon," Parrott said, "then we'll find them shortly." He braced the barrels against his thigh and snapped closed the shotgun's breech.

Legg watched him. "You sure done that clever, having yourself made deputy marshal of Hays City. Getting them warrants was smarter yet."

"Quite," Parrott said absently.

"There's times, John, a person just has to marvel. You think of damned near everything."

"I make a point of it." Parrott turned and looked up at Bayard, who was still sitting his horse. Bayard's eye sockets were deeply sheltered, giving no clue to his thoughts or feelings. He looked chiseled, so that from Parrott's perspective it was like looking up at an equestrian statue set in a park.

"You did us a piece of work," Parrott said. "Now you can wait here. If they come back, don't molest them. That's a privilege reserved for our Mr. Legg."

Legg cawed his laughter. Bayard did not answer, but Parrott was becoming used to such nonresponses. In a moment Bayard slid lightly off his horse and stood where moonlight hit him, his face still giving no indication of what he thought about anything.

"All right then," Parrott said, and he nodded, supplying his own agreement. Parrott handed Bayard the reins to his horse and then turned abruptly—a big man on long legs, wearing a buckskin hunting coat. At the movement, the coat's fringes flowed like water. Legg got himself up stiffly from the rutted yard in front of the livery barn.

"Mr. Legg, I'd hate to think you were too bushed to do your work," Parrott said. "After all, this is your specialty."

Legg stretched, then yarded out his Winchester from a scabbard on his horse. "Hell, I just had a saddle nap. A bit of a stroll to limber up and I'll be fresh as a daisy."

"Good," Parrott said, summing up. He made a small adjustment in the set of his hat. "Let's go hunting." He tucked the shotgun high up under his right arm and began walking.

Legg held out his horse's reins to Bayard, who took them without comment. "You be a good redskin," Legg said, "and when we're done with these fellows, I reckon John'll let you scalp 'em. That's one kind of cutting I don't go in for."

Legg laughed his dry laughter and hurried to catch up. Parrott chuckled at what Legg had said. Then he thought of something further he could say to Bayard. He stopped walking and turned. "Of course when our Mr. Legg is done with them, hair is damned near all that's left."

25 · RILEY

RILEY STOKES WAS HAVING MORE BOTHER THAN HE'D EVER HAD with a beer glass. The fact was, he found cheating far more vexing than playing square.

The lens, the part of the beer mug Cass called the eye, went dark unless he got his face right up to it. Then if he happened to breathe on it while his face was so close—which a person naturally would do while struggling to see anything—his breath would promptly cloud it.

Even when the picture came clear as creek water, Riley had a devil of a time, for the image was both inverted and reversed right to left, like that in the glass plate of a camera Riley had once peered into. Then too, objects loomed and yawned at him, sometimes stretching tall and skinny, and other times, depending how he held the mug, all squished fatly together. It was like seeing oneself in the wavy mirrors county fairs often had.

Hardest of all, despite the beer mug's magnifying powers, was homing in on a player's cards. Riley usually saw the cards as mere blurs of movement, and when he tried to follow that movement by rotating the mug, the image's backwardness and invertedness confounded him. Even when a player held his cards still, a poker hand appeared no more than a scattering of red and black dots on a white field. The only thing the cheater's mug showed clearly, in fact, was Cass's face, upside down, so that he seemed to wear his nose below his mouth, his eyebrows below his eyes, and his hat suspended from a wide, bearded chin.

The sole consolation was that while Cass was mostly scowling due to the uncertain signals Riley was sending, the scowl, appearing inverted, looked to Riley like Cass was having a high old time. Riley had to keep reminding himself they had nothing to feel chipper about, for certainly Cass's stake of greenbacks was not growing any larger. As far as Riley could see, Cass had barely half of it left.

The hand signals they'd agreed upon presented their own set of problems. Even when Riley managed to home in clearly on a hand of cards—say a pair of jacks with a ten-high on the side, held by the man sitting in the number three position—conveying the information to Cass required a whirligig of hat-brim tugs, finger waggles, and nose scratches. It made Riley look like a man who heard voices. Then too, his signals often miscued, forcing him to shake his head violently in an effort to erase them.

It was a trying business, and all in all, Riley felt he was doing as well as could be expected of him. Imagine, Riley thought to himself, a person spending a single evening studying a foreign tongue, and the next night going out and trying to hobnob in it. Anyone would make mistakes.

While thus justifying himself, he saw a piebald flash of face cards slip past in the mug's eye, too quickly to make out any of them. He looked up from the mug in frustration, noticing again that Cass's inverted smile was actually a scowl. Riley shrugged, not seeing what Cass had to be cross about; Cass was the lucky one, having only to tap a finger on his temple to say "I understand you," or else tug an ear to mean "I don't understand you." It was sure a bunch easier than all of Riley's antics.

Now, as Riley watched, Cass tugged furiously on one earlobe, all the while scowling fiercely. Riley responded with another shrug, which, though not a signal they had agreed on beforehand, seemed to get through well enough. All it did, though, was make Cass madder.

Cass shut his eyes in evident frustration. Riley felt bad about the collapse of their signal system but he didn't see what he could do about it. He believed they were getting what cheaters deserved, their good cause of raising money for Tai Hei notwithstanding.

When Cass's eyes reopened, they instantly narrowed, then

locked on the doorway beyond Riley's shoulder. Then the eyes went big as dollars—an interesting phenomenon to watch.

Concerned, Riley swiveled to take in the bulk of Terrible John Parrott filling the doorway, a shotgun under his arm. Behind him was the wool-capped man they'd called the shill, a Winchester rifle held port arms at his chest.

Cass swept the remains of his stake into his hat, a deft movement under the circumstances. Riley, abandoning the beer mug, dropped to the floor, his four-day mustache seeming too slender an object to hide behind.

Among the bar's drinkers and card players, there was an instant and dramatic and complex sound that can be made only by many panicked humans in a confined space. It commenced as a choral intake of breath and progressed to the scraping back of dozens of chair legs, some chairs clattering completely over, then to eighty booted feet scuffling, then to two score of voices pronouncing sudden oaths tending alarmingly toward the blasphemous. And then there came a massed scratchy thudding as whole squads of patrons simultaneously hit the sawdusted floor, each man moving with remarkable alacrity.

"It's them!" Parrott's voice bellowed, followed by the roar of a shotgun of major gauge, a tremendous blast that hammered Riley's eardrums and tapered off into a glissando of broken glassware.

Then Riley was scuttling on hands and knees through spit gobs and cigar butts, while at the same time being scuttled upon by a dozen others scuttling for their own lives on their own hands and knees, all moving through the furniture like rabbits in berry brush. Riley scuttled as quick as any of them, but he had no idea where to go, since Parrott and his crony blocked the front door and Riley and Cass hadn't bothered beforehand to scout out a rear one.

A second shotgun barrel roared, causing Riley to figure Cass had probably bought it, knocked down like a pheasant in his frock-coated plumage. Then Riley caught a glimpse of the side window. Gripping a chair before him to shield himself from cuts, he scrambled up, took two running strides, and launched himself at the glass.

At the height of his trajectory, a rifle blasted. Riley Stokes believed that just before a person died, his whole life flashed before him. Summoned by conviction, this phenomenon now happened, a magic lantern show at locomotive speed, scenes hurtling one upon another.

There was his mother at the cookstove, brushing sweaty wisps from her forehead, her face flushed and frazzled. Then Riley himself swinging in the oak tree and looking skyward at his own little bare feet. Then the cow that had kicked him senseless as he'd tried to milk her, and he was forced to endure that episode all over again, even down to collapsing into fresh manure. There was an axe he had dropped down the well and was waiting to be punished for. Then the first girl he'd loved, laughing at him, nipples like friendly eyes and auburn ringlets splayed out against straw. And then his years in the war and much death and destruction . . .

And then he was back in midair again and diving through a saloon window. It added up to a paltry sort of life, all yanked away before it was half over; he had a feeling of being badly shortchanged, and was more than a little sore about it.

The window mullions, of substantial strength, slowed him as he crashed through them. Even so, his dive carried him squarely through the window. He plunged into a well of darkness, and was falling, releasing the chair and falling—falling many feet farther than he had expected to, for the saloon floor was at boardwalk level, well above the street. He panicked and clawed out, grabbing fistfuls of nothing, and then landed largely on his head in a walkway between buildings, a space graveled over in broken liquor bottles.

He was bruised and stabbed and, for all he knew, probably shot and killed as well, but having no time to reflect on the tragedy of it, was instantly up and running, glass crunching underfoot, heading for the rear of the building. As he rounded the saloon's corner, the back door burst open, causing Riley a surge of panic. A figure windmilled out the doorway, more flying than running, a tall and fast and coattailed shadow that was Cass McCasland.

This time Riley kept up, benefiting from his practice run in Hays City a few days earlier. They pounded in tandem like a runaway team, going headlong down a coal-pit alley, jumping stray dogs busy with garbage, then veering away from the business district on a road rutty with wagon tracks.

"This is getting to be habitual," Riley managed to say, though he put most of his breath into running. Shots sounded behind them, but they were mere pops, lacking conviction. Even so, he and Cass ran most of a mile before slowing, then wheezing to a walk. The lights of Front Street made a glow in the west. The same as last time, Cass laughed his silly head off. The same as last time, Riley was furious.

"*I could have been killed in there!* I had to jump out a window! My whole life flashed before me!"

"I'd wager, being your life, it was awful boring," Cass said, straightening his tie.

"Hmpf," Riley fumed. "I hope I never get like you, where I have to get shot at every few days for life to stay interesting."

"You'll admit it's a stimulation."

"We won't ever get that wagon back to Hays City now," Riley said. "Parrott and his boy are going to be beating the bushes. There goes my sixty-five dollars."

"Umm," Cass said. "Parrott must have tracked us, same as we tracked the whiskey wagons."

"I suppose we still got Parrott's money. I could go to Topeka or someplace."

"Yes, you see there? You're still ahead of the game," Cass said. "The tragedy is we lost that beer mug."

"Buckshot is flying like bee swarms and you're sorry about a hunk of glass," Riley said. He spoke mournfully. "We are a whole different breed of cat, you and me. I should've seen it from the start."

"Well, somebody's going to pick that thing up," Cass argued. "They might get suspicioned and conclude we were cheating. Kentuckians maybe don't value their good names, but we Texans sure as hell do."

"Oh, for Pete's sake," Riley said. "I don't believe I care to associate with you any longer. I really mean it. Partnering up with you was the worst—"

"Send it down the river," Cass told him. "You're not hurt any."

"Gol-danged if I'm not." Riley looked himself over. "My hands are bleeding. My ears are ringing like church bells."

Cass had started them walking, though to where was a mystery. It seemed to Riley there was the business district of Buffalo City on one hand, and on the other, one awful stretch of plains. He did not much fancy either alternative. The road led over open ground between widely spaced residences, most with small barns and woodsheds. Picket fences pretended to citification. A tethered dog barked at them. A mile away, the business district was a scattering of yellow lights—holes in the night.

"Shush!" Cass said. Riley shushed, feeling new alarm rising. They listened, hearing giddy voices, distant music from Front Street saloons. But new sounds came from the opposite direction. There was a clear tinkle of piano music, its source a narrow, two-story-and-dormers frame house on the town's fringes, a place as lit up as a riverboat, as merry as Christmas.

"What do you make of it?" Cass said.

"'My Old Kentucky Home,'" Riley said. "Being from there, I always did like it."

"The building, you simp. I'll bet it's a sporting house. Come on. We stand here and we'll be hunted down. A sporting house is a sight better than sleeping in another barn."

They jogged toward the house, keeping wary eyes on their back trail. The piano assayed "Camptown Races," the music lurching doggedly through a thicket of misfingerings. Horses stood drowsing at a hitch rail. A gate fronted a neat flagstone walk. Cheery lamps, dizzied by june bugs, flanked the door. They tiptoed up painted porch steps.

"Seems safe enough," Cass whispered, peering in a window. "Parrott and his boy could hardly have got here ahead of us."

"I'm not really in the mood for a cathouse," Riley said.

"What a mama hen." Cass tugged on a bell rope. "This is the best way of lying low I can think of."

The piano, still wrestling with "Camptown Races," stopped abruptly, leaving a *doo-dah* dangling. A red-haired woman in a peekaboo-topped dress opened the door and exclaimed over them with professional sincerity, saying, "Just in time for the party, gents."

They were let in. Riley grabbed a last anxious glance out the front door before the woman closed it. "There's a party?" he asked.

"Every night but Monday," the woman assured them. She pinched Riley on the cheek and Cass on the behinder, then abandoned them in the foyer to an even bustier woman in a dress of black silk.

"Maggie Rose?" Cass said. "Maggie Rose Land?"

"For the love of Mike—Cass McCasland. Looks like you got scalped of your mustache."

"I haven't seen you since Abilene," Cass said. "A lot of the strut went out of that town when you left it."

"And you'd be something or other Stokes," she told Riley. "I recall your mug from Newton."

"It's Riley," Riley said, "and it was Wichita. How in the world you been?"

"McCasland and Stokes, a regular pair of jacks," Maggie Rose said. "And all partnered up, looks like. From what I know of the both of you, I reckon you deserve each other." Riley and Cass exchanged looks.

"Say, I am getting a cyclone in my noggin, seeing you two together," she said. "I will wager you just come in on a freight wagon from Hays City, or I am Mrs. President Grant."

"Parrott tell you that?" Cass said. He peered into the dining room. Riley's hand slid to his gun butt.

"*Parrott?* Terrible John Parrott? I ain't seen the bastard and hope not to," Maggie Rose said. "No sir, it was a little birdie told me you two was in town, though I didn't know it was you two till just this minute."

Yet another swap of blank looks.

"Wait'll you see what's in my kitchen," Maggie Rose said. "I believe you two are the scalawags to blame for putting little Tai Hei in the street, poor thing."

Riley's eyeballs may have rolled over completely. "Tai Hei?" he said stupidly.

"What do you mean *scalawags?*" Cass said.

"Don't try and slither out of it. Here's a little slip of a China girl working buffalo men on Front Street, a babe clutched to her bosom, and the both of them just been through hell—captured by Kioway and shot up by trash. You oughta be ashamed of yourselves."

"But she—"

"You so-called gents couldn't even get her a proper dress."

"No, but she was just—"

"She must not of et decent in *weeks,*" Maggie Rose said. "You should of seen her demolish the meal I just give her!"

"Well, sure, but this Dr. Tweed—"

"Pimping her off on buffalo men is some shameful way to serve a poor wretch is what I say. It's good fortune a person of feeling come along. I'd treat a mule better'n you done that girl."

"That's ridiculous, to think we'd do a thing like that," Cass said.

"We went way out of our way for that little gal," Riley said.

"And in the second place, who's going to pay to go with a skinny thing like her?" Cass said. "Tai Hei doesn't hardly have enough meat on her to be taken for a woman."

Maggie Rose's smile broadened. She beckoned the red-haired woman to her and they laughed conspiratorially. "Let's give 'em an eyeful, Dolly." Dolly, bustling with a secret, vanished into the dining room.

"What sort do you take us for?" Riley demanded, though he supposed what sort was clear enough.

"Hush now, and mind your manners." Maggie Rose got a puffed up look, like a mother hen. There was the creak of an inner door opening, a rustle of stiff fabric. The division between dining room and parlor was implied by a wide archway, with plump-legged, plaster cherubs poised on tiptoe on either side. Into this frame stepped an elegant miniature, a figurine in a sweeping, much-petticoated dress of royal blue satin, with puffed, leg-o'-mutton sleeves bracketing an umblemished expanse of shoulder and neck, down which cascaded tresses so gleaming that the hair dimly reflected the dress's color. Crowning all was a shining face: shy, hopeful of pleasing, somehow quite familiar.

"By God." Cass's voice was as hollow as a barrel.

Riley said, "Well, my lands."

"Are you liking me?" Tai Hei said.

Cass said, "I just don't believe it."

"What do you think of my little creation? I expect that color was made for her." Maggie Rose went to Tai Hei, hovering and adjusting. "You come on into the parlor, honey. These tongue-tied gents like you just fine. I reckon they never seen you in a real dress. Well, sir, they don't know how handy a low cut like that is for nursing babies, do they? You just take a deep breath, honey, and you will pop yourself right out of it."

Maggie Rose went prattling on in that vein. Riley found he had his mouth open as though he were going to say something. But then the doorbell rang, cutting through whatever thought he'd been forming. Then he realized who and where he was—and why—and he and Cass recoiled from the door.

"Quick—hide us!" Cass whipped out a revolver and cowered behind the piano. Riley ducked behind a divan, cocking his cap and ball. Maggie Rose shook with laughter.

Dolly opened the door on a trio of buffalo hunters, holding their hats in their hands and grinning like apes.

"Oh, mother," Riley breathed. Cass straightened, struggling for dignity, though his color had not come back.

"This little doll ain't available." Maggie Rose pointed out Tai Hei to the buffalo men. "Don't you even think about it." Dolly led the men to the curving bannister and Riley heard big boots tramping up the stairs.

Maggie Rose turned back, her smile amused. "So—it's plain you two got somebody on your back trail. John Parrott or you wouldn't've mentioned him."

"It's all a big misunderstanding," Cass said.

Maggie Rose laughed. "I always did read men like a book."

"It comes awkward for a gentleman to ask a favor of a lady," Cass said, "but we could use a place to lie up. A couple days would do us."

"I trust it don't look like I'm running a hotel here," Maggie Rose said.

"Have I ever asked for a favor before?"

"Lots," she said stiffly. "Besides which, I don't care for shooting in my house. What I'll do is give you a safe way out of town." She sent Dolly for someone named Dash. A tall skeleton of a Negro appeared so quickly that Riley figured he'd been listening from the kitchen. Maggie directed him to harness up her buggy.

"It still *is* hitched," Dash said. "I been all this time watching that little gal eat."

"A buggy is just the ticket," Cass said. "How can we repay you?"

"I aim to tell you," Maggie Rose said. "I got conditions." Riley and Cass swapped new looks. "This poor girl's story is like to break your heart. You know she ain't got a way in the world to get her little boy back. Little Eagle Feather—three years old and I'll bet cute as a button. Was you gents to track down these child thieves I would be disposed to view it favorable."

"That's asking a whole lot," Riley said. "Some rough whiskey outfit has got that boy. Somebody-or-other Hollenbeck. Why not just call in Parrott and let him shoot us? We're dead men either way."

"Bug-eye Hollenbeck?" Maggie Rose considered. "Then I'd go about it awful gingerly—not that I took the likes of you for heroes. You can buy the boy back, maybe, or win him at cards. Cards is what you're supposed to be good at, ain't it?"

"Look—" Cass fished out ten dollars. "We'll each take a girl upstairs for the night. We can talk about this Tai Hei business in the morning."

"We will talk about it now," Maggie Rose said. She moved to block the stairway and stood, a bastion of stubbornness. "You will take this girl to find her darling lad or I will fetch Parrott myself and bullet holes be damned."

Riley peeled a curtain and peeked at the road. "I got no hankering to go out there again."

"We'd need somebody to go around the Dodge House and fetch our outfits," Cass said in a subdued voice. There was a Confederate for you, Riley thought sourly. Always surrendering.

"Dash can do that," Maggie said. "He's a pal of the night manager."

Cass sighed. Riley was doubtful.

"I am glad of you do this for me," Tai Hei said, and Riley had to admit he had never seen such a plea in pretty eyes.

"And don't get no notions about whores with hearts of gold," Maggie Rose said. "I got gunmen who owe me favors." She aimed a finger like a pistol. "You bring my rig back or I will have your pelts for a bedspread."

26 · RILEY

THE BEARDED MAN DRIVING THE HIDE WAGON BLINKED REPEATEDLY and then had to spit. It was as though he'd never seen a high-topped buggy on the plains before, being driven by a man in Sunday clothes with an Indian girl in a blue satin whore's dress sitting slap up next to him. That Tai Hei held a new baby seemed to double his consternation. That a second Sunday-dressed town gent was slumped up asleep in the buggy's backseat only compounded it.

"Was you folks out taking the air, I'd venture you took a wrong turn somewheres," the wagon driver said. A younger man sitting next to him laughed at this wit.

The baby, little Kam Loi, was kicking in protest, while Riley and Tai Hei screwed up their faces and held their noses. The stench rising off the wagons—putrefying flesh on buffalo hides—was enough to scorch the nostrils.

"*Is it them?*" Cass asked excitedly from the buggy's backseat. His face came smeary out of sleep.

"It is not them," Tai Hei said. "It is shameful hunters of buffalo."

"Just hide hunters," Riley told him. He turned back to the men on the Murphy wagon. "We're trailing a party of whiskey haulers. Got a message for them."

"Bug-eye Hollenbeck's bunch?" the man said in some astonishment. He found it necessary to spit again. "Met 'em yestiddy."

"He have any Indians with him?" Riley said.

"Why, there was a squaw or two, waren't there, Pa?" the younger man said.

"Expect there was. Don't know as I'd trail along after Hollenbeck myself. It's courting trouble."

"How about a little Indian boy traveling with them?"

Cass said from the backseat. "Three years or so." He put out a hand beside the wheel to about the height of the buggy floor.

"No, sir—nothing like that. Hollenbeck would only have use for the squaws, if you take my meaning. A'course a feller don't want to look over Hollenbeck's outfit too close lessen he take exception to you. I seen him pop his eye out at a feller once. Then knife him when he stood consternated. I take it you know the man."

"Know of him," Riley said. "Any idea where he's headed?"

"That I do—seeing there ain't no other place. Mooar's Town, same as we just come from. It's a trading post and buffler hide drop-off. A place to get liquored and kick your heels. Pure hide runner's town."

"We're obliged." Riley touched his hat brim.

"Want a piece of advice free gratis? You ain't obliged to take it."

"Why not," Riley said.

"I would not go down there in no high-topped buggy. Mooar's Town, I mean. Fact is, I would not go a'tall."

"Why not?" Cass said.

"Buffler range pulls in all kinds. This outfit here, we're God-fearing, mostly. But a place like Mooar's Town ain't nothing but a devil's den. There's no law to it any which-way, and in some, that brings out the beast. Whatever I'd do, I wouldn't take no woman with me." His eyes settled on Tai Hei.

"She's right comely for her kind," the younger man said.

"Cyrus, you shut your mouth. I reckon we all got eyes." He turned to Riley. "We been on the plains too long. That brings out the beast in itself."

"I din't mean nothing," Cyrus said.

"Thanks for the warning," Riley said. He was uneasily aware of Tai Hei sitting beside him.

"Maybe we can catch Hollenbeck before they strike this Mooar's Town," Cass said.

"Not likely. Lessen they have a bustdown, they'd already be acrosst the Cimarron. Mooar's Town's only a day or so below that, on the North Canadian."

Riley looked at the thin trail ahead, shallow ruts going off who knew where, and thought of buffalo men and beasts. It seemed a fine place to turn around.

"Well, gentlemen, you'll pardon our dust," the man said. "We're aiming for Buffalo City by nightfall."

The younger man, Cyrus, leaned forward in the wagon seat. "Going to wet our whistles," he assured them.

"The wages of sin is death," his father admonished him. "Good luck to you," he told Riley, and then let his eyes rove once more over the three of them, as though getting the details right for retelling the story later: two town fellows in Sunday suits and an Indian girl in a blue whore's dress.

"Stink follows them," Tai Hei said in some disgust as the procession of wagons lurched into motion.

"Some awful smell, all right," Cass said. "I couldn't hunt for hides if they brought twenty dollars apiece."

"You must not," Tai Hei said. "You are too honored to do such poor hunting."

"Too honorable?" Cass said, surprised.

"Yes, honor-able. This thing you do makes great warriors of you among all white men. Songs will be made in your honor."

Cass tugged his hat lower and looked away, then back at Riley. Riley was grinning.

"All that just for hauling you to the Territory?" Cass asked her.

"Not for to haul. For to catch these whiskey men and rub them out. *Kggsshh, kggsshh, kggsshh,*" she said, shooting. "All dead."

"Shooting," Riley said, "is that what you're expecting?"

Her brow troubled up. "How else to make free my people?"

Riley's expression was an appeal for help. Cass only shrugged. Riley shook his head. He said, "Tai, Hei, ma'am, I don't have no kind of clear notion. But if the only way to get your people back is shooting, you have got yourself the wrong pair of gents."

27 · BAYARD

LOUIS BAYARD PADDED INTO THE HOTEL SITTING ROOM IN KNEE-high moccasin boots and stopped in front of the bannister. He didn't shy from going into the occasional, uncrowded building, but he felt climbing to a second story was pushing his luck. Once a true man got off the ground—which, after all, was his mother the earth, upon whose breast he'd spent his entire life—he was disconnected from all that held him. He might float right up to the sky, maybe.

Still, Bayard worked now for a white man, one rather particular about what he wanted, and who at that moment slept in a room on the second floor. Bayard's alternative to climbing the stairs was to wait with the horses, or to go back and lie in the wagon belonging to the men they were hunting, thus passing the day as he had passed the night, dozing sometimes, mostly just thinking. It was not a good alternative, Bayard thought, for this big white man, this Parrott, would want to learn immediately the news that Bayard had for him.

Bayard sighed and studied the stairs with apprehension. There seemed to be no help for it.

"You there—no loitering on these premises," a man's voice said. The speaker wore a high white collar that held his head as rigidly as if stuck on a pole. He stood behind the long counter where people did their hotel business. Bayard, having no interest in him, turned back to face the stairway. He would rather cross a swift, icy river than climb those steps.

"Are you deaf or what? Shoo on out of here." The clerk was beginning to sound annoyed. "We don't allow Indians in any case."

Bayard extended a hand to feel the bannister's newel post. It was a roundness like the breech of a cannon, except fashioned from wood instead of iron. He put a foot on the first step and felt its strength and took heart. He would climb one floor higher and then no farther. He would grip the railing and be careful not to climb away from the pull of the ground. By holding to the wood, it would be done in the manner of climbing a tree to steal a bird's eggs.

"You don't comprehend English?" the man demanded of him. "I won't have redskins scaring our guests."

Not caring for the scolding tone in the man's voice, Bayard put his hand on his knife hilt and his eyes on the man. It was a long, grave look that weakened the man's power and soon made him blink. Though Bayard didn't know it, the look also sent the man's imagination reeling through scenes of scalpings and burnings at the stake.

"I go up," Bayard said, and began padding up the steps, moving deliberately and gripping the railing. He moved as though each step required a separate decision. Below him, the counter man cleared his throat.

As a demonstration for Bayard's benefit, Parrott had drawn in the dirt the mark that would be on the door: two bent numbers like a pair of men stooping. Bayard assumed one number stood for Legg and the other for Parrott. He found a door bearing this mark exactly as Parrott had drawn it. Bayard was familiar with doorknobs—the roll of the knob, the feel of a mechanism moving against a spring, like parts in a gun.

Bayard went into the room, which hemmed him in with flowered walls. On the bed the white men lay like corpses, tangled in bedding, the smaller, weaker one with an arm thrown over his eyes, snoring like a dog. The window was shut tight and the room smelled of white men.

Parrott convulsed, a mountain coming alive. There was the snicking back of a revolver hammer and Parrott's face came slackly out of sleep, the eyes struggling to focus. The pistol's muzzle sought Bayard, quickly steadying. Bayard put a hand on his knife hilt while Parrott glared at him. The standoff was broken by Legg falling out of bed.

"Christ Jesus—don't you know enough to *knock?"* Parrott demanded, his face purple. He struggled to get his ghostly bare feet onto the floor. Bayard kept a hand on his knife.

"I don't stand for being snuck up on," Parrott said groggily. "Next time, by God, I will blow you straight to hell."

"Damned sneaking savages anyway," Legg's voice said from the floor on the far side of the bed.

"You keep out of this," Parrott muttered. "Anybody who's so frigging afraid of fire we can't lock a hotel room doesn't rate airing his opinion. Can somebody tell me why I have to work with *imbeciles?*" Parrott let his revolver hammer off cock and sat glaring in his underwear, eyes still unfocused, face lumpy. His lips moved distastefully, sampling his sleep.

"One reason is I don't cost much," Legg's voice said limply from the far side of the bed.

Parrott shifted the gun to his left hand and reached up and gripped the bed's headboard. Legg, wearing badly grayed long underwear, got up and put on his cap.

"There better be some excuse for this." Parrott rummaged for clothes. "You find out anything?"

"They travel now to the Indian Territory," Bayard said. "They have a high-wheeled woman's wagon. They have also the woman and the woman's little one."

"A woman's wagon? A buggy?"

Bayard nodded.

"Why in hell would they be going to the Territory?" Parrott said irritably. "They must be going to double back. They're heading for Hutchinson, maybe. Or Newton or Wichita."

"They travel to the Territory," Bayard said. "They too follow someone."

"Why do you say that?"

"They follow whiskey wagons. I do not know why they do this." Bayard considered. "The woman with them once wore moccasins of the Kiowa. Now she wears the sharp heels of a white woman. These whiskey wagons also carry the tracks of Kiowa moccasins. Squaws." For him it was a long speech, and it emptied him. He would let Parrott draw his own conclusions.

"You're saying there's a connection?" Parrott said. Bayard stood; he had speculated enough. "How do you know they're whiskey wagons? You saw them with your own eyes?"

"I smell them," Bayard said brusquely. He did not like having his expertise challenged any more than he liked being scolded or having guns pointed at him. He pointed to his nose, as though dealing with the stupid.

"You got a sharp nose for liquor, do you, redskin?" Legg asked him.

28 · CASS

THE FRONT HALF OF THE DAY HAD WORN AWAY. THE HORSES trampled their shadows. The buggy wheels rolled hypnotically, inducing drowsiness. Cass sweltered. Tai Hei had not spoken to them since their argument about shooting. She sat singing her ching-a-ling song with its short and ringing words and its tune that started nowhere and went noplace. As usual, little Kam Loi liked the singing, sometimes cooing in response.

Cass stopped them and set out the buggy weight. There was not a tree within a mile; the patch of shade under the buggy might have been the biggest patch in Kansas. The cessation of movement brought Riley out of reverie. With his brown eyes looking sleepy and diluted, he climbed out of the buggy's backseat. At the same time, Tai Hei got down and went behind the vehicle, her petticoats rustling. Cass looked away, allowing her her meager modesty.

"Let's you and me go fishing," Cass said.

"Fishing? You getting sunstroke?"

"It's an expression. Come over here a minute." Cass walked a couple of rods off the wagon trail. The buffalo grass, already sun-cured by early June, was sparse underfoot. He had stopped them on a rise, the highest point for miles, from which the land fell away in a sea of subtle rises and depressions, etched by dry washouts and dry creeks. The world hinted it was spherical.

"It looks the same from over here," Riley said. He looked up and frowned at something in Cass's face. "What's eating you anyhow?"

"I thought I saw movement back there where we just came from," Cass said, glancing back.

"I don't see nothing."

"You just woke up."

"More buffalo hunters, maybe," Riley said, sounding optimistic. The word unspoken was *Parrott*.

"I hope so. Probably my imagination." Cass looked at the distant swells of land awhile longer and then away, to where Tai Hei busied herself behind the airy screen of the buggy wheels. He saw browned bare legs. "I need to plumb your mind on something," Cass said. "You think we're on a fool's errand?"

"I thought that before you did."

"We're not doing her a favor if we get her and her baby killed."

"That is a point," Riley said. "I don't care for getting killed myself."

"I'm wondering if keeping my word to a whorehouse madam is all that important to me. I believe I could turn around and still manage to sleep nights." Cass looked at the endless trail ahead. Indian Territory. It was like running off the edge of the world.

Riley nodded agreement. "The smart thing would be to strike off for Wichita. The railroad just reached there."

"She is not going to like hearing it," Cass said. "She's got her heart set on finding her boy, and who can blame her?"

"Maybe we could sort of wander off the trail, then swing around without her knowing it."

Cass was doubtful. "She spent four years as a Kiowa. I reckon she knows south from north." At his own mention of it, he looked south, seeing visions of disaster.

"Then we'll just have to talk her out of going farther," Riley said. "Let me take a crack at it."

"You've got the knack, do you?"

"Folks say I've got a sympathetic face," Riley said. Had Cass felt like joking, he would have said those folks were only being polite to him. But it was too hot for joking, too hot for anything. They shouldered back to the buggy, two men in dusty town clothes. Sitting spang on the plains, the buggy looked both as festive and incongruous as a lattice-work bandstand. All it lacked was bunting.

"Are you decent?" Riley called. Tai Hei stepped around the buggy's rear. She had taken off the dress and the layers of petticoats and her button shoes and changed back into the rag of a buckskin dress, with the doctor's old dress shirt worn under it. The reversion to being Indian was startling.

"What's that for?" Riley said.

"The blue dress I save to show my people. I will wear it to show my sister-wife, who will burn from wanting one." Tai Hei laughed happily.

"We wanted to talk about that," Riley said. "Seems we don't know where the heck we're going. Fact is, we're loster than blind fish. The smart thing at this point would be to turn back. You'd like it in Wichita."

"There's a railroad there," Cass said. *"Choo, choo."*

Tai Hei looked delighted. "Such funny men. It is much lucky I travel with two such."

"We're running out of food," Riley said. He made spooning signs.

"You have a long gun," Tai Hei pointed out. "You must shoot a buffalo. My people hunt them with bows and lances. With a long gun it is much easy." She smiled and mimed aiming a rifle. *"Kggsshh.* Much easy."

"Oh, cripes," Cass said. "Shooting is her answer to everything."

"I'm saying we think turning back's the best thing," Riley said, sounding mournful about it. Cass thought Riley was overdoing the mournfulness; he could hang his face as mournful as some old coon dog. "It'd be best for you and your baby both," Riley said. "Maybe even best for your boy. Those whiskey men are not just going to hand him over."

Tai Hei's happy expression collapsed. "You made your promise-word to Maggie-of-the-high-house." Tai Hei put the bundled dress and petticoats into the buggy and kept her back to the men.

"Maggie of the high house ain't here helping," Riley pointed out.

"It is so what is said of all white men," Tai Hei said angrily. She picked up little Kam Loi from where the baby had been nestled on the ground, sleeping in her blankets, and walked out past the buggy in determined steps, heading toward the Territory, the whiskey wagons, toward Mooar's Town where men were beasts. In ten steps, she turned on them.

"I see you speak together your secrets. This turning back, it is that you are no warriors and you know this. You lack . . . braveness," she said, apparently considering it a crushing condemnation.

"She's got us there," Riley said.

"White men know not honor. They are the women-men." Cass said, "Now just a darned minute here."

"Honor and braveness. Your hearts know not these things. Only money." They fidgeted.

"It's money makes the world go round," Riley said lamely.

"I too have my secret, which I tell of now," Tai Hei said. "I have one thing only of my old life, from Hong Kong and the great ship and the city of San Francisco, by the sea of California."

"We know. Your son," Riley said.

"Not my son. He is a Kiowa and will grow to be a *Koitsenko,* one of the Ten Bravest, as was his father Two Horses and grandfather Eagle Man. A society of Kiowa soldiers," she said. "And also my little Kam Loi is Kiowa and bears one day great warriors." Cass looked critically at his boots; Riley, at the plains.

"This thing is not of the Kiowa, yet a great thing to have. My father has given it, saying, 'You must never to part from this thing except saving a life.'" Her eyes held them a long moment. "White men desire only money, and so I offer this thing for you now, for it seems I must pay for help."

"What is it?" Cass said.

"It is an eye of God. A stone. I do not know how you call it. It is colored like the spring grass. It is given of the earth, yet holds in itself the light of sun and moon and stars."

"You mean a gem? A jewel?" Cass guessed.

"A jew-wel," she said, "green as new leaves in the moon when ponies shed."

"An emerald, must be," Riley said.

"Green as grass, big as the fruits of the nutmeat trees," Tai Hei said.

"As big as a *walnut?*" Cass said.

"Such big." She circled a thumb and forefinger. "From China. The jew-wel sits honored by a ring of silver, and is tied by a chain going here." She gestured, circling her neck.

Riley whistled. Cass said, "A thing like that might be worth thousands."

"Where is this here stone?" Riley said.

"It now protects my son, for the medicine of a young one is much weak."

"Then they've already found it," Riley said. "Hollenbeck's bunch."

"No. My Eagle Feather has it." Tai Hei spoke firmly. "It protects him. This I feel in my heart."

"For Chrissakes," Cass said.

Tai Hei went to the buggy and got into the front seat, facing resolutely ahead. "You shall set free my little *Koitsenko* in some honored way with shooting or in some other way. Then shall I give to you this eye of God, which thus saves a life as my father instructed."

Riley toed a whitened buffalo bone and then looked back toward Kansas. Cass made a circle of his forefinger and thumb and stood studying it. "Just how big of a walnut would you say, exactly?" he asked her.

"Confound it, I thought you were for turning back?" Riley said.

29 · RILEY

THE SUN WAS LOWERING BY THE TIME THEY SAW THE RIVER, A DARK line of elms and cottonwoods cutting across the wagon trail.

"The Cimarron," Cass said. "The exact boundary to the Territory is just a line on a map. As for a marker a person can see, the river will do right enough."

"It's said any man venturing below the Cimarron can expect to get his hair lifted." Riley shuddered at the thought. "You might as well stick your head in a rain barrel and forget to come up."

"There's no use in that kind of talk," Cass said. "I went through there on a cattle drive and it wasn't bad. Just dry, is all."

"What you did in company with a bunch of cowboys and two thousand cattle is not hardly the point," Riley said. "You got awful brave since you heard about that jewel."

"What *is* the point? You fixing to do yourself in while we sit here and watch?"

"I am only saying this jewel business ain't worth shelled corn if you don't live to spend it. Before I ever left Kentucky I gave being captured by Indians considerable thought. I reckon I'd do myself with a pistol before I'd be taken alive. Redskins torture a person for days on end."

"Such is only for brave warriors," Tai Hei said starchily. "In order to make them much honor."

Cass breathed theatrically, pretending relief. "See there? It doesn't apply to us."

"It is your people we must have fear of," Tai Hei said, "not of my people."

Riley urged the horses into the shallow river valley. The buggy's top shook and rustled and its wheels skittered in dried ruts. The buggy's shadow stretching on their left was as tall and somber as a church. Unbidden, the horses picked up the pace.

"They smell their water now," Riley said.

A greenness of grass, virtually a meadow, thrived along the river. The trail was flanked with cottonwood and elm. In moments they were beside the Cimarron, which was broad and shallow, a stately processional slipping eastward, bound for the Missouri. Riley unhitched the horses and let them drink even before removing their harness, as they'd had a long day of it. Being whorehouse horses, Riley figured, they were probably not used to such labor.

When the horses slowed their drinking, he pulled their muzzles from the river, believing a lathered horse foundered if overwatered. He turned and became aware that some critical element in their situation had changed. Tai Hei on the bank, stooping to swaddle her infant in a blanket, had stopped in midmotion. Cass beside her had his shoulders hunched in sudden tension.

At the rear of the buggy stood an Indian, as still as if whittled from oak, his face pocked, his features resting. He wore a red rag as a headband, a blousy, polka-dot shirt, knee-high moccasin boots, and trousers with the crotch cut out to make leggings of them, the bare space covered negligently with a breechcloth. One arm cradled an old muzzle-loading rifle. The other arm was moving, extending slowly till its dark hand rested possessively on the iron rim of the buggy wheel.

There was a rustling. Riley whirled and reached for his gun, realizing belatedly that he'd taken it off before watering the horses. A pair of white men stepped noisily out of a thicket.

"I believe you've not met our Mr. Bayard," Terrible John Parrott said, indicating with a gesture of his shotgun muzzles the chiseled Indian. "A remarkable man in many ways. He has been smelling you coming for the last hour and a half."

30 · BAYARD

WITH HIS MUZZLE-LOADING RIFLE IN THE CROOK OF ONE ARM, Louis Bayard turned back from his task of hobbling the horses in the meadow. Five horses were a considerable wealth to have gathered in one place so far from a town, especially when they were not Indian ponies but long-legged white men's horses, well shod with iron and their ribs covered with grain-fed meat.

Bayard came back to the river to find a circle of light, the usual bonfire that white men liked to make for their camp. He was thinking of how good it would be to own such a wealth of horses.

"That was some ride we done today." Legg liked to speak to everyone at once, like an army general. "My rear end's so tender I can't sit down."

"Mr. Legg has a point," Parrott said, speaking to the captured men. You have put us to considerable bother." Parrott, too, did many things Bayard did not care for. He had a way of scolding like a squaw that Bayard did not like to hear, even when it was directed to others than to Louis Bayard.

The captured white men had been made to sit against the buggy wheels, and Bayard, as he'd been ordered, had stuck their wrists through the spokes and tied them securely. Bayard had helped the army bring in renegades; he knew how to tie a man, first wetting thongs and then drawing them tight around the flesh until the captive cried out. These whites had whimpered at the first squeeze, like women, Bayard noted. Then he saw the error of this thought. They cried out only like white men—for no Indian woman would have cried out so easily.

Parrott approached the captured white men. He spoke to them while pointing a burning stick at the taller one's face. Then he brought the stick toward his own face, lighting a cigar.

"If this all's a matter of getting that beer mug back, we'll gladly buy you another one," the shorter of the captured white men said. Squatting by the fire, Legg laughed hoarsely. His voice was like a crow calling.

"What this is about is you and I," Parrott said slowly. He tossed the stick toward the river, so that its flaming end looped crazily in the darkness before hissing into the water.

The woman bent over the fire, her movement distracting Bayard. He watched her closely, this Kiowa who was also not-Kiowa. She was small and comely, with waist-length black hair that a man might wrap around his wrist when he wanted to draw her to him. He watched with appreciation her slim flanks working under the dress. The sight of her touched him. It had been a long time since he had been with a woman.

The woman, Bayard realized, was another kind of wealth, and he suddenly had a powerful sense of great riches: horses, woman, firearms, money. Such wealth in combination with the remoteness of their camp on the Cimarron River, on the rim of Indian Territory, and at the limit of the white men's reach, was a rare thing, dizzying with possibilities. It was more dizzying, he felt, than the sight of the woman moving or the smells of rabbits roasting.

"What's she still fussing around for?" Legg said. "I'd say them creatures are done enough to eat." He stepped around the woman and bumped hips with her, so that she took a lurching step to keep her balance and then quickly backed away from him. Legg laughed his crow laugh at this action and then squatted to the naked, spitted carcasses. Bayard did not like to see the woman butted by a white man, even though he knew it had not hurt her.

"I should be living in a good hotel somewhere instead of

eating bunny rabbit in the moonlight," Parrott told the captured white men, scolding again. "As I say, you've put us to considerable trouble. The fact is, I'm sorely tempted to let Mr. Legg start in on you."

For emphasis, Parrott kicked the taller of the captured white men in the soles of his boots. This time, the captured white man did not cry out. "I know better than to let him do it on an empty stomach, though," Parrott said. "He'd likely get in a hurry about it, which would be a great pity. Taking one's time at such things is damned near the whole point."

Legg left off gnawing a rabbit haunch to laugh his crow laughter. Then he drank from a bottle. Parrott went over and sat down by the fire, close to it as a white man always sits, so that the firelight seemed to make feathers of flame of his bushy side-whiskers.

"Pass the brandy," Parrott said to Legg. Bayard swallowed dryly as he watched Parrott pour from the bottle into his cup and then drink deeply. Then Parrott selected a piece of the rabbit meat and gingerly tasted it. "Hmmm—I conclude a woman's touch is just what this camp circle has needed."

"We maybe oughta take her on with us," Legg suggested. "She could be real useful. I bet she don't eat much." Legg seemed to find his comment a great jest. After laughing his coughing laugh he took the bottle from Parrott and poured liquor into his cup.

"Considering the occasion, I think a toast is in order," Parrott said. "You'll pardon me if I don't stand up to do the honors, it's been a long day." A foolish gladness, Bayard heard, had come into Parrott's voice.

"Why sure," Legg said.

"To our successful expedition," Parrott announced, sitting cross-legged and lifting his cup. He looked about him in victory. "Whoopsie," Parrott said. "Our Mr. Bayard ought to have a nip. The man certainly played his part."

"That he did," Legg acknowledged. He belched.

"Bayard, man," Parrott said. "You'll drink with us, surely. I doubt I ever heard of a temperate redskin."

Bayard stood graven. Parrott sometimes used unfamiliar words. It made Bayard wary of being played with.

"Come, come, good man—your cup." Parrott held the bottle high, comically threatening to pour liquor on the ground if a cup were not placed under it.

Bayard wore his tin cup at his belt as habitually as he wore a knife. He loosed the thong holding the cup and stepped cautiously toward where Parrott sat with the bottle upraised. It seemed to Bayard that now that they had caught the white men, his job was over. Yet, he could not leave before being paid. Until he had his money, it was wisest to obey this Parrott—especially if that meant drinking free liquor.

Bayard glanced at the woman, who was setting a pot of water for coffee at the edge of the fire. She was closed into herself, her eyes locked down as was appropriate to her situation. It was a good sign of obedience, Bayard thought approvingly. He propped his rifle against a saddle and stooped to the sitting man with difficulty, for he held himself carefully around white men. Two fingers of brandy glugged into Bayard's cup. He raised the liquor to his lips.

"Whoa now—just a moment here!" Parrott waggled a scolding finger foolishly. "Not a drop till we all drink together."

"Some folkses' manners," Legg said.

"Now then. To a satisfying finale to our little expedition," Parrott said, "and to . . . well, precisely to what?"

"To fun." Legg glanced over at the captured white men to make sure they were paying attention.

"Exactly so," Parrott said. "To an enjoyable evening of entertainment."

"Here-here," Legg said happily.

"Now drink," Parrott instructed, as if talking to a child. Bayard felt he was being made fun of, but he raised the cup and drank. It was good, sweet liquor and he immediately wanted more.

"Another taste or two wouldn't go badly, eh?" Parrott poured more brandy into Legg's cup.

"Good stuff," Legg said.

Bayard promptly squatted and extended his cup. "Well, by all means, fellow," Parrott said warmly. "It's about time we saw you unbending a little. You've been so . . . *wooden.*"

He laughed and poured Bayard more brandy, spilling some because of the laughing, which seemed to Bayard a squandering of wealth.

"Wooden Indian!" Legg whooped and then laughed his crow laugh. Bayard thought it probable that the laughter was at him.

Parrott sighed, coming back out of the laughter. "I think I have just struck upon the perfect way to commence these proceedings." He glanced toward the captured white men, and then looked to Legg, who dug obediently into a hip pocket and came out with a clasp knife. Legg opened it; the blade was thick and hooked.

"No, no, Mr. Legg. I mean the buttons. By all means, let's . . . *show them the buttons!"* There was now in Parrott's voice a great foolishness.

Legg's face came alight and he got up in an instant, weaving a little from brandy. Bayard stood where he was and drank gravely, this time making the liquor last several swallows. He watched Legg rummage among piled saddlebags, moving quickly as a rat. The liquor was as good as Bayard had ever tasted, and much sweeter than whiskey. It made his insides feel happy to drink it.

Legg proudly displayed a small bag of soft leather. It hung weightily.

Parrott said, "Show *them,* you idiot. Not me."

Holding the bag like a great prize, Legg scuttled to the captured white men. Their faces were far back from the fire, but even so Bayard could read their alarm: eyebrows arched, eye-whites big, the expressions heightened by the firelight. Bayard thought such alarm foolish, for nothing very fierce could be captured within such a small bag.

"I suppose I'll have to shed some light on the subject," Parrott said, "else they'll miss the import of what we've got here." He groaned as he got onto his haunches and then stooped to the fire for a burning stick. He picked one up and waved its flame playfully at the woman, who squatted across the fire from him, nursing her baby. The woman recoiled and regarded Parrott with hatred. This was a fine woman, Bayard thought.

Parrott laughed and got stiffly to his feet and approached the captured white men. Legg crouched, his back bent like a man gaming with dice. Parrott got down on his knees beside Legg. The burning stick reddened the captured men's faces.

"Pour them all out," Parrott said. "I haven't had a good look in a while myself." There was a pouring sound, like dried beans or corn flowing.

Bayard was curious and wanted to see, but he wanted the brandy also. He stooped quickly and got the unguarded bottle and stealthily drank. His eyes met the woman's. She said nothing.

"By God, just look at them all," Parrott said, marveling. "Mr. Legg, that's getting to be quite a collection. How many, would you say? Enlighten our friends here."

"A hundert and thirty-nine exactly," Legg said proudly. "All cut from dead men's clothes."

Parrott whistled. "And dispatched by yourself, every one of them. How many men is that *in toto?* Perhaps a dozen?"

"I never kept no count of the men," Legg said, sounding reproving. "I only count the buttons."

Parrott laughed foolishly. "Mr. Legg, you are a one."

Bayard heard the words and wanted badly to see the buttons, but first he wanted more brandy. He upended the bottle, sucking liquor straight to his stomach. At the same time, he stepped away from the fire toward the kneeling men, who huddled over a place on the ground with their backs toward him. Bayard still could not see the buttons. What he saw most clearly were the faces of the captured white men as they looked at the buttons. Their expressions, in the lick and dance of the burning stick, were aghast.

"Bayard, man—you'd appreciate a look at this." Parrott turned and started to get up on one knee. But as Parrott's face came around, side-whiskers catching the firelight, the expression changed. His jaw dropped from a kind of foolish happiness, quickly hardening to anger.

"Put down that bottle, you half-breed arsehole!" Parrott shouted. "By God, no man steals my liquor behind my back!"

Parrott was a big man and no longer young; getting up from one knee cost him a struggle, all the more so because of the long day of riding. He put one palm on an upraised knee and pushed himself up angrily, and with the other hand pointed the burning stick accusingly at Bayard.

Louis Bayard, almost lazily, a man accomplishing a small matter, swept a white man's bowie knife from the sheath at his belt. Taking one long step forward, he plunged the whole blade into Parrott's soft middle.

Parrott, his expression disbelieving, groaned and sank to both knees. He sucked in breath. Legg rose up, his face gone to shock, his palms still displaying buttons. Bayard took three steps back to the fire for his rifle, taking time to set the bottle down carefully and even so getting the gun before Legg could react. He shot Legg with a single blast across the firelight. Legg's upper body convulsed forward; at the same time, his feet took two steps backward, a chickenlike movement, till he tripped on nothing and sat down abruptly with his feet out in front of him. It was so comical that Bayard laughed.

Legg struggled to get a revolver from his holster. Had Bayard's rifle been a repeater, he could have shot again. But since it was an old muzzle loader with its one shot, Bayard stepped carefully around Parrott, who had fallen forward on his face and knees and was still moaning, and kicked Legg over out of his sitting position before the man could get his revolver out.

Bayard moved in to scalp Legg. He plucked off the wool cap and flung it into the bushes. But then the gleam of the buttons caught him. The buttons were many, and he stooped to feel them, but at that moment the woman sprang to her feet and ran, clutching her baby, so that Bayard was obliged to run after her and catch her. He brought her down carefully, both of them rolling in weeds in the darkness. As he fought her, he was mindful of his knife and of the baby, for a baby, too, could be a kind of wealth, since it was a thing many people wanted, although surely this baby was some kind of mixed blood, and from Bayard's experience in his own life, mixed bloods were not worth much to anybody.

He dragged the woman back to the firelight by her wrist and cast her down where she had been sitting. She did not cry out or whimper, but only glared at him with a flaming hatred and then looked away, all of which Bayard felt was a proper way for her to act.

The faces of the captured white men were as startled as masks, looking all holes: eyes, mouths, nostrils. Legg had quit moving and making noises but Parrott still moaned. Bayard went to him. Putting his foot on the back of the big man's head, he carefully scalped him. It was thin hair, and mostly white—not much of a trophy. He stabbed Parrott a couple of times with the knife to silence his moaning.

Legg's scalp was thicker and tight to his skull. It was thick hair but short. The scalps amounted to very little, Bayard realized, but the other wealth was considerable: horses, woman, firearms, money. Even white captives, if he wanted them, although having men to look after could be a great bother.

Bayard stopped and looked about him. He had a sense of something he'd been about to do. The woman sat by the fire, drawn in to herself and singing to her baby. Bayard felt things had quit happening, that nothing further would happen for a while.

Then he remembered. He picked up Parrott's burning stick to give himself light and he bent to the buttons. He grabbed them up in handfuls, letting them run through his fingers. Many were black rubber, others wood, and many others shiny brass or pewter. It was a treasure in buttons, in themselves a kind of wealth. He picked them up methodically, breathing audibly from his exertions and the brandy, and put them one by one back into the leather poke. The poke he stowed in a saddlebag, which he then patted thoughtfully.

When he finished, Bayard felt like spending some of the wealth immediately. There was no store or trading post nearby, of course, but there was the woman, and also the brandy, both representing wealth that could be enjoyed at once. The woman, being an Indian, or mostly an Indian, could keep, for she would not quickly lose her head like a white woman would do. The brandy, in its glass bottle, probably would not keep, for bottles were brittle and easily broken. Bayard stepped to the bottle and hoisted it. He drank a long time.

31 · TAI HEI

THE POCKMARKED MAN WHO HAD BEEN CALLED LOUIS BAYARD ate a rabbit while he finished the bottle of spirits. He regarded Tai Hei across the fire while he chewed and drank. He said, "You will not run again or I will kill your baby," speaking in English and at the same time gesturing in the language of signs.

Then Bayard stood up. Drinking over half the bottle of spirits did not make him stagger. What it did do was make him move with a heavy deliberation, as though while he drank the earth had grown in strength under him. Seeing him move so deliberately was even more alarming, Tai Hei thought, than when he had lashed out like a cougar, thrusting his blade into the white-whiskered man and shooting the other one. Riley and Cass looked frightened also; their faces, blanched of their own color, were only the color of firelight.

She told herself to be Bird of Morning, a Kiowa, but she was afraid anyway, not only for her baby but for what Bayard might do to the white men. As for herself alone, a young woman was always of value to a man, even if only as a bad kind of property. Another fear was for her people, those captured by whiskey men. She was afraid this Bayard would use her roughly and then take her away she knew not where, so that she would never be able to fulfill her duty.

Bayard wiped his chin on his sleeve, then wiped his knife on his trouser leg before sheathing it. He paused to upend the bottle and claim the last drops of liquor, and then threw the bottle into the bushes. He moved to the smaller of the two dead men, moving as ponderously as a great chunk of ice down a river, and began to go through the man's pockets, finding a clasp knife and a few pieces of money.

Bayard shifted to the bigger dead man, rolling him over with difficulty. This man's clothing gave up more coins, then a pair of dice that Bayard played with for some time. In the man's inner coat pocket Bayard found something shiny and flat, like a piece of jewelry. Tai Hei saw it was a kind of metal picture, a star within a circle. Bayard was fascinated by this object; he angled it one way and another, watching how it reflected the firelight. With much fumbling he fastened it to his shirt and stood with his chin down admiring the flashing metal. Looking pleased, Bayard dug farther into the dead man's coat pockets and came out with crisp sheets of papers with black writing on them.

At once Bayard's expression changed. He dropped the papers and backed from them. Tai Hei assumed they were the kind her people called talking papers. She knew they carried power, but even so, she was surprised by Bayard's reaction. Bayard looked from the papers to the shining star-in-a-circle, then he ripped it from the shirt and dropped it beside the talking papers. Watching Bayard, Cass's and Riley's faces were as open and empty as if their minds had stopped working.

Then Bayard was moving, no longer like an ice floe down a river but like a cougar again. He came at her in quick strides and caught her and pulled her roughly to her feet. Tai Hei had the baby cradled in one arm and could not fight him. He pulled her back into the darkness, where Tai Hei was blinded after having sat near the fire. At one point she stumbled and nearly fell. Bayard, however, moved as surely as though within his own tepee, as though he did not need eyes to see.

When she grew more used to the darkness she saw he was gathering up the horses, stooping to cut the hobbles with swift strokes of his knife and then collecting them by the bridles.

In a moment Bayard was pushing her ahead of him toward the firelight again. Not wishing to provoke him, Tai Hei walked woodenly, her eyes downcast, as was proper for a captive. Bayard came up behind her leading the horses. He turned her by pulling her shoulder and she came around and saw his eyes, which were bad eyes, having the dull shine new bullets have when poured by warriors at a campfire.

"If you have things, now get them," Bayard told her in English. It was startling to hear his voice again.

Tai Hei stood a moment not knowing what to do. Her duty, she considered, was owed to her baby and to her people who were captives of the whiskey men. In order to fulfill either duty she would have to protect her own life. She put little Kam Loi down on a blanket and began gathering up her satin dress, the petticoats, and her white woman's shoes. Besides those things, she had extra wrappings and a blanket for the baby and a wool man's coat given by Maggie-of-the-high-house. She picked up little Kam Loi and stood waiting while Bayard bent to his work. He dragged the dead men one after the other to the river and launched them into the current, not looking to see where their bodies drifted. He gathered up all the firearms and the saddlebags, then he saddled two horses and fastened the saddlebags behind the saddles.

Uninstructed, Tai Hei put on her man's coat, for the night would be chilly away from the fire. Bayard grasped her and the baby together and grunted as he lifted her onto one of the horses, setting her astride. She smelled the liquor and the man sweat on him and struggled to get a leg over the horse. When she was seated, the pain from having given birth welled up. It was a tearing pain, and yet good, for it sharpened her mind, making what was happening seem less like a dream.

Bayard took a shiny pistol that had belonged to one of the dead men and put it in his belt. Then he stopped where Cass sat tied to a buggy wheel and in a swift movement pulled his knife. Cass stiffened and drew his legs in, but Bayard stepped around and cut the bonds so that Cass sagged away from the buggy wheel. Bayard cut Riley's bonds with the same swift movements. He put the knife back in its sheath and drew out the revolver.

"You are the friends of soldiers," Bayard said. "I know this for I have followed you."

"That's right," Cass said.

"What was done at this camp was not your matter." Bayard's words came thickly, Tai Hei heard, and what she saw was his back—how he stood a little bowlegged in soft Indian boots. His blousy shirt. The white man's trousers split in half to make leggings and the space between covered with a breechcloth.

"Also the woman," Bayard said. "She is not your woman."

"No," Cass said. "Not really."

"When next you speak with soldiers, you will tell how this thing that was done was an Indian matter." Riley and Cass seemed to be caught by the man's power. They sat massaging their wrists, looking up at him.

"I take your horses and guns that you do not follow, but I do not kill you," Bayard said. "Beyond the river I leave a gun that you may hunt on your way to Buffalo City. Do not cross the river before the sun rises. Do not follow. If again I see you I will kill you." Bayard stood looking at them. Little Kam Loi was making cooing noises, but even so, Tai Hei could hear the man's breathing.

Bayard stepped back from them, standing where the talking papers lay, and stooped and picked up the star-in-a-circle and tucked it into his belt. The papers he regarded some time longer, at one point stooping to pick them up and look at them closely. Then he looked at the fire, so that Tai Hei thought he would feed the papers to the flames. But what he did instead was lay the papers on the ground with great care and then pick up a burning chunk from the fire. He carried it to the buggy and set it on the floor beneath the rear seat and soon flames climbed to lick at the seat's underside. Bayard watched until the flames had gathered strength.

"I do not like a woman's wagon," Bayard told the white men. He turned and took the reins of Tai Hei's horse. He put a foot into his stirrup and swung up and then set his old rifle across the pommel. He thumped the horse's sides with moccasined heels and started forward, and when Tai Hei's horse was tugged forward she felt the animal's withers working under her. She looked back at Cass and Riley, seeing them stand like husks of men, and seeing the other horses follow in a line behind her.

When they splashed into the dark water, her horse became alarmed and snorted, so that Tai Hei had to hold tightly to the mane while her other arm cradled Kam Loi. It was a small matter that the river wet her feet and ankles.

Bayard reached the far bank and drew Tai Hei's horse up behind him. There was enough light from the stars for her to see him throw down the old rifle, along with a blanket and some other objects. Then he regarded her, although she could see nothing of his face.

"Do not think any longer of these white men," he said to her in English. "They will not help you." And he turned and urged his horse deeper into the darkness.

32 · CASS

ONCE BAYARD AND TAI HEI AND THE FILE OF HORSES HAD DISAP-peared into the darkness of the river, their attention was taken by the flames, which quickly engulfed the buggy, transforming it into a blazing skeleton of spidery rails and axles and crescent springs. Then even that much began falling down.

When the flooring collapsed, it broke them from a trance so that they moved together, sinking to the ground and picking up the papers Bayard had handled and examining them in the light of the burning buggy.

"They're John Doe warrants," Cass said. "I read long enough for the bar to see that much."

"'For apprehension of Caucasian male,' et cetera, et cetera," Riley said, reading. "'Wanted for the commission of assault and armed robbery upon persons of John Galt Powers and Enoch Legg, employed as manufacturer's repre-sentatives, of Chicago, Illinois, in Hays City, Kansas, the evening of Twenty-ninth May.'"

"It's the same on this sheet," Cass said. "Then it goes on with a description of you, more or less."

"This one's of you."

"Both warrants signed by a judge," Cass said. "Parrott must have got himself deputized in order to make killing us legal. I guess it explains that lawman's badge we saw Bayard take."

"I believe I'd ruther be chased after by Parrott and Legg and a whole damned posse," Riley said, "instead of having just that Bayard after me."

33 · RILEY

In the morning they waded the Cimarron, finding the gun, a canteen, an old trade blanket, and a rusty skinning knife a few yards up the bank. With grass closing around them, the various articles looked as forlorn and useless as if they'd lain there for years.

They stood trouserless and bootless, for a moment doing nothing but letting their shirttails flap, holding their clothes and looking at each item in turn. The gun was the ancient flintlock muzzle loader Bayard had used to shoot Enoch Legg, its stock as weathered as a fence post. Brass tacks had been nailed in it for decoration.

"What a piece of junk," Cass said.

"Harper's Ferry rifle. I know every kind of old gun, as my pa used to fix them for people." Riley picked up Bayard's rifle, which was warm from the sun. With it was a buckskin poke holding a handful of lead balls, a piece of linen cloth for patching, and a tin flask of powder, only half-filled. Cass began drying himself with the blanket.

Examining the gun made Riley feel a little better. The bore was bound to be rusted, but some rifling still showed at the muzzle. "We fought off the British in eighteen-twelve with these things. What I'm saying, we could do worse."

"Some consolation." Cass pulled on trousers and buttoned them, then sat down on the bank and brushed sand off his feet. "What we ought do, being there's warrants for us in Hays City, and being Parrott and his boy have lately turned into fish bait, which could lead to complications, is go up to Wichita or someplace. The last thing we ought do is go farther into the Territory."

"Don't I know it," Riley said unhappily. He could not help but notice Cass was getting dressed on what he considered the wrong side of the river. He frowned as he stood on one leg to pull on his trousers, then he sat down on the bank beside Cass, wetted a patch with river water and poked it down the gun's bore with the ramrod. It came out

127

as black as boots. The second patch, though, came out cleaner.

"You are not getting any argument out of me," Riley said to renew the subject. "It is one time you are right as rain."

Cass looked off across the river. "Maggie Rose will be some sore about her burnt-up rig."

"And Mr. Herbert up to Hays City is starting to wonder where his team and wagon are at," Riley observed.

"Well, it is surely a comfort to be so widely missed," Cass said, at which they both chuckled, although Riley noted it went quickly hollow. He sighed and brushed sand off a foot with a balled-up sock.

"One thing about me is I hate to follow my own back trail. Where you backtrack just to get to where you've been already. There's no progress in it." Cass pulled on a boot and looked at it doubtfully. "You know that feeling?"

"Sure do."

"Like when I hit Abilene with that trail herd. The other boys just blew off their wages and were ready to go do it all over. Not me. I like to go from one thing to the other without sliding back. Otherwise it feels like retreating. Some deep thinker might say it's got to do with me coming out on the short end of the war."

"Even having been on the long end, I know right enough what you mean," Riley said.

They sat without speaking, Cass regarding his boots. Finally he said, "These high-tops are going to give me blisters."

Riley watched the river slide. In his eyes it was an equator, dividing the safe half of the world from the half that had Louis Bayard in it. He swiveled around and looked down the thin trail leading deeper into the Territory, seeing soapweed tufts and pale buffalo grass, all harmless enough. Cass turned and looked too. Riley wondered what was happening at that moment to Tai Hei and her baby. Then he got a vague notion of Mooar's Town, where men were beasts, and finally an awareness of the whiskey men and of Tai Hei's little boy and her women relatives. A lot of elements were strung along together.

"It is both of ours bad luck, I reckon, to have been raised

up to be a certain kind of person." Cass grunted as he got to his feet. "Different as we are in most ways."

"Yes, it is," Riley said. "I expect too it's the kind of fool thing I will look back on when I'm older and just shake my head over, providing I *get* any older." He stomped his foot down into a boot heel. "One thing it for damned sure is not, is a matter of that jewel."

"Not a bit," Cass agreed.

"And it is not like Tai Hei's expecting us."

"Oh, with her notions of white men and bravery and whatnot, she will figure we turned tail," Cass said.

"One good thing is the half-breed's not expecting us either," Riley noted, "or he wouldn't of left his old gun."

"I guess that's the only point in our favor, then," Cass said.

"I guess so." Riley put on his vest. He took up the rifle and was ready.

Cass had picked up the blanket and canteen and the old skinning knife. He said, "Shall we stroll?"

"After you," Riley said.

34 · BAYARD

LOUIS BAYARD WAS DISAPPOINTED. HE HAD EXPECTED TO TRAVEL hard to make up for his meager progress the day before, when he'd been tired and sick from drinking and from lack of sleep. Even worse, they'd had to make a wide swing around a party of buffalo wagons, which was necessary because Bayard did not like to be seen. He was afraid white men might take exception to a half-breed traveling with five white men's horses and with a woman who was perhaps not an Indian.

Bayard was finding that wealth, far from making him happy-foolish as he had seen it do to white men, was bringing him worry, for once wealth had been attained, great care seemed required to hold on to it. The horses, to take one example, were tedious to lead. Any number of horses could be comfortably driven ahead of two riders. But since he was one man alone, and had to keep an eye on the woman besides, the horses had to be led rather than driven.

It was not that Bayard minded working, for all of life was effort. But now he was finding that looking out for his wealth was more tiring than scouting for the army or scouting for foolish white men. He had to do all the work and all the thinking besides. It was a job without end—which came as a disappointment, for Bayard was now a wealthy man and was primed for easy living.

Given this direction his thoughts had been tending, finding the water hole had seemed a gift. It was no more than a pool four steps wide in an otherwise dried-up creek bottom, but there was enough water to sustain a grove of cottonwoods and bunches of hackberry and sumac.

Bayard watered the horses, as any man owning five good animals would do to keep them sound for traveling. He was hot from having the sun on him and frustrated with having to lead the horses and keep their ropes from tangling, so that the cool of the shade was tempting. He was a rich man and felt like spending something on himself, even if all he spent were time. Accordingly, he swung down from Parrott's tall horse and lay himself down. The woman, seeing that they were halting, slid down and sat a few strides away, nursing her baby and not looking at him.

For the first time that day, Bayard was comfortable, but at the same time it bothered him that some of his horses had to stand with tight cinch straps. He thought about how uncomfortable it must be for them until he had to get up and loosen the straps.

Then it occurred to him how the saddles, having had their cinch straps loosened, might slip around until they hung under the horses' bellies, where the horses might easily step on them and break the stocks off the rifles. Bayard had once broken an old musket at the wrist by falling on it. Repairing it with rawhide and white man's copper wire had been much bother and turned out poorly anyway. He had lost interest in the gun after that and had soon traded it.

He grunted, acknowledging there was no help for it but to get up again. He took off the saddles and stacked them, being careful of the rifle butts. He looked at the equipment on the ground and it suddenly seemed he had done well nigh everything but make camp for the night, and here it was hardly midday. Wealth was spoiling his mobility.

Which brought Bayard to another truth about wealth: how having so much property made him long for a place in which to keep it. For the first time he envied tepee men, those Indians who stayed with their tribes—not the hang-around-the-fort people but the real tribes still free on the plains. Also enviable, he realized with a start, were those tribes now tamed and placed on government lands, for if one among them had wealth he would also have a place in which to protect it.

Bayard thought how fine it would be to have his things of value, the guns and money, safely put away inside a good tepee, while the horses grazed nearby and the woman cooked for him and kept the tepee clean. It was a good kind of dream to enjoy there in the shade, seeing pictures floating before him of the woman's child toddling around the tepee, growing up to be his own, and of the woman willingly lying down at night to be his woman.

He closed his eyes, hearing the baby suckling and the horses whuffing and pulling grass, enjoying the dream of living with the woman in a tepee, surrounded by wealth. Then it seemed he was going two directions, for the sweeter the dream became, the stronger a feeling of wariness became at the same time. Soon this second feeling became so pressing that he had to get up and pace around and worriedly survey his wealth. Finally he realized what bothered him was not within his mind nor within the campsite at the water hole, but something out there, on the plains.

He went to the trees and stood a long time looking at the country, seeing a pair of hawks spiraling and distant dots of buffalo. What he saw was in no way alarming; the alarm was in what he felt.

"They come," Bayard said in Absaroka, and he felt bad the way a man feels when he discovers he has made a mistake. He looked at the woman then, for surely they were coming for her. She looked back at him evenly, her hatred glowing like coals. She said nothing, which he felt was fitting. She acted well, this one.

"My eyes do not see them, but they come," he said in English. He went to his things and drew out the long Sharps rifle and slung its belt of cartridges around one shoulder. Then he realized a further responsibility of his new wealth, for his need was to go out there and hunt the white men, rather than let them come hunting him. He could leave the horses and the guns well enough, but the woman was a problem. He was struck that the woman must be some special woman for the white men to want her so badly. Bayard had not thought so earlier, but perhaps she was the woman of one of them—or for all he knew, of both of them.

"You are as I am," Bayard said with some sympathy, "dwelling between whites and Indians. It is a poor place. I know this, for I have always been there."

"I am Bird of Morning," she said in English, startling him. "A Kiowa." It was the first time she had spoken to him and he was pleased to have drawn a response.

"No, you are as I am," Bayard insisted. "Why then do they come for you?" He felt it was an honest question. She looked up but her flat cheeks and narrow eyes gave nothing. He recognized that she was no Kiowa. The baby had quit nursing and had gone to sleep, but the woman still held it to her nipple, as though the baby were protecting the woman, rather than the other way around. Perhaps it was, Bayard thought, for without the matter of the new baby and the soreness childbearing brings women, he would have lain with her by now. He was being tender, he admitted, because he wanted her to come to him on her own. Having her want to be his woman would make the pleasure all the sweeter.

"Your thinking is much wrong," she said. "They come not."

"I do not know your tribe," Bayard said. "You are no Kiowa."

"About this too you are wrong. You know much little." A fire warmed her voice, pleasing him.

"You scold like a prairie dog."

"I am Bird of Morning, wife of Two Horses, one of the great *Koitsenko*, the Ten Bravest. He will kill you and hang your scalp from our lodgepole."

Again, her fire pleased him. How lucky he was that she was not a white woman. "These words are like smoke which blows away," he said. "I could sell you. Instead, I choose to honor you. You shall be my own woman." She scowled, which pleased him further.

The white men were nowhere in sight, but he felt they were coming, for the breeze and waving grasses told him so. It would be easy to move on from this spot and put a half-day's ride between himself and the white men, who were afoot, after all. But then it seemed troublesome to move, for there was water here and shade and buffalo not far off. He felt it would be good to remain here until he had it over with, this matter of the traveling white men. They were a bother, but he was still feeling very lazy.

He loaded the Sharps rifle. It had a strange encumbrance behind the hammer that he had not seen on a gun before. He puzzled at it for some time before deciding it was a new kind of sight, an awkward affair that stood up close to where he placed his eye, annoying him. He did not care for such a sight and he decided that later he would twist it off.

He lay down with his head against a saddle where he could watch her easily and he cocked back the rifle's hammer.

"Do not think I sleep," Bayard said. "If you move, I will kill your baby." He lay still, dozing a little. At one point he roused at some noise and caught her beginning to stand up. He extended the rifle, pointing at her. She looked at him with contempt, then placed the baby carefully on the ground, stood up and walked behind the hackberries, moving deliberately. He admired her boldness and then heard her making water and had to laugh. She defied him very carefully, Bayard thought. This was a fine woman.

The sun was a palm's breadth above the horizon when he again stirred. He had really slept this time and he awoke with a sense of alarm, coming out of the tangle of sleep like a man caught in brush. The woman sat singing to her baby, the song sounding to Bayard like cartridges clinking softly in a leather pouch. He decided it was good after all that she had the baby, because it meant he did not have to watch her so closely.

35 · RILEY

THEY WERE IN A DRY WASH THAT CUT THROUGH A THICK STAND OF hackberries. The bushes suggested there might be water, but ten minutes of digging with the skinning knife produced only damp sand. Giving up, they picked up the old rifle and the canteen and blanket and scrambled up the wash bank, having to run a few steps to get up momentum. Cass, on long legs and with no old rifle to encumber him, made it easily. He paused atop the bank and turned and gave Riley a hand up. There was an odd jump of dust ten feet in front of them and then a shot rolled out of a distant stand of cottonwoods. They dove back into the wash like frightened badgers.

"Oh, mother!" Riley said.

"He must've laid up all day," Cass yelled. "I had no idea we'd catch him up so quick."

"There goes our surprise. I believe you said it was the only point in our favor." Riley poked his head up and saw a dim outline of horses tethered in the trees some quarter mile ahead. He put his hat on a stick and stuck it up. Another bullet splashed dust angrily and then the shot sounded. Rifle smoke blossomed in the distant trees.

They hunkered in the wash. Riley reclaimed his hat and put it on carefully. "You know, it's funny. Two days of walking and we cussed it all the way, and now walking looks like the easy part."

"I'd take a horse anyday," Cass said.

"That goes without saying," Riley said. "I wasn't picking walking over riding, just over fighting."

"I'd ruther be eating than either one," Cass said. "I hate fighting on an empty stomach. I never thought I'd say it, but I wisht we had another jackrabbit."

"You said yesterday's was tough as boot tops."

"At least it stayed a spell in the belly. Just because it was tough doesn't mean I wasn't glad to get it."

"There's times criticism is just not called for," Riley said grumpily. "I was lucky to've hit it and you are lucky you got to eat at all."

"All I said was if a person had to eat jackrabbit, it ought to be stewed. You stew it some hours and it soaks out the toughness."

"Now you're wishing for a stew pot. You might as well wish for a restaurant to go with it, and a hotel with that."

"There's nothing wrong with wishing," Cass said sternly. "I expect craving improvements has caused every good invention that ever came along. When it gets to where a person can't wish for something better, we might as well all turn up our toes and die."

He got up looking disgusted and walked a few steps down the wash and stood spread-legged to urinate. Riley was going to say more but he thought better of it. Cass, after all, was subject to highfalutin notions, in Riley's view a kind of disease. Riley was glad his own wants were not so particular.

"I don't see where you're getting the moisture," Riley said, to change the subject. "I ain't peed aught but dust since yesterday." He hefted the canteen, finding it a quarter full. It was tempting to gulp some while Cass's back was turned.

Cass stooped for something and came back with a long, bent stick. He studied it awhile and then hacked a piece off it with the skinning knife.

"I wouldn't of given you any jackrabbit at all had I known it would turn you crazy," Riley said. Cass tossed away part of the stick and then held up what he apparently considered the good part like Riley was supposed to admire it.

"Congratulations—you invented a stick. Must of taken a power of craving."

"With that dogleg in it, it looks like a rifle," Cass said. He brought it to his shoulder and aimed at the dirt bank.

"Maybe you can wish it into shooting."

"It'll look convincing from a distance. The idea being Bayard will think I've got the rifle, and all the while you'll be sneaking up on him."

"I'll be doing no such thing." Riley got up and snuck a worried peek over the dirt bank. Bayard's horses were still in the clump of trees. Bayard would have to advance across four hundred yards of open prairie to get at them, which meant he and Cass were safe enough at the moment. But now this sneaking up business. Riley resolved he was not

flipping any damned coins with Cass McCasland about it;
that much was final.

"One of us has to," Cass said. "Once it's dark, he'll come
down and kill us."

"You're a sneakier type of person. Besides which, it's your
idea."

"We'll flip for it," Cass said.

"Fresh out of coins." Riley smiled and patted his pockets.

"We'll do hand-overs for it." Cass threw the stick so that
Riley, still holding Bayard's old rifle, had to catch it
one-handed. Cass stepped over and gripped it just above
Riley's hand.

"I can't imagine why I'd agree to this," Riley said, but he
put a hand above Cass's. Cass went again, then Riley did,
and they alternated until Riley got his whole hand securely
onto the stick near its end, covering all but the last quarter-
inch of it. Cass's hand hovered. Riley had never noticed how
tapered his fingertips were. They were long fingers and
slender as a woman's. Cass managed to get a thumb and two
fingers over the stick's muzzle, or what would have been the
muzzle had the stick really been a rifle. He stood triumphant, holding the stick by the very end.

"Son of a bitch," Riley said. "I knew it."

"You ought to be tickled to get the real rifle," Cass said.
"Bayard takes a notion to come at me, I'll have nothing but a
piece of stick."

"I don't relish any kind of sneaking up, especially against
Indians."

"You shot the jackrabbit," Cass pointed out reasonably.
"I haven't shot the gun, while you've got it all studied out."

"One old jack. Took me two shots on account of the sights
pull left."

"Just what I'm saying." Cass explained how he would
poke his head out of the wash every so often and draw
Bayard's fire while Riley snuck around behind and got his
shot.

"I'd have to go miles to sneak around somebody in open
country like this," Riley said sourly.

"The more reason to get started. When the sun starts to
set I'll get real busy distracting him. I'll wear your coat
sometimes and mine sometimes and he'll think he's seeing

both of us. You run in close and shoot him. It's just simple enough to work."

" 'Run in close and shoot him,' " Riley mimicked sarcastically. "You and your plans. This better not turn out like that beer mug business."

Riley swore while he stuck his head out of the wash. He put his hat on the old gun's barrel and waved it till he saw a puff of smoke, then dropped down quickly before the bullet came.

"See there? He hasn't moved," Cass said cheerfully. Riley stuck his tongue out at him. Sundown, Riley noted, was no more than an hour off. The alternative, though, was as Cass had said: sharing the night prairie with Louis Bayard.

36 · BAYARD

BAYARD KNEW HE OUGHT TO TIE THE WOMAN, THEN GO DOWN AND hunt the white men like deer. It would be little trouble, since white men were unwary. But tying the woman would be a shame, as she was part of his wealth and he did not like to hurt her. Then too, while its mother was tied, the baby might come to some harm. Most of all, he felt a man should not have to tie his woman to make her obey him. Tying a woman reflected poorly on him as a future husband.

The traveling white men, Bayard saw, were very foolish. As he watched, one showed himself, skulking poorly in a pitiful attempt to move closer. Bayard sighted down the heavy Sharps rifle and fired. He looked up quickly over the barrel to see the man scramble comically to the safety of the dry wash. The recoil hurt his shoulder, but nevertheless Bayard chuckled. They were trying to run him out of ammunition, these foolish white men, but they had no idea just how much ammunition Bayard had. They did not appreciate that he, Louis Bayard, was a man of wealth.

That big white man, however, that Parrott, had bought himself a poor gun, for the big Sharps had a tall and very awkward rear sight. Bayard had to take care when aiming that it did not poke his eye. Worse, the rifle kicked fiercely, pushing the gun back and the sight closer yet.

The other white man showed himself and Bayard fired, closing his eyes so that neither eye got poked, then opening them quickly to see the dust kick up and the man dodge for the wash. It was enjoyable, but it seemed, though, that he enjoyed each shot less than the previous one. The more he resisted the rifle's kick, the more savagely it reared back at him.

Bayard stood up, not caring that he showed himself, for the white men had only the old muzzle loader and he knew well how poor a gun it was. He moved to his pile of saddles and gun scabbards and dug through them, first finding revolvers, which were useless at this distance. There was the shotgun Parrott had made the gunsmith cut. Then there was the other white man's Winchester rifle, a slender and graceful weapon.

This gun was to Bayard's liking, for it fired a smaller cartridge and had a sight he understood. Also, it was a repeater, a kind of gun Bayard had never before owned. He took the rifle and a box of cartridges and lay down in his former place, watching for the men.

Soon an object showed above the wash, perhaps a hat, which was a foolish and pitiful diversion. Bayard fired anyway, grateful for a target on which to try the Winchester. The new gun made a pleasant noise and kick, but he could not see where the bullet hit. Another of the white men showed himself and again Bayard fired, but again no dust flew. Shooting at such long range, no matter what kind of gun one had, was an unrewarding business.

Then Bayard saw one of the white men stand on the edge of the wash and dash forward to a clump of sage, pausing before he ducked down to turn and gesture to the other one. This running white man carried Bayard's old rifle. Bayard fired, again not seeing so much as a puff of dust. The white man lay shielded by only the sage, which, of course, would stop no bullet.

But instead of shooting again, Bayard raised the Winchester and considered his problem. Soon it would be evening, for already the sun lowered close to earth. What he should do, he saw clearly, was tie the woman and go hunt the white men and be done with it.

At that point, a small rustle of noise tugged at his

attention. He turned, his head still busy with the problems of shooting, and did not at first take in what had changed about the woman—that she now knelt beside the pile of saddles and gun scabbards and that she held the shotgun with its twin muzzles pointing. The infant lay on the blanket where the woman had been sitting, but she herself was not sitting there now. Instead she knelt, the shotgun muzzles big as owl eyes and directed straight at him, and the woman's face a fist of effort as she struggled to cock the hammers.

Bayard at first felt pride—that this fine woman, with her fire and bravery, would someday be truly his own. Having such a woman could only reflect well upon Louis Bayard. He glimpsed a future time in which he would live in some village and be respected for his wealth and accomplishments and his fine child and woman.

And then the feeling collapsed, for the click of one of the hammers sang out and she raised the shotgun, her face as intent as any warrior's. Bayard jerked upright and swept his rifle's muzzle to bear on her—knowing all the while there was no such village, Indian nor white, where he could live thus respected, for he was Louis Bayard, and only of his own kind, and the respect of others would never attach to him, whether he were wealthy or poor or had a fine family or none.

Her shotgun blasted just as his rifle came to bear on her. Bayard had one leg tripped out from under him. His rifle discharged as he fell. He landed painfully with his face against his rifle's breech and saw the world's colors dim to blackness and then come back swirling and roaring. Pain like fierce jaws ripped him. He lay as helpless as a fallen calf being torn by wolves.

He heard himself groan; he felt his rifle's steel against his cheek; he smelled its oil and burned powder and he tasted his death. Urgency clamored in him. He knew his task was to raise himself and shoot the woman, but it was bothersome keeping the task clear enough in his mind so that he could accomplish it.

The world steadied. He heard the baby crying and the echoes of the shotgun's blast. Then the world cleared. Bayard raised his head to see that the woman had crept closer. She stood crouching, wary as a hunter, the shotgun pointing at his head. He looked at her face and for the first time felt disappointment in her, for she looked, not triumphant as one should look when vanquishing an enemy, but terrified, her eyes as wide as a wounded doe's, though it was she who held the shotgun and he who lay with his leg guttered. Well, he thought, she was no warrior, but only a woman after all.

"You have done a foolish thing," Bayard said in English. "You were my woman. Now I will have to kill you."

She blinked and trembled and he laughed, although poorly. But as he laughed, the woman did an odd thing: She stooped and grasped the end of his rifle barrel, all the while keeping her shotgun pointed at his head and looking both terrified and determined. She began pulling, digging her heels and making a face of effort. He was angered by how freely she defied him. He tried to protest, but the words came in Absaroka. He was angered to feel the rifle being pulled from under him. Still she went on, grunting with effort, steadily pulling.

The rifle was slipping away. Bayard wriggled his fingers so that the movement would tell him where his hands were. He was angered but saddened too, for moments earlier he had been wealthy and already he was less so. Things changed quickly. His leg was smashed, which was a bad thing. He would have to kill the woman, and without woman's milk, the baby would die also. Now the rifle was slipping from him, which made him angry all over again.

Bayard lunged forward and tugged at the rifle so that the woman was startled and cried out. When she dug her heels more fiercely and pulled, he released the gun, spilling her. As she tumbled he stabbed the ground with his bowie knife and pulled himself to it, one stab after another, moving quickly, urgent as any animal, dragging himself a hand's breadth at a time. The woman screamed and tried to get away but Bayard got her by an ankle and held on tightly.

37 · RILEY

RILEY WAS THINKING, TO THE EXTENT HE COULD THINK AT ALL with his heartbeat pounding in his ears, his mouth dry as cotton, and his palms cold and sweaty, that he was lucky Bayard lay up at a water hole. The water hole, a wide spot in a creek bottom, was a low point on the plains, allowing Riley to creep around to the west of Bayard's camp, staying behind rises, and get within a hundred and fifty yards without being seen. From here on, the going would be more difficult, for once he showed himself, Bayard needed only to turn and look and then start screaming rifle bullets at him.

Riley risked a peek over the rise, seeing the horses' backs in the trees. He did not see Bayard or Tai Hei, but then he did not expect to.

A big rifle boomed, startling him. Riley could not see Cass or even the distant wash that sheltered him. What he could see was a plume of smoke pushing out of Bayard's camp as Bayard fired what must be some big buffalo rifle. It surely made a lot of smoke.

Riley decided he would have to get almost to the edge of the trees before shooting off his one shot. Getting so close would require great luck, and also require him to move quietly. He tried to think of what he'd heard about the keenness of Indians' hearing. Some people, he remembered, claimed Indians could hear a man's eyelids blink, while others said they could hear thoughts tick by in a white man's head. Others yet held it was all moot, for an Indian would not have to hear you; he could smell you coming a mile away, and upwind or downwind was all the same to him.

Riley banished such thoughts and glanced at the sun. No more than a few minutes remained before he would have to creep forward. The next shot surprised him because it was a crack, obviously coming from a lighter rifle. Riley didn't know what that could mean, but he decided he was in no position to puzzle it out. Cass was still drawing Bayard's fire and Bayard was still shooting—those were the essentials. Probably Bayard had simply changed guns. It crossed

Riley's mind that if there were a second man in the camp, some confederate with whom Bayard had joined forces, Riley was sure as hell going to be sore about it.

He was wiping his palms on his trouser legs and was just about to start forward when he heard two reports come almost as one—the one heavy and echoless, like a shotgun, and the other a sharper crack, maybe from the light rifle he had heard before. He showed his head over the rise. In Bayard's camp, nothing appeared to have changed, although a lot of gun smoke drifted out of the trees.

Riley got cautiously to his feet. No shot came his way. The fact was, there was no sound whatever. He glanced at the sun, thinking Cass should be making a big display of himself by this time, for the sun was touching the horizon. Hoping for the best, Riley crept forward, a crouching, skulking man on the wide plains.

He heard no shots, no sound at all, which meant Cass must not be doing his job, for Bayard should be firing. Riley crouched forward; he covered seventy yards, then a hundred. He was close to the trees now. One of Bayard's horses whinnied, scaring the life out of him.

Then out of Bayard's camp rose the cry of the baby—a chilling wail, gathering strength and outrage, all the world's misery in that one lonely voice. Why didn't Tai Hei comfort it? The cry struck him as so abandoned, so . . . motherless.

Great weights shifted in Riley's mind. He had a vision of Bayard attacking Tai Hei, raping her, Bayard so busy that he paid Cass no mind, cavorting as Cass supposedly was a quarter mile off and trying to draw Bayard's fire. The instant this thought dawned on Riley, it seemed all too likely. Anger blared in him. He gathered himself and charged the last fifty yards to the camp, boots thumping. The horses erected their ears at him. He hit the trees and flailed through cottonwoods, making a terrific din in hackberry brush. Thorns tore him, branches whipped his face.

A clearing opened and Riley burst into it, trying to cover every direction at once with the old rifle. He came in running to behold Louis Bayard sprawled forward, gripping a bowie knife in one hand and Tai Hei by the ankle with the other, struggling to draw her to him while Tai Hei kicked out with bare heels, fighting like a wildcat.

Riley couldn't shoot because they lay together fighting. Instead, he galloped in on boot heels, never slowing, and kicked Bayard in the side of the head, rolling the man over and splaying him out. Bayard cried out and tried to rise on an elbow. Riley glimpsed a bloodied, fist-size gouge where Bayard had been shot high up on one thigh.

Riley raised the old rifle and sighted, but the man had his eyes squinched shut in pain and Riley could not bring himself to pull the trigger. What he could do was kick him again. He kicked the toe of his boot into Bayard's bloody wound. The effect was like a lightning strike: Bayard's eyes bulged out and then fisted shut; he cried out and stiffened, his back arching. Then he subsided like a bridge collapsing and lay without moving, though still moaning a little.

Riley backed away and tried to get Tai Hei to her feet, but she was so insensible she flailed him with her fists.

"Tai Hei, stop it now!" Riley said it over and over, but she went on hitting him. He said, "Your baby. Tai Hei, your baby needs you!" which made no difference either. Then he tried to hold her while she tried to fight him. It was awkward for him, because at the same time he had to watch Bayard. The only good part was that Bayard showed no further inclination to move.

Finally, Tai Hei quit trying to fight him. "Riley," she said then, which startled him, both because he had never heard her say his name and because he hadn't even known she knew it. She clung to him tightly; he felt her convulse in silent sobs. He stood that way, holding her and saying it was all right until eventually he began shaking. It started in his legs and took over all of him.

"I just got to set a spell," Riley said, embarrassed that his legs were shaking so much. He sat plop on the ground and put the rifle on Bayard, although the rifle was shaking too. Weapons were strewn all over. Riley crawled to the Winchester rifle and levered in a fresh cartridge. How many rounds were in it, Riley did not know, but holding the Winchester made him feel better than holding the old flintlock muzzle loader.

Then little Kam Loi's crying stopped and Riley looked over to see Tai Hei holding the baby. She came to him, walking woodenly, and sat down close by him and they stayed that way, Tai Hei beside him and holding her baby, sitting with her head bowed forward and her hair covering both her own face and the baby so that Riley could not see either of them.

They were like a family grouping, and sat together until Riley realized he could hear Cass yelling in the distance somewhere, sounding frantic, still trying to get Bayard to shoot at him.

Bayard's wound looked bad enough to anchor him, bad enough that eventually it would kill him. Riley resisted an impulse just to shoot the man and have it over with. Once Riley got his shaking controlled, he got up and went to the edge of the trees and called for Cass to come on in, all the while keeping the Winchester trained on Louis Bayard.

38 · THE GENTS

BAYARD LAY ON HIS BACK LOOKING UP AT THE STARS. HE HADN'T moved since Riley had kicked him. Along his left leg, the ground was soaked dark with his blood.

"When next I see you, I kill you." Bayard looked up at the night. "All of you."

Riley stopped what he was doing and stood marveling. It seemed a brassy thing to say for a man bleeding to death, his leg axed open by a ten-bore shotgun.

"You said pretty much the same thing the last time," Cass told him, "and yet, here you lie. It's plain making threats doesn't agree with you."

"Yes sir, was I you I'd say my prayers," Riley said. "A man's a goner with a leg tore open like that." Bayard did not respond. Neither Cass nor Riley had taken a very close look at Bayard's blasted leg, considering the man too dangerous to handle, disarmed or not, wounded or not. What they did do was give Bayard some water.

Then they sat huddled to the fire, although the evening was warm, and ate while Tai Hei nursed her baby. There was little food, and no sunlight left for hunting anything. Riley thought that an empty belly was a small discomfort that did not even begin to offset the pleasure of being alive and whole, with his scalp still on and a good gun in his hands. He also liked the popping sounds of the campfire, the accompanying spectacle of sparks hurrying up to the stars. A growling stomach, in fact, reassured him he was still alive.

Tai Hei sat looking into the fire, weariness masking her face. "I don't suppose after all this you could be talked into going back to Kansas with us?" Cass said gently. "Turn around now, I mean." He noted that he did not sound very hopeful about it.

Tai Hei looked down at her baby and then away to the south, as though her eyes could penetrate the dark and see all that lay down there. She sat that way for some time, her eyes working.

"My little Eagle Feather was in his first winter when he lies burning with fever. My husband, Two Horses, was to go with some warriors and steal ponies from Comanches. It was his place to lead, he being a *Koitsenko,* but he felt strong his duty and stays with me and with our little Eagle Feather, who soon becomes better.

"None among these warriors was seen again," Tai Hei said heavily. "Just as my little Eagle Feather in this time saves a life, so must I now save his. Was it your son, you would not ask me this turning back."

"I don't expect so, no," Cass said.

"And then also would you not get the jew-wel green as grass," she reminded him. "The whiskey white men would have it."

"The famous eye of God," Cass said. "It's funny but I had forgotten that." He thought a moment, wondering if what he'd said were true. "I don't be careful, I'll get to be as bighearted as Riley here."

"This jew-wel is not why came you for me?" Tai Hei looked at them, from one to the other. There was something in the eyes besides worry, Cass thought, and besides exhaustion. There was an insistence, a need to know.

"No, it damned sure wasn't your precious jewel." Cass could have said more, but he only shrugged. She looked at him till it was clear he would say nothing further, then she looked to Riley.

"I don't think I know exactly why we did it," Riley said. "It seemed we had to, is all."

"Some things a person can't abide," Cass said.

Tai Hei looked troubled. She studied the fire, following her thoughts through the licking flames. Finally she lifted her head. "Now I see white men have a white men's kind of bravery and honor. It is different of the way of Kiowas, and yet they have it."

Riley elaborately readjusted his hat. Cass said, "That is a mighty nice thing to hear," and then busied needlessly with the coffeepot. Riley got up to check on Bayard, who lay with his eyes closed, giving no clue to whether he was dead or asleep. Do us all a favor, Riley thought. Hurry up and die.

Watching Bayard, Riley had a fresh urge to shoot him, but then remembered that he himself was a man of bravery and honor, if only in the eyes of some little Chinese girl who thought she was an Indian, and who was still all too likely to get them killed. But the truth was he felt a smidge like a man of bravery and honor to himself as well, shaky legs that afternoon or not. It was a fine feeling as feelings went, easily reason enough to give Louis Bayard until morning to die.

When Riley came back to the firelight, Tai Hei's head was nodding over her infant. "Tuckered, I expect."

"We're all pretty much tuckered." Cass unrolled his blankets.

Having gotten their money back, they flipped a coin to see who would take the first watch over Bayard. It was no surprise to Riley that he lost. Cass rolled up in a blanket, his Colt's army in his hand. Riley took up a post with his back to a tree. About midnight, he roused Cass for his turn.

Riley got comfortable in his blanket. He did not dream of Bayard; he dreamed of men as beasts, men hunkered like wolves over a buffalo carcass, devouring it raw.

The baby cried. Riley awoke in dread, his hand finding his pistol and then holding his pa's old watch to catch light from the embers. It was three-twenty-five; Cass should have awakened him at three. He got up alarmed, hearing Tai Hei fussing with the baby. Cass, Riley saw, sat slumped against a saddle with a rifle in his arms. Riley stepped quickly past him.

Finding the empty space where Bayard had lain was like falling headlong down a well: Riley's stomach churned; his heart drummed high in his throat. He crouched and pivoted, sweeping the camp with his gun muzzle. He stepped back to Cass and nudged him awake with his boot.

"Wha . . . ? What is it?" Cass said thickly, less than half-awake, his expression already protesting innocence.

"He's gone!" Riley whispered. "You went to sleep!"

"The hell! I was awake the whole time!"

"Like hell you were!"

"Like hell I wasn't!"

Tai Hei was sitting up, holding little Kam Loi to her. Moonlight glinted off the skinning knife in her hand. Riley got her Parrott's shotgun, figuring she had already shown well enough that she could use it.

Holding their breaths, fighting disbelief, Cass and Riley searched the camp, finding all the saddles and guns in their places. They searched the trees, finding one horse gone, the tall bay that had been Parrott's. Somehow the half-breed, badly wounded, had mounted the horse and walked it away in the night. An unarmed man with a guttered leg, now out in the dark somewhere.

39 · BAYARD

BAYARD RODE SLUMPED, HANDS GRIPPING THE MANE. HE KEPT the falling moon on his left and headed north, following the trail toward the Cimarron River.

The wracking pain of getting onto the horse had emptied his mind, but now his thoughts were gathering. He felt bad about his shot leg, and worse that the wound had been given to him by a woman. Worst of all was how poor he was, who had lately been wealthy. In fact, he was worse off than he'd been in years. He had a fine horse under him, that was true, but the trade for that horse was a leg so mangled that he might never be whole again, which was a very bad bargain. He no longer even had his old rifle.

He rode north, gripping the horse's mane. North was the Cimarron, whose water would be life-giving. But north was also Kansas and the dominion of white men, and Bayard was one who had recently killed two whites, one of whom had carried a nickeled badge and strong-looking talking papers.

Remembering the papers was troubling. Did not the army ride many leagues just to carry talking papers? They brought papers to various tribes, in order to get their marks upon them, then carried these papers to the forts again. Very important and powerful, these papers, and because Bayard could not read, he feared them. He saw now that leaving the papers after killing Parrott and the other had been as great a mistake as not killing the traveling white men. Had not his luck gone bad immediately? Up in white man's country, perhaps much trouble awaited him regarding those papers.

Bayard considered the south, where lay the Canadian, also life-giving. The lands to the southeast men called the Nations, the country of the five civilized tribes, those Indians long ago tamed by whites. These were the women-men, squash and corn planters, and Bayard did not respect them. Straight south, on the other hand, was the country of the free-raiding Kiowa, and farther yet, the Comanches, both of which Bayard considered true men. Bayard smiled then at his own foolishness, to think any Indians might take him in. He was a breed, a man purely his own kind, dwelling in neither world.

But then he remembered that to the south was another element: the whiskey men, whom Bayard felt to be enemies of these traveling white men. Why else would men follow other men except to catch and kill them? These whiskey men had much food, for Bayard had examined the remains of their campfires. Perhaps they had among them someone who could doctor him. A drink of whiskey, too, would be a blessing, for whiskey was the enemy of pain. He was cheered by this pleasant turn of thinking.

He pulled up the bay, and then tugged feebly on the halter rope until the horse, unwilling, followed its head around and stood facing the new direction. Bayard would have to skirt wide around the camp of the traveling white men and their not-Kiowa woman, but much of the night yet remained. The Indian side of him, the Absaroka, had settled upon an Indian notion, yet one few white men would have found foreign. It was this: that the friendless man turns for succor to the enemy of his enemy.

Bayard held the horse into the new direction—south—till the animal ceased to fight him. Then he thumped its flanks with the heel of his good leg and started.

40 · TAI HEI

TAI HEI AND THE MEN SAT OUT THE NIGHT WITH THEIR BACKS against trees, guns across their laps, occasionally drifting into filmy sleep. When sun woke them, they stood up, dew dampened, thick headed, constricted in their clothes.

While Tai Hei set a fire going, Riley pointed out that the bay's hoofprints were closely spaced, indicating a slow walk, and that they led east. They packed up and followed Bayard's trail, finding where the tracks circled north and finally merged with the sparse trail that led back to Kansas. Where Bayard had made his turn, Riley found traceries of blood, already sun dried a rusty brown.

"Heading back to the Cimarron," Riley said.

"He won't get far, shot up as he is," Cass said. They looked again at the thin line of blood, taking comfort.

"Traveling with him wouldn't of been any picnic anyhow," Riley said.

"What means this picnic?" she asked them.

Cass said, "He means Bayard would've been a trial on everybody."

By midmorning on the trail to Mooar's Town, they struck a running creek. Tai Hei handed Kam Loi to Riley and got down and untied her bundle. While the men led the horses toward the creek, Tai Hei nestled the baby in the shade. Dogwillow whispered around her. The men were busy watering the horses and talking so she went alone down to the water, carrying her things.

"Well, we ought to have *some* kind of plan," Cass was saying. "You don't want to just barge in on them."

"I've had enough of your plans," Riley said. "They always turn out with me doing the dirty work."

Their bickering tone at first disturbed her, for if the white men lost heart and turned back, Tai Hei's mission, her duty to her people, would be made vastly more difficult. She eavesdropped another few moments and then put away her fears. Just as Sky Calf always talked to her in a joking manner, so too these white men often pretended to be angry with each other. Even Kiowa men often acted this way, attempting to hide the regard they had for one another.

She untied her bundle and spread out her things on the man's wool coat Maggie-of-the-high-house had given her. The blue satin dress caught the sun, dazzling her eyes and gladdening her heart. This was the garment she would wear for Sky Calf, her sister-wife, and for Hears Snow Falling, the mother of her husband. She pictured how they would greet her—she, Tai Hei, wearing the dress and holding her baby, whom they had never seen. Then she imagined the pleasure of telling them the daughter's name—little Kam Loi, or Good Things Coming.

But then she was startled to realize the name would mean nothing to them, not Good Things Coming or anything at all, for they were Kiowa women, while she, and her baby too, were also Kiowa, but something else as well. Once they rejoined the Kiowa, Tai Hei realized, Kam Loi would get a new name. Her throat got a pinched feeling over this matter, and she admitted to herself that a new name would not please her.

Perhaps she was thinking too much like a Chinese. Or more and more since being in a white world, thinking like a white woman. It was something to study on further. Meanwhile, she had a need to clean herself, and would take advantage of the little creek.

The men sat on the bank some distance downstream, one of them smoking tobacco. "What I got in mind is we could pose as whiskey buyers," Cass's voice said. "Since they've got all this whiskey to get shut of. It'd be a way of getting into Hollenbeck's camp without their suspicioning anything. We'd get a look at the boy and the women and make sure everybody's all right."

"They'd want to know why we'd want so much whiskey," Riley said grumpily, "meaning we'd have to concoct another story. We'd just get in deeper and deeper."

Tai Hei peered back into the shade at Kam Loi, who slept peacefully. The men were out of sight behind sumacs. She slipped out of her moccasins and her buckskin dress, then stripped off the shirt the doctor had given her and waded naked into the water, which was surprisingly cold, although shallow.

"I suppose we'd have to make out we were going to sell the whiskey to Indians," Cass's voice said. "Which is why we have Tai Hei with us. Because, um, she's a Kiowa princess. She'd be our connection to the Kiowa and the reason we could travel safe down to Kiowa country while nobody else could. Anybody would believe that part."

"So that story gets us into their camp," Riley said. "So then what? We can't just buy whiskey and leave again."

Tai Hei lay back on her elbows, letting the current buoy her body, hearing their voices without listening. Where the sun touched her, her skin was warmed, but everywhere the cold water touched, her skin firmed itself, resisting the cold.

"Hell, I don't know," Cass said, sounding out of sorts. "Think of something."

Tai Hei turned onto her stomach, letting the sun play over her back. The current tugged her. She raised her chin out of water and for some reason was moved to begin singing the song about the swans. How they were awkward on land but became graceful the moment they floated out on the broad river. Little Kam Loi's song.

"I suppose for appearances we'd have to buy a few barrels," Cass said, "however many we could afford. But see, we'd want to buy the boy and the women as part of the bargain. No Indians, no whiskey."

"Now you're talking," Riley said, which made Tai Hei laugh to hear it, as the men had done little but talk all morning. White men were funny, Tai Hei reflected, but they had their own kind of honor and bravery.

"We'd say it was this way," Cass said. "Without the Indian captives, the whiskey'd be no good to us, because we'd never get safe into Kiowa country. We would tell Hollenbeck the Indians were going to be our safe conduct to Kiowa country."

"You just now said Tai Hei would be," Riley pointed out.

"Well, in that case, she couldn't be," Cass said. "We'd

have to leave her out of it because there's got to be some reason to get the Indians as part of the bargain."

The current had towed her. She stood up and the air closed coldly around her. Despite the bright sun, she shivered.

"You'll have to admit it's the only way," Cass said. There was a pause. "Riley?" he said. "What in hell you looking at?"

Riley's voice said, *"Cats' sakes alive."*

Tai Hei heard the change in Riley's voice and was suddenly afraid for her baby, for herself. She hurried to the bank, the sun flashing on her. Perhaps Bayard—

But Riley stood on the bank, mouth agape, a man of wood. Beside him, Cass had gotten halfway to his feet and then had frozen in midcrouch. Standing thus stupidly, he slowly took a cigar from his mouth. Both stared and looked very foolish. She glared back at them.

"A person does not look so at one who bathes," Tai Hei said stiffly. "Once more, white men show they do not have honor."

41 · SILE COOPER

SILE COOPER STOLE A LOOK AT THE YOUNG SQUAW. WHAT HE wanted was a couple days in the settlement. A whore and a drunk, a meal that was not buffalo meat, somebody to talk to who was not that annoyingly silent old Useless Falk.

For here they sat, just three or four miles from Mooar's Town, yet camped spang on the plains like any night on the trail. Hollenbeck said they were waiting on whiskey buyers, who would show up soon enough, for news of whiskey traveled faster than prairie fire. Yet to Cooper, who was young and correspondingly impatient, it seemed the rumored buyers were in no apparent hurry. Meanwhile, Cooper thought, what use was a town if you couldn't go turn the bear loose in it?

Cooper knew better, though, than to complain directly to Hollenbeck. The man was unpredictable even in his sweetest tempers; in his worst he was downright savage. Like attacking those Kiowa for no good reason when they could have ghosted their wagons past and not been bothered. Sile Cooper had no love for Indians—on the contrary. But he believed if they weren't pestering you, the smart thing was to leave them be.

It was a progression of thinking—from the delights of town to Indians—that brought him straight back to the squaw, who, Cooper finally admitted, was starting to work at him. She was a plumpish thing and still lively and cheerful despite being a captive and having been used badly by Hollenbeck a couple of times. She stood out there now, not fifty yards from the wagons, gathering buffalo chips for fuel with the old woman who might have been her mother.

She was young and round, which was what Cooper liked in women, yet not so plump as to hide her womanly contours. The fact was, her womanly contours stood out all the more, making the broad face and the coal eyes that stayed bright even through her rough treatment all the more inviting.

Well, eyes and face were admittedly attractions. But it was her stooping that gave him twinges, the display of rounded haunch under the buckskin dress, the occasional glimpse of dark-nippled breasts. Cooper knew he should look away, for his own peace of mind if for no other reason, but instead kept looking anyway. By gol, he thought, staring, then remembered Hollenbeck had staked a claim on her, which made the whores of Mooar's Town a whole lot safer. Cooper could surely use a trip there now.

The way a smart man got a message to Bug-eye Hollenbeck, though, was to complain *past* him, address somebody else in the outfit and let Hollenbeck overhear. Address somebody innocuous and irrelevant, like that stringbean, Useless Falk.

Speak of the devil, Useless himself picked that moment to stroll meditatively out onto the prairie and take a leak like a horse, his water running out of him in a fat, pressureless stream. Still thinking of the squaw, Cooper rehearsed his sentences, so that when Useless came wandering back, face blank as a board and fingers grappling with trouser buttons,

Cooper was ready for him. Hollenbeck himself was not far off, sitting on a wagon tongue, reloading cartridges and—of all things—humming.

"By gol, Eustis—that squaw's looking better to me by the hour," Cooper said, nodding toward the younger woman. He glanced over at Hollenbeck, who was too close not to have heard. "I reckon if we don't get a chance to howl down to Mooar's Town pretty quick, I will likely bust my britches."

Eustis stopped uncertainly. Rarely a target for small talk, he was wary. As Cooper had just done, he looked toward where Hollenbeck perched on the wagon tongue, seating primers in cartridge cases, an apparently ticklish job that required holding his mouth just so. But Hollenbeck's humming, Sile Cooper noted, had stopped already.

"I ain't that hard up," Eustis said.

"Female's a female, I reckon," Cooper said. He had raised his voice for Hollenbeck's benefit. "'Course like you say, them couple whores down in Mooar's Town would do a sight better."

"I never said it." Eustis looked down at his feet as though surprised to find he'd stopped. "Last trip they had sorghum beer down to Mooar's Town," Eustis said, brightening. "I would admire a taste of that."

"Sure, anybody would." Cooper glanced again at Hollenbeck, who was looking up at them.

"Excepting Bug-eye says we are staying put," Eustis reminded Cooper cautiously.

"I only thought a change of scenery would do us a world of good," Cooper said. There was a little too much appeal in the statement; he heard it and felt it. Getting careless could be dangerous.

Hollenbeck's brass voice piped up from the wagon tongue. "When we get something to celebrate, Cooper, we will go and celebrate." He seated another primer, having to tuck his tongue carefully to do it. "We got some whiskey to get shut of first, by God—or hadn't you noticed?"

"Well, son of a bitch," Cooper said in frustration. The words just leaked out before he could think. He looked at Hollenbeck and then too quickly away, letting his eyes rest on Eustis, who had blanched at such dangerous talk and now stepped away from Cooper as though he might draw gunfire.

"By God, what was that, Cooper?" Hollenbeck put down his tools and stood up, now fully interested. There was a vein of trouble in his voice that even the Indian women recognized. They straightened from their work and looked back toward the half circle of wagons.

Sile Cooper was afraid he might be in for it, but as the youngest man in the outfit, he felt he could get away with saying things an older man could not. "I said it just don't seem right to me."

"What don't?"

"All this damn sitting on the plains. We could just as well be funning ourselves in town as sitting here."

"If you're that itchy for it, go stick it in a gopher hole," Hollenbeck said. "Too bad you ain't as tall as Useless, you could bugger an ox." The other men laughed—mostly, Cooper saw, out of relief that Hollenbeck had chosen humor over anger. Cooper considered them a yellow bunch, but then they had known Hollenbeck longer.

"Aw, Bug-eye," Eustis muttered.

"Useless here been buggering that brindle all the way from Hays City." Hollenbeck's voice carried like a bugle. "Next calf she drops going to be baldheaded and have a droopy mustache." Again the men laughed.

"I never done it once," Eustis said seriously.

"Well, just when are these buyers of yours supposed to get here?" Cooper said, letting out more exasperation. At the words Eustis went wide-eyed, a clear warning to anybody. Cooper knew well that nobody butted into Hollenbeck's business, but it was high time, he considered, that somebody stood up for the rest of them. He looked at Eustis with satisfaction, then at the circle of other men, letting them know he felt entitled to a little information. If they were any kind of men, they'd demand information too.

"By the powers, the pup is cheeky," Hollenbeck said mildly. "Not that it's none of your business, I reckon they will get here about when they get here."

Cooper nodded, feeling relief, but at the same time he had

learned nothing. Hollenbeck stretched. "Getting antsy ain't going to hurry them," Hollenbeck said, his voice changing because of the stretching. "We already put the word out, so there ain't nothing for it but wait."

"Maybe they won't come a'tall," Cooper suggested. He was proud to be speaking for all of them.

Hollenbeck splayed his fingers over his stomach under green suspenders and stepped speculatively away from the wagon tongue. "They always done before," Hollenbeck said. "Let me straighten your thinking on something. This here outfit sells liquor. We don't do it in Mooar's Town on account of it ain't good business. But oncet we get shut of the lot of it, we go down to Mooar's Town and have our fun. Then on to Buffalo City and have more. Then we go back to Hays and do it all over again. That's how the business works."

"Well, maybe having Useless put out the word ain't the best way," Cooper said. "He don't say two words a week. Besides which, a town trip is wasted on him anyways. He don't even take time to get whored."

"And better not neither," Hollenbeck said thickly.

"Well, I guess next time you want to put the word out, you can send me," Cooper said. Saying it made him feel reckless, almost giddy.

"You got better sense than most of these coons, do you?"

"I guess I got more sense than old Useless," Cooper said.

"Come over here, Cooper," Hollenbeck said, crooking a finger. Among the others there was a stiffening of postures.

"What for?"

"Just come over here." Hollenbeck's thick hand beckoned. Cooper, utterly startled, looked around the camp circle. Eustis, Grubb, the others, even the Indian women— were all watching him. His head waltzed. He took one hesitant step.

"Right over here." Hollenbeck pointed out the spot. Cooper was towed by force of command to within a yard of Hollenbeck. Obedient as a hound, he stopped. Hollenbeck regarded him sternly, the beard bristling, the good eye fixing him, the bug-eye staring off, as if it had other things on its mind.

"How'd you like yourself one of these here bug-eyes?"

Hollenbeck's tone was reasonable. "I could fix one of your'n up like mine. It don't take but a little bashing around."

Cooper's gaze fixed on the bug-eye. He should have known what was coming for he had heard the stories, but it seemed he could neither think nor look away.

"With an eye like this here, you get a rutting urge, you just pick out a female and give 'er the bug-eye. Directly she comes a-running."

Cooper could only gape.

"You just fix on 'em like so, like I'm doing on you now," Hollenbeck said. "You give 'em a little come-on look and then hold your breath and do this here—" He brought his horrible face spang up to Cooper's. He puffed his cheeks till his face flooded red. Cooper was alarmed and tried to look away, but before he could shift his focus, there came a squishing, squirting sound and Hollenbeck's bug-eye popped out of its socket and hung swaying, the socket a red hole where the eye had been and the muscles strung down and glistening ropy as snot and the eye hanging out of the socket but still looking somehow, wickedly, at Cooper. It even seemed the eye was smiling.

Cooper covered his mouth and felt strangely light-headed. He tried to back away, but he tripped over nothing at all, clumsy as a colt, and fell down on his rump. Hollenbeck laughed hugely, a great bullish blaring with his face screwed up in vast merriment, till the others started laughing too.

And then almost immediately the laughter aged and fell away, and Hollenbeck's face changed like weather, becoming terrible, twisted, still horrifically gap-eyed. It was a transformation to mark and remember, Cooper thought, and it was a thought that came as clear and solemn as words chiseled on a headstone.

"You're not telling me my business, are you?" Hollenbeck thundered. The eye swayed below its socket. Cooper, lying on the ground, his stomach lurching, could no longer read the face—the expression, the emotion that any human face held. It seemed, in fact, no longer human at all, all twisted and black-bearded and the eye still hanging. He got a vague inkling a response was called for.

"No," Cooper said, his voice strangled.

"And you by God had better not!" Hollenbeck said.

"Useless does his own job! When next I got a job of work as requires some squirt running off at the mouth, I reckon you to be the first I will think of."

One of the men—it could have been Grubb—laughed tentatively.

Cooper tried to answer but his words came out a gargle. Hollenbeck kicked dust on him where he sprawled on the ground, which Cooper didn't much mind considering what worse could have happened. Then Hollenbeck spat on his fingers and put the eye back, so that he looked human again except for being red-faced and huffed up a little.

Cooper put his hands behind him to brace against the ground but didn't know whether it was safe to stand up or not; in fact, it suddenly seemed too great a decision. He was saved by some ruckus out beyond the wagon circle.

"Rider," Eustis Falk was calling. "Rider coming."

The men became fluid—rushing about and finding rifles and cartridge belts. Hollenbeck got a long army Springfield and steadied it on a wagon corner. Cooper, getting shakily to his feet, could see only the distant horse, walking slowly, still nearly a mile out but coming straight on at them. In a minute or so he made out what might have been a rider slumped over the horse's neck. Hollenbeck elbowed him aside and sat on the ground, then steadied a brass spyglass on a pair of shooting sticks.

"Injun," Eustis said.

"That Useless has got the eye for redskins," Hollenbeck said, looking through the spyglass. "An Indian is just what I make it. He ain't got no hat on and I can see his black hair swinging."

Eustis knelt swiftly and brought a Remington sporting rifle to his shoulder. At the sound of the hammer cocking, Hollenbeck started.

"There now, not so quick," Hollenbeck said in mock alarm. "By God, that Useless sees an Injun he right away wants to kill it. Let's find out what he's after." Hollenbeck peered again through the spyglass. "Anyhow, he looks to be hurt or tuckered or something. If he don't turn out amusing, we can always kill him later."

42 · BAYARD

Louis Bayard lounged against a wagon wheel, his bandaged leg stretched in front of him and his back padded with a buffalo robe. The whiskey men had built a big white man's fire, using both wood and buffalo chips for fuel. The flames thrust upward as though trying to reach the sky.

Bayard looked around him, seeing the heavy wagons, smelling the oxen and the white man smell and the cooking meat. Under all was the odor of spirits.

"I wish whiskey," Bayard said. There was an empty space, then laughter roared all around him. It seemed he had made a great joke.

"Shore—give him a drink, just a itty-bitty one," one of the white men said. He had a strange eye, a big fierce beard, and the look of a killer. Bayard had seen many foolish white men—foolish with whiskey or wealth or weakness, a smiling sort of harmlessness that was the most foolish of all. He had seen many foolish white men, but this one, called Hollenbeck, did not seem to be one of them.

Bayard was offered a cup with whiskey in it and he took it gratefully. The liquor was not so good as Parrott's brandy.

"Food, water, doctoring, now my store-boughten whiskey," Hollenbeck said to him. "Just how you planning to pay for all this?"

"I wish to talk."

"Ain't that just like 'em," Hollenbeck said humorously. "One drink loosens 'em right up. How'd you larn English so good?"

"Many times ride for the blue soldiers," Bayard said. "On scout." Some of the white men had come in closer to listen. There were seven in all, and also two Kiowa women, one young, one old, the women whose moccasin prints he had often seen on the trail. He said no more about the blue soldiers and his ability with English; no one would be interested in a breed's story.

"I wish to pay with infor-mation," Bayard said, having trouble with the long word. Hollenbeck laughed and said information was generally a cheap commodity. "Two men follow you," Bayard told him. "White men. They hunt you."

"Just what do you mean, *hunt us?*" Hollenbeck demanded.

"Two men." Bayard displayed fingers. "They trail your wagons from the town which is by Fort Hays."

"Who? Lawmen? You by God had better not be leading lawmen down on us. It'll be the worst mistake you ever done."

Bayard winced. He had not liked Parrott's scolding tone and he did not like to hear it from Hollenbeck, either. He did not ordinarily lie, nor did he speculate on questions to which he had no answers. The traveling white men now had the nickeled badge; perhaps they even had the talking papers. It was possible these things now made them lawmen, although Bayard was not sure of it.

Hollenbeck started to say something further but Bayard said, "I do not lead them. I do not know what they are."

"I expect it was them as shot you," Hollenbeck said slyly, looking like a person does who pretends to know everything.

"I am shot on account of them," Bayard said.

"What in creation could they be after us for?" a young white man said. "The breed's maybe got his story all balled up."

"By God, it don't make a lick of sense," Hollenbeck agreed. He kneaded his beard awhile, as though searching for answers in that tangled mat of hair.

"There maybe ain't nobody trailing us a'tall," the younger man said. "It's some trick, is what it is."

"Cooper, you shut your yap," Hollenbeck said. "We took ten buckshot outen his leg, didn't we? You figger he shot hisself that bad just to look convincing?"

43 · CASS

"THEIR TRACKS HEAD STRAIGHT INTO IT, BUT I SURELY DON'T SEE whiskey wagons there now," Riley said.

They sat their horses on a last rise before the river and looked down on Mooar's Town in the red, shadowless light, the river looping beyond it as silvery in dusk as molten lead. The town itself was a score of low buildings, a few of chinked logs, the others mud colored, all with buffalo grass growing off sod roofs. Some were dugouts, set deeply into hillsides, little more than dens. Cass had a notion of primitive men, neither white nor Indian, more akin to the bear and wolf. Sounds of wood chopping carried to them. A dog barked. A single rider moved along the road that meandered through town.

"The plain fact is, I don't see much of anything," Cass said.

Riley grunted as he swung off his horse and stood kneading his rear end like bread dough. In two days of riding they'd made poor progress. Tai Hei, deprived of the luxury of the buggy seat and still sore from giving birth, had to sit a horse sideways. It made for a precarious perch, all the more so since she held Kam Loi in her arms. Cass and Riley had talked about cutting poles to rig a travois, but had decided against it, thinking that dragging such a contraption would only slow them further.

Tai Hei handed down the baby, which began to cry as soon as Riley took it. Then she slid down with Cass's help and reclaimed her daughter. Tai Hei struck up her song and the baby gradually quieted.

"At least there's somebody gets some benefit from that singing," Riley said. Cass noticed that Tai Hei made a picture standing there on the trail, wearing the blue satin dress and holding the baby, and with the soft light gathering around her. Lavender streaks of sundown reflected off her hair.

In a moment, Riley noticed her too. They stood wordless, looking at her. She was like one of those hazy portraits of Greek maidens that folks stuck up on parlor walls. At the picture's bottom a title would be stated in scrolled letters. "Blessed Motherhood," maybe, or "A Little One's Sweet Bliss."

"Might be a big mistake going charging in there with Tai Hei and all," Cass said finally, breaking the spell.

"I will help in shooting them," Tai Hei offered.

Riley said, "You think some whiskey men are still in town?"

"Seems a poor idea whether they are or not," Cass said. "It's likely a rough place. We keep hearing how we ought not bring a woman so deep into Indian Territory. There's bound to be good reason behind the warning."

"You're saying somebody stays with Tai Hei and somebody else goes down alone. I'm glad you're volunteering for once." Riley looked at Cass and then away, and then snuck glances from the corner of his eye.

Cass was thinking again about men living like wolves. "I'll match you coins for it." He dug into a pocket.

"I don't know why I'd risk it. I never win anyhow."

"Was my luck as good as you claim, I'd be rich by now," Cass said. "Pick it yourself if you're so skittish. Sames or differents."

"All right, it's high time you got a comeuppance," Riley said. "I guess sames." Cass arced up a half dollar. Riley flipped up his own coin, caught it, and slapped it against his wrist.

"Heads," Cass said.

"Same here," Riley said stiffly, not looking up. "You do the scouting."

"Did I ever mention I can tell when you're lying?"

"Well, confound it, McCasland—you win every time! I don't see how you do it."

"While you're at it, find out about someplace to stay," Cass said. "Someplace we can sneak Tai Hei in and out of."

"Cripes," Riley said, disgusted.

"And then if it seems to come up natural in the conversation, ask about the whiskey men. Say we see by their tracks they came through here. Ask about the Kiowa women and the boy, if it doesn't suspicion anybody."

"Don't any of this falsifying come natural to me," Riley said. "That's your department. I don't see why you don't do it. Besides which, I was the one had to sneak up on Bayard with an old muzzle loader."

Cass, irritated, looked down on Mooar's Town. The first lamps were glimmering in greased-paper windows. He blew out a long breath. "I suppose if you're going to get all contrary about it, I will have to do it myself. Even though I did win the toss."

"Don't expect me to feel guilty about it," Riley said

owlishly. "It's high time somebody else stuck his neck out—especially being you make all the plans. Was we going according to my notions for once, I'd feel different."

"So much of foolish talk," Tai Hei said.

Cass was putting on his frock coat. He stopped with one arm in a sleeve. "Well, just what *is* your notion?" Riley looked off at the afterglow and mumbled something.

"I didn't hear it."

"I said in this case I ain't got one," Riley said. "When I get one, I'll let you know."

"Jesus, he gets a funny streak sometimes," Cass told Tai Hei, who looked doubtfully at both of them. Cass decided it wasn't worth going into any further. He checked the caps on his revolver.

"You and Tai Hei hold the horses off the trail a ways where some rider coming in won't see you," Cass said. "Once it's full dark you can breathe easy because it'll be a long while till the moon pokes up." He looked around at the featureless plains. "Let's remember whose turn it is next time some extra chore comes up."

"Just don't take all night about it," Riley said. "Don't get playing poker like you do. And bring us back some food."

"I said I'd do it and here you are telling me how. A person might as well keep a wife as go partners with you."

"Same for you," Riley said sourly.

"Cripes," Cass said. Tai Hei resumed her song, probably to shut out the arguing. Cass swung up onto his horse and looked again at Mooar's Town. The buildings had blended into the rising dark, replaced by a few greasy lights.

"Mr. Cass," Tai Hei said, startling them, for she rarely used their names. "This is much honor-able work you do for us." He knew she meant for her and her children, both the one in her arms and the missing boy. Cass regarded her a moment. Since they'd rescued her from Bayard, he'd had his mind on the emerald. A person might have to go clear to St. Louis with a thing like that just to get top price. The rest of her words caught up with him and he made a face.

"Not honor. There's too much lying and deceit involved for there to be honor." Cass nudged his horse and went down the trail, keeping between the wagon ruts.

44 · CASS

As Cass reached the first buildings, a dog welcomed him, streaking out in the near dark and barking fiercely. It scared the bejesus out of Cass's gelding, who went into sidestepping, picking his hooves up high and being loath to put them down again. The lone dog was a herald of others. Soon Cass trailed a pack of five ribby-chested, dutifully barking mutts, all with stiff tails and their backs ruffed up. They took turns faking runs at the invader, keeping Cass's horse skittish.

Accompanied by the yapping escort, Cass wound between the buildings, which squatted in no particular relationship to a bend in the wagon road. He had a sense of the North Canadian lying ahead. Just when he was tempted to throw the dogs a pistol shot, the dark form of a man materialized behind them, swearing prodigiously and shaming them to silence.

"Was there a place of business still open, I'd be obliged to hear of it," Cass called out to him.

The man let off his swearing. "Mooar's Fort," he called. One arm cantilevered slowly, pointing toward the river.

"Fort?"

"Sort of trading post, tavern, and whatnot. Mr. Cable will have hot grub."

"Much obliged," Cass said, not slowing his horse.

The last building before the river was long and narrow, sod walled on one end, log walled on the other, surmounted by a pole roof heaped with sod chunks. Oval gun ports in the walls gave Mooar's Fort the aspect of a blockhouse; yet despite its solidity, it looked as though it had risen without fanfare straight out of the dirt. It sat on a tongue of ground jutting into the river, a horseshoe in the North Canadian.

Cass tethered his horse. The door was a buffalo hide pegged over the doorway. He drew himself up, tugged down the front of his vest, and then ducked through the flap.

45 · EUSTIS FALK

IT SEEMED TO EUSTIS HE'D BEEN WATCHING THE LICKING TONGUES of fire and the chunks of wood slowly collapsing, and then, magically, he'd been a boy at home in Ohio again, herding milk cows in from the pasture at suppertime. He'd been dozing, he supposed, something he'd done a lot of since the German's outfit had quit traveling and was squatting on the prairie, waiting for whiskey buyers.

Eustis began watching the fire again, still resentful that he always had to be the one to go fetch in the cows. But then he became aware that he was not watching the fire in Bug-eye Hollenbeck's camp circle but a fire built in a log-and-daub fireplace inside the smoky cave of a tavern called Mooar's Fort. He must really have slept.

Guiltily, Eustis straightened in his chair, hearing excited, liquor-fueled voices. Two buffalo runners were shaking dice at a plank table near the door, slapping a tin cup mouth-down on the planks with enough noise to rouse the dead. Another pair were throwing knives at a scarred mark on the log wall. They exclaimed, barking with idiot laughter, every time a knife stuck quivering.

Eustis ran a hand over his stubbled face. He reached for his cup of sorghum beer and had a syrupy taste. All Hollenbeck's outfit hauled was whiskey, but what Eustis liked was sorghum beer. He seldom got it, and when he did he liked to make it last for hours, taking small sips.

That big-mouthed Sile Cooper had wanted to bet him that he, Eustis, would go down to Mooar's Fort and would not dare order even one drink, lest he get too frizzled to do his job proper, thus risking getting jumped on by Hollenbeck. Well. If Cooper could see him now, Eustis thought, he'd see he would have lost his money. For here Eustis sat, feet propped on a fire grate and his hinder planted on a proper chair, by God, drinking the landlady's sorghum beer and pleasuring himself like a proper gentleman.

He sipped again, noting a ringing falsehood in his thinking that partially eclipsed his enjoyment. For if he were

165

enjoying himself, Eustis asked himself, then why was he so anxious for these men to show up, this pair of town fellows the breed had warned were following them?

Bug-eye Hollenbeck, who never lacked for all kinds of notions, had told Eustis privately that he believed the town gents to be Indian Bureau men from the east or even Federal marshals out of Fort Smith, Arkansas. Not men with warrants, necessarily, but men out to make names for themselves, so as to curry the favor of whomever they worked for. The German usually knew the ins and outs of every damned thing, but these notions struck Eustis as farfetched, being there was plenty of other lawlessness going on in the Indian Territory, the squelching of which would make a man a bigger reputation than hauling in whiskey runners. Bug-eye, if confronted, would just claim anyhow they were hauling liquor to Texas, which was legal enough although not half so profitable. Besides, any fool looking to make a name for himself could go to Missouri and catch Jesse James.

But it was not so much the story the breed told that Eustis doubted—or even Hollenbeck's interpretation of it. It was the teller himself, that damnable half-breed. Eustis hated Indians, but with a whole Indian you at least knew where you stood. You killed him and were quick about it, before he made shift to do the same to you. A breed, on the other hand, was neither fish nor fowl. And here this one had come straggling in half-dead, leg shot to beef hash, and what does Hollenbeck do but take the breed in, like they were big-hearted farm folk instead of whiskey runners to the Indian Territory.

The thought of his mission—spying out these men, whoever they might be, providing they even existed—made Eustis bestir himself and sit more upright. He took his feet off the grate. He'd been getting too comfortable.

Then he was startled to hear an unfamiliar voice in the room. He turned with a reeling, unguarded motion, his mouth jerking open on black stumps of teeth, and looked up and beheld this, this *gent*, as tall a man as Eustis himself, standing by the plank bar and talking to the Mooar's Fort's missus. The gent had a fairly new town haircut, wore a stiff-brimmed hat and dark wool pants, and—of all things—a frock coat and fancy vest. Except for trail dust and being some rumpled, he looked as spruce as a state governor.

The man was asking about a room for the night, Eustis realized, his brain catching up—a room in Mooar's Town, just like they had a hotel or something. Mrs. Cable laughed, and then a couple of the bar loungers did, at which the town gent smiled perceptibly and then gave them all a steady, appraising look, faintly challenging, which was a surprise considering how dandied-up the man was. Indian Bureau men and lawmen be damned—what the gent looked like was a riverboat gambler!

It was a muddler and then some. And so to puzzle it out, Eustis decided he'd get crafty. When the gent resumed his talking to Mrs. Cable, Eustis picked up his beer cup and migrated, taking a chair just five steps from the bar.

"I have been traveling hard and am pretty well used up. A roof for the night would make a welcome change," the gent was saying. "Besides which, I've got people joining me directly."

Mrs. Cable snorted, which is just what Eustis figured he himself would have done. The gent would most likely ask next for a hot bath and gin cocktails.

"Travelers in these parts is mostly buffler hunters," Mrs. Cable said. "And mostly sleep outdoors, which is a blessing for everybody, as oncet they get the hide smell on them they are enough to curl paint." She regarded the men standing across from her in a joky way. "Myself, I am spoilt by proper upbringing. I am used to quality, being original from Texas." A buffalo man laughed sarcastically.

"Well, it is the gospel," Mrs. Cable said stoutly. "We was getting on all right, my Amos and me. Had wallpaper in the parlor and whatnot. Then he taken a notion we would go up to Kansas. Start us a store, he says. Get rich on the railroad coming. Well, sir, Kansas was bad enough, but then we had to come down to *this* hog wallow. I give up being a lady in Kansas, but I give up being a female entirely the day I set foot in Injun Territory." She set a corncob pipe in her sparse teeth and nodded. "I reckon now to be a feller in skirts," she said seriously, and the buffalo men cackled gleefully and slapped their legs.

When the gent said he too was from Texas, Mrs. Cable's face took on a light, to where Eustis could see she'd once been almost pretty. The both of them talked about Texas. It seemed they'd lived in neighboring towns, which in Eustis Falk's understanding of the place didn't necessarily put them within two or three hundred miles of each other.

"Well, my lands," Mrs. Cable said, "since it seems you're nigh to kinfolk, I reckon I can let you have the cabin."

"The cabin," the gent said.

"Yes, sir. Got a daub-mud fireplace draws a sight better than this one. The charge is two dollars."

The gent said, "A night?"

"Of course, a night—don't sound so grateful. We got the expense of keeping it up through the times there's nobody in it."

Eustis could see the gent was bristled up at the price, which did seem sky-high if Mrs. Cable meant the cabin Eustis remembered, no more than a squat adobe a few miles down the North Canadian. He'd heard it had been the Mooar Brothers' original headquarters back before they'd built Mooar's Fort and then sold out to Cable and his missus and moved down to Jacksboro. As Eustis watched, the gent paid his two dollars. Then he bought a pail with food in it and paid cash money for that too.

"You can't hardly be hunting buffler, dressed up so," Mrs. Cable said. She bit a dent in one of the gent's coins and seemed satisfied.

"We're looking to buy whiskey," the gent said, "me and the people I work for. Maybe a wagonload of it."

"By God, a whiskey runner," Mrs. Cable said, putting on like she was some surprised. "Here I was just starting to take a shine to you." She was enough older than the gent, Eustis saw, that she could mother-scold him a little.

"It pays for a person's necessaries," the gent said.

"I never would've figured it, you dressed up so," she said. "Besides which, I hold that to be kind of a shameful business for a Texan. Some among us still got our pride." She was being joky but the gent looked at her in that steady way.

"There's considerable pride in any business, if you go at it right," the gent said. "At any rate, we heard of a whiskey train in these parts but we don't seem able to find it."

"That'd be that son of a bitch Hollenbeck's outfit," Mrs. Cable told him. "They come down with barrels and barrels of it."

When the gent asked how he would find this Hollenbeck, Eustis Falk's neck hairs prickled.

"No need to," Mrs. Cable said. "When he gets in this country, he sends his half-wit bootlicker to find buyers for him. Yonder he sits. Name of Useless Falk." She looked out past the gent and pointed a skewering finger smack dab at Eustis, who felt boxed in the ears to hear his own name given out.

The gent turned and looked at Eustis. Mrs. Cable was still looking at him. Two or three buffalo men lounging against hogsheads turned and looked at him too.

"Is that a fact," the gent said. He had chilly blue eyes, almost transparent, and when they settled on Eustis they gave him a shiver. "I'm obliged," the gent told Mrs. Cable, and he moved thoughtfully away from the plank bar and walked spang up to Eustis.

46 · RILEY

RILEY STOOD HOLDING THE REINS OF THREE HORSES, A CONSIDERable chore given the way two would crop grass at the same time another would insist on shaking its head. They'd been bridled and bitted the whole day and they chafed to be free to graze. Riley knew also that it galled an animal to stand there thirsty when it could plainly smell the river.

From time to time he studied the ragged string of yellow lights that was all he could see of Mooar's Town. He regretted after all that he hadn't gone down himself. Cass had mentioned how when the next chore cropped up, it would be Riley's turn again. And since they were getting close to the whiskey men, that next chore might turn out infinitely more ticklish. Cass volunteering made Riley suspect he was being outfoxed. He held himself no slouch as a thinker, but Cass McCasland always seemed to think one situation ahead of him. Riley vowed he would begin thinking one situation ahead too.

Tai Hei paced, singing her cowbell song to soothe her baby. Her petticoats rustled every time she turned. Riley was always more aware of Tai Hei as a woman when she wore the blue satin dress. Probably if it hadn't been a whore's dress, leaving her shoulders and half her front open, he'd be more comfortable with it.

Glimpsing Tai Hei's bare throat, he couldn't help but picture the emerald necklace or pendant or whatever it was, with the jewel itself hanging there above the two mounded breasts where her baby nuzzled.

Riley wondered how Tai Hei could give the jewel up, this keepsake that had come down through her family. It wasn't like she didn't appreciate pretty things; it was clear, for example, she had a great fondness for the blue dress, for she had talked several times about wearing it for this Sky Calf, the Kiowa woman friend of hers. Whether her little boy, Eagle Feather, would like the dress too, Tai Hei had never said. Maybe the boy would be scared by it, having never seen a whore's dress. In any case, Tai Hei in that dress was a sight. Maybe it was because she had the dress that she didn't mind giving up the jewel. At least he hoped so.

Riley was still regarding her when he felt her eyes playing back on him. He looked away quickly, and kept his eyes away until it got uncomfortable having a direction in which he couldn't look.

Without being asked, telling himself she might find the evening chilly, he dug a blanket out of a saddle pocket. It took him a while because he had to shift one set of reins to his teeth to free up a hand. When he pulled out the blanket, a soft, metallic noise sounded on the ground, as though a rifle cartridge had been loose in the blanket. Supposing there might come a time they'd need every cartridge, he squatted and searched the ground between the horses, finally having to strike a match to see anything. Something gleamed at him; it was the nickel-plated deputy's badge that Parrott had once carried. Riley retrieved it gingerly. He didn't care to handle it, for it was a reminder of the warrant that had been issued for his arrest.

He got the blanket and went to her, the horses resisting and having to be towed by the reins. Tai Hei looked up with frank eyes. He held out the blanket to show his intent, and then wrapped it around her. Instantly, she looked to be an Indian again, or whatever she was when she was not dressed like a whore. Then her eyes shifted, and she jerked her head as though she'd heard something.

"Traveling with a woman in these parts is a bad business," a hailing voice said. Riley wheeled, aware he should have taken the horses farther off the trail to do his waiting, but he hadn't wanted Cass to miss them when returning in the dark. With the horses milled around him, Riley had to swing out in a half circle just to see who was talking. Moving with the horses in front of him gave him a chance to draw his revolver.

"I say, you picked a hell of a poor place to bring a woman," the voice said.

A man stood in the road, outlined against what little was left of the sundown. He was carrying a long gun in one hand, probably a shotgun, and what appeared to be a wild turkey in the other, holding it by the feet. The dead bird seemed a considerable weight.

Riley had never much cared for unasked-for advice, all the more so when he had no intention of following it. "We're Mennonites," Riley informed him. "One of your more worldly sects—you might've heard of us. I'm just now waiting for the rest of my wives to come up. We're looking for a place to herd our goats. Seems a great deal of space hereabouts, which is what we're after, as we've got thousands."

"What in holy Hades?" the man said.

"Mind your French," Riley said, "for the wages of sin is death." He'd heard that just recently.

"Worldly Mennonites!" the man marveled. "Goats!"

"We expect to take over the whole country directly," Riley told him as the man began walking. "We drop young'uns faster than rabbits."

The man hurried, turning and looking back every three or four steps. The story served him right for sneaking up like that, Riley thought. He chuckled. Tai Hei was looking oddly at him.

"Mennonites are sort of like Mormons," Riley said. "Or like Baptists, only a lot quieter about it." Her look stayed blank. "They're like different tribes of white people." She stood like an Indian—or maybe a Chinese, he didn't know which—giving no sign she had either heard or understood. He felt his explanation must not have helped much.

"You must be awfully anxious about your boy," Riley said, just to change the subject. "Now that we're so close to him, I mean." He winced. The boy, the Kiowa women captives, all might easily be dead by this time. He hoped he hadn't merely reminded her of sore subjects.

The horses chuffed grass, uprooting it with ripping sounds. In the trees along the river, katydids put up a distant racket. The two sets of noises did not add up to much. In all the space that was not filled with noises, Riley could as good as hear long seconds ticking.

"Yes," she said finally, again leaving the conversation hanging. Riley made a vow never to play poker against Chinese; he'd be outdeadpanned at every turn. Among his own people, Riley's statement would have been recognized as an opening, an invitation for both parties, if they had any kind of civil tongues in their heads, to share their fears about the kidnapped boy, even though merely saying out loud what both parties already knew. His people held it lightened burdens to share them.

Still she said nothing. He itched to ask about the emerald: what she thought it'd be worth, where he and Cass might sell it to get the best price. Another sore subject, he decided, in light of the jewel being the only thing left from her old life. A sore subject and a tasteless one, and he felt vaguely guilty.

"Have you thought of what you and your little family will do," he said, having come that far, "I mean, when we get your boy back?"

"I am a Kiowa," she said. "The land of my people lies below the Mother Canadian. It is now not far."

He knew she meant the main course of the river, as opposed to the north branch of it that they were on. "No hankering at all to see your Chinese folks?" Riley asked. He'd heard about people being rescued from Indians after long captivity. Some, strangely, only pined to go back.

Cynthia Ann Parker, he remembered, white mother of the young Comanche chief Quanah, had been a famous case in point.

"No," Tai Hei said, "my people are Kiowa." She looked away and he was soon back to hearing the horses and katydids. Conversation, he reflected, was often just an idle way of passing the time anyhow.

He was about to turn away and start checking the bridles when she said, "We traveled eastward from the city of San Francisco, my Chinese father and brothers and I. They were sellers of tin pots and spices, all things Chinese need. My father had buy a wagon of two wheels—"

"A cart?" Riley suggested.

"Yes, a cart. We followed the iron rails to where Chinese men worked. It was near the place of Julesberg."

"Julesberg, Colorado? I never heard there was Chinese there."

"People called it only Julesberg," she said. "We camped at sunfall by water. They came so soon among us—I mean so fast—that there was no chance. All others were killed. I did not learn till a long time it was Arapaho took me."

"I'm awful sorry," Riley said.

"I was given to Cheyennes in a bargain for horses and then again given to Kiowa, who treated me well." She looked up at him. "It is why I must now be a Kiowa."

Riley looked away, feeling guilty. He had indeed brought up sore subjects, although Tai Hei had told the story matter-of-factly, as if it had happened to somebody else. He supposed in a way it had.

While he was glancing for the hundredth time toward Mooar's Town, a sound came, traveling clearly in the stillness, a distant horseshoe scraping stone. Riley could barely make out a rider—no, two—separating from the buildings and angling up the trail toward them, walking their horses.

"Mr. Cass is one," Tai Hei said, looking intently.

"How in the world can you make out that?" Riley said. The shapes were merged—one rider against the other, dark upon dark against the grasses near the river.

"One rides not like another," Tai Hei said. "The behind

one is Mr. Cass." Riley stared till his eyes dried and itched. There was the distant flicker of a match—one of the men lighting a pipe or cigar.

"He speaks to us with fire," she said.

"He signals? How do you figure that?" The glowing ember of cigar was a pinpoint; sometimes he could not see it at all. The riders were coming up the trail, beginning to start up the hill, making a wide arc toward them. Just as Riley began to feel exposed on the rise, to feel that he and Tai Hei would be seen, the riders veered eastward, following a line that must have paralleled the river.

"We must follow," Tai Hei said, and as she spoke the trailing rider moved the glowing cigar tip in something resembling penmanship: wide loops and scrolls.

"By gol, maybe so," Riley whispered. He took the baby while Tai Hei got up on her horse. For once, the baby slept deeply and did no more than stir when he held it. Then Riley swung onto his own mount and set out leading Tai Hei's horse and the spare.

"If that's not Cass and he comes back and don't find us," Riley said quietly, "he sure is going to be sore."

47 · CASS

CASS EMERGED FROM THE BUFFALO-HIDE DOORWAY CARRYING A tin pail of buffalo stew and a burlap poke of corn dodgers. Eustis Falk came out behind him and without a word clumped toward the near corner of the building. Cass guessed Falk had a horse back there and he swung up on his own mount in order to be ready.

This man Eustis Falk barely spoke at all. As Cass understood it, Falk had agreed to guide Cass to the adobe cabin Cass had rented from Mrs. Cable. Then in the morning, Falk would bring down his boss, this Bug-eye Hollenbeck, to discuss the sale of the whiskey. In a moment Falk reappeared, riding around the building's corner on a suitably skinny-chested, long-legged animal, a match for its master.

"Here we go," Cass said, sounding to himself like an idiot.

Falk said nothing. Falk had a way of hanging in the saddle, all limbs, loose as a scarecrow. His hat was collapsed, more bag than separate crown and brim, and served to hide his features.

"About your whiskey, I'm sure we can come to an understanding on price," Cass said as Falk walked his horse past him, taking the lead. Cass tried to sound unconcerned, as though he bought a whiskey train every week. "Just how many barrels are we talking about?"

Falk presented a silent back, elbows flapping even though the horses moved at a walk. He said something Cass didn't catch.

"What?"

"Lots," Falk said louder. "More'n you can haul, not having no wagons."

"Oh—wagons," Cass said dismissively. Wagons indeed —he and Riley had not talked about wagons. "Well, wagons have never been a problem other times," Cass said. "I mean, hell, where there's whiskey, there's always wagons." His words rang with hollow cheer and he tried to cover that fact by chuckling. "Maybe we'll just buy your wagons right along with the whiskey," Cass suggested.

"Not likely," Falk said. "Bug-eye's fussy about 'em." Cass let the man's elbows flap on awhile in silence. He'd rarely seen so sloppy a rider. They rode out of Mooar's Town on the same route Cass had come in, past sod hovels, soon rousting the dogs again, who gave them a raucous send-off until the same man as before came out and cussed them.

The trail led out of town. It was too dark to see anything, but Cass had a sense of Riley and Tai Hei at the top of the rise to his left, a hundred yards off. He wasn't sure they could see him and Eustis Falk at all.

"I thought we'd be going downriver," Cass said, still trying to sound offhand. He'd no sooner said it than Falk angled his horse away from the wagon ruts, following a trail no wider than a cowpath, angling east to front the river. Cass risked a look toward the rise. The sky was just perceptibly lighter than the ground. He made out dim shapes, nothing more.

"Give me a second," Cass said. He reined up and hooked

the stew pail over his saddle horn. He fished out a cigar and made a show of lighting it, using two matches. "I'm a slave to the infernal weed," Cass said. "Can I offer you a smoke?"

"Got a chaw," Falk said, and turned in the saddle and urged his horse forward, presenting a mute back again. Unbidden, Cass's horse followed. Suddenly inspired, Cass waved the cigar wildly, doing loops and scrolls, waving it until he thought Falk might have looked back at him. "Only way to get these damned twists going," Cass explained. "Next time I'm buying Havanas."

48 · EUSTIS FALK

EUSTIS WAS GLAD HE'D HAD HIS NAP BY THE FIRE IN THE MOOAR'S Town tavern because it was turning into a tiring night. Not tiring because of the ride itself, for he led the town gent down the North Canadian at the kind of fast walk he and his animal could keep up for days. Instead, tiring because of the uncertainty of it—because he didn't know what kind of fellow this town gent was, or what he was up to, or how much, if anything, he, Eustis, ought to be telling him.

The fact was, there was so much to think about when being with this fancied-up gent that Eustis, a simple man, could barely keep check on it. When Hollenbeck was around, which was most of the time, Hollenbeck did his own thinking and everybody else's too. Left on his own hook, Eustis liked to think about things one topic at a time. When thoughts came all in a rush—and he felt them bearing down on him now like a buffalo stampede—a person's mind could not sort one item from another.

They rode along the river, hooves clopping, katydids fiddling in the grass, the gent gabbing with no letup. "There was a lot I couldn't very well go into back there in the tavern," the gent was saying. "A man doesn't want to flap his jaws too much in this business."

Now that was plain enough, Eustis thought; surely he needn't add anything to that. The gent, though, picked away at him.

"I'm sure you'd agree, Mr. Falk."

"I ain't much of a talker," Eustis ventured to say, hoping to shut the man up.

"Still waters run deep, is that it? But when a man like yourself has something to say, I'll wager folks pay it full mind."

Eustis was about to shrug the statement off, but then saw the shine of truth on it. Folks did indeed hush up whenever Eustis was fixing to say something. He sat up a little straighter. "Well, sir, I expect you're right," he heard himself tell the gent. But then when he did say something, Eustis reflected, half the time folks just laughed. The German, especially.

"What I hear, this Hollenbeck's a tough nut to do business with," the gent said. "Or maybe I've been steered wrong in that department."

"He's particular," Eustis conceded.

"Exactly. That being the case, I don't know how he might react to the, the more unusual parts of the deal we'd like to make."

Eustis said, "Umm."

"The thing is, along with whiskey, we are going to require something to ensure our safe conduct, being we're taking the liquor into Indian country."

Now what was the damned gent getting at? Nothing in the world could ensure a whiskey runner safe conduct in Indian country, short of a regiment of cavalry. Which then would slap you in the guardhouse and shoot you in the morning. Though words reeled in his head, Eustis rode on in silence. Hooves clopped, katydids fiddled, and Eustis Falk's ears hummed with anticipation.

"The fact is, we had in mind buying Indian hostages," the gent said. "To be exact, Kiowas."

Kiowas? The word jolted through Eustis like snakebite. He swallowed uncomfortably. He rotated his shoulders to relieve a knot there. First it was whiskey, then wagons if the gent could get them, now Kiowa captives! This town slick had more notions than Hollenbeck. What would he be hankering to buy next—the German's old bug-eye?

"Now this may be a touchy subject, but I'm going to say it

straight out," the gent said. "A party of buffalo hunters the other day told us your outfit might be holding Kiowa women."

Startled, Eustis nearly dropped his rifle. He began to turn in the saddle, then caught himself and forced his attention forward. Why, the damned gent seemed to know every blessed thing about them! Eustis held his breath and squinched his eyes shut, afraid of letting out information that Hollenbeck would have him skinned for.

"A couple-three Kiowa captives," the gent said, talking as ordinary as if about the weather. "At least, so I'm told."

Eustis sat hunched, his mind locked, afraid of admitting anything. But then he began to worry that his silence might be taken for assent, that he was thus revealing the very things he struggled to hide.

"I ain't saying we got 'em or don't got 'em," Eustis said finally. Which seemed safe enough. He let his horse clop awhile, feeling the pressure lift from him, taking satisfaction in what he decided had been a shrewd answer. "I don't give turds about redskins one way or t'other," Eustis added, and reckoned that showed him.

"You play a close game, Mr. Falk," the gent said. "And rightly so, under the circumstances. Well, sir—to lay my cards on the table, we're particularly interested in buying the little Kiowa boy you're holding. We'd want the whiskey, the women, and the little boy—all part and parcel of the same deal."

Eustis could hold it in no longer. *"Boy!"* he exclaimed, turning in his saddle as though yanked by ropes. "I fer damned sure don't know nothing about no *boy!"*

49 · CASS

ONCE EUSTIS GOT HIS BACK UP, THEY DID NO MORE TALKING. Cass had pictured the cabin on their side of the river. Falk, though, brought him some four miles downriver on the North Canadian, where they were welcomed by a rising half moon. Abruptly, Eustis reined in and pointed into the dazzling bar of reflected moonlight that rode, shattering and reforming, on the river's current.

"It's across?" Cass said, letting his surprise show. "How deep is the water?"

"It won't give a horseman no trouble," Eustis said, with the implication that Cass might be no horseman. Eustis spat tobacco, then bridled his horse around, aiming for the open plains.

"Hold on a minute," Cass said. "You'll bring down the whiskey in the morning?" Anxiety crept into his voice, which was careless of him, but the man had been so silent that Cass was not sure whether they had an arrangement or not.

"More whiskey than you seed afore," Eustis said.

"When can we expect you? First light, or what?"

"I reckon directly," Eustis said. "Bug-eye don't let no grass grow under him."

Cass could think of nothing more to say. He supposed he had to take on faith that there was a cabin across the river. Eustis resettled his rifle on the saddle pommel, then kicked up his horse and set off, hooves clomping hollowly. In a minute, he was gone, leaving Cass with the gliding river.

Cass shrugged and then urged his horse down a three-foot embankment. There was a muddy strand before the water started. He faced his animal squarely to the water and sat frowning. What was worrisome was the surprise in Falk's voice, the sudden heat with which he had said he knew nothing about a boy. Cass thought wearily of all the distance they'd traveled, and for what? Likely nothing at all. Then too, Cass was angry with himself for being too eager. Maybe he'd pressed the man too closely. Still, the surprise in Falk's voice concerning the boy had sounded genuine enough.

His horse shied off, reluctant to enter the shining water. Cass was angry and took it out on the horse, bringing its head roughly around, aiming it rather than guiding it into the moon's wavering reflection. Even then he had to thump the animal's flanks until they started forward. Once the horse was well into the current, Cass had no further trouble, except for wetting his legs. Sudden, cold water spilled over one boot top and he cursed aloud at the annoyance of it.

He found the cabin a hundred yards back from the river, hulking in the moonlight amid scattered elms and cotton-woods. It was a square adobe with a sod roof and a plank door on leather hinges. A rude corral was set thirty yards to the left of the building. He inspected the peeled sapling rails for breaks before loosing his horse into the corral. The saplings were lashed with rawhide strips and stood sturdily enough.

The horse was not sweated, but since it had had a wetting in the river, he rubbed it down with dried grass. He was halfway to the house, walking with his saddlebag over one shoulder and the Winchester in his hand, when he sensed movement. *"Who's there?"* Cass called, his challenge shushing crickets.

"Just old us," Riley's voice said, coming from Cass's side of the river and surprisingly close by. "You alone or what?"

"I'm alone. Come on in." In a moment they were there, Riley and Tai Hei towering on horseback, the moonlight catching at them in odd angles, sloping off Riley's chin or Tai Hei's smooth cheek. Cass had a hard time looking at her; he knew it was because the news he had—or rather, lack of news—of little Eagle Feather, her son.

"You must have crossed farther up," Cass said.

"It seemed smartest, in case you were keeping that feller you were with in the dark about us."

Cass told how the man was one of the whiskey traders. "He's some suspicious," Cass added. "He thinks whiskey buyers ought to have wagons."

"I suppose we ought at that," Riley said, "though it's a little late to be thinking about it."

Cass opened the heavy door and lit a match. He stepped aside to let Tai Hei carry her baby into the adobe, which was a single room housing only a rickety table and chunks of stumpwood to serve as stools. The floor was packed dirt, but reasonably clean. A fireplace had been sculpted into one corner.

"Some lodgings," Riley said.

"I will make a fire if you give matches." Tai Hei put her hand out, causing both men to dig into their pockets. She'd apparently been an Indian long enough to find matches a great wonder.

"Adobes put me in mind of my old south Texas stomping grounds. Besides which, I like the thickness of these walls." Cass smacked the adobe with the flat of his hand. "Hard as brick."

"Bulletproof, you mean," Riley said. "Sounds like this party you're planning will likely get rambunctious." He moved to check the windows—wood frames set into raw adobe casements and covered with greased skins, thin as parchment. There was one window per wall, evidence that the adobe's builders had given thought to defense.

"Not necessarily. But it is some comfort that a couple men could hold off an army from here." Cass slapped the wall again. "At least till the ammunition ran out."

"That's some comfort, all right," Riley agreed, with no more than usual sarcasm. He went outside, probably to tend his horses.

Within a few steps, Cass was beside him. "We ought to talk."

Riley grunted like he'd been expecting as much. "This feller you followed. You spring the business of Indian captives on him?"

"I did," Cass said. "It was like pulling teeth getting the drift of his thinking, him being one of those wordless bastards. I expect this Bug-eye Hollenbeck does all the brain work. But I did want to plant the notion of Kiowas in his head. No Indian captives, I said, no deal on the whiskey."

"So he admits to holding them," Riley said. They unsaddled and corraled the horses and left the saddles on the corral rail. The animals circled to investigate their confinement.

"I kind of tricked it out of him." Cass glanced back at the adobe. "One thing, though—the boy's not with them."

"What do you mean, *not with them?*"

Cass shushed him. "I'm saying this Falk claims they haven't got the boy. In fact, never even saw him."

"Lying like a snake, I expect."

"The way I read him, he's too simple to be much of a liar."

"Well, *hell and hallelujah,* if that don't put us in a fix," Riley said in disgust, and he angrily kicked a corral post, startling the horses.

Cass turned reluctantly to face the cabin. He'd been

avoiding looking at it because Tai Hei was in there. Yellow firelight already shimmered in the greased windows, giving a homey aspect. Fragrant woodsmoke reached him, and soon after, a dizzying smell of heating food. He tried to imagine telling Tai Hei about her boy being nowhere within a hundred-some miles and he could not think of the words he should use to tell her. He couldn't even think of how to begin.

Riley kicked the corral post again.

"I hope your mad gives out before that corral does," Cass said.

Riley huffed until he got a grip on it. "I expect then they've killed him."

"I got a notion otherwise. Most likely when the whiskey men attacked, Tai Hei ran off one way and the boy another, neither knowing the other had got away."

"Well, that about caps the climax," Riley said. "This whole trip was a fool's errand. I should've stayed in Hays City and nailed roofs for a living. Now I got a warrant out for me and no prospects anyplace!"

"You're making the animals jumpy kicking that post like that."

"Well, gol dang it anyhow." Riley turned his back and muttered something else.

"What?"

"I say, how old's this youngster of hers supposed to be?"

"Just three."

"Indians are mighty resourceful," Riley said hopefully. He looked at Cass, who made a face.

"A sprout that little on the great big prairie," Cass said.

Riley said, "It's like to kill her, finding this out."

"Let's not tell her anything at all till we're sure. There's no point in upsetting her."

"Well, we know they got the women," Riley said. "Tai Hei will want to get them back in any case."

They stood, unwilling to go to the cabin despite the compelling smell of food. Cass had an urge to mention the emerald—the great, green jewel that was supposed to have hung around the boy's neck, protecting him. He let it go unsaid, though he figured Riley was thinking about it too.

The cabin door opened, letting a long wedge of yellow light splay out. Tai Hei's figure darkened the doorway. "The food cooks," she called.

"In a minute," Cass answered. It was as though they were menfolk on some granger's spread, being called in for supper.

"So you got any kind of picture how this is going to go tomorrow?" Riley said.

"This Falk thinks we ought to have wagons. I expect the whole setup smells wrong to him."

"We'd maybe be best off dropping the dodge of buying whiskey," Riley said. "We're maybe not fooling anybody. We haven't got all that much money anyway."

"And just offer flat out to buy the Indians?" Cass considered it. "It amounts to a ransom—though we wouldn't call it that. At worst, doing that might tell them we know how they got those Kiowa."

"What of it?" Riley said. "To you and me, maybe, attacking Indians for no reason seems a shameful business, especially when they got women and sprouts with them. But I expect to most folks hereabouts, killing Kiowa is about the fastest way to get popular."

"Could be you're right. And selling off those Indians is maybe what these men had in mind all along," Cass said. "But there's still the matter of Tai Hei, whether she'll even take their word about the boy. It'll go hard on her to hear they never even had him." Still, he didn't see what else they could do but try to buy the women.

Cass had a saddlebag draped over one shoulder. He climbed the corral rails and loosely saddled what he figured was the freshest horse, then tied the saddlebag on behind.

"What are you up to?" Riley asked him.

Cass slapped the saddle pocket for luck. "Figuring an ace in the hole. Parrott's money is in there. If we have to skedaddle in a hurry, either in the night or after Hollenbeck gets here—like for instance, if bullets start flying—we'll still have the money. We can saddle the other animals in the morning."

"I take it you don't expect them to just take our money and leave us the Indians," Riley said.

"It feels a long way from civilization down here. Which brings out the beast in fellers, remember?" Cass slapped the saddlebag once more and climbed back over the corral fence.

50 · BAYARD

LOUIS BAYARD LAY LIKE TWO MEN. IN ONE PART OF HIM, PAIN BORE steadily. His leg throbbed; it was that that had woke him. But at the same time, he had popped into wakefulness with a buoyant heart, feeling with certainty the return of his former wealth. The traveling white men were bringing it: horses and guns, the money and the not-Kiowa woman. Yes, the woman—he was surprised to acknowledge—the woman most of all.

It was a many-sided business, of course, so many-sided that it would have been good to talk it over with others, as Indian men did it around a council fire. For besides these traveling white men and the riches they carried, there were the whiskey men, who had riches also—more guns and animals, and much strong drink. And too, their Kiowa women, one of which was an old grandmother and worthless, but the other who was young and useful, though not as comely as the not-Kiowa.

A many-sided matter, but Bayard had no one with which to discuss it, for he was of his own kind and alone. Keeping so many thoughts separated was difficult. To Bayard, it was the feeling that came clearest, the feeling of something that once was his and soon would be his again—but only if he guided the feeling truly and acted well to further it. The only obstacles in his way were the various white men, two camps of them, enemies of each other. He would let the white men fight until the power of both camps was reduced. When that was accomplished, he, Bayard, would see just whom he would have to deal with.

He changed position, resting the shot leg on a pad of buffalo hide placed on the wagon tongue. Keeping the leg high kept the blood out of it, so that the bandage oozed less.

The wonder was that the bone had not been broken. He lay still and banished the pain to a far part of him and let his thoughts return to savor his riches. But for some reason, these thoughts would not come clear. The whiskey men's fire had burned to coals. He heard oxen whuffing where they were staked off in the darkness. A sleeping man passed wind.

Then it seemed he felt iron-shod hooves approaching. His nostrils worked. He reached for his knife, then remembered he'd lost it after being shot by the not-Kiowa. The pain was a great weight on him, but he rolled to his side and stiffly got up. He was weak, yet the feeling of approaching hooves sustained him. He moved through the camp, stooping to appropriate a cartridge belt and a long rifle of the kind the blue soldiers carried. They were good guns, these rifles.

When he got away from the wagon camp he saw the low moon that was shaped like a stone axe riding the sky. The farther from the white man's camp he hobbled, the better he could see and hear and smell. He began to make out details on the ground: buffalo droppings, scraggly sage, and soapweed. He felt rather than heard the thudding hooves of a horse walking, coming from the river. He put his moon shadow on his right, faced toward the river and hobbled, using the rifle as a crutch, its butt on the ground and his left palm over the muzzle and tucked into his armpit. When he saw the rider, he crouched.

Bayard let the slow rider come within a bowshot, then half a bowshot. Then he rose up as though straight out of the sod, rising and at the same time cocking the rifle's hammer. At the movement, the rider's horse snorted with surprise and bounded sideways. The man's arm shot skyward, seeking his lost balance. A rifle slid off the saddle pommel and thudded to the ground. The whole sight was so comical that Bayard laughed.

The rider fought his horse, finally controlling it and then sitting frazzled and huffing while the horse rolled its eyes, staring at Bayard as though he were the devil incarnate.

"Lord and Savior," the man breathed, and then he too stared at Bayard. In a second he pulled his revolver and tried to look threatening. Bayard laughed again.

"I hear your hooves like drums beating." Bayard knew

this tall, skinny, comical man would do nothing without Hollenbeck's approval. "Also I smell you coming." Bayard eased his rifle's hammer off cock and let the barrel's length slide through his hands until the butt grounded. He leaned his weight on the gun and allowed himself to savor his accomplishment. It was enjoyable to laugh at a white man and to have him know it.

"You give my animal a fright," Eustis said, trying to work up outrage. "You got no call to do that." He eyed Bayard's gun again before swinging stiffly down to pick up the rifle he had dropped. His legs looked shaky when he stood on the ground.

Bayard heard movement in the wagon camp. *"That you, Useless?"* Hollenbeck's big voice called.

"We go in," Bayard suggested to Eustis. He motioned toward the camp with his rifle barrel.

"There's redskins I've shot for less," Eustis said sullenly, and he turned and walked, leading his horse.

"By God, that Bayard beats any watchdog," Hollenbeck said as Bayard and Eustis came into the half circle of wagons. Other men were sitting up in their bedrolls, roused by Hollenbeck's blaring voice. "What'd you find out, Useless?" Hollenbeck demanded. "You come back early so you musta larned something."

Eustis gave Bayard a lethal look. Then without looking at Hollenbeck or Bayard or at much of anything, he told about the town gent he'd escorted to Mrs. Cable's cabin. The man was alone, but had mentioned others were planning to join him. The gent claimed to be a whiskey buyer, Eustis said, though Eustis had seen no wagons.

"Whiskey buyer!" Hollenbeck said. "Wal, no wonder these gents was follering us!"

"This gent had heard on the trail we got Kiowa captives," Eustis said. "Though I never said we had them or didn't. Appears he wants the captives as bad as the liquor, as he's got a notion to sell spirits to the Kiowa." Eustis breathed a moment.

"The *Kioway?*" Hollenbeck said. "By God, I'd a sight ruther sell to Choctaw or Cherokee in the Nations—hell, any of them but Kioway. A man might as well skelp hisself and cut off his own stones and be done with it. These fellers evidently got whiskey peddling mixed up with suicide."

"And then he kept on about some Kiowa boy we're supposed to of got," Eustis said.

"Boy?" Hollenbeck's voice cracked, so that the word trailed off to a whisper. Hollenbeck looked from Eustis to Bayard to a young man, who stood in grayed long johns. "One of you coons hiding a boy in your bedroll?" Hollenbeck demanded, enjoying his joke.

The young man laughed. "Useless, most likely."

"I never," Eustis said.

"I didn't never see no boy noplace," Hollenbeck said, "excepting for the little buck you kilt that day, Useless. You recollect the one you skelped."

"Wal, I plumb forgot," Eustis said, his voice marveling. "This here gent only said a boy. He never did specifize how big."

"So they want the Injun women and the whiskey all in the same deal." Hollenbeck consulted his beard, twisting the kinked hairs around a finger.

"The gent said he'd maybe buy your wagons too," Eustis said, making Hollenbeck cock his good eye skeptically.

"Must have a power of money, these fellers," the young man said.

"Could be they do," Hollenbeck allowed. "This town gent, he was well turned out, was he?"

"Sunday go-to-meeting," Eustis said. "Frock coat and whatnot."

"How about as for being a lawman?" Hollenbeck said. "Din't look to be any kind of badge-toter, did he?"

Eustis shook his head. "Talked too damned much."

"By God, it don't figure a'tall. I need me a drink of thinking whiskey." Hollenbeck took a tin cup and set off toward one of the wagons, but quickly turned again. "Bayard, you put up that rifle where you found it. Seeing a redskin with a gun in hand don't ease my mind none."

Bayard let himself down on his pallet, using the rifle as a crutch. When the young man came forward to take the rifle, Bayard gave it up. Inwardly, Bayard was entertained. It was the way of white men to complicate a simple thing. What matter was it what the traveling white men wanted? It was enough that they were here, far from the white man's power—the soldiers and marshals.

Hollenbeck stood with his back turned, tapping a whiskey keg. The young man said to him, "If this gent has got money enough for liquor and wagons and Indian women and whatnot, we might could make ourselves quite a haul."

Hollenbeck looked up. "Don't no pup need tell me my business, Cooper." He sipped whiskey and made a face. "But now you mention it, suppose we made out of these gents a pair of stew-pot chickens? Just who in the world, I am thinking, is ever going to miss 'em?" He looked happy with himself, like he'd said something clever, then he sipped whiskey noisily, making Bayard want some.

"Killing white men is bad business," the young man said. "Even in the Territory."

Hollenbeck stood only a few strides beyond Bayard's pallet. "I would drink whiskey," Bayard said. "To ease my leg that is shot."

Hollenbeck guffawed. "Whiskey and redskins is poor partners. Ain't no skin off my arse you got yourself shot." He sipped again, making a show of enjoying his liquor, then he tipped his head back and drained the cup. The beard thinned low on his throat and it was there, Bayard thought, that a true man should slash with a skinning knife.

"There's a bunch to this deal, though, that just don't figure up. Selling whiskey to the Kiowa—by God, nobody's that fool-headed, not even town gents," Hollenbeck said. "Cooper, you and Useless rouse them squaws. Haul 'em over to the fire here."

"What for?" the young man said.

"Just hop to it. Bayard, you speak any Kiowa?"

"Kiowas know the speaking of hands," Bayard said.

"Wal, shoot—sign lingo," Hollenbeck said happily. "Up offen your arse, Bayard. You other coons drag that young doe-eye up to the fire here. Grubb, throw some fuel on the fire. I got me a notion we are about to larn something."

With difficulty Bayard struggled to his feet. Since he was a kind of captive of the whiskey men, it was best for now to do as he was told. He felt his wealth returning to him, steadily, steadily; yet, until he had it, he was reminded of something he had concluded earlier: that while many white men acted foolishly, this Hollenbeck was not one of them.

51 · EUSTIS FALK

THE BUSINESS WITH THE KIOWA SQUAWS WAS THE KIND OF THING that made Eustis feel life in general was not worth a turd and life on the plains not worth half that. Eustis had no love for Indians and would kill them however he could. Any buck that carried a bow or gun was fair game to him. But unlike some, he drew the line at sprouts and women.

Then too, there was considerable difference between torture on the one hand, and on the other a quick shot from a rifle, or even a slashed throat or a bashed-in skull to finish the job, the way he would dispatch a wounded buffalo cow or stick a shoat before butchering. Torture, though—pain dealt for the joy of it—was something that turned his stomach.

"Them screams like to give the stock jitters," was what Eustis said about it, then he slunk off beyond the wagon circle under the pretense of making sure the oxen were staked tight. He carried a sledge and went to each ox in turn, indifferently testing stakes with his boot for looseness, tapping a few for the sake of appearances. He did it quietly, lest iron ring upon iron and call the men's attention to him.

The oxen paid the woman's screams no mind at all, as if they'd long since lost interest in the affairs of humankind. What they did was stand, either monstrously stupid or wise beyond all appearances, or else lie down with their hooves gathered under them, chewing cuds.

The woman's screams, though, cut right through Eustis, turning his stomach bilious and spurring his blood, so that he could neither bear to watch nor not watch as Hollenbeck had Sile Cooper and Grubb pick up the younger squaw like an elm log and hold her head to the fire. The flames leapt up and caught her long hair and climbed quickly for her head. The squaw held herself rigid and her face like a fist and then as the flames jumped she screamed and kicked till Cooper and the others dunked her head in a water bucket, putting out the flames but also holding her under longer than they needed to, the men laughing and Hollenbeck braying like a mule.

Then they did it again, except that with what was left of the squaw's hair sopping wet by this time, they had to hold her longer in the fire to get a good yelp out of her. Eustis figured one ear and the side of her head got roasted before they dunked her the second time. It made him sick to see it and the burning hair smell was more sickening yet.

In the darkness beyond the camp circle, Eustis needlessly checked another stake. Long shadows of the frolicking men fanned out to touch the oxen. Finally, they threw the young woman to one side and got hold of the older one, whose gray hair gleamed in the firelight on account of she had bear grease or some such rubbed into it. Eustis figured greased hair would go up like a torch.

He saw the half-breed watch the hair burning with no more expression than you'd watch somebody harness a mare in a rig. The men marched forward, holding the old woman level to the ground like a battering ram. When she struggled, he was reminded by the weak way she moved of how old she was. Surely she was grandma to a passel of Injun sprouts.

They no more got the old squaw close to the fire when the younger one came up off the ground and tore at them. They pushed her away at first and turned back to their work, but she came back at them. Then it was Bayard who stepped forward and said something Eustis didn't catch, and the men all stopped and were looking at the younger one, who was a sight, with her hair burned short and her face bumpy with heat blisters on one side.

Then she was moving, sobbing at the same time, moving her hands and her twisted face, making motions and gestures so fast that Bayard caught her wrist and slowed her. She began motioning again, but more controlled this time. The screaming part seemed over. Curious, Eustis was drawn to the edge of the camp circle, still holding his sledge.

"She knows nothing of these traveling white men," Bayard told Hollenbeck. "She knows not why they follow."

"Ask her about that little doe-eye what got away from us up on the Pawnee," Hollenbeck said. "I got me a notion about her."

Bayard moved his hands, making the signs, then she motioned in response.

"She says she and the other are wives of Two Horses, who was killed in that fight," Bayard said. He motioned again and Sky Calf responded. Bayard translated, saying, "This missing one is called Bird of Morning—a Kiowa, but she was not always such. Bird of Morning was big with child that day. The child by now would be here in the world—"

"Meaning born, I expect," Sile Cooper suggested, and looked smart-eyed till Hollenbeck shushed him.

"Bird of Morning has the eyes of a not-Kiowa, she says, but she is not white," Bayard said, and then he turned from Sky Calf and spoke for himself. "I have seen this not-Kiowa."

"By God, an eye for an eye is what this here is about," Hollenbeck said, "there ain't no whiskey business to it. White town gents helping a Kiowa squaw get her piece of vengeance." Hollenbeck shook his head in wonder, then said, "Can you feature that?" It sounded to Eustis like an honest question.

Bayard let go of the young squaw so that she sagged to the ground. The two women wept together, holding each other and rocking. Eustis reckoned white women would have done and sounded about the same.

"I expect we will visit these town gents first thing in the morning," Hollenbeck said. He looked at Cooper. "Whiskey buyers!" he said, and laughed his big laugh.

"Fun's over," Grubb said, and started for his bedroll. Eustis came walking back into the camp circle carrying the sledge.

"Good thing we had this half-breed in camp," Hollenbeck told Eustis in a joky way, with Bayard standing there hearing himself praised. "I expect there's times an Injun's worth his keep."

Eustis gave Bayard a look and then rolled into his own bedroll. He'd had a longer night than the others, for he'd been the one to go meet the town gent in Mooar's Fort and then ride half the night while the others went to bed. And then Bayard had scared daylights out of his horse and gotten away with it. And also, he thought sourly, it seemed anymore that to get on the German's good side you had to speak sign lingo, as though speaking sign were not merely a thing all Indians were born knowing. For Eustis Falk, it had turned out to be a galling evening.

Eustis lay in his blankets feeling hollow as a stovepipe. The Kiowa women went on sniveling and sobbing until somebody threw a piece of kindling at them.

The fire burned to coals. Eustis shifted to his other side, his stomach aching dully. He found he had been awake a long time, kind of half thinking about things, or else had slept and had awakened—he didn't know which. The camp was still except for oxen whuffing out beyond the wagon circle. The moon had arced to the west and was hanging low someplace over the North Canadian; Eustis couldn't see the moon on account of a canvas wagon cover, but he could read its position by the shadows it cast.

Then there was movement in one corner of the camp and Eustis knew even without rising up on an elbow what it was. It was Bayard, moving stealthily, which alerted Eustis all the more. Bayard was creeping, not like creeping just on account of his bad leg or so he wouldn't wake anybody while he went to take a leak, but creeping like he didn't want to be seen. Eustis held his breath to watch.

Bayard reached the corner of a wagon and pulled himself up by the wheel. Eustis lay still as a log while Bayard looked out over the sleeping camp. Then Bayard snuck to a wagon box and drew out the long army rifle and a cartridge belt from where Sile Cooper had cached them after taking them back earlier. He took something else, too—maybe a skinning knife.

So, Eustis thought, a gun thief, but he kept his head down so that Bayard wouldn't notice him.

When Bayard looked back at the camp, the Indian women had halfway risen up and were watching him. Bayard regarded them without a trace of expression that Eustis could see. Finally, Bayard went out beyond the camp circle to where his horse was tethered. In a minute Eustis heard faint hoofbeats.

In another minute, Eustis Falk's spooky feeling over

watching Bayard sneak around had changed to a glad feeling. He was happy the half-breed had turned out a thief. He always said you never knew where you stood with a half-breed, but now this one had showed his true colors.

What Eustis could have done was roll out and get a horse, go after Bayard and shoot him. But shooting in the dark was a tricky business and you never could tell how things would go. The two of them might end up fighting with knives, a kind of fighting Eustis had never been good at.

It was better all around to let Bayard go. For one thing, it would serve Hollenbeck right to lose an army rifle, which was what came from paying mind to half-breeds. It was cheap riddance, really, getting shed of one like Bayard at so little expense. But cheap riddance or not, Hollenbeck would be mad as a bull when he discovered the theft. He'd be apt to throw firewood. Eustis savored a picture of it, smiling, his eyes closed. A few moments later he slept.

52 · TAI HEI

"CASS—DANG IT, WAKE UP! YOU DIDN'T MOVE THE HORSES IN THE night, did you?" At Riley's shouts, little Kam Loi began crying. Tai Hei came awake reluctantly. She'd had a hard night with the baby and would have liked to sleep longer.

"Wha . . . ?" Cass said.

"All four horses!" Riley insisted. "The corral's wide open!" Cass vaulted to his feet, a pistol in hand, and lurched for the door. Riley grabbed up one of the long guns the men called a Winchester. With Tai Hei following, they spilled into thin dawn light and sprinted to the empty corral, barefoot men in underwear. Tai Hei was also barefoot and wearing only the doctor's dress shirt. She tried to hurry, holding Kam Loi closely.

The corral gate hung forlornly. The men said, "Son of a bitch," almost in unison, and crow-hopped around on their tender, milky feet, peering into the trees, shading their eyes, and examining the low hills.

"There's a trail here a blind man could follow!" Cass yelled, and he dashed into the trees. "They couldn't have wandered far. Come on!" Tai Hei could hear he was trying to make the best of it.

"Yes, they could," Riley said.

"What do you mean?" Cass spun around and his excitement seemed to leak out of him.

Riley was studying the pieces of thong that had held the corral gate. "Cut clean."

"I am seeing the saddles also are gone." Tai Hei pointed to the corral rails.

Cass said, "Gol dang it to hell anyway, if somebody didn't steal our horses!" It was not like Cass to say aloud what everybody knew. She saw his anger, that his eyes had gone ice colored. "Son of a bitch," Cass said. "And the saddlebag with Parrott's money in it. Well, *turds!* That just about cuts it." He looked back at the horse trail he had started to follow.

Riley inspected the ground around the corral. "I'd say that's somebody's track right there." He toed a spot. "Just the heel of it and the rest wiped out by a horseshoe track."

"Well, you're the tracker," Cass said.

"It's for sure no bootprint. Probably Hollenbeck's men sneaking sock footed or wearing moccasins, paying a social call. Unless it was Indians." Once Riley had said that, both men looked at Tai Hei.

"*I* did not take them," Tai Hei had to say.

"Think they'll find the money?" Cass said.

"If you stole a horse, you'd look in the saddlebags, wouldn't you?"

"Son of a bitch," Cass said again.

"This changes a lot," Riley said. "Without that money, it don't leave us much to bargain with." Again, both men looked at her. They appeared stricken—the way a person does when sitting by the bed of one who is sick and dying.

"You would try to buy my Kiowa with white man's money?" Tai Hei said.

"That was the general idea," Riley said. "Not anymore, though."

They straggled back to the cabin, the men scanning the low hills, the far riverbank, looking everywhere, Tai Hei thought, except at her and her baby. Once inside, she put little Kam Loi down on her blanket and for a moment watched the baby sleeping while the men dressed. Riley said, "I doubt you're going to need that necktie in a gunfight."

"It gives me confidence, is all," Cass said.

Tai Hei used matches to make a fire and heat the last of the stew. Cass stepped over and looked into the stew pail. He frowned and said that if they all had to fort up inside the cabin, they'd have little to eat for the rest of the day. "As for tomorrow and beyond," he said, "we'll have nothing at all."

Riley began setting out their firearms with belts or boxes of ammunition beside each one. There were a lot of guns. Cass had his own revolver and Riley had two. Then there were shiny revolvers that had been Legg's and Parrott's. Riley leaned two brass-framed Winchesters against the wall and the men looked at them absently while they ate.

"I will do shooting with this one," Tai Hei said, and went over and picked up the shotgun she had used to shoot Bayard. The gun was heavy but it shot two large shots before needing to be reloaded.

"You just hold your horses with that thing," Cass told her.

There was one other gun, a heavy long-range rifle that Bayard had used to shoot at Riley and Cass. Riley said it was a Sharps, the favorite gun of buffalo hunters. It had a tall rear sight that Riley looked at closely and called "a fine piece of machine work."

"Don't you and your sprout take alarm," Riley said to her, "but I think it'd be smart if I sighted this field piece in." He carried the long gun outside, sat down in the dirt and rested the heavy barrel on one knee. Cass went out and stood watching him. Riley opened the rifle and put a cartridge into it that was as big as his thumb. He told Cass, "This sight looks to have enough elevation that a man could shoot a mile if he wanted." His voice changed as he sighted through the sights.

Cass said, "You think it's smart to shoot with Hollenbeck coming?"

"Well, listen who's the worrier now," Riley said. "It won't hurt to see where she's sighted. Besides, a gunshot or two will remind those boys we're armed. I reckon it a hundred yards to the river, two hundred, give or take, to the far bank, and two and a quarter to that white rock where the hills start swelling up. What do you make it?"

"It's all of that," Cass said.

Riley nestled himself against the gunstock. Tai Hei stepped deeper into the cabin and cupped her hands around Kam Loi's ears. She was curious, though, and pushed a stump-stool with her foot so that she could sit down and see out the front window.

"That rock atop the front sight looks like a pigeon on a fence post," Riley said, in a voice that came squinched against the gunstock. Abruptly, the rifle bellowed and both her own body and little Kam Loi's gave a start. She saw an explosion of dust on the ground beyond the river.

"Two feet out at four o'clock," Cass said. Kam Loi's eyes opened brightly in wonder, saw her mother, and then dimmed and closed sleepily.

"About what I figured," Riley said. "City fellows buy a fancy rifle and don't know enough to sight it in." He worked on the rear sight with a pocketknife. Again, the rifle roared like a bull.

"Hit!" Cass said. "Some shooting!"

"Where?" Riley said.

"Oh, a tad left but a good hit," Cass said. "Don't worry about it."

Tai Hei looked out to see Riley working again on the rifle sight. That they were getting ready to fight the whiskey men was something to think about. She had thought it would be more honorable to take back the captives by fighting than by buying them, but the bellow of the rifle gave her doubts. Anyone could be struck once many bullets began flying. She could see where it might have been smarter just to buy them. But the men had said their money was gone, so it was too late for that now.

Riley fired a third shot, smashing the rock into two large pieces and a debris of smaller ones. The largest piece disappeared behind a clump of soapweed.

"By gol," Cass said.

"This here is some gun," Riley said. He offered Cass a cartridge. "Here, you try one."

"No sir. I could never top that."

"Then you give the bore a quick cleaning," Riley said. "I'll take a Winchester and go out on scout so we have some warning when they come down on us. I might kick up a rabbit before the day heats up too much. It wouldn't hurt to have more food."

"Don't wander off," Cass said. "That Eustis Falk said they'd be coming directly."

"As if I ain't well aware," Riley said. "You scared?"

"Are you?"

"Hell yes," Riley said.

Cass tried to laugh but he did a poor job of it. "It doesn't seem to spoil your shooting." Tai Hei thought a Kiowa warrior going into a fight would never have told anyone he was scared, but then she remembered the white men had shown their own kind of bravery.

Riley leaned the big rifle next to the door before going inside to pick up a smaller one, then he went out, heading for the trees behind the adobe. When he was gone Tai Hei spoke to Cass. "It is too late for hunting," she said. "The sun is now this high." She demonstrated with an outstretched arm. "It is too warm already for animals."

"I expect he knows that right enough," Cass told her. "He's just too fidgety to wait in the cabin."

53 · BAYARD

LOUIS BAYARD LAY FACING WEST, HIS BACK TO THE COMING sunrise, on a swell of prairie overlooking the river valley. The traveling white men's horses, the renewal of his riches, he had both tethered and hobbled in a grassy swale behind him.

Perhaps half a mile on his left and across the lightening expanse of river stood the adobe and its empty corral, although he could barely make out the adobe and nothing at all of the corral. The valley, the silver-blue river, even the cabin—all seemed components of his new wealth, nearly as palpable as the greenbacks he had spread out in the grass before him. He was hungry, and immediately after choosing his spot had searched the captured saddlebags for food. He found only white men's money, which was a fine thing in a town or trading post but useless on the plains. Besides which, he eventually would have gotten the money anyway. What he could have used then was food—and a dulling drink of whiskey.

To still both his hunger and pain, he made himself a pleasant dream in which he and the not-Kiowa woman were founders of a new tribe. They were not-Absaroka and not-white and not-Kiowa; they were a new race, wintering here along the North Canadian and in summers following the buffalo. They had a life surrounded by many horses, by the babble of children. The dream soothed him. He dozed.

In time, the day's growing warmth woke him. With the sun climbing, Bayard could look off down the gradual slope, over waving grasses, and see the empty corral and the back of the cabin with woodsmoke trailing from the chimney. He rolled to his good side and tried to ease the guttered leg. As he moved he heard a shot roll up from the river valley, reverberating like thunder.

Bayard propped himself on an elbow. The traveling white men seemed to be shooting guns for play, rather than fighting anyone. It made no sense to Bayard, but then white men's actions seldom did. The reports rolled twice more, then died away.

Some time after the last shot sounded, movement attracted him. On a far rise across the river, the horizon fractured and a canvas wagon cover appeared, lurching comically against the sky. Tiny oxen drew tiny wagons; tiny men walked alongside, shouting and popping whips.

White men always acted as though they were the only people in the world. Bayard would let them go on thinking that a short time longer; he would be the hawk who sits in the sky, wheeling slowly, riding his high perch and seeing everything, watching the white men fight each other, thus reducing their power. But when that power was weakened enough, he would shed his hawk's feathers and become the wolf, whose powers must be reckoned with. Then he would ride down—he, Bayard—to take the winnings from the winner.

54 · CASS

CASS SQUATTED IN THE SUNSHINE IN FRONT OF THE CABIN AND looked out across the river at thinly grassed hills climbing beyond. Without having meant to, he found himself studying the backtrail of his life. It meandered from dim beginnings in south Texas, picking up speed as it went along. In the war, he'd been as far east as Virginia, as far north as Pennsylvania, though not to Gettysburg, as his unit had arrived late for the battle and only met the shattered Confederate army on the rebound, straggling columns of ragged, hollow-eyed men.

Cass's father had been Constant McCasland, a fighter against Santa Anna in the old days, later one of the first English-speaking ranchers in that part of Texas. The firstborn son was Noble Houston McCasland, who took to managing the business of grass and beeves and hired hands as naturally as he took to horseback.

He, Cass, was second born, named Prosper and only later called Cass. Cass the Itchyfooted, not content to ranch in the shadow of his brother. First he had to go off warring when he could well have stayed out of it, for raising beef for the Confederacy was considered honorable enough.

Like many another soldier, Cass came home restless, used to perpetual movement. So next it was trail driving to Kansas, a laugh and a half considering he could have had life easier tending longhorns on his family's own spread, and made more money to boot.

Then the wide-open Kansas towns, Cass fancying himself a cardsmith. Dressing the part: a gent. And now partnering up with a damned Kentuckian, a Union veteran besides.

It was funny, now he thought of it, how having been on different sides in the war counted for so little in the face of all they had in common—the experience of the war itself. They had both called this trip across the Cimarron plains a fool's errand; they probably had a fool's partnership, too, he and Riley. Maybe there was something that happened when they were together that brought out the worst in both of them. But then Cass eyed the heavy Sharps rifle leaning in the doorway and remembered Riley's great shot on the piece of rock. No, sir, he decided—the best.

A rustling of fabric made his ears perk. He thought maybe he could help Tai Hei in some way; besides which, he was getting antsy. He got up and went into the cabin, finding Tai Hei swaddling her baby. She again wore the blue satin dress, along with the petticoats. To her, he figured, the morning promised to be some kind of occasion, a family reunion. He had a nótion to break the bad news, her son was dead. He had a second notion to point out that the women held by the whiskey men were, strictly speaking, no kin of hers. There was still time for any of them—Tai Hei, Riley, Cass himself—to change their minds. They could trek back to Mooar's Town and trade extra guns for horses. In three days they'd be safely above the Cimarron, sleeping in bedsheets in Buffalo City. Save what you can, Cass wanted to tell her: your life, your baby . . . hell, my and Riley's lives too.

He said none of it. Her face was too serene to disturb. Her eyes, though, were heavy with stored feeling.

"Penny for your thoughts," Cass said.

She looked up, her expression that was no expression at all holding unchanged. Tai Hei, Cass considered, could look longer into a man's eyes without blinking or speaking or turning away than anyone he'd ever met. A white person unused to it could take it for rudeness; a white man observing her beauty might take it for sexual interest.

"It's just an expression." Cass smiled to show harmlessness. "It means you tell me your thoughts and I'll give you money for them."

"Whites pay for one's thoughts?" she said.

"It's more like a joke. They don't really pay." He sighed, wishing he hadn't gone into it.

Tai Hei's eyes drifted, then sharpened. "My thoughts say it is good to see my people. But also there is a bad feeling. Something has happened."

"You don't know that," Cass said, more quickly than he should have. And then he could have bitten his tongue for saying it at all. Had she suspected the worst about the missing boy all along? He had often thought Indians gleaned information differently from whites; it came to them on the wind, or the trees whispered it. But Tai Hei was Chinese, he reminded himself. At any rate, he should start letting her down easy, not sustaining her hopes.

"It's a bad business all around," Cass said limply. There was truth to that, though it hardly needed stating. "I'm afraid there will be a fight."

"Yes. I also fight." She took the shotgun and sat on the dirt floor beside her baby, and as she'd been the evening before, she became a picture, though not the kind folks hang on parlor walls. Fierce Motherhood, this picture would be titled. In the light of morning, Cass saw the blue dress was reaching a point where even washing and mending would not save it.

Cass didn't know what more he could have said, so it was a relief when he heard Riley's hailing voice. He took up his Winchester, stepped into the sunshine, and spotted Riley coming off the low hills and through the trees behind the cabin, hurrying in long strides.

"Four big Murphy wagons," Riley called, half out of breath and his face urgent. Cass saw red points of flush had appeared high on Riley's cheeks. "Looks like they'll draw up spang across the river from us." Riley went past Cass and purposefully into the cabin.

"There's too danged much open country up behind us," Riley said. "We'd best mind our fronts and backs both." He poked a rifle muzzle through the greased rear window, making the skin pop like a drumhead when he broke it.

55 · TAI HEI

THE WAGONS APPEARED IN PROCESSION ON THE FAR SIDE OF THE river, four white-topped freight wagons, the bodies painted green, the wheels red, lumbering at ox pace.

"You see our horses among them?" Cass said. He stood at the edge of the doorway. Tai Hei was beside Cass, both kneeling at the window.

"Only other horses," she told him.

"I can't tell from this far," Riley said, as though she had not spoken. "I don't see more than three or four horses all told anyhow. It's a sure bet they would've come down with a few mounts of their own."

"I'd have thought so too," Cass said. They saw teamsters walking beside their animals, heard the popping of bull-whips. The wagons drew even with the adobe, squarely across the river. There was a round of hollering and the procession halted.

"Nice of them stopping where I shot that rock," Riley said.

"I ought to fess up something before the ball opens," Cass said. "I never could shoot for beans."

"You can't shoot?" Riley said, sounding startled.

"Not like you can," Cass said. "I mean I can shoot off a gun right enough, I just can't hit much. For a Texan, it's embarrassing."

Riley made a face like he'd eaten bad meat. "Well, it amounts to the same thing, then, doesn't it?" He sounded strongly of anger. "If that doesn't about cap the climax, I don't know what the hell does!"

"I'm fair across a card table or barroom," Cass said quickly. "But put range to it and me shooting is mostly a waste of ammunition." His eyes sorrowed like a dog's. "I've been meaning to practice, but what with one thing and another I never did get around to it."

"Damn it, you were in the *war!*" Riley said.

"Cavalry. A lot of dashing about and firing off pistols. I never got much good at it."

Riley huffed as Tai Hei had seen buffalo bulls do. He said, "By God," through his teeth while holding in some of his breath.

"I expect I should have told you this morning when you were shooting the Sharps," Cass said.

"When you should've told me was back in Hays City!" Riley said, the words slapping the walls. "I for damned sure wouldn'ta gone out on the prairie—" He had to take a breath.

Cass said, "Riley," quite softly.

"—with a person whose idea of shooting is a *derringer* across a *card table!*" Riley kicked a table leg and it caved in, and Kam Loi's cry rose up at the noise.

"Well, me being sorry and you losing your head won't

help matters," Cass said over the crying. "The thing is to make the best of it."

"I shall shoot," Tai Hei said, surprising them. She gripped the two-barreled gun and held her thumb as though to cock the hammers.

"Well, if that ain't a comfort," Riley said, and he huffed out another breath and turned back to the doorway. "You want to be helpful, shush the young'un. A person can't hear himself think in here."

Tai Hei picked up Kam Loi, leaving her gun leaning against the wall. When she got back to the window a pair of riders had separated from the whiskey wagons and were coaxing their mounts into the river. The horses floundered a moment and then began swimming, making slow headway, the current sweeping them downstream about as fast as they surged forward.

"Eustis Falk is the skinny bird on the left," Cass said. "I figure that makes the other one Hollenbeck."

Tai Hei said, "Eus-tis Falk and Holl-en-beck," getting the names right. "These are much hateful men." Cass turned with his face close to hers and looked at her in wonder.

For a time the riders disappeared, sheltered in the lee of the near riverbank. Then they came into view again, first the men's hats, then their faces, and then the horses. Finally, their mounts scrambled up the bank, vaulting at the steepness until getting solid footing.

"That one feller's eye bugs out like advertised," Cass said. "What kind of gun has he got?"

"Spencer repeater," Riley said grimly. "The skinny one's carrying a single-shot Remington, which is a piece of luck for us. Let them come in close as they like. The closer they get, the farther they've got to scuttle back to that riverbank."

But as he spoke, the riders reined up, horses wet and gleaming. The bearded man wore a wide hat with the brim pushed up in front, letting the sun play on his face.

"Eighty-yard shot," Riley said. "Not exactly acrosst a card table."

"All right, since you're the gun artist, I'll do the talking," Cass said. "Just remember this much—whatever direction I take, you follow along." He gripped a small leather poke that looked to Tai Hei as though it held white man's money.

"Just what in the world are you cooking up?" Riley said. "What's there in the poke? I thought you said we were about flat busted?"

"Come on out and say howdy," a big voice blared from the near riverbank, causing Tai Hei to stiffen. She had heard that voice in the attack on her people, and since then had heard it in dreams.

Riley gripped his Winchester and looked to Cass. "Just follow my lead," Cass said. Riley gave him an odd look and they went out together into the sunlight, but Cass immediately stuck his head in. "Watch out the back window with your shotgun," he told her. "And keep this door open. We might be coming back in a hurry." He winked one eye, looking merry and at the same time very serious, and was gone.

Tai Hei looked out the back window, which was high in the wall, seeing nothing but elms and cottonwoods, the leaves nearly motionless. Then she was drawn by need and curiosity to the front window, where she watched Riley and Cass walk twenty steps before stopping in the cabin yard. The men at the riverbank sat their horses.

"We heard us some shooting down here earlier," the bearded one who was called Hollenbeck said in a hailing voice. He and the taller, thinner one, named Eustis Falk, made no move to get off their horses.

"Doing a little hunting," Riley said. "We like to start the day with a full larder."

Hollenbeck said, "Pretty rifles," noting the brass-framed Winchesters, but neither Cass nor Riley responded. Hollenbeck spat tobacco and wiped his mouth on a sleeve. "Eustis says you are interested in doing business, but that you ain't got wagons, which don't figger square to me. I got a general proposition to make, just so's we start off the proceedings on the right foot."

"What would that be?" Cass said.

"I ain't a one to dance around the fiddler," Hollenbeck said. "You din't come way down to the Territory on account of no liquor."

"True enough," Cass said. "We're more interested in buying Indians."

"You fellers, I swan," Hollenbeck said, and he looked at

Eustis Falk and laughed. "Happens we got a squaw or two, but we kind've taken a shine to them. I would hate to part with a good woman excepting for the right offer."

"Since we're laying cards on the table," Cass said, "I expect it was you who stole our horses."

Hollenbeck's face troubled up. "Wal, *hell* no!" he said. "Besides oxen, we ain't got but four saddle horses. All brung down from Hays City."

"You didn't steal our horses last night?" Cass said. "Right out of the corral there?" All four men looked at the corral as though staring hard enough would make horses appear.

"Nobody stands with a rifle and says I stole horses," Hollenbeck said thickly. "We never done it."

Riley said something so quietly that Tai Hei could not make it out and Cass nodded without looking at him. "I guess the horses will have to be our problem," Cass called out.

"That is for damned sure," Hollenbeck said.

"Our offer is four hundred dollars," Cass said. "It's all we're carrying. For which we want the Kiowa women you've got—and the boy."

Riley turned urgently to Cass and this time Tai Hei heard him. He said, "But we don't have more'n twenty, thirty dollars!" with his face scowling. Cass only looked at the whiskey men and raised a hand to shush him.

Hollenbeck was laughing. Eustis Falk said in a whining voice, "Bug, I tolt you they kept on about some boy."

"More horseshit talk," Hollenbeck said. "The only Injun boy we saw was about so high." He put his hand out to indicate a youth, causing Tai Hei to think instantly of Iron Bow. "And that little buck is someplace he won't get no taller," Hollenbeck said. "What we have got is two squaws we was Christian enough to give free transport, for which considerable bother we will take your four hundred in cash money, and also them pretty Winchesters. We'll leave you your belt guns, not being the greedy sort."

"No deal," Riley said sharply.

"I expect we'll have to take your word about the boy," Cass called. He still had not looked at Riley.

"Damned right," Hollenbeck said. "So are we getting the Winchesters or ain't we?"

"All right," Cass said, causing Riley to give him a bad look. "Let's see the women," Cass called, and only then turned and looked at Riley. He might have made a face.

"That's in due course," Hollenbeck said. "First show us some money."

It seemed to Tai Hei that Hollenbeck's demand brought them to a sticking point. She knew she should look out the back window in case shooting started, but just as she began to move, Cass surprised her by reaching behind him and coming out with the leather poke, its neck tied with a thong. Cass stepped forward a long-legged stride and as easily as a person piling up firewood pitched the leather poke half the distance to the riders. It thumped metallically and raised dust, making Tai Hei think many coins were inside.

Hollenbeck said, "Kind of a poor tosser, ain't you," and then looked at Eustis Falk and said something else. Falk raised his reins, looking like he was about to come forward and get the poke, but Cass pivoted, bringing his rifle around on the whiskey men. Falk hesitated.

"Leave the money lie," Cass said. "The women come over next or we don't have a bargain."

Hollenbeck smiled a flash of teeth through the beard. He looked at Eustis Falk and then turned in his saddle and looked back to his wagons. "Cooper!" he blared, and he waved someone over, putting his whole arm into it. "Bring over them squaws!"

From behind the leading wagon a single horse and rider appeared. Then another horse, its neck extended because of being led. Tai Hei could see that the second horse carried two Indian women wearing buckskin dresses. The riders went down the bank and started into the water and began steadily coming over. At the sight of Sky Calf and Hears Snow Falling, excitement swelled in Tai Hei's chest. She felt summoned into the yard, perhaps in order to see better or to welcome and encourage the women, or to somehow ensure, doing whatever she could, that this bargain that was happening did not break apart. She felt the summons strongly.

She put Kam Loi on a blanket, where she lay looking up with the dark eyes that were the eyes of her people. Then Tai Hei went to the doorway and stepped out into the sun, holding the two-barreled gun along her leg in the folds of her white woman's dress.

Riley must have heard the rustle of the dress's fabric for he turned and made a strong, sour face, then motioned strenuously for her to go back. His movement caused Cass to turn and look as well. But Tai Hei's eyes were fixed beyond the men, following the progress of the riders fording the river.

Hollenbeck whistled. "Well, lookit here," he said happily. "I reckon this here's little Bird in the Morning we heard so much about. Ain't you gents going to introduce us to so pretty a lady?"

"No," Cass said.

Tai Hei watched the women coming on, an unnameable feeling intensifying. She felt what she had felt earlier that morning: Something had happened. *"Tai Hei—get back inside!"* Riley hissed at her, but she neither moved nor responded; she kept her eyes fast on the approaching women.

The second pair of horses scrambled up the bank and grouped up with Eustis Falk and Hollenbeck. The rider Hollenbeck had called Cooper carried a rifle. The two Kiowa women, wet to their thighs, sat double on the horse. When they saw Tai Hei their faces changed; they exclaimed and gestured toward her. Again, Tai Hei's heart surged.

"Get back inside!" Riley demanded of her, but she did not so much as flick her eyes toward him.

Cass did not turn again. "Start the women forward," he called to Hollenbeck. "When they pass the money bag, you can come pick it up. Do it otherwise and we start shooting." These words appeared to alarm Riley, for he began looking everywhere: at the men on the riverbank, at Tai Hei, up into the trees behind the cabin.

Hollenbeck laughed. "You gents got your brass, I'll say that. I maybe oughta point out there's seven of us all told. Fact is, we got rifles trained on you." It made Riley look again into the trees, his face frowning.

"We won't start it," Cass said.

Hollenbeck regarded the Indian women and then the leather poke and then he said something to the young man called Cooper, who swung down and motioned to the women. Sky Calf skinned off the horse, moving well and uninjured. She reached up to help old Hears Snow Falling. They conferred excitedly, gesturing toward Tai Hei. Tai Hei heard the Kiowa words and felt relief about her bad feeling, but then she saw something was changed about Sky Calf's head: her hair was singed tight to the scalp and her face on one side was darkened.

"Don't forget them repeaters to boot," Hollenbeck called.

Cass answered, "I'm not forgetting."

Hollenbeck said, "Go on and start 'em." Cooper shoved the women forward and they started walking, their faces both excited and apprehensive. Their inclination was to go around Riley and Cass, who after all were grim-faced white strangers holding rifles.

A horse nickered elaborately, the sound coursing Tai Hei's nerves. Then, from within the cabin, little Kam Loi began to wail for her mother.

"Now fetch us that poke," Hollenbeck commanded. Cooper, a young man, started forward carrying his rifle, his eyes wary. He trailed Sky Calf and Hears Snow Falling by no more than five or six steps.

"Best you let Cooper pick up them Winchesters," Hollenbeck called. Cass shifted his stance so he could look behind him as easily as ahead. Tai Hei saw him glance back at her, and then Cass was talking, his face taut but his voice coming easily.

"Tai Hei," Cass said, his voice smooth, "tell them to run." Riley clicked back his rifle hammer.

Tai Hei could not think what to do. If the women were to run, it might cause shooting to start. Riley and Cass were trading money for her beloved ones—in her eyes a very good bargain. Tai Hei's duty was being fulfilled. Except for Sky Calf's burned face, it was all happening like a good sort of dream, but her telling the women to run could only break it.

"Tai Hei—tell them," Cass said more urgently, but then she was distracted by Cooper, who quickened his pace to the leather poke. Sky Calf and Hears Snow Falling had already passed that point, coming on to safety, Sky Calf babbling excitedly in wonderful, familiar Kiowa. One side of her head, Tai Hei could see clearly, was burned dark, the skin crinkled and the ear badly twisted.

Moving swiftly, Cooper dropped to his knees. He cut the thong off the leather bag with an impatient jerk of his knife and poured into his hand what might have been bright coins. Tai Hei watched transfixed as Cooper's face changed.

"Son of a bitch—it's all gol-damned *shirt buttons!*" Cooper said, looking in disbelief at his outstretched hand. Still on one knee, he wheeled toward the whiskey men. *"Bug! They're gypping us with buttons!"*

"Tell them to run!" Cass commanded. "Yell it! *Now!*"

Tai Hei saw the dream breaking and she screamed out in Kiowa, telling them to run, *run!* The women's faces stretched in alarm and they scuttled forward, Sky Calf tugging old Hears Snow Falling. In a moment the women were abreast of Cass and Riley and then running past, making frantically for Tai Hei where she stood in front of the cabin.

At the riverbank, Hollenbeck threw up his gun and fired, knocking Hears Snow Falling onto her face. The dream was shattering, exploding.

Moving in jerks, Eustis Falk brought his rifle to his shoulder but Riley swung up and shot the man from his horse, so that he leaned out and fell like a tree. Cass shot too, making Hollenbeck's horse scream and rear up. Cooper fired from waist level and wood splintered off Riley's rifle and he dropped it as though it were hot. Cass fired two quick rifle shots at Cooper, cutting him down.

Tai Hei ran to Sky Calf, who was shrieking and trying to raise Hears Snow Falling. Riley drew his revolver and shot at Hollenbeck. Cass turned, his face a mask of effort; he dashed to Hears Snow Falling and scooped her up. Bullets screamed past, some throwing dirt; smoke shrouded everything. Tai Hei grabbed for Sky Calf's hand and they ran together to the cabin. Cass ran fast and went in, carrying Hears Snow Falling, and then Tai Hei pushed Sky Calf in through the doorway.

"Riley," Tai Hei said, remembering, and she turned to see Riley alone in the cabin yard, as rooted to the spot as a

Kiowa *Koitsenko,* pivoting to fire twice at someone up in the trees behind the cabin, a haze of powder smoke drifting over him. Beyond him at the riverbank, one horse stood trailing its reins where Eustis Falk had fallen; Cooper's horse was loping off with stirrups flapping and Hollenbeck's horse reared with its rider onto hind legs, screaming as shot horses do, its rider clawing to stay in the saddle. The picture of these things held her fixed in the doorway.

Hollenbeck, struggling to control his horse, shot his rifle one-handed from the shoulder. The bullet, meant for Riley, buzzed past Tai Hei's ear and whocked inside the cabin. She raised her own gun but Cass yanked her deeper into the room. Even so, she saw Riley whirl and crouch under the smoke. He extended his arm with the revolver and fired.

Cass fired from the doorway. Riley steadied deliberately and fired again, and Hollenbeck, looking flustered, his hat gone, slid off the rearing horse and hit the ground like sacked corn. Before either Riley or Cass could shoot again, Hollenbeck rolled himself over the edge of the riverbank and was gone.

Sunlight burned through the rising smoke. Cass yelled, *"Run, you idiot!"* Riley spun on a boot and sprinted toward the cabin. Shots sounded from across the river; others, from behind the cabin. Dust exploded at Riley's churning feet and a bullet whocked into the adobe's front wall. Kiowa words were flying up in the room, speaking of the wounded Hears Snow Falling, but Tai Hei's need was to help Riley. She sprang to the back window and half a bow shot from the cabin saw a man stepping out from a tree, raising a rifle. She got one hammer cocked and stuck the two-barrel gun out the window. Riley flew in the doorway as wild-eyed and sudden as a horse and slammed the door behind him. Tai Hei pulled a trigger and the gun boomed and pushed her backward. She tripped over Hears Snow Falling on the floor and fell beside little Kam Loi, whose tiny face was clenched with crying.

"Stay clear from that door!" Riley yelled. *"It won't stop bullets!"* Inside the adobe was blue smoke and madness: crying and wailing and yelling and Cass saying, "Son of a bitch!" over and over.

"They got at least one man up behind us!" Riley hollered over the noise. He grabbed the heavy Sharps rifle and in three steps reached the back window as a bullet screamed in. He poked the barrel out and shot, not looking where the sights were aligned. The report was deafening in the little adobe room.

56 · RILEY

TAI HEI AND THE BURNED WOMAN LAID THE GRANDMOTHER ON A blanket and keened over her and babbled in Kiowa. Riley saw a bloody wound just above the old woman's knee. The grandmother appeared pale and shaken, but she was alive and awake and doing her share of the talking. Riley had never heard so much Indian talk up close. It was a revelation that Tai Hei could speak a river of Kiowa, faster and with more expression than she ever spoke English. It transformed her, making her bigger and stronger, a larger force.

A steady succession of gunshots came from across the river and bullets thocked regularly into the adobe. Riley overturned the table and leaned it against the door but the next bullet splintered through both door and table. "Big help that was," Cass observed.

"By God—*buttons!*" Riley said. "When you run a bluff, McCasland, you surely do it up big."

Cass had to grin. He held the front window, poking his carbine out and firing at the wagons. "I figured it was like poker. It's not the cards you hold, it's how you play them."

Riley risked a peek out the back. He was trying to remember which tree Hollenbeck's sniper was covering behind. "That's worth remembering next time I play poker against you." Riley fired the Sharps again. For the time being, he figured, the two end windows would have to take care of themselves.

"The rifleman up behind us might've skedaddled," Riley said. "He's not much of a shot or I'd be dead already." He turned to Tai Hei. "That scattergun of yours won't reach him, but I do appreciate the effort." He shifted to Cass's window and looked out the front. Smoke blossomed along the wagons and more bullets slapped the adobe. Riley's Winchester lay in the dirt twenty yards out and he could not think why he'd dropped it. Farther on, Sile Cooper was sprawled dead. At the riverbank was the crumpled body of Eustis Falk, with Hollenbeck's horse beside him, now down and kicking in its death throes.

"By gol, you fight like a wild man," Cass told him, grinning. "I might have to treat you with more respect."

"I tend to get mad," Riley said. "You shoot better than advertised yourself. Trade windows with me. I want to try out this Sharps." They exchanged places, moving hunchbacked. Riley put his old coat on the window ledge and rested the Sharps barrel on it. He was surprised to find a piece of splintered wood from the shattered Winchester sticking out of his hand, the blood running freely. Behind him, he heard Cass reloading and the flood of Kiowa and the baby crying because of the shooting.

Riley waited for another shot to whock into the adobe and then he showed himself at the window, quickly getting the sights on a span of oxen. The Sharps roared and he ducked back without seeing the shot's effect.

"Speaking of those buttons, I own it was sneaky of me," Cass said, "but I had to make them think we had something they wanted. Otherwise, why would they give up the women?"

"What I don't see is why didn't you tell me." Come to think of it, Riley was a little sore about it. "I can keep a secret as well as anybody."

"Not hardly. Folks read you like a book. You got a face deceit won't hide behind."

"The hell," Riley said. He tried to see the comment as some backhanded compliment, but it was like saying somebody was as honest as the day was long—the kind of weak praise folks reserved for those considered simple. He decided it had been an insult any way he looked at it.

He waited for another bullet to hit the cabin, then popped up with the Sharps. Just before he squinted and hunkered into the sights, he was gratified to see both oxen he had shot at lying dead in their traces. His previous bullet had pierced both of them. He aimed amidships at one of the wagons and the Sharps boomed and butted his shoulder.

"Hitting anything?" Cass said.

"I killed two oxen with one shot. Now I'm working on

wagons. I figure a whiskey barrel makes good cover so long as it's not your whiskey." The answering fire was dying out. He risked another look, seeing movement and hearing commotion along the line of wagons. "I believe that last shot tapped a barrel," Riley said. "Expensive stuff to water the prairie with." Tai Hei had gotten the baby to stop crying, which was always a relief. Riley breathed a moment. "Those boys are probably realizing they've got a lot to lose."

"How badly did you hit Hollenbeck?" Cass said.

"Not hard, I don't think."

"A pity."

"I expect he's easing himself down the current to a place he can cross safe," Riley said. "Depends how bad he's hit. He'll be hurting worse every time I shoot an ox, though." He raised up again and steadied the rifle barrel. No more shots came from the wagons. Two men, fully exposed, were working frantically on the downed oxen, probably cutting the traces. "By gol, they're pulling out," Riley said. He could hear the whips popping.

Cass scuttled to join Riley at the front window. Together they watched the wagons pull out, angling away from the river in a panic to gain the shelter of the hills above them, the oxen laboring, teamsters keeping to the cover of the wagons and driving the oxen forward with whips. The whole maneuver was a race to get out of rifle range.

Riley steadied down the Sharps again, but then considered. Hollenbeck had said there were seven men all told. With Falk and Cooper dead, Hollenbeck wounded and slipping down the river, and another man who'd been in the trees behind the cabin still on their side of the river, it left only three men to move four heavily loaded wagons. It occurred to Riley the fight was over. The whiskey men had too much to lose to come at them again.

"I believe I won't shoot another ox just yet," Riley said. "Best thing might be to let them skedaddle."

"They found out we bite pretty deep anyway," Cass said.

57 · BAYARD

LOUIS BAYARD WATCHED THE FIGHT IN THE CABIN YARD WITH detached amusement. The traveling white men seemed to have gotten the better of it, for they had managed to get the Kiowa women and themselves safely into the cabin and were still shooting. The young white man called Cooper lay dead in the yard. The foolish skinny man, Eustis, lay near the river. Hollenbeck, easy to pick out because of his black beard, had tumbled from his horse and then rolled over the bank's lip. It was a comical sight and Bayard had laughed to see it.

Another whiskey man had fired at the back of the cabin from a hiding place in the trees. But he had acted badly when shot at and soon ran away. Then the traveling white men began firing the big-sounding gun, knocking down two oxen with a single shot, clear across the river. Such far shooting surprised Bayard, who liked to do his own shooting close up. Evidently, it had surprised the wagon men too, for they made haste to get out of range. The traveling white men did not fire again, although they could have, and this part was puzzling.

The wagons topped a rise and hurried on behind it, leaving their leader in the lee of the riverbank. Bayard figured Hollenbeck would slip on down the river, riding the current, rather than risk sticking his head up and getting shot. Slipping down the river, at least, was what Bayard himself would have done had he been in that fix.

The whiskey men had been foolish to bring their wagons into the fight. Bayard figured the whiskey men had used the wagons for cover before, and so felt safe behind them. They would have been smarter to have stalked up close and begun firing all at once. White men, though, had their own notions about fighting. Perhaps Hollenbeck was another foolish white man after all. Then Bayard thought how he would like to add barrels of whiskey to the wealth he was already counting on: the horses, weapons, and the women. It would be good to ease his shot leg with many drinks of whiskey.

214

Still, there was no whiskey on top of his rise, from which he looked down upon the back of the cabin and out across the North Canadian to hills where the whiskey wagons had vanished. He figured he had seen only the first part of the fight and that other parts would follow. He hoped the whiskey men would not wait until dark to make their next attack, as Bayard had no food with him and did not care to wait so long. Now that great wealth was again within his grasp, he was anxious to have it.

It was sleepy on the rise with no more fight to watch. As the sun slowly arced to its highest perch of the day, Bayard struggled to keep his mind clear. His leg pained him. He rolled onto his good side to see his horses grazing peacefully, then he pillowed his head on his arm. He closed his eyes for a moment, for healing oneself from such a gunshot demanded much resting.

58 · RILEY

FROM FIRST SHOT TO LAST, THE FIGHT TOOK A QUARTER HOUR; once the wagons were out of sight, the day dragged. Riley and Cass studied landscapes out the windows while the cabin cleared of powder smoke.

Tai Hei and the young Kiowa woman, Sky Calf, tended the grandmother, who was called Hears Snow Falling. She had been shot through the back of the leg above the knee. It looked to Riley like a clean wound, if it did not go bad. The old woman was in evident pain, but her eyes were shiny black, her color had returned, and she spoke with animation. Within an hour, Hears Snow Falling was holding little Kam Loi and cooing to the baby as any grandmother would, Riley figured, whether Indian or white or Chinese or whatnot.

The blue dress, as Tai Hei had hoped, did indeed make an impression on Sky Calf, who seemed not to notice how bedraggled it had become. Tai Hei in turn made much over Sky Calf's singed hair and blistered face and ear.

"These hurts want buffalo fat," Tai Hei announced in English, speaking of Sky Calf's burns. Cass apologized for not having any. It was a pity, Tai Hei told them. Even so, the mood of the women was becoming lighter. The flow of Kiowa was like a tumbling stream, the women catching up on each other. Before long they were shrieking with laughter; even Hears Snow Falling laughed frequently. Then Tai Hei made a kind of speech, with many gestures toward the baby, causing Sky Calf to hug both of them.

"What did you tell them?" Cass asked.

"I say my duty is finish," Tai Hei said, her face shining. "The two parts of me, the Chinese and the Kiowa, are made as one. My own Sky Calf and Hears Snow Falling are much happy to know my little Kam Loi, who will one day wear a Kiowa name." She added something in Kiowa and the other women brightened and chattered in response.

The more lighthearted the women became, however, the longer-faced Riley felt. Something important and tragic, he felt, was going unobserved.

"Tai Hei," Riley said, breaking in on the party. He let his face go heavy, showing he was going to speak seriously. The women stopped their laughter and looked at him.

"Tai Hei," Riley said again, mournfully this time, "I expect it's clear those whiskey men don't have your son." At mention of the boy, Tai Hei's eyes lowered. The women caught her change of mood. Cass, gripping a Winchester, looked first at her and then Riley. He appeared as strained as Riley felt, unreadable thoughts crossing his face.

"So it is," Tai Hei said. She did not look up.

"I wanted to say how sorry I am . . . how bad Cass and I both feel about the way things turned out," Riley said. She flicked her eyes up, then averted them. She took her baby from Hears Snow Falling and rocked it in her arms.

"I reckon if you want to go back up on the Pawnee and find out just what become of the little feller, Cass and I will take you on up there." Riley waited, expecting she would thank him, but she said nothing.

"Why don't you ask her why the only boy Hollenbeck's outfit ever saw was about so tall?" Cass said strangely. He extended a hand to roughly Tai Hei's height.

"What?"

"Go on," Cass said, "ask her."

Riley said, "What in holy hell's wrong with you, saying that? Look how bad she feels."

"Because something around here doesn't figure. And the fact is, it never did." Cass turned brusquely on Tai Hei. "The truth is, you never had a son. You lied about it from the day we found you."

Riley said, "Cass, for pity's sake——"

"Didn't you?"

Tai Hei's face was as heavy as stone. She looked down at her baby. To Riley's amazement, she said, "Kam Loi is my firstborn."

"Son of a bitch!" Cass said. "She suckered the both of us!" He punched his palm, then stalked to the west window. He looked at Tai Hei and then out the window again, his movements angry. "And you the one always talking about your damned honor."

Tai Hei looked as light as leaves. Sky Calf put her arms around both her and the baby, then said something in Kiowa and said it again when Tai Hei would not answer. Tai Hei finally murmured awhile in Kiowa and Sky Calf looked up at the men in sober understanding.

It took Riley a while to get his mind working; he sort of had to butt-kick it. "Then what about that story of your little Eagle Feather. Him being sick and your husband staying home from a raiding party?"

"This thing has happen in some other family," Tai Hei said.

"By gol, if you didn't put us through all this on account of that damned *emerald!*" Riley said finally, feeling stunned. The anger inside him was like an ugly red sun coming up. "All this about your boy was just a big fat . . . *concoction!* A way of getting us to help get your precious jewel back!"

"No, no," Tai Hei said.

"What were you aiming to do once you got it—sneak off? We like to've got ourselves killed a half-dozen times over in all this!" Riley's voice rang in the little adobe till the baby began crying. He knew he should stop himself before he really got going.

"No," Tai Hei said. *"No, no!"* She sagged against Sky Calf, who had to hold her up. They stood together, the two women with the baby crying between them. From the floor, the grandmother launched into some long-winded observation, complete with gestures.

"Son of a bitch, you said it," Riley told Cass. He kicked the overturned table and one of its legs fell off. "I guess no piece of shiny rock is worth getting killed over!" He knew he was acting badly but he went ahead and did it.

"Riley," Cass said.

"So let's see it!" Riley demanded of her, talking too savagely. "Let's see this famous gol-danged stone you think so much of that we all almost got shot for it! And might still, for that matter."

She raised her head and looked at him with eyes dark and still, till he felt bad, like a father wrongly punishing children. "Who the hell's got it?" Riley insisted, feeling cruelty twist his face. His eyes settled on Sky Calf. "You?" Sky Calf backed cautiously. "Maybe old grandma," Riley said wildly.

Cass cleared his throat. He looked suddenly tired. "There never was a jewel either, was there?" he suggested gently.

Riley felt mule-kicked.

"It was all a story," Cass said, "the kidnapped son and the jewel. To get us to take you below the Cimarron, chasing the whiskey men. I expect these women were the whole reason you did it."

Tai Hei put her back to the wall. She held her baby defiantly. "At that time I did not so much know you, you or any white men. Kiowas teach that white men have not honor, that they act only for gain. In some way this was so, for you would have not taken me on the plains only to free Kiowas."

She was making a brave front of it, all the more so for having to wade through it in English. Cass and Riley consulted with looks—Cass guilty, Riley stunned. "You're right about that much," Cass admitted. "I don't reckon we would have."

"These are my people," Tai Hei said, gesturing fiercely. "Sky Calf is my sister-wife. Hears Snow Falling is mother of my husband. They are the only ones in my life who are good to me. Never did I have a Chinese family. I was purchased by men in Hong Kong and taken. In San Francisco I was a wife for money, lying down with many men. We are called the sing-song girls and feel very bad about what we must do. Then American men purchased me and teached me English and took me east, I and others, to lie with men who built the train road. My words of the attack of Arapaho are true. They killed the whore men and I was much glad. In the end I came to the Kiowa, who became my people." She held her hand tenderly to Sky Calf's cheek. "Saving these ones was a duty," she said. "Have you never had a duty, then I pity you."

"I just . . . I just never realized," Cass said. It came out half-voiced.

"I made lies," Tai Hei said bitterly, her mouth twisting, "and I am much glad I did such. No one would have helped me otherwise."

Riley looked at her in astonishment till he had to turn away. He stooped and took the table away from the door and tried to right it but it collapsed because of the broken leg. He was moving badly, as though grown suddenly old, shaking a little from having been mad and then having the anger drain so quickly.

He went out into the sunshine, carrying the heavy Sharps rifle. The rifle was his ballast, holding him down, because he himself felt as insubstantial as an empty sack. The sun was warm; he heard the river, heard birds chirping. The threat of whiskey men seemed vastly unimportant.

He leaned the rifle against the outside wall where the adobe was pocked by bullets and moved into the expanse of dirt in front of the cabin, hardly aware of what he was doing. Cottonwood down drifted past, catching sunlight. Cass came out carrying his Winchester.

"I reckon those fellers had enough," Cass said quietly. He looked more hangdog than Riley had ever seen him.

"It's lucky a person don't feel this much of a shit too often," Riley said. "I'd go drown myself in the river." Rather than look at his friend's face, he looked around at the encircling hills. It was empty country.

Sile Cooper lay dead as dirt, amid bright points of scattered buttons. So much stupid death, Riley thought, as he retrieved the Winchester he'd dropped earlier. The forearm was split by a bullet and the magazine tube bent but it would still function as a single shot.

His mind was so hollow it echoed. He tried to remember the reason for the killing and it came to him: the rescue of loved ones. Duty. Putting aright a tragic wrong. At once he felt better. Of course he had sometimes acted out of duty; it was why he had gone to war, why he and Cass had followed Tai Hei when Bayard took her. It suddenly seemed that he and Cass had done a good thing after all, fighting these men—although maybe for the wrong set of reasons.

Out of the riverbank, Hollenbeck's horse lay with one eye blinking. Without thinking much of anything, Riley put a cartridge in the Winchester's chamber and directed the muzzle to a spot below the animal's ear. He looked away to avoid seeing the eye and pulled the trigger.

Eustis Falk was still alive, in a bad way with a bullet through his lungs. His lips labored to say "water," but no sound came out.

Riley picked up Falk's battered hat to fetch him water. He walked three yards to the riverbank and suddenly stiffened and drew up. Below the bank, Bug-eye Hollenbeck lay sprawled in the mud, one arm in the river's current, staring at Riley with one eye and at what might have been hellfire with the other, not seeming to mind the flies on his face.

59 · TAI HEI

THEY DRAGGED EUSTIS FALK INTO THE SHADE ALONG THE ADOBE'S east wall. His breathing had a whistle in it. Drinks of water revived him somewhat, but Riley said he had never seen a man shot through both lungs who did not soon die, and in the war, he said, he had seen a lot of them. Tai Hei looked at the man with curiosity, but Sky Calf would not go near him.

By midafternoon the men felt emboldened enough to scout wide from the cabin. They went up into the elm grove behind them and came back with empty cartridge cases from where a whiskey man had fired at them.

Tai Hei cut flank steaks from Hollenbeck's dead horse, for

they were all very hungry. Cass was for crossing the river and butchering a haunch off one of the fallen oxen. Beef was beef, Cass said, and was a sight better eating than horsemeat. Riley cautioned against it, arguing that if firing started, whoever went would be caught on the far side of the river. When the men were finally done arguing they built a fire in the adobe's hearth and Tai Hei roasted the horsemeat, which all shared without complaining.

The thing to do, Cass said, was to slip out in the afternoon, in case the remaining whiskey men found new courage. He said the sooner they got on the open plains and far from the whiskey wagons the safer he'd feel. Riley's shooting with the Sharps, he said, was good enough to hold an enemy at some distance, at least so long as it was daylight.

They gathered up the best guns. Rather than leave them for the whiskey men, Riley threw his broken Winchester and Hollenbeck's and Eustis Falk's rifles into the river. He kept Cooper's Henry rifle, saying it was nearly as good as a Winchester.

With Tai Hei instructing, the men cut cottonwood poles and fashioned a travois, fitting a blanket tightly over the frame. They fixed the travois to the skinny horse that had been Eustis Falk's and on it gently loaded Hears Snow Falling, who lay back looking stoical and holding little Kam Loi. Tai Hei cut off more chunks of meat from Hollenbeck's slain horse and they started, walking west, following the river upstream and keeping to the trees as much as they could.

Within a mile they found the unsaddled roan mare on which the Indian women had forded the river. The mare was skittish and shied from them, but to Tai Hei's surprise, Cass approached it matter-of-factly, speaking in a low voice, and then calmly grasped its bridle.

"Some kind of Texas horse talk, I imagine," Riley said to her. Cass rode the mare back to them in triumph, saying he would like to catch Cooper's black as well, but they saw no sign of it.

Sky Calf, Tai Hei thought, was looking increasingly anxious and kept trying to hurry them. When Tai Hei asked what was wrong, she responded in a torrent of Kiowa.

"What's all this?" Cass said, seeing the look on Sky Calf's face.

"My sister-wife say there was with the whiskey men an Indian," Tai Hei said, translating. "She knows not which tribe."

"So?" Riley helped Tai Hei climb up on the mare and then helped Sky Calf up behind her. Sky Calf spoke excitedly all the while, imploring Tai Hei to tell the white men that they should travel in the river so as to leave no tracks.

"It means this Indian man can track us," Tai Hei explained. "He has left the whiskey men only last night so he is nearby."

Sky Calf dabbed at her cheeks with fingertips. "A cruel man," Tai Hei translated, "having holes in his face." Riley jerked around, startled.

"Pockmarks?" Cass looked at Riley. "He'd surely be dead by now." It was more question than statement.

"I hope to hell," Riley said. Sky Calf talked on excitedly, then drew a finger along one thigh in the position where Bayard had his wound.

"*Bayard,*" Riley said. Tai Hei froze as though struck.

"*Bay-arrr,*" Sky Calf said, so clearly it chilled them.

Cass said, "Son of a bitch," without force.

"It is Bayard who in the night has taken the horses," Tai Hei said with conviction.

Riley said, "You know, I will wager she's right."

"I wish to hold the two-barrel gun," Tai Hei said.

"Not a bad idea." Cass handed her the gun from the travois. When she had it, Tai Hei thumped her heels against the mare's sides and started it toward the river.

"Hey—hold on here!" Cass said, catching the bridle. "We don't know for sure he's following. We haven't talked yet about where we're going."

Riley said, "Mooar's Town is closest."

"They'll be expecting that," Cass said. "I vote we head for Camp Supply. It's probably sixty miles down the North Canadian on Wolf Creek, but the army keeps a contingent there. We'll eventually get an escort up to Kansas."

"We do not. We go to my people—to Kiowa land." Tai Hei told Sky Calf and Hears Snow Falling the same thing in Kiowa and Sky Calf agreed vigorously. From the travois Hears Snow Falling chimed in, one thin arm gesturing weakly.

"Camp Supply is better," Cass said. "We'll feel safe there with the cavalry."

"As long as we've got the women to protect us, I think we're better off with the Kiowa," Riley said. "The army might consider these women contraband."

"Then I vote for Mooar's Town," Cass said flatly. "Having too many Indians around gives me the bejeepers."

Riley shook his head. "Too dangerous."

"We'll flip coins to decide it," Cass said.

"Not with me you won't."

"We'll break a stick," Cass said, looking suddenly clever. He broke a stick off a dead cottonwood branch.

"This is much foolish," Tai Hei said. She tried to start the horse forward but again Cass caught the bridle.

Looking wary, Riley picked one end of the stick. "You couldn't of planned this—so why am I leery you could of planned this?"

They gripped opposite ends of the stick and began to bend it. Sky Calf went on pleading that they leave at once. Tai Hei saw the stick bend deeply very close to Riley's end.

"Confound it, suckered again," Riley said. But when the stick could bend no deeper, it suddenly snapped in a different place, close to Cass's hand. Tai Hei told Sky Calf in Kiowa that she had seen quite enough foolishness. She thumped her horse and started toward the river.

"Would you look at that—I got the long end!" Riley said. "By gosh, *I won!*"

"It doesn't matter anyhow." Cass tossed his stick and hurried to catch up. "Any fool can see the ladies got their minds set."

60 · BAYARD

LOUIS BAYARD AWOKE FEELING THAT TIME AND OPPORTUNITY
had passed him by—that he would never be wealthier than
he was at that moment, with five horses and an army rifle
and a saddle pocket of white man's money. He tried to shake
this feeling, for he badly wanted the other guns and the
women, especially the little not-Kiowa. It had been a
pleasant dream, he and the not-Kiowa beginning a new tribe
of true people along the North Canadian.

The day had raveled to evening. He was stiff from sleeping
but he rolled to his good side and got painfully to his feet.
Because of his wound and steady loss of blood, he had slept
away most of the day, as softheaded as a baby.

He heard no firing, saw no whiskey wagons; he saw no one
except a single dead man—Cooper—lying in front of the
cabin. Then Bayard saw that the other dead white man, the
foolish Eustis, was no longer where he had fallen near the
riverbank. With a start, Bayard realized the whiskey men
could have closed in on the cabin and killed the traveling
white men, in which case they would have captured the
wealth that was rightfully Bayard's: the not-Kiowa along
with the other women and the guns.

Bayard hurriedly tied on his saddlebags, his feeling of
loss sharpening. He opened one of the pockets and thrust
his hand inside, reassuring himself with the feel of
the crisp paper money. Then something bit him. He
sucked blood off a finger and examined a tiny puncture
wound. He dug carefully into the saddlebag and drew
out a shiny object—the lawman's badge that Parrott had
once carried.

Bayard's first impulse was to hurl it from him, but then he
noticed its beauty: its shiny surface and the way the soft light
of sundown caught it, then its shape—a star within
a circle—which seemed to Bayard a kind of picture of the
sky. In all, it was too pretty a thing to leave on the prairie. He angled it in his hand, playing with the light coming
off it.

Suddenly inspired, he pinned the badge to his shirt front and stood straighter. He had killed two white men and perhaps would kill more. He was himself, Bayard, a true man, and was in the Territory, beyond the reach of white men's law. He decided the badge would make him his own lawman. It was a strong feeling that banished the sense of loss he had felt earlier.

He mounted the big horse that had been Parrott's, set the army rifle across the pommel and thumped the horse's ribs with his good leg, setting off down the grassy hills, trailing his wealth of horses behind him. Perhaps five bow shots downstream and out of sight of the cabin, he turned squarely toward the river, picking his crossing where low banks indicated shallows.

After crossing, he rode partway up the hills and dismounted. He tied his reins to sagebrush to anchor the line of animals, then crept up to the hill's low summit, keeping his head down and using the army rifle as a crutch.

The whiskey wagons were drawn up together, their canvas covers silhouetted against a fiery sun. Bayard heard singing, as though the whiskey men were celebrating a victory. His nostrils flared at the smell of their distant campfire. He had a picture of the white men drinking whiskey, drinking and celebrating, which was what Bayard himself would have done had he won a victory. The celebrating meant, he thought, that the traveling white men had been killed while he had slept, and that the whiskey men had taken back the Indian women and the not-Kiowa as well. He was too late; his bad feeling had been a true one, for much of his wealth was gone.

Bayard struggled painfully onto his horse and recrossed the river directly in front of the cabin. To his surprise he came upon the whiskey train's leader, Hollenbeck, lying dead at the river's edge.

Bayard took caution from the sight and approached the cabin warily, passing the dead man, Cooper, and—oddly—a scattering of buttons. He tethered his horses in the trees and took his rifle and crept closer to the cabin. All was stillness. He came up on the southeast corner of the adobe and leaned a shoulder against the chimney, finding it cool to his touch. No light came from the cabin's windows.

He circled to the front, making no sound. The door hung open, revealing within only a deeper darkness. He took a breath and stepped through the doorway, his eyes wrestling gloom.

A white man's voice said, "Grubb?" Bayard froze. "By God, Grubb, I was ascairt you wasn't coming." The voice came flooded with relief. It was the foolish white man called Eustis, lying wounded on the cabin floor. He was unarmed, so Bayard took him by the feet and dragged him outside, ignoring the man's weak moans of pain.

"Where have they gone?" Bayard said.

"You . . . Injun!" the foolish white man said. His eyes reeled, apparently unseeing. Bayard kicked him and repeated his question.

"Lit out," Eustis said, groaning through pain. "Give a man a drink, for pity's sake."

Bayard knelt and scalped him alive. The foolish man began screaming but Bayard stuck the knife in his throat so that the screams turned to gurgles. Bayard wiped the knife on the man's trouser leg and then thrust it into his sheath and went back to his horses. He did not scalp Cooper or Hollenbeck because other men had killed them.

The trail was easy to follow—two white men in boots, walking with a burden, and two Indian women in moccasins. Within a short distance Bayard found where the men had captured horses. Then they had made a travois. At first the trail was as plain as the white man's iron rails, but then the tracks led down to the river and entered the water. Bayard forded, but found no tracks emerging on the far side.

So, Bayard thought, they were keeping to the river to hide their tracks. It was good the women were not in the hands of the whiskey men, for it meant he was not too late after all. He grunted satisfaction at this truth, mounted his horse and rode along the bank, crossing and recrossing the river to find where they had come out.

61 · RILEY

THEY WADED UPSTREAM IN THE SHALLOWS. THE RIVER MADE horseshoe bends. Along the outside of each bend the water deepened and the current gained strength, forcing them to cross to the inside where the water was shallower. They made slow progress, so that it was hours before they passed Mooar's Town in the darkness, seeing lights aglow in Mooar's Fort.

On the river's south bank, they found a well-marked wagon trail where the inhabitants of Mooar's Town regularly forded. They went a mile past the ford before finally leaving the river, heading straight south and deeper into Indian Territory.

Once they had climbed away from the North Canadian and reached the broad openness of the plains, they sat the horses double, Sky Calf with Riley and Tai Hei with Cass. Hears Snow Falling held Kam Loi on the travois and they made a dozen miles, walking the horses until morning. The place to rest, Riley said, was on the open plains in broad daylight where he could fend off with the Sharps rifle anyone who approached them.

62 · CASS

BY MIDMORNING CASS THOUGHT THEY OUGHT TO BE MOVING. THE horses had grazed and the men had taken turns dozing until the sun got too hot. The horses had drunk their fill in the river the previous night, but he figured that by midafternoon they would need to drink again. He had brought Mrs. Cable's stew pail, supposing he could pour water from a canteen into the pail for the horses. But even a whole canteenful was not much of a drink for a horse.

"Company coming." Riley got up from where he'd been lazing and jerked out the Sharps. Cass sprinted to the travois for his Winchester.

227

A single rider flanked them, keeping his distance a good half mile out. He rode a tall horse and led four others in a string behind. "It is him," Tai Hei announced. "Bayard."

"You can't be sure at this distance," Cass said.

"One rides not like another," Tai Hei said simply.

"And what do you bet there's our horses?" Riley buckled the belt of Sharps cartridges above his revolver belt and then tucked two cartridges between the fingers of his left hand for quicker reloading. He said, "I figure I'll teach him to keep his distance," and sat down on the prairie, supporting the heavy barrel on one knee.

"Wait—he's getting down," Cass said, watching the rider. The distant figure busied himself alongside his horses. Then he remounted a different horse, taking a long time to struggle into the saddle, and began riding straight toward them. Seeing Bayard coming on, Sky Calf shrieked and Tai Hei let out a long, excited string of Kiowa.

"Everybody quiet down," Cass said. Tai Hei gave her baby to Hears Snow Falling and went to Sky Calf, who kept speaking excitedly and gesturing toward Bayard.

"She say he is a terrible one," Tai Hei said. "She say Bayard has help the whiskey men hold her in the fire."

Cass said, "It figures."

"Hell and hallelujah, that is close enough," Riley said. He raised the rifle and sighted.

"Damn it, hold up," Cass said. The distant figure was waving his rifle, the barrel going back and forth like an upended pendulum. He had tied a rag to the muzzle and was waving it as he came walking his animals on toward them. "He wants to parley," Cass said. "We'd best hear him out."

"I got nothing to say to that bastard," Riley said, but he looked up over the rifle sights and watched the rider come on. When the man was less than three hundred yards out Riley lay the Sharps on the ground and took up Cooper's Henry repeater.

The rider trotted to within a hundred and fifty yards before Cass could see he was indeed Louis Bayard—not that he'd really doubted it. Bayard was dressed the same as ever, with a blackened bloodstain down his left leg. One arm was bare; Bayard had cut or torn off a shirtsleeve to fashion his truce flag. He came on, trotting his horses. A hundred yards. Soon fifty.

Riley called out, "Far enough."

Bayard slowed to a walk. Cass saw he had Parrott's badge pinned to his shirt. "I would talk," Bayard announced.

"We hear you right there," Riley said, but Bayard did not slow. Riley threw the Henry rifle to his shoulder and fired, raising a brief-lived puff of dust off the prairie and making Bayard's horse shy. Bayard halted.

"It is the truce flag," Bayard pointed out.

"So say your piece," Riley said. "Nobody's stopping you." Behind the rider, Bayard's extra horses fanned out. Cass could see the saddlebag on the horse that had been Parrott's. He wondered if the four hundred dollars were still in it.

"Here is my bargain," Bayard said. "I could have killed you once and yet did not. Also you could have killed me and yet did not. Perhaps it is not meant we kill the other. You white men go in peace—it is not far to Mooar's Town. The women and the horses and the guns you will leave for me."

Riley sniggered. "Now hear our terms. You get out of sight real quick and I won't put a bullet through you."

Bayard looked at the far horizons. He raised a hand, palm up, as though pointing out the brute facts of the situation—the expanse of plains, the fact of no help coming, the absence of any authority to appeal to.

"These words are foolish," Bayard said. "I have seen you shoot the gun that shoots far, but in darkness a gun's eyes are blinded. You must sleep sometime, for you are only white men."

Riley said, "Well, you arrogant son of a bitch," but on top of his words Sky Calf called out a sudden warning, its meaning coming as forcefully as if she'd spoken in English. Cass wheeled, finding Tai Hei stalking forward, the shotgun held close into the folds of her dress.

"Tai Hei, no—" Cass said, but Tai Hei set herself with a leg braced behind her, tucked the shotgun's stock high up under her armpit and fired off a barrel. Bayard threw up his arms to shield his face. His horse shied badly, then lashed out with hind legs, kicking another horse in the process,

trying to shake off the buckshot that stung it. Tai Hei struggled to cock the other hammer but Cass dove in low to tackle her and they rolled on the prairie together. The second barrel went off alongside his head and the concussion set his ears ringing. Angered, he wrenched the shotgun from her and flung it away.

Bayard's horse circled crazily, trying to buck him. Blood spots gleamed on its flanks. Fear spread to his other animals and Bayard struggled with all of them, fighting the horses and laughing high-pitched, though in obvious pain because of his leg. His laughter was an eerie sound on the emptiness of the plains.

"This is a woman of much fire." Bayard laughed again and jerked his horse's head around.

"She gave our answer plain enough," Riley said. "You best git."

Then Bayard yelled, a kind of war whoop that coursed Cass's spine as cold as a blizzard. Bayard thumped his horse's flanks and dug off at a lope, leading his horses and raising dust. When he was a quarter mile out he wheeled to one side, yanked the shirtsleeve off his gun muzzle, and fired the rifle at them one-handed. Riley fired a shot in return but he was still holding the short-range Henry and Cass did not see where the bullet hit.

"I told you talking to that bastard wouldn't do us no good," Riley said.

63 · RILEY

ALL DAY BAYARD DOGGED THEM. RILEY THOUGHT THE DAY MUST have been the hottest of the summer. Their horses were stumbling from thirst and exhaustion, making riding double out of the question. Most often he and Cass walked, carrying rifles. Tai Hei and Sky Calf rode the horses, while Hears Snow Falling and Kam Loi lay in the travois, the old woman talking at least half the time. She was a game old bird, Riley thought. Himself, had he been shot anywhere, he would have wanted enough whiskey to damper the pain.

Bayard kept a distance between them, some eight or nine

hundred yards of open prairie. Cass called a halt and they rested, sitting in meager shade cast by the horses. To prevent Bayard from sneaking up, they had to keep to open ground, avoiding washes with their cool shade of plums and cottonwoods, and where—given luck—they might have found water.

In the war, Riley had watched the work of long-range snipers, whose job was to harry the enemy while the rival armies were entrenched in stalemate. He had been fascinated by such long-range shooting: the fussy preparations, then the abruptness of the shot; the seconds-long wait for a puff of dust to indicate the strike. Then a spotter with field glasses would call out the degree of elevation or wind correction for the next shot.

Hits were seldom occurrences, which was just as well. Riley himself had no stomach for killing an unoffending soldier a thousand yards out, enemy or not, when no particular battle was on. Potting a man going peaceably about his business—ambling back from a call of nature, maybe, or fetching water for tea—was to him akin to murder, especially when taking one trooper's life made not a whit of difference in the outcome of the war.

Louis Bayard, though, was another matter. A damned nuisance by day, by night he would be a lurking, murderous presence loosed on the plains. Neither Riley nor Cass would get any sleep this night.

Riley checked for Bayard, finding him and his string of horses the usual half mile out, seeming to swim in mirage.

"Keeping his distance," Cass noted. Riley fetched down the Sharps rifle and sat with it, resting the barrel on one knee. The rider was a flyspeck, shimmering in heat, an impossible target under the best circumstances. And even as Riley sighted, Bayard slipped down behind his horse's neck to present no target at all.

Riley said, "Damn."

"He'll come up in the night," Cass said, "just like he said."

Riley nodded. "So we'll take turns sleeping in the day while the other keeps watch. That way, we'll be fresh enough to stand guard all night. We dasn't move at night for fear of blundering into him."

"It'll make for slow travel," Cass pointed out. "Besides which, eventually we'll get hungry."

"We'll butcher a horse," Riley said.

"Thirsty, too."

"By gol, you're cheerful."

"I was only stating the facts," Cass said.

They set off again, with Riley and Cass riding for a time, letting Tai Hei and Sky Calf walk, an arrangement that Riley found offended his sense of chivalry. Worse, the men's extra weight only tired the horses.

It was nearly evening when Riley veered them west. They were on a rise, heading directly into the sun, Bayard trailing at his half-mile distance. Between prey and hunter was a series of swales, folds in rumpled prairie fabric, each one bottoming in a finger of dry wash.

Saying nothing, Riley halted. He upended the stew pail on the ground, bunched his coat atop the pail, then lay down on his stomach with the Sharps rifle cradled on the coat. Tai Hei slid unaided off her horse and stood watching him.

"If you're going to get down, let Cass up in your place," Riley told Tai Hei. "And don't let Sky Calf get down too. It's supposed to look like we're only stopping a moment."

"What exactly you got in mind?" Cass said. Mounted, he was a tall silhouette against the sundown.

"It's soon dark, so it's now or never," Riley said. "I've got him looking at us spang into the sun. My hope is he can't see what I'm up to." He flipped up the tang sight, loosened the adjustment screw, and raised the aperture cup nearly as high as it would go.

"Assuming this here's a thousand-yard sight—which it may be or may not—I figure sliding it most of the way up will put me in the general vicinity. I make him at nine hundred yards."

"Highly scientific," Cass said.

"I might hit a horse or something," Riley said. "Remind the man that we can still sting."

He sighted. It was late enough in the day that the mirage did not bother him. Just as Riley set the trigger for a hair letoff, Bayard appeared to sense danger: he had been coming straight on toward them, but as Riley readied to shoot,

Bayard tacked abruptly, trying to move his quarry, from his perspective, out of the setting sun. The change of angle gave Riley a target that moved sideways instead of coming straight on.

"He's ruint my shot now, but let's try it anyhow. He's not moving fast. Even so, I figure at this distance I'll hold two horse lengths ahead of him."

"At least there's no wind," Cass noted.

"We make a prayer for this shooting," Tai Hei said. "Little Kam Loi and I." Cass shushed her.

Riley aimed a long time, tracking the sights well in front of the rider, who moved steadily, leading his procession of horses. When Riley touched the trigger, the rifle bellowed and set back violently. A white cloud billowed in front of him.

Riley looked quickly over his sights through churning smoke. Two seconds were a long wait—three, an eternity. Bayard's horses walked steadily in procession. Then the erect figure on horseback threw one hand skyward and toppled from the saddle. The line of horses stopped and waited.

"I don't believe it," Cass said, his voice awed. He slid off the horse and stepped closer, still staring toward where Bayard had fallen. Behind him, the women burst into animated discussion.

Riley left his rifle cradled on the stew pail and stood up, trying to see better. Cass's attention was still locked forward. As Riley watched, a couple of the distant horses lowered their heads to investigate the grass. There was no other apparent movement.

"I just flat don't believe it," Cass said. Then a ragged whoop erupted unwilled from Riley's throat. Cass was badly startled and nearly dropped his Winchester.

"Was that some shot?" Riley demanded. He gave his old pal Cass a sock in the shoulder, a little harder than he'd intended. He bounded like a deer to Tai Hei, lifted her off the ground and hugged her, which first bewildered and then pleased her, so that she covered her mouth in surprise and laughed, her eyes delighted.

"Son of a bitch!" Tai Hei said sweetly.

"What?" Riley said.

"Son of a bitch," she said, becoming hesitant. "Do you not say this?"

"Oh—right!" Riley said. "Son of a bitch, son of a bitch!" they sang together, and with Riley leading took two circle-lefts on the prairie in time to inaudible music. Sky Calf and old Hears Snow Falling babbled with great animation at each other, talking at the same time.

Cass was still watching Bayard's horses. He said, "I don't know, Riley . . ."

"My sister-wife say you have great medicine," Tai Hei said, laughing. "One who shoots like the lightning strikes."

"That was . . . that was the best shot I ever made!" Riley said. His chest felt overinflated. "Hell, what am I saying? The best shot I ever *heard of!* Cass, you old horse thief, shake my hand. Just tell me I'm not dreaming."

"I don't know . . ." Cass took the proffered hand without enthusiasm. "I'm thinking it didn't look right."

"What do you mean, *didn't look right?* You saw him drop. Ka-*Boom!*" Riley's fist punched a hole in the air for emphasis. "That old Sharps' ball took him clean out of the saddle!"

"He maybe heard the shot and ducked before the bullet reached him," Cass said worriedly.

"The hell!" Riley sniffed treason. "The sound and the bullet would've reached him together. It's plain you don't know boot polish about long-range shooting."

"Or he saw your powder smoke and hit the ground on purpose," Cass said.

"Not likely," Riley said, sounding less sure than he'd intended. "You're just jealous it wasn't your shot. Gol-dang it, Cass, a body's got a right to crow over a shot like that."

"I will own it was the best shot I ever saw or ever will," Cass said, "but only if we go find him lying dead."

"Oh, hell." Riley was disgusted. He picked up the Sharps and extracted the empty shell. "Ye of little faith," he said to Cass accusingly.

"You know yourself we have to make sure," Cass said. "He's got our horses and money. We'll have to trek over there sometime."

"Son of a bitch," Riley said. The women's faces were becoming crestfallen. He walked past Tai Hei and lay the

Sharps in the travois, where Hears Snow Falling touched it with reverence, as though hoping the gun's magic might rub off on her. Riley took Cooper's Henry rifle because it was lighter to carry. Or was it because the Henry was handier for close-up shooting? Already, he noted, doubt itched at him. And Cass, damn him, had planted it.

"Don't move from here till we get back," Cass told Tai Hei. "Sit tight and be ready to move."

"Doubting Thomas," Riley said sourly.

"You can just drop that talk," Cass said. "You know yourself we have to go look."

They began walking, their backs to the falling sun, their shadows, tall as masts, probing jaggedly ahead. The closer they approached Bayard's string of horses, the more deliberately they moved, so that their advance had the feel of an attack on entrenchments.

"He had an army needle gun," Riley observed. "I don't care to walk up into the muzzle of one of those."

"Look who's the doubting Thomas now," Cass said.

They closed to within two hundred yards and then powwowed, deciding to split up and come in from two directions. The horses began to notice them, from time to time lifting their heads.

It was nearly dark when Riley crept within seventy yards of the rise where Bayard had fallen. The dapple gray Bayard had been riding had grazed itself a ways down the slope. The other horses stood tethered in a line just back of the high point.

Riley stared until his eyes burned but could make out nothing on the ground except soapweed bunches and a scattering of fresh horse apples. Riley had no cover except the curve of the hill, and the closer it got to full dark, the more Bayard—if he lived—would have the advantage. The smart thing, Riley considered, was to work around behind what he figured was Bayard's position, even though it would mean facing into afterglow.

He hurried, circling, keeping his head low, his eyes tugging against the growing darkness. When he was within twenty-five yards, creeping like some humpbacked night animal, he cocked his rifle hammer, jacked up his courage and charged the hill—where he met Cass charging from the other way. They scared the bejesus out of each other; they nearly shot each other dead.

"He's gone!" Cass breathed, wheeling his rifle muzzle, waltzing in an attempt to cover the whole rise.

"Can't be!" Riley said, disbelieving. It seemed that Bayard had been swallowed by the earth. He searched the open ground, finding no body, no Springfield rifle. Below them, the humped prairie fell away to swales that rolled down into a crease furred with stands of hackberry bushes. Farther yet was a wash with what looked to be elms and cottonwood. It was nearly full dark.

"He's maybe drawing a bead on us right now," Cass said, crouching like a skirmisher. He dropped to one knee and held his Winchester ready.

"Look at this," Riley said. He pointed out a great gout of blood darkening the grass. At one end, the fresh stain was smeared away. "The bastard crawled off," Riley said, marveling. There was a regular high road of blood leading off the rise, heading toward the hackberries.

"I swear. That half-breed took a four-hundred grain Sharps bullet. Just yesterday that was enough of a dose to drop two oxen. But that danged Bayard just crawls away. By gol he's a hard man to kill."

"I'd give odds he's holed up in the brush yonder," Cass said, "waiting for us to go in and get him."

Obeying impulse, Riley stood upright. Cass hissed at him to get down but Riley figured it was too dark to make much of a target. *"Bayard!"* Riley called, putting his voice behind it. It was a feeble sound against the immensity of plains, the vastness of coming night.

Riley called again, echoless, useless. The plains swiftly repaired its silence.

"We ought to get back and protect the women," Cass said. "A man like that, he could be anywhere."

They caught up the gray Bayard had been riding, and then the string of four others and mounted hurriedly.

"I won't feel safe till we're twenty miles from here," Riley said, and despite the enclosing darkness and the danger of prairie dog holes, he set them in a lope toward the women.

64 · CASS

THEY RODE OUT THE NIGHT, THE STARS THEIR ONLY SIGNPOST. Sometime after midnight they crossed Wolf Creek, tributary to the Canadian, where they stopped to fill canteens and water the horses. Then they pushed on, seldom speaking, often dozing in their saddles.

At dawn Riley surprised a badger and shot it with his revolver. The animal, though well hit, chugged doggedly into its burrow, where it lay up and died. Made resourceful by hunger, they cut a hook in a willow stick and fished out the carcass. The women made a breakfast fire. Cass, normally particular about the kind of meat he was eating, was too starved to be squeamish. The five of them ate the badger down to the bone marrow, then lay back against a creek bank and slept like corpses.

By midmorning the sun's heat woke them. They rode, the sun on their left, evolving to overhead. Sometime in the afternoon they topped a rise to see the southern horizon bristling with horsemen. Tai Hei declared they were a Kiowa party; Sky Calf excitedly confirmed it, though Cass and Riley could make out little at that distance.

"They could be anybody," Riley argued. "Comanches, even."

"No, no—Kiowa," Tai Hei insisted. "One people ride not like another."

"So you keep telling us," Cass said to her.

Whatever Indians they were, they remained wary, for more than an hour keeping off to the southeast and dogging them as Bayard had done. Then, suddenly emboldened, they galloped closer, yipping like coyotes, fourteen warriors trailing extra horses.

"You see I am right," Tai Hei said. "Anyone now sees they are Kiowa." The Indians split into two troops and flanked them, loping abreast and then going past, never looking directly at the gents and their charges.

Though Tai Hei scolded them for it, Riley and Cass rode with repeating rifles across their pommels, keeping careful eyes on their visitors. Finally, taking the initiative, Tai Hei trotted out to the warriors, who reined up and sat with grave faces. Feeling great unease, Cass watched her with the Kiowa men. Just how much influence, he couldn't help but wonder, could a Chinese woman have with Kiowa warriors?

"They're coming in," Riley said. From both sides, the Kiowa riders converged on them. They were taut-faced men, Cass observed uncomfortably, who regarded the whites with suspicion and contempt.

"These are not of our home band," Tai Hei told Riley and Cass when she came up. "They say traveling with white men is a much bad thing. Anyway we shall ride with them and come to the country of my people, who camp for this time on the mother river. What you call the Canadian."

"Tell them we understand," Cass said.

They rode the rest of the day, exhausting their horses. Though Cass and Riley bristled with firearms, the escort gave Cass a disturbing sense of captivity; his neck grew stiff and his shoulders tightened. Not until full dark did they stop to make camp, squatting around tiny fires and sharing warrior rations. Cass and Riley chewed warily, not looking too closely at what they'd been given.

They spent a tense night with the Kiowa, all the more so because the weather turned cool. Before dawn a misty rain slid in. In the morning, they rode two hours by Cass's watch, maintaining a fast walk and sitting hunched and well chilled. Then at some invisible signal, the warriors set up their coyotelike yelping, kicked their mounts to a lope and split off from them. Riley said he was sure not sorry to see those boys go.

The reason for the warriors' departure was soon obvious, for over the next rise lay the Canadian River. They traced it upstream until nearly noon, when they surprised two Kiowa boys fishing with bows. Wearing only breechcloths despite the cool air, the boys stood astounded at the sight of the three familiar women accompanied by white men. Sky Calf chided them, causing them to bolt and dash on ahead, apparently vying for the honor of announcing the return of the missing ones.

Within another mile the riders entered a village—

perhaps three-score tepees strung along the north bank, the smoke of campfires hanging low in the damp weather. Skinny dogs barked dutifully while Tai Hei's Kiowa people milled out into a loose, silent assembly that opened in disbelief to accept the riders, and then closed around them in growing excitement.

65 · RILEY

RILEY AWOKE IN THE NIGHT TO A CRASH AND ROLL OF THUNDER and fierce rain beating on the tepee's hide walls. He changed position and snuggled deeper in his buffalo robe, feeling warm and dry and the comfort of food in his belly. Within minutes the sharpest crashes passed over; the rain settled down to a steady drumming on the tepee walls that soon carried him off.

Sometime in the morning two women entered and started a fire in the ash pit in the tepee's center. While Cass and Riley drowsed, the women prepared food, dropping chunks of meat and pieces of roots into an iron pot, then sprinkling in salt and herbs. Riley looked up to catch them giving the men shy looks.

The tonic of rising food smells woke the men fully, although for a time they lazed in their robes, the tepee's width between them, talking of where they would go. Riley remembered they were only a few miles from Texas. It was understandable, he said, if Cass wanted to head home while he, Riley, went back to Kansas.

"No prodigal son act for me," Cass said. "I'm not going home till I've made my pile."

Up in Hays City, Riley reminded him, there were warrants issued for them.

"I was getting tired of Hays City anyhow," Cass said.

"Old Julius Herbert won't ever get his wagon and horses back."

"So he keeps our wages," Cass pointed out. "It comes out about even. Besides which, we've got all of Parrott's money."

They settled on Buffalo City because it was the closest town in Kansas. Riley figured for the time being, it was all the destination they needed.

The Kiowa women made insistent gestures, the meaning clear enough. "Chow time again," Cass observed. They were served gourd bowls and they sat up and ate. Any time the level of what proved to be a tasty stew dropped appreciably in either man's bowl, one of the women insisted on refilling it.

About the time Riley was stuffed to busting, footsteps came up and Tai Hei's voice sounded outside the tepee.

"It is I who stands here," she said.

"Come on into our abode," Riley said. Tai Hei stepped in wearing a new buckskin dress that was cleverly fringed and ornamented with shells and porcupine quills. She circled to the left as befit a female entering a lodge and sat down on a folded buffalo robe. Her hair was washed and brushed and decorated with strips of shiny blue satin—unmistakably remnants of the dress given her by Maggie Rose Land. It made Riley a little sorry to see it, for the demise of the dress meant the end of other things too. It was a reminder they'd be moving on soon.

Cass, though, whistled appreciatively.

"What means this noise?" Tai Hei said.

"It's what a fellow does when he sees the prettiest girl in town," Cass said.

"Yes, I am more prettiest as Kiowa than Chinese. To be much prettiest as Chinese, one must have bound-up little feet."

"I heard about that custom," Cass said.

Riley looked at Tai Hei's feet, which had always seemed dainty enough. Her moccasins were new too. "All females have pretty feet," Riley observed, "lessen they're bigger than my own."

"Riley is much funny a man," Tai Hei said cheerfully. She peeked into the stew pot and said something to the women, who answered elaborately, with many gestures toward the white men. "Ah—you are placed in great honor," Tai Hei said. "Riley is called Kills Far, a maker of great gun medicine."

"Wounds Far would be more like it," Riley said.

"And Cass is Tall White Man, friend of Kills Far."

"Oh, dandy," Cass said. "I get to play second fiddle."

"This buffalo stew is also much good. We Kiowa have many wonderful foods."

"It savors right well, I'll say that," Riley said.

Tai Hei spoke again to the women, saying something they obviously disagreed with, then something further that pleased them. The women laughed and looked at the men gratefully.

"Don't you go marrying us off," Riley said.

"I tell them you say such food is too much honor for you," Tai Hei said. "That you, you *de-serve* . . . ?"

"Deserve, yes," Cass said.

"That you deserve not such. This kind of talk much pleases all Kiowa, though then they must say it is poor food. I tell them you never have eat such good food, for white women's cooking is known as very poor." She laughed.

Perhaps feeling left out because of all the English, the two women got up with more smiles for the great Kills Far and his friend and went out, leaving the tepee flap open to yellow sunlight and a triangle of blue sky.

"So, Tai Hei—what will you do now?" Cass said.

Her first response was a shrug, as though the answer were plain enough. "Again I am Bird of Morning. I have little Kam Loi, who in time shall have a new name. In time also I shall perhaps have a new husband." For a moment her eyes drifted, so that Riley imagined she was seeing her Kiowa life all laid out ahead of her. Then she focused, manufactured a brief smile and shrugged again, summing up.

"The Chinese of San Francisco are your people, too," Cass suggested.

"I have seen how big is the world—Hong Kong and San Francisco and Buffalo City," she said, as though the places were on a par. "I am much glad in a small world."

There followed a silence that Riley found edgy. "Well, us—we'll be heading back to Kansas." He wiped his hands on his trouser legs. "Fact is, we ought to get riding."

"No, you must not. Tonight there shall be a big eating." She made encompassing gestures. "All the people."

"A banquet?" Cass said.

"A big eating. All people sitting to make you honor. Long Knife leads it, our headman."

"I've heard of this Long Knife," Riley said. "The army's after him."

The comment subdued her. "Long Knife and all Kiowa love not the blue soldiers, who offer poor lands in order they may take the rest. We do not like it there. Much trouble shall soon happen over this."

They sat absorbing it. Riley wanted to say the blue soldiers were many, and there were more where those came from. He saw it would be awkward, though, pointing that out.

"I'm real sorry to hear it," Cass said.

Her face changed then; she put on false cheer, which did not become her. "When war is end, it will be like the days which old ones speak of," Tai Hei said. "This is so, for many have dreamed it."

Riley felt his face going doubtful. He looked to Cass and saw the same face on him. "No war is for always," Tai Hei said. "Anyway you must now come. The day is much fresh and I have much things to show."

66 · THE GENTS

THE MORNING AFTER THE FEASTING IN THEIR HONOR, AFTER MANY retellings of the shoots-far gun and the rescue of the women, Cass and Riley dressed for the trail. They cut out four of the seven horses they'd brought in, not wanting to appear greedy, and saddled up and tied on saddlebags. They did not see Tai Hei about, nor did they know which tepee was hers. The village, in fact, took scarcely any notice of them; it was as though the previous evening's festivities had accomplished the good-byes.

Once they had shoved their rifles in the boots, however, and Cass had swung up into his saddle, Long Knife and a delegation of elders materialized, as though they'd been waiting in the wings for the big moment. The festive mood Cass and Riley had seen the previous evening was gone entirely. The Kiowa men did little more than acknowledge the whites with frank looks. The Indians stood graven, officiating.

"By gol," Riley said, checking a cinch, "everybody's about as stiff as cold lard this morning."

Riley indicated through gestures that the horses they were leaving would belong to the tribe, though communication was difficult without Tai Hei around. Even so, the gift went over well, as they heard murmured approvals and saw brightened faces.

Riley wanted to ask about Tai Hei; he could not accept that they would not see her. He wanted to say Tai Hei, her Chinese name, but then remembered that would be useless. He wanted to say Bird of Morning, but of course, that was only an English translation. Finally, he pantomimed as best he could a woman with a baby, playing to an audience of blank looks. Feeling foolish, he soon gave it up. Perhaps it was bad manners for a recently widowed Kiowa woman to see white men off.

Riley mounted. Virtually in unison, the Kiowa men stepped back, giving the horses room, a clear invitation for leave-taking. Cass figured if you were dedicating a bank or a railroad or something, it would be good to have a bunch of Kiowa in attendance; they were that impressive at formalities. He threw Long Knife a military salute, showing Riley was not the only one who could make grand gestures. Long Knife responded with a decent imitation, and then all the men did it.

"It helps to remember they're friendlier than they look," Cass said.

"I surely would hate to have them mad at me," Riley said. He squinted north, picking a route. "Well, sir, here we go. It doesn't seem right not seeing Tai Hei. I expect, though, that they do things different."

"Send-offs are maybe men's business," Cass said. He encouraged his horse and drew the packhorse behind him and preceded Riley out of the village. Once they were moving, women looked up from their tasks and children dashed out and paced them. They looked in vain, though, for Tai Hei and her blue satin ribbons.

They aimed squarely north, taking the shortest line to

Kansas, wanting to cut their chances of striking some roving band who might not have heard of Kills Far and Tall White Man. It was a fine morning, although the plains heat was building and within another day would be insufferable again.

The backs of their necks itched, making them turn often to look back. They saw the Canadian lying in a trough of its own making, winding among low grassy hills. They climbed a final rise; in another fifty yards they would be out of sight of the village.

At that modest summit they reined in and studied the scattering of tepees, smoke penciling from the smoke holes, pony herd grazing, morning sun blazing off the river. Riley had a thought that time did not exist down there, at least not the kind he and Cass were used to.

He dismounted and checked his cinch strap, feeling foolish when he realized he had just checked it. Cass readjusted himself in the saddle, saddle leather creaking, then fussed with a canteen just to get a modest swig of water. Riley saw that Cass was as reluctant to leave as he himself was feeling. They exchanged baffled glances.

"I know what you're thinking," Cass said. "That it just doesn't seem right not saying good-bye to her."

Riley's face had taken an intent expression. Cass heard voices from the village. "Somebody's coming," Riley observed.

Cass turned to see a rider on a long-legged white man's mount and trailing a packhorse. As he watched, the rider detached from the village and began following the same uphill route the men had taken. For some time, both men studied the approaching figure.

"One rides not like another," Riley said.

"Yes sir, one sure doesn't." Cass's gaze followed the approaching horses, the rider's features slowly resolving, till he made out Tai Hei's new buckskin dress. She carried the baby in a cradle board on her back. When she was closer he could see the gloss of her hair and the blue satin ribbons.

"By gol," Cass said.

She did not hail them, but rode until she came up to them. Her face was serious. Riley found the silence hung heavily.

"Nice morning for a ride," he said, sounding clumsy to himself.

"The sister of my sister-wife has given this prettiest cradle board," Tai Hei pointed out, turning her back to show it off. Little Kam Loi's round face nestled there, dark eyes regarding them with an uncertain focus. "Kiowa make much clever things," Tai Hei said wistfully.

Both men praised the cradle board, going on a little too long about it, even while their eyes ached for the true subject.

"My people are much sad," Tai Hei said finally. "All talk is of agent Lawrie-Tatum, called Bald Head, who is angry we leave the poor lands he has for us. Already he has send blue soldiers to chase after us. Our great chiefs, Set-Tainte or White Bear, and Addo-Eta, called Big Tree, lie in a soldier prison in Texas. There shall be this summer no sun dance."

Cass looked at the village, which sat deceptively peaceful.

"All Kiowa bands now choose," she said. "Some walk the white man's road in poor country, where they labor to be the corn growers. Those who would follow the true life and hunt the buffalo join with the war chief Lone Wolf."

Riley breathed audibly.

"My own people," she said, her eyes averted, "have choose with Lone Wolf."

In the Kansas towns and forts, Cass had heard plenty of talk about a new war with the Kiowa. Most whites considered Lone Wolf a bad egg.

They sat a long time like that. Riley remembered that to Kiowa, time was different.

"Well, you . . ." Riley said, but he had to clear his throat. "You and the sprout look like you're fixed for some riding."

"So it is. My duty is with my new little one. If we may some way live apart from war, my new one and I, then I think I must choose that road. My sister-wife has laugh and say I am anyway a poor Kiowa," Tai Hei said ruefully. "A Kiowa would not have changed one's mind."

"I think you've made a good choice," Cass said.

"We ask now to ride with honored men, Kam Loi and I. We are much used to traveling."

"You ought to know white men don't lift a finger without

somebody paying them," Riley reminded her. He tried to sound stern, but his voice rose up a little giddy at the end of it.

"I speak not false of some valued thing which I have to give for you," Tai Hei said. "I have no such."

"But had you something—say some valuable jewel or the like, some big emerald, let's say—I am sure you would offer it," Cass said.

"Yes," she said, "but I have not one." She managed a smile to acknowledge their teasing.

"I expect in that case you'll just have to owe us one," Riley said, and he reined his horse around and started them all toward Kansas.